BREAK OUT

A Riot MC Next Generation Novel

KAREN RENEE

eBook ISBN: 978-1-957194-27-1

Paperback ISBN: 978-1-957194-28-8

Paperback ISBN: 978-1-957194-37-0

Cover Model: Joey Berry

Photographer: Furious Fotog/Golden Czermak

Cover Design: Bee at Bitter Sage Designs

Editor: Barbara J. Bailey

For the sassy women who love a bad boy

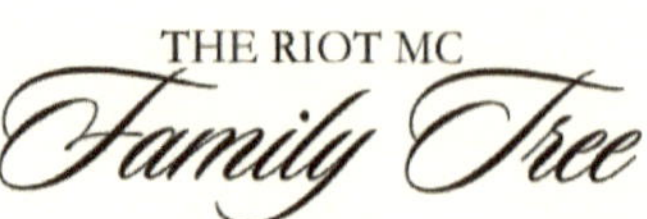

THE RIOT MC
Family Tree

PARENTS	CHILDREN
HENRY "VOLT" ADLER JACKIE ADLER	SIMONE BOBBY
CAL "CALLOUS" ROBERTSON MALLORY ROBERTSON	ALEXANDRA
HOMER "ROLL" ROLLAND TRIXIE ROLLAND	RAFFERTY JASMINE
CARY "VAMP" SULLIVAN LORRAINE SULLIVAN	GABRIELLA
GAGE "GAMBLE" GARRISON VICTORIA GARRISON	KILLIAN RYAN MICKAYLA

AUTHOR NOTE

This book is intended for mature readers 18+. It contains a surprise pregnancy, discussions about pregnancy, a morally gray hero, profanity, abduction, and violence. Do not read if this content might trigger you.

Playlist

YES I'M A MESS by AJR
THE LESS I KNOW THE BETTER by Tame Impala
ALL MY LIFE by Foo Fighters
COMEDOWN by Bush
HOW SOON IS NOW? by The Smiths
MASTER OF PUPPETS by Metallica
RUNNIN' WITH THE DEVIL by Van Halen
HIGHWAY TO HELL by AC/DC
RUN AWAY WITH ME by Cold War Kids
FIRE AND THE FLOOD by Vance Joy
SO FAR AWAY by Dire Straits

CHAPTER 1

JADE

SIMONE

I crossed University Avenue with my eyes on Vicious Vinyl feeling relief, accomplishment, and excitement. I'd done it. The final exam for my last class was over, and my Computer Engineering degree was in the bag. To say this was cause for celebration was an understatement.

The only thing weighing on me was that Jordan, my boyfriend, wouldn't be getting his degree this December, too. He'd dropped an important class earlier in the semester, and resigned himself to finishing next spring. Once it was clear I would graduate in December, Jordan arranged to move in with his buddy, Chet. Jordan had finished his semester earlier this week, and he'd spent the last few days boxing his stuff.

I'd asked him on Tuesday if things were cool with us. He'd smiled and said, "Of course they are."

Still, that little voice wouldn't leave me alone. Then again, I hadn't seen him much the last three days because I was studying or sleeping while he was packing. Our Friday night tradition was to meet up across from campus at Vicious Vinyl, a "high-end dive bar." I didn't understand how a true dive bar could be high-end. (Weren't they supposed to be seedy?) But I loved the contrary notion, and their Old Fashioned couldn't be beat.

As I squeezed through the crowds inside, my excitement grew. Finally, I found the usual suspects I called friends. Everyone stood in a circle since tables were hard to come by after finals. I moved so I stood behind Jordan, but I didn't push closer since he was mid-conversation.

"Oh, man! Don't get me started," Jordan said, leaning toward Chet. I smiled because I loved how animated he became. "I don't know what was worse. How she latched onto a single phrase saying it over and over again, or how immature she could be. Putting olives on all of her fingers and buying those cheap-ass vanilla ring cookies so she could wear them on her pinkie."

I did those things with the olives and cookies, but he'd always said I was cute.

He wasn't talking about me, was he?

"She doesn't glom onto phrases," Lisette said.

Jordan's head reared back and he almost bumped into me – proving he was oblivious to my presence. "If I had a fuckin' dollar for every time she asked me 'Have you've lost your mind,' I could pay for all of our tabs tonight."

To be fair, I rarely asked him, I outright said he'd lost his mind. At this juncture, he sure as hell *had* lost his mind.

I felt eyes on me, and noticed Tennyson staring at me. She cleared her throat and touched Jordan's bicep.

He turned, blanched for all of a moment, and then shrugged. His hazel eyes had the tell-tale sheen that comes from being tipsy, if not drunk. "Simmy, what are you doing here? We're done. I thought you figured that out." Jordan's voice hit me harder since the blaring pop music inside the bar forced him to yell.

My rage split like a two-headed beast coming to life. Did women named Kim get as outraged at being called 'Kimmy'? Maybe not, but it was one helluva stretch to take Simone and use Simmy as the diminutive.

Add his condescending tone, the fact our four closest friends were gathered around, and the way Tennyson stood so close to him, I felt like laying into him with the force of a sledge hammer.

Yet, as my dad and all my 'uncles' had taught me, that gave assholes the upper hand. Every time.

I glanced at everyone in the group. Their discomfort was visible. I nodded, considered saying something, but turned around and left.

"Simone!" Lisette yelled after me.

I looked over my shoulder – tears threatened, but I blinked them back.

She caught up to me. "I honestly didn't know—"

"That makes two of us. Have a great night."

"Do you need anything?"

I needed a stiff drink, but I'd be damned if I stayed here.

After a deep breath, I aimed a blank expression at Lisette. "No, thanks. I'm gonna head home. His stuff is all gone, and if it isn't, I need to move it into the hallway."

She went back to the group and I shouldered my way through the crowd to the sidewalk. The December air hit me like a smack in the face. My nose stung with gathering tears. I clenched my teeth to will them away – never successful with that before, but it seemed today that record might change.

The door opened behind me, and I refused to look back.

"Simone, wait," Jordan called.

I stopped. Lord knew why, because every instinct said to run, not walk to my Vespa. Problem was, it was on the other side of campus.

"Let me explain please," Jordan said from behind me.

Ever the fool, I turned around.

One glimpse of him and clarity hit me. I recalled a strange interaction between us earlier in the day. I'd come out of the bathroom and into the living room where he sat sifting through his stuff. After a sideways glance of me in my form-fitting, black dress pants and dressy blouse, Jordan had asked if *that* was what I was wearing.

My bone-colored faux-leather top only bordered on being conservative since it looked like leather. I wanted to be slightly conservative for my Product and Process presentation. Bonus, it wasn't dressy enough that I'd stand out like a sore thumb at the dive bar.

"Yeah, it is. Is there something wrong? A stain or something?" I'd asked.

His lip curled up a little. "No, it just looks like something a biker bitch would wear."

Seeing as the top was a gift from Aunt Abby, wife and old lady to Blood, the Vice President of the Riot MC, Jordan wasn't exactly wrong. Motorcycle club life had been *both* a point of connection and contention between us. My parents had encouraged me to move away for college and get out of the biker lifestyle. Jordan's father wasn't just an MC president, he was president to a mother chapter. Jordan hated that about his dad, because his dad had left when Jordan was five years old. He couldn't fathom how a man could abandon his family for years. Any time I asked him which club his dad ran, Jordan refused to talk about it. He was that bitter.

With my hands behind my neck, I clasped my jade necklace. "To be fair, Jordan, a biker bitch would get this top in blood red or black, and she wouldn't be in dress pants."

His brows furrowed. "Those are dress pants?"

That conversation should have been my sign that things weren't okay. Hell, the fact we hadn't had sex in almost two months should have tipped me off – but I figured we were both busy.

A harsh gust of wind brought me out of my thoughts and I blew out a sigh. "What do you want, Jordan?"

He opened his mouth, closed it, and finally said, "It's not that I don't care about you."

I stared at him and my chin lowered an inch. His words held no sincerity – not that I'd have believed him anyway.

He shrugged. "You're from a family of bikers."

"You knew that," I reminded him.

"You even ride a Vespa around campus."

I laughed. "You've got to be joking! A *thousand* other girls ride those things around campus and nobody looks twice. Please. Riding that thing is nothing like a bike. Hell, my dad and all his brothers want to get me off it. If you only heard the flack I get for my helmet alone."

He shook his head. "Whatever, Simone. I need someone... different."

I glanced past him. Tennyson stood holding the purple door of Vicious Vinyl open.

My focus shifted back to Jordan. "By all means, Tennyson's waiting for you."

"Don't be like that, Simone. I'm trying to be... nice." Jordan said.

I nodded. "Mission accomplished."

My brain had felt like mush when I turned in my final exam. Now, my body moved as though some other force drove me. I wondered how I'd missed the signs, but then I realized I hadn't. Not really. We'd been living together for more than two years, but his insistence on moving in with his buddy should have given me more cause for alarm. I'd argued against it, but in the end I gave in much easier than I would have a year prior.

As much as people talk about the power of love, it boggled my mind how falling *out* of love could be such a gradual experience. Things didn't always end with an epic blow-up, and on some level that was more blindsiding. My heart was breaking, but it felt like a scab that had been reopened. I hadn't understood how deep the cut ran until I'd been forced to acknowledge the pain.

I turned around and walked up the block. In a haze, I passed a coffee shop, a convenience store, and a few other places where I could have stopped and pulled myself together. While I waited for a walk signal to cross a side street, I contemplated an upscale tapas restaurant. A large group of guys sat outside. They were loud and getting rowdy. I didn't want to be around that scene.

The signal changed and I kept moving. At the end of the block, I saw a hotel that housed a pizza place Jordan had refused to try. Some bullshit excuse about any restaurant inside a hotel was either over-priced, no good, or worse: both. The red door for Pi House caught my eye and snapped me out of my fog.

It seemed as though my life had turned to shambles with Jordan's bombshell, but I still had plenty to celebrate. The more I thought about it, Jordan had done me a favor. He wouldn't be around any more to criticize me or keep me from doing the things I wanted to do.

Yep, it was definitely time to party. Even as a mere party of one.

MY STOMACH GROWLED AS I tugged open the heavy red door. The aroma of roasted garlic, fresh bread, and tomato sauce hit me the moment I stepped inside. From four feet to my left a middle-aged man with a pot belly crowed, "A girl like you should smile more."

Rather than roll my eyes, I lifted my chin and walked toward the bar on the opposite side of the restaurant.

One empty bar stool beckoned to me even though two men who were probably in their forties sat on either side of it. I pulled out the stool, perched my ass on it, and slid my ID and credit card out of my pocket.

"Don't listen to that prick," a man with a deep, rumbly voice said.

I turned my head in his direction.

Ho... Lee... Schnikes, as Aunt Mallory would say. I had been wrong. This man wasn't in his forties, more like late thirties. He had the sexiest wavy hair and wore a black t-shirt which struggled to encase his well-inked biceps. The dark stubble lining his angular cheeks almost distracted me from the gray hairs at the side of his head, but those grays only enhanced his appeal.

His brown eyes danced over my face, but I sensed malice would shine from his irises just as easily. He had an energy about him, like he was a leader and accustomed to being in charge. Then it hit me.

Power. He oozed *power.*

I shook myself out of what felt like a trance. "I'm sorry, don't listen to what?"

His lush lips tipped up. "That asshole who told you to smile more. Don't listen to him."

That made me chuckle. "Trust me. No woman ever smiles because some dickhead tells them to."

A deep rumble came from his direction and I realized he'd chuckled. "Good to know."

"I'm surprised you heard him," I said.

His teeth flashed in a small smile. "Hard not to. He's been obnoxious since I got here, drunk for about the last hour. If I'd wanted to deal with that, I'd have gone to the college bar five blocks down the street."

"The same one I just left," I muttered.

"Not your scene?"

I raised my brows and smiled. "Not any more. After today, I'm done being a college girl."

The bartender made his way to me. "What can I get for you? If you have your student I.D. we have half-price shooters and slices."

I felt my eyes light up and I put my student I.D. on the bar. "Fabulous. I'll take a slice with pepperoni and black olives and two fingers of Jack Daniel's Honey."

The bartender grimaced. "Discount is only for well drinks."

I shrugged a shoulder. "That's cool. Believe me, today calls for the JD Honey."

The bartender turned to enter my order and the man next to me chuckled again. I glanced at him.

"Doesn't look like you're *done* being a college girl."

I tilted my hands up. "What can I say? I'm a sucker for a deal."

He stared at me, those brown eyes weren't dancing any more. They examined me. It should have made me uncomfortable, but I adored having his scrutiny.

His full lips formed the slightest smile. "Why does today call for Jack Daniel's?"

I grinned. "Honey, don't forget the honey."

He closed his eyes and I watched his chest rise with a deep breath. His brow arched and he opened his eyes. "Right. What's the occasion, Jade?"

Did he just give me a nickname?

I loved that even more than him staring at me.

"I finished my degree today. That's a pretty big deal in my book, and anything worth celebrating deserves Jack." My head cocked to the side. "Why did you call me Jade?"

He brought his left hand up to stroke his chin. No wedding band on his finger... though he wore two very thick, heavy-looking gold rings on his index and middle fingers. What was wrong with me? Why did I care about a wedding ring? He had a good eighteen years on me, and I'd just been dumped.

His deep voice cut into my thoughts. "Don't know your name yet. I noticed your jade necklace. The name Jade suits you. Great piece, by the way."

I blushed and grabbed my jade dragon out of habit. "Thanks. It's one of my favorites."

He kept staring at me and I couldn't tear my eyes from him. Heat gathered in my belly.

He should scare me, but I couldn't remember ever being so attracted to someone.

The soft thud of a glass hitting the bar in front of me interrupted the moment. I turned to see the bartender walking away, a high-ball glass of amber liquid sat on a cocktail napkin.

I grabbed the glass. Thick, warm fingers curled around my wrist. The warmth of his fingers practically seeped into my skin and that warm sensation shot straight to my breasts.

"It's not a celebration without a toast," he said.

I twisted my body an inch toward him. "You're right."

He let go of my wrist and picked up his glass which was half-full. "To great pieces..." He paused while his eyes went to my necklace. He continued, "And higher education."

The inuendo in that toast had to be in my head. It was a very bold and sly toast, even if it bordered on being crass.

I clinked my glass to his. "Cheers."

I took a huge swig of whiskey and swallowed. That burn was like nothing else and boy, did it cure what ailed me.

The man sitting next to me helped, too.

He leaned toward me and nudged my shoulder with his. "Not judging here, Jade, but Jack was made to be sipped."

I smiled. "It's not all gowns and tassels in my world..." I paused, trying to find a decent nickname for him on-the-fly, but I failed at shit like that. Finally, I said, "Handsome."

He chuckled. "You think I'm handsome?"

With a pointed look, I pursed my lips. "Like you don't know. But, I don't know your name either."

Warmth filled his eyes. "Steel."

I looked at him expectantly. "That's it? Is that your first name or last name? Or is that some sort of dramatic intro? Steel... Jim Steel."

He huffed out another chuckle. "No, Jade. Everyone calls me Steel."

I dragged my fingernails under my chin to scratch an itch. Steel seemed like a road name for a biker, but that was ludicrous. For one thing, he wasn't wearing a cut, and the Harley dealership was out near I-75 with plenty of hotel options nearby. For another thing, I sensed he was here on business – and not of the biker variety. The name fit him though, and it was a common last name.

After a moment, I nodded. "Okay, Steel. I'm Simone."

He nodded slowly. "Gorgeous name. From what you said, you're not just celebrating."

I shrugged and sipped my drink. "Pretty much, but the more I think on it, I'm pretty sure a lame break-up is worth celebrating more than my degree."

He looked at me askance. "You got dumped?"

I nodded and finished my drink. "It was a slow dump, too. Which makes me feel like a dumbass."

Steel scoffed. "*He's* the dumbass."

The bartender brought out a plate of wings for Steel and put my plate of pizza in front of me. He spied my empty glass. "Another Jack Daniel's Honey or something else?"

I nodded and handed my credit card to the bartender.

Steel said, "Add hers to my tab. And I'll take another Old Fashioned."

"Yes, sir," the bartender said.

"You don't have to do that," I said, looking up at Steel.

His eyes darted side to side as he stared into my eyes. "Yeah, I do, Jade. A gorgeous woman like you has something huge to celebrate, she doesn't pick up that tab. I do. Eat your pizza."

The authority in his tone lit something inside me. Normally that something would be my temper, but with him, it was like all reason went out the window.

"You're bossy," I blurted.

"Look at me Jade," he said.

I did as ordered. There it was – a hint of malice shining from his eyes along with the power. That was so attractive, I felt it in my nipples, my pussy, and right down to my tingling toes.

He grinned. "You have no idea *how* bossy I can be."

My teeth sunk into my lower lip. "Then show me."

Oh shit! Did I really just say that?

My girl Alexandra would smack me upside my head if she'd heard that. Then she'd remind me that it's better to keep your cards close to your chest. Something about being with Steel made me aggressive and assertive.

He eyed me for a long moment. Just as I expected blatant rejection, he said, "I'll think about it. Now eat your pizza, Simone. I don't like to repeat myself."

"Yes, sir."

Chapter 2

Naughty

Steel

*Was I going to **do this?***

Who was I kidding? Of course, I was. The moment that damned door opened for the thirtieth time, letting the coldest gust of air inside, I'd turned to glower at whoever stood there. One look at her, though, and my glower faded like waking from a great dream.

She was a dream. Shiny, brown hair that fell to her mid-back, big brown eyes, and lips stained in a shade like red wine. She was tall and slender, but had curves exactly where a man would want them. That leather top had me itching to rip it open.

I turned away since I knew the bartender was watching me – waiting for my order.

"An Old Fashioned, please, and I'll have the wings. Medium heat, and ranch on the side – not blue cheese."

He nodded, but before he turned away, I said, "And one more thing, if that woman who just walked in sits anywhere at this bar, you hold my food until she gets hers."

He glanced at college girl and back to me. "And if she doesn't?"

My eyes widened a touch. "Then bring it when it's ready."

The man on the other side of the empty seat shook his head and chuckled. "You're dreaming."

I ignored him because the asshole who had previously vacated the empty seat for a small booth on the other side of the restaurant heckled her, telling her to smile. That man couldn't tell a mule to be stubborn. I wanted to punch him, but I didn't want to cause a scene.

The way she entered the room, it was clear something was wrong. Like she was jaded, but wouldn't let that interfere with her life. My sense was that despite whatever was wrong, she was going to face it and overcome it.

That made her even sexier.

When she sat down, her soft, floral scent invaded my nose. I thought I would struggle to keep my eyes off her cleavage. Instead, I'd struggled to take my eyes off that necklace. The sterling silver dragon clutching a ring of jade struck a chord with me, like I'd seen it before, but I hadn't. It looked like jewelry found at Bike Week or Biketoberfest in Daytona.

Even if I hadn't spoken to her, I knew it suited her, the dragon and the jade.

Then she'd asked me to show her how bossy I could be... but, fuck. Was I thinking about it?

Why was I thinking about it?

I'd ordered her to eat her pizza and she faced forward and obeyed. With a 'yes, sir' to boot. That pleased me to no end. Every time I thought she couldn't make my cock harder, she amped it up another notch.

She had finished her pizza and sat back with a satisfied groan. I stared at this bombshell brunette. She stared back at me like she could take any amount of scrutiny from me. My cock throbbed as I envisioned tying her naked to my bed at home and staring my fill. Unbidden, I saw myself marking her with my cum.

That thought jarred me.

For fuck's sake, she couldn't be more than twenty-two years old. Until six months ago, I'd thought I had a son her age. He was why I was in this God-forsaken town. My efforts at calling, texting, and emailing had all failed.

I hadn't been able to find him today. An hour ago, I'd visited the address his mom gave me. A neighbor across the hall said he'd moved out *just today*.

Simone's eyes caught mine, a devilish light shining from them. "This has to be the best *and* worst pizza I've ever had."

I chuckled, and realized I'd laughed more since she sat her lush ass next to me than I had all year. "That doesn't make sense, smart girl."

One eye brow went up and down. "It's the best because it had the perfect blend of oregano and garlic in the sauce, plus they were generous with the olives."

I nodded. "Gonna take your word for it."

She lowered her voice. "It was the worst because the more I ate the hungrier I felt."

I faced forward. It wasn't hard to read between those lines since they were triple-spaced. She wasn't alone. The sexual tension between us was killing me.

I focused on wiping hot sauce from my fingers with a wet-nap. "Why was it lame?"

She angled her body toward me. "I'm sorry, what?"

My lips tipped up and I couldn't help but feel pleased at catching her off-guard. "You called it a 'lame break-up.' What made it lame? Or is that just old slang coming back as new slang?"

She stared at me for a long moment, and it was the first time I couldn't read her.

She shook her head. "Not new slang. He made arrangements to move in with a buddy of his last month, and part of me thought something was up then. I asked him point blank earlier this week. He said we were cool. Apparently he lied and gave me a slow-burn break-up."

My eyes widened and I stared at my cocktail glass. "Jesus. What a pussy."

The bartender sidled up to us. "Can I get these plates out of your way?"

Simone smiled and handed him her plate. "Thanks."

He grabbed my plate. "Another round?"

I glanced at Simone.

She grinned at the bartender. "Yes, but make mine an Old Fashioned. It'll be fun to see if it's as good as—"

"Vicious Vinyl's?" the bartender asked, returning her grin.

I wanted to punch him, grinning at her like that.

Simone nodded.

"Mine's a thousand times better, miss."

I propped an elbow on the bar and leaned closer to her. "Do you like Old Fashioneds?"

She mimicked my posture, leaning closer. "Love them."

The urge to kiss her overwhelmed me, but I wouldn't do that in public. Instead, I lowered my lips to within an inch of her ear. "Can you handle that much whiskey, Jade?"

Her head turned and those lips were a breath away. "You can't imagine how much I can handle."

Our gazes held for a long, loaded moment. I hadn't wanted a woman this fucking bad in years.

"Have you thought about it?" she asked, her hand gripping my thigh.

I reached down and laced our fingers together. "Haven't thought of anything else. Are you trying to be naughty?"

"Definitely," she whispered, grazing her nose against mine.

I sat back in my seat, breaking part of her spell. To keep her from being disappointed, I squeezed her hand. "Good to know, woman."

Her brown eyes roved my face. "Do you like naughty?"

The bartender garnished two glasses. I waited until he delivered our drinks before I answered. "There's a time and place for everything, Jade. The better question is whether you can handle the consequences."

With her left hand, she swirled the red stirrer in her glass. "Consequences?"

I moved our hands to her upper thigh and leaned forward. In a low voice, I said, "Naughty girls get spankings where I'm from."

Any other place, that ghost of a smile would have made me groan. The man to her left watched us avidly. He'd been watching all along, but he'd been better about hiding it. I didn't want him witnessing anything between me and Simone other than our very sexually-charged banter – even that was too much for his ass.

"Where are you from?" she asked, sipping her drink and setting it down.

Mentioning the word 'Georgia' in this college town could start a fight. "Not from here," I said, letting go of her hand to grab my cocktail.

"And you're just ... passing through?"

There was another thing that appealed to me about her. From her tone alone, I could tell she didn't want an attachment, but she damn sure wanted me.

That was mutual, and not just because she was fucking gorgeous. She wanted me because of that undeniable attraction between us.

Not because I was president of the Devil Lancers.

Not because it would give her more status with a bunch of sweet-butts.

I loved that she didn't know who I was. She oozed sweetness and sexiness that wasn't geared to catching a man like me. Her question made it clear, she damn sure didn't want to trap me.

She was perfect.

"I hit the road at noon. No offense to your alma matter, but I won't ever come back here. Hard to say which '-ville' I hate more, Gainesville or Jacksonville."

Her face twisted fast in my direction. Those gorgeous eyes were wider than ever, but then she shuttered the outrage, nodded, and a calculating look took its place.

That wasn't good. Seeing as I'd come to the bar to drown my thoughts about my shitty luck and bad timing, maybe this chance encounter was going to crash and burn like everything else had today.

"Thinking awful hard over there, Jade."

She took a sip of her drink. "Not really. Just marveling at how life turns out sometimes."

"And how has life turned out?"

She leaned closer as though she didn't want anyone to hear us either. "My lame ex-boyfriend dumped me slow-burn style, and I wander into a place he swore wasn't any good. He was wrong though, because it's fucking excellent, and unless you're too chicken, I'm gonna get exactly what I want."

My nose grazed hers. "And what do you want, Simone?"

She took her time dragging her nose along my neck until her lips were centimeters from my ear. "I want to get laid for the first time in over two months." Her hand squeezed my thigh and she slid it up to my groin. "And I'm going to be very naughty, because of those consequences." She let out a breathy chuckle, the warm air forcing a shiver down my spine. "Well, that, plus I'm pretty sure you know *exactly* what you're doing."

Goddamn she was a temptress. But I hadn't had this much fun in over ten years. Maybe I didn't hate Gainesville so much after all. If all I got out of this trip was a great fuck with a college co-ed, that made the five-hour ride down from Augusta well worth it.

I moved her hand back to her lap and tilted my head back, staring at the dark ceiling. After a calming breath, I righted my head and looked at her. "What I ought to do to you...you should—"

She smirked and spoke in a flirty tone. "I should what? Are you going to tell me to smile more?"

My eyes flared. "Fuck, no. I'd rather *give* you something to smile about."

Her teeth sunk into the side of her lower lip and I knew we were on the same wavelength.

The bartender had left the bill close to my drink. I opened the small leather folder, signed it to my room number along with a hefty tip and slammed it shut.

I stood and picked up my cocktail. The man on her left watched me closely. I put my lips next to her ear so he wouldn't hear. "Let's go, Jade. Grab your drink, we'll finish it in my room."

FOR THE SECOND TIME, I couldn't get a read on her. She had been cool, calm, almost poised during the elevator ride up to the fifth floor. Once my room door closed, she seemed skittish.

I set my Old Fashioned on the credenza near the flatscreen. "Come here, Simone."

She faced me, her gaze locked with mine. Her chest rose with a deep inhale. It felt like an eternity waiting for her to take that first step, but then she did and I exhaled. Gently, I took her drink and set it on the corner of the credenza.

Even if it struck me as being outlandish after our chemistry downstairs, but there were many ways law enforcement tried to capture outlaws like me. For all I knew, this could be a set up and she'd accuse me of forcing myself on her.

I hated having to ask this, but the question had to be raised. "You having second thoughts?"

Her eyes slid to the side and back to me. "No. It's just... you haven't even kissed me."

Relief washed through me. I closed the slight distance between us, one arm going around her waist, my other hand at her cheek, fingers splayed wide.

My control felt like a rubber band stretched to the hilt. One false move and I would snap. The things I wanted to do to her. Once I started, I wasn't sure I'd be able to stop. It was the only problem with an arrangement like this. The clock was ticking and I only had two condoms on me. If one night wasn't enough...

"Are you just gonna stare at me?" she asked.

My arm at her waist gave her a squeeze. "Maybe."

Those tantalizing lips curled. "Good to know."

She paid attention downstairs. I liked that.

Her nose ran along my neck. My control snapped. I pulled her closer, used my hand at her cheek to tilt her head back, and I grazed her lips once before crushing my mouth to hers.

Downstairs, I'd thought I'd noticed everything about her, but I'd missed her fingernails. Feeling them in my hair forced a groan from me, and I dropped my hand from her cheek to wrap that arm around her shoulders.

Her mouth opened. My tongue accepted her invitation and I got my first taste of her.

Whiskey and pizza. She tasted so much better than I'd expected.

Fuck.

Her hands left my hair, and she tugged my shirt free of my jeans. Downstairs, I'd noticed her eying the tats on my arm, which felt nice, but I didn't want her to see all of the tats on my body. Those questions led to sharing which led to intimacy – a level of intimacy I wouldn't give her or any woman.

I tore my mouth free, but rested my forehead on hers while I caught my breath. "Goddamn, woman."

She gave a breathy chuckle. "Backatcha, handsome."

I wasn't handsome, but I'd let her keep that misguided notion. "Let me get the lights. It's too fuckin' bright in here."

Her head cocked to the side. "Too bright? I don't get to see you?"

At the entryway, I opened the bathroom door and turned on the light. Then I tagged the main switch for the room. The only light came from a desk lamp on the far side of the room and the bathroom, but it was enough to see each other. Yet not enough for her to make out too many of the details of my tattoos. In a half-crouch, I yanked off my boots and socks.

Barefoot, I stalked toward her, while unbuckling my belt. "That work for you, Jade?"

"Yeah," she whispered, her hands going to the bottom of her fake leather shirt.

"Stop right there," I said with all the authority I could muster.

The sound of her sucking in a breath made my dick harder. I undid my jeans and pulled the zipper down, letting them hang open. Her eyes went straight to my groin.

"Don't worry, you're gonna get a very good look at my hard cock."

Her legs fidgeted.

I pulled my shirt off, tossing it toward my duffel in the corner. My jeans crept down my legs and I shoved them to the floor along with my boxer briefs.

"Good God," she whispered. Her eyes met mine. "You don't need me to tell you this, but you are impressive. You're inked... almost every-where."

My fingers gripped the lower edge of her shirt. "Are you inked, baby?"

The light from the bathroom was just bright enough for me to see her eyes flare. "Not yet."

My brow arched at those words.

Too bad I wouldn't be the man inked on her skin. That fucking thought really jarred me and I yanked her shirt up harder than I'd intended.

I dropped the material to the floor and took in her breasts which were hidden behind two scraps of off-white satin with my favorite fruit embroidered on the cups.

"Cherries," I murmured.

"Yeah," she whispered.

It was like she was made for me. That was insane.

"You are a goddess."

She scoffed.

"Are you trying to anger an old man?" I asked, but the words *your old man* were on the tip of my tongue. That wasn't right.

She smiled. "You're not old, and age is just a number."

I cupped her breasts with my hands, determined to ignore that state-ment. "Not sure if I want to take this off you or not."

Her hands went to my waist and slid up to my chest. "Why not?"

"Because I fuckin' love cherries," I said, before I kissed her, harder than the first kiss.

Her hands were pinned between our bodies. My dick scraped against her pants, and I pulled back. "Get your pants off, Simone."

Her eyes gave her away, but I recalled her words down at the bar about being naughty. Rather than do what I said, she dropped to her knees. Her hands took hold of my aching cock just before she ran her tongue up and down the length of me.

I tipped my head back, hissing, "Fuck me."

She let out a breathy laugh. "That's the general idea, Steel."

This wasn't part of my plan. My hands went to her underarms and I hauled her up, then lifted her up in the air. She wrapped her legs around my waist and kissed me. My hips moved reflexively. I needed inside her, but I wasn't going to do that until I tasted her.

Every lush ounce of her.

I laid her down on the bed. She smirked up at me and Mona Lisa could learn a thing or two from Simone.

"Pleased with yourself, I see."

"I didn't say that."

My fingers searched for the button on her pants, but didn't find one. I slid my hands around for a zipper, but then she raised her hips and shoved the waist band down. I dug my fingers in to make sure her panties were part of the deal, and I tugged them off.

"Naughty on purpose, weren't you?"

"Maybe."

With her ankles in my hands, I flipped her to her stomach. The globes of her ass were round and firm. I wanted to sink my teeth into one, but first, somebody needed to learn about consequences.

Simone

OH MY GOD. JUST when I thought I couldn't get any wetter, Steel grabbed my ankles and twisted me to my stomach.

I was so fucking turned on, anything might make me orgasm.

He kissed like a dream. That bossy streak lit a fire in me I didn't know needed lighting, and those tattoos. God, I couldn't wait to take them all in with my eyes, fingers, tongue... maybe even my teeth.

He was delicious. Or what little of him I'd tasted.

Older men, who knew?

His finger skated along my pussy, delved inside, and then withdrew.

I looked over my shoulder at him. "What was that?"

Those fierce, dark eyes burned on me. "Taking stock, you might say."

I narrowed one eye at him, but didn't say anything.

Fire burned across my ass and I heard a resounding smack. He'd spanked me. I gasped and moaned a little. My hands fisted the downy comforter when his finger pushed inside me again.

"Oh, yeah. You like that, baby."

Did I ever.

He delivered a smack to my other ass cheek and pleasure radiated through my body. It scored a path straight to my breasts. I didn't even try to hide my moan. His hands came to my hips and lifted. I shifted back on my knees, eager for him to give me more.

I didn't realize how wet my pussy was until he slid his finger inside me again. 'Taking stock.' Steel could take whatever he wanted from me tonight. That was certain. I rocked back when his finger retreated and he pushed it back inside while making a tsking sound.

"Greedy and naughty, baby."

He pulled away and put that hand on my hip. I expected another spanking, but from the corner of my eye, I saw him hunch over me. The next thing I felt was a warm pinching sensation. I glanced over my shoulder and saw he had his mouth on the globe of my ass.

"Oh God!"

"You've got a fucking fantastic ass, Simone. We had more time, and some lube, I'd fuck this ass."

I bit my lip. Part of me wanted that, but he was right. We didn't have time. I shifted back on my knees to get closer to him and that glorious cock.

He gripped my hips tight. "Simone... patience."

"Steel, I need you to—"

He shifted me to my back and hovered over me. "Know what you need, baby. Gonna give it to you, but I'm gonna savor every bite, every lick, every fucking moment of making you come."

I slid my hands up his taut arms. He had tattoos aplenty, and I couldn't believe how attractive they were on him. A large tat on his chest looked like a grim reaper, but not quite. Rather than carry a scythe, the figure carried a strange looking sword. The art reminded me of an MC patch, but it didn't have any script or rockers. No, he wasn't an MC man -even if he had the energy and power to command a chapter.

His eyes were locked on mine and he seemed pleased watching me ogle his body and tattoos. With a heavy sigh, he lowered himself to me and kissed me.

I lost myself in this kiss, it was so good. Possibly the best ever, so I could only imagine what having sex with him would be like. And God, was I ever here for it. I lifted my hips, letting his cock rub through my slick folds.

He backed away. "Ah, ah, baby. Patience."

Rather than kiss me again, he lowered his lips to my neck and gave me a nipping kiss. It caught me off-guard and I gave a slight hiss.

"Too much?" he asked against my shoulder.

"No, just... unexpected."

I felt him smile against my skin. I liked that entirely too much. He dragged his lips down to my breasts, nipping at me along the way.

"Love this fuckin' bra, baby."

"I'm glad," I breathed.

He pulled the cup down and took my nipple in his mouth, sucking hard. Harder than anyone else had, and I realized he definitely knew what he was doing.

My hand cupped the back of his head. "Yes, Steel, don't stop. That feels so freaking good."

He chuckled and pulled away. Then he yanked down the other cup of my bra and lavished that breast with attention.

Need built inside me like never before, and I rocked my hips, wishing I had his cock, his fingers, anything.

He lifted his head with a grin. His eyes seemed to twinkle with mischief in the dim light. "Your tits are delicious. Gotta find out if your pussy is, too."

Like a snake, he slithered down the bed, grabbing my thighs as he went. He shoved my legs up and over his shoulders. My body jerked like a live wire when he put his mouth on my pussy because he went *right* to the spot. He didn't need any words from me, he *knew* a woman's body.

My high pitched moan filled the room and I draped my arm over my mouth. He reached up and tweaked my nipple. "Oh, no, Simone. I want to hear you, and I don't give a fuck who else hears you. Gonna make you come so fuckin' hard, and I want to see it, hear it, and taste it."

I grabbed his hand at my breast, bucked my hips and hissed, "Jesus! Your dirty talk is fucking hot, Steel."

He chuckled and his fingers dug into my ass. "Thanks, baby, but I prefer *doing* over talking."

The way he latched onto me, he proved that to be true. I couldn't stop my orgasm if I tried. I ground my pussy into his face with abandon. His hands gripped my ass like a vice. There would be marks there, and I loved that. Everything about this had the potential to be addictive. I didn't want to come down from this high.

After a moment, he lapped at me as if he were finished.

I had no shame. "Again."

A full-fledged smile split his lips and my belly pitched. He was hot, no doubt, but when he smiled like that.

Fuck, yes.

He was everything any woman would want.

He bit my inner thigh and I squirmed. "Baby, it's like you said downstairs. You're gonna get exactly what you want, but my cock is fit to fuckin' burst. Time to pound you into this bed and *really* make you scream."

With my coyest grin, I asked, "You think so?"

He chuckled, planted his lips on my other thigh and sucked hard on my skin. His eyes slid to mine and my breathing picked up. He let go of me with a pop. "Yeah, woman. I know so."

In a series of fluid movements, he shifted my legs off his shoulders, rose up on his knees, grabbed my ankles and flipped me to my belly again.

"On your knees, naughty girl."

I grinned into the pillows, but pushed up on my hands and knees.

Within seconds, he spanked me again and I moaned.

"Thinking you like that too much."

"I don't like it," I muttered.

His hands rubbed both of my cheeks. "Are you lying to get more punishment, baby?"

Reflexively, I pushed back against his big warm hands. "I'm not lying. I don't like it, I *love* it."

The sound he made was somewhere between a groan and a growl. "You're lucky I gotta get a condom, or you'd pay for that, baby."

The bed jostled, then I heard his clothes rustling.

I looked over my shoulder mesmerized by the sight of him rolling on protection. "You're so good at it, who wouldn't love it?"

His brows arched. "Point taken, but you're gonna love my cock even more."

Considering how much I loved everything he did to me so far, I knew he spoke the truth.

The bed dipped when he came back. He spread my legs wider and rubbed the globes of my ass again. "What I want to do to you, woman," he murmured.

I reached back and stroked his hand. "Then do it, Steel. I want everything you can give me, any way you want to give it to me."

He made a sound again, but this time it was one-hundred-percent growl. His cock entered me, but didn't get too far.

"Oh," I cried out.

"How are you so fuckin' tight, Simone?"

"Could it be that you're so fuckin' big?"

He chuckled and smacked the side of my ass. That perverse pleasure surged through me and he thrust inside another inch.

"Yes," I hissed.

"You feel so fuckin' good, Simone," he whispered and gave a slight thrust.

It took some time, but his cock finally bottomed out inside me. He had his chest pressed to my back, his hands next to mine on the bed.

"You are perfect, Simone. Gripping my cock so fucking tight, and so wet."

He brought his fingers to my clit and I nearly collapsed.

"You on the edge, baby?"

I shook my head. I'd heard of edging, but I didn't think this was it. "I don't know. I need you to fuck me, Steel. Please."

He gathered my hair in his fist and placed a kiss on my neck. "Hang on tight, baby."

His heat left my back, but he kept tight hold of my hair. He put his free hand on my hip, pulled on my hair, and pounded into me.

I didn't know if I screamed or I moaned, but no one had done anything like this with me. This was next-level fucking.

His hand at my hip reached for my breast. "Push up, woman," he ordered.

He stilled enough that I was able to push my weight up. His hand at my breast moved across my torso and he pulled me back so I was sitting on his lap.

"So fuckin' gorgeous," he breathed.

I held his hand to me, waiting for him to pound into me.

His fingers played with my nipple. "Jade, you gotta ride me."

I tilted my head back until it hit his shoulder. Our gazes caught in the dim room. I grabbed his neck and pulled his lips to mine.

He cut the kiss short. "You've never had it like this? Doggie-style meets reverse cowgirl?"

My teeth sunk into my lip. "No, but I'm a quick learner."

His body jerked with a laugh, then he sank his teeth into the soft skin at the nape of my neck. "Damn right you are. Now ride."

The way he said those two words. It wasn't just bossy, it was as though he said those words frequently. Ocala wasn't too far away, maybe he'd come to town on horse business. I forced my mind back to the moment, and rode him.

It was so freaking good, I screamed with pleasure. Turned out, Steel lied. He cared if other people heard my pleasure because he covered my mouth with his and swallowed my screams – like they were his and his alone.

STEEL SAUNTERED OUT OF the bathroom, and I didn't care if he saw me gawking at his tats. The problem was, he had so many I couldn't focus on a single one before he moved out of the light. Not to mention, his thick cock hung between his legs and that stole my attention.

"You are something else, Simone."

"I could say the same about you, Steel."

He climbed under the covers and settled next to me. "I ought to give you the choice to go home right now."

My brows furrowed. "What do you mean?"

He rolled to his side, propping his head in his hand. "That was intense fucking, baby. You might have had your fill and want to go home. But the thing is I'm not letting you go anywhere right now."

I chuckled. "Why not?"

He grinned. "For one thing, it's cold and rainy outside. Nobody needs to be out in that shit. For another, it's just after midnight. I don't give a damn if you live at those over-priced, pretentious apartments across the fuckin' street, or across town, you aren't goin' home alone this late at night."

I bit back my rejoinder of, 'Okay, dad.' Instead, I asked, "Is that all?"

His eyes raked my body. "No. The most important reason I'm not giving you a fuckin' choice is because I'm not finished with you."

I smiled my closed-lip smile as warmth swirled through my insides. "Good, because I'm not through with you either. Someone told me I'd get up close to his cock, and he's yet to deliver."

He made a low roaring sound, reached out and pulled me on top of him. I kissed him before he kissed me, but he took full control of it. Our tongues danced around each other, and it turned into a make-out session like no other.

I felt his hard cock poking against my leg. I dragged my lips along his jaw line. "Can I finally give you a blowjob?"

He gathered my hair in his hand, and tugged. I stared into his dark eyes. "You never have to ask me, baby. I'll always take that sweet mouth on me, but first, give me another kiss."

CHAPTER 3

NEEDLED

STEEL

MY BLADDER WOKE ME up at a quarter after three. I trudged to the toilet, wincing against the bright light.

I finished my business, washed my hands, and stepped out of the bathroom. I caught sight of Simone in the bed and I wished I had another condom. She was so fucking beautiful with her olive skin and that mane of hair spilling over her shoulder. I recalled gripping that hair tight while I railed her from behind.

Fuck.

I turned off the light so I didn't stand here staring at her and getting hard – or harder. She had taught me something, though. I needed to find a woman who wasn't in the MC life. A crazy-ass part of me wanted to drag her back to Augusta, but I knew better.

Hell, the more I thought about it, the way she reacted to my name, I got a feeling she knew about bikers – but that had to be my imagination. A powerful yawn reminded me I needed more sleep before a five-hour ride. When we woke up, I'd give her another orgasm by eating her out. That sounded like a plan.

On my side, I pulled the covers up to my shoulder. She let out a sleepy sigh and her body shifted toward me on the king-sized bed. Her sigh sounded similar to the sounds she made when I'd used my last condom and fucked her missionary-style. Somehow I'd restrained myself and took her slow and gentle. That memory had me craving a repeat, but I was out of condoms.

That was my life. I had planned a meeting with my 'son,' but wound up meeting a college girl who turned out to be phenomenal in bed.

I rolled to my back as I wondered if there was another way I could corner Jordan. He needed to know the truth. I wasn't really his father – though I would always be his dad. In reality, I was the dumbass his conniving mother had fleeced for twenty-one years. Maybe he could learn the value of a paternity test, even if I didn't.

My thoughts had distracted me from Simone's sleeping form next to me, which was exactly when she rolled so she was facing me and put her arm over my waist.

I should have shifted her off me. I never let women sleepover. Having her warm, soft body next to me like this felt like a rich dessert. Decadent in more ways than one. Her pressing against me, it felt as though she were mine. Something about this felt satisfying and right.

I hadn't had that even when I lived with Debra and Jordan. She didn't sleep close to me or gravitate toward me in her sleep.

I allowed myself to indulge one last time and held Simone close while I fell back to sleep.

I had steeled my heart to women. I'd reinforced that barricade after I learned about Debra's deception. No woman would ever be in my bed permanently.

HOTELS NEEDED SILENCERS FOR their doors. While that would never happen, it sucked waking up to multiple doors banging and slamming.

I rolled over and my hand hit rumpled sheets.

"The fuck?" I whispered, propping myself up on an elbow and opening my eyes wide.

The emptiness in the room felt like a weighted blanket. I fell to my back.

"Goddamnit," I bit out.

How the hell had that slip of a woman snuck out on me? I was a light sleeper. Talk about plans going to shit. I hadn't woken up with such hard morning wood in months. Simone's sweet mouth would have been the perfect remedy.

Shit.

My disappointment had me muttering to myself, "Get your shit together."

It also bothered me that the flirty bombshell had taken a play out of my book. Love 'em and leave 'em.

The rational part of my brain said it was better this way.

No awkward goodbyes or any of that shit.

With my eyes closed, I fisted my cock and gave it a few good tugs.

I couldn't get the vision of her entering that restaurant out of my head. She would make some lucky man very happy.

Jealousy coursed through me, weakening my erection. Everything was out of whack in this damned town. I didn't struggle with the green-eyed monster, but I hated the idea of another man having her.

Yeah, it was good one of us had been smart today.

After a shower and breakfast, I stood next to my Harley in the hotel parking lot. The sun glared off the surrounding vehicles and the apartment windows across the street. At least it wasn't raining.

I gave Jordan one last call. It rolled to voice mail and I locked my cell into the phone mount on my bike. Even though Simone had ditched me without saying goodbye, I didn't hate Gainesville as much as Jacksonville

But it was high time to get home.

I PARKED MY BIKE behind the Devil Lancer's clubhouse at five o'clock. As I approached the clubhouse, the back door opened. Torque, my Vice President, sauntered out with a groupie under his arm. His sandy brown hair was pulled back in a low-ponytail, and his cheeks appeared to be shaved.

He shot me a lazy grin. "Yo, you made great time, Steel."

I nodded. "Yeah. Everything good here?"

His grin widened to a smile and his light brown eyes gleamed with mischief. "Very. You missed a helluva bonfire last night."

After giving him a chin lift, I went inside. The scent of smoke wasn't as strong as usual, but the bonfire would have kept everyone outside. I rounded the bar toward the corridor to my room.

Josie, a sweet-butt I'd never been with, came out of the kitchen and stepped into my space. It was fifty-two degrees outside and she wore a black, lace-up corset – her breasts nearly spilling out, along with tight black short-shorts. She left nothing to the imagination.

After last night, that didn't appeal.

She skimmed her fingers down my arm. "Hey, Steel. Wanna fuck? Put one of those two condoms in your wallet to good use."

My mind tripped over her words. Once they sunk in, my body tightened.

I stood straighter, towering over her. "What the fuck did you just say?"

"What?" she asked, fake innocence dripping from a single word.

"Repeat yourself," I thundered.

I didn't know if she was stupid or brave, but she didn't cower at my tone or volume.

"I asked if you wanna fuck."

My eyes widened and I vaguely heard the back door open.

"And?" I demanded when she went silent.

"And what? Everyone knows a man keeps a condom in his wallet."

My fury had a stranglehold over me.

"That's not what you said," I roared.

Torque moved into my line of vision. "Brother. What's the problem?"

I took three deep breaths. They didn't calm me, but I controlled my rage. I glared at Josie. "How did you know I have two condoms in my wallet?"

Fear hit her blue eyes for a second, then she shook her head. "I didn't say that. I said one of the two—"

She realized her fuck-up and snapped her mouth shut.

I turned my head and blew out a long exhale. This woman had no idea the wrath I wanted to rain down on her right now. I faced her. "One goddamn question – and you better answer it the first fucking time. Did you mess with my condoms?"

I watched Torque's face cloud with anger on my behalf. Our brotherhood ran deep.

The silence stretched.

"Answer him," Torque shouted, making her jump.

The fear returned to her eyes and she spoke in a simpering voice. "Only the ones in the opened box... and your wallet."

"How the hell could she do that?" someone asked.

That didn't matter. I couldn't believe this shit. Two months ago, I found out I wasn't Jordan's father and had been trapped twenty-one years ago, only for this bitch to fuck with my stash and—

"Fuck!" I yelled while thoughts of last night hit me like a hail of bullets.

Simone needed to know about this... and I had no fuckin' way of reaching her.

"Get her out," I hissed, turning away.

"What? I didn't—"

I whirled on her. "You fucked with my wallet. I'd kill a man for less. Count your fucking blessings, bitch."

"Let's go," Torque ordered, grabbing her arm.

I stormed to my room, yanked open my nightstand drawer and threw the box of condoms against the wall.

A primal yell tore out of me and I shoved my fingers into my hair.

That action reminded me of Simone's nails dragging along my scalp not even twenty-four hours ago.

"Goddamnit," I whispered.

Someone had the balls to knock on my door.

"Go away!" I yelled.

"Not happening, brother. Let me in," Torque demanded.

"Come in and make it quick, motherfucker," I hollered.

He came inside, shut the door, and eyed the box of condoms on the floor. His lips pursed and he kicked the box toward the en suite bathroom.

"Guess you won't need those any more. I'll get a prospect to take out your trash."

I paced the room, my hands still in my hair.

Torque wasn't known for being patient. "Jesus, man. She got to your wallet, fucked with your rubbers. You went to visit Jordan, not get laid. But you're acting like you went to a fuckin' orgy bare or some shit."

In two strides, I grabbed Torque by the throat and had him up against my door. "You think I want to be trapped by another fuckin' woman? You think I want to bring another kid into the world without knowing a bitch planned on that?"

"No, man. I get that," he rasped out.

I stared at him a long moment and finally let him go. I hated that I'd harmed Simone. My anger wasn't dissipating. I paced to the other side of the room.

"What the hell happened in Gainesville? Did you talk to Jordan?"

I scoffed. "No. My fucking shit timing... I went to his apartment, a woman across the hall told me he'd moved out, get this, *that fuckin'* day."

He shook his head. "Your timing sucks, man. But, what's got you so pissed? I'm guessing you got laid."

Just thinking about my time with Simone calmed me down, a little. "Yeah. It's a long fuckin' story, man. You seemed to be on your way somewhere. I'll... figure shit out."

Torque scoffed. "Screw that, Steel. I'll go get a bottle of Jack—"

"No," I snapped, my eyes boring into him.

His head reared back. "Christ. You always drink whiskey, man. What the fuck is up with you?"

I closed my eyes and exhaled. How had she gotten so up in my head? I couldn't drink Jack Daniel's without thinking of her, I couldn't stand that I might have impregnated her and she didn't even know it yet.

I opened my eyes. "Bring some beers. I can't afford to get shitfaced tonight, no matter how much I want that."

Torque came back with a bucket of beers on ice and a bottle of Johnny Walker Blue label.

My vice president poured two shots, slid one to me and we downed them without preamble... or fucking toasts.

Christ, every damned thing reminded me of her.

Torque uncapped a beer and handed it to me. "Tell me about her. A woman across the hall told you Jordan moved, did you bang his neighbor?"

I took a swig of beer. "No, fuck, no. Once I found out he'd moved, I should have packed up and left, but I couldn't get out of my room reservation, so I went down to the bar and had a drink."

"Okay."

"This fucking asshole wouldn't shut up. He ignored me when I told him to keep it down."

Torque shook his head. "Didn't he read your patches?"

I let my head tilt. "I wasn't wearing my cut. A prick at the front desk had insisted gang emblems weren't allowed on the property."

"Fuckin' bullshit," he muttered.

"Yeah, finally the asshole at the bar yelled something inappropriate and a businessman took it up with the bartender. Asshole went to the other side of the fuckin' restaurant."

"What's this guy got to do with any damned thing?"

I swallowed more beer. "He gave me my in with the hottest brunette I've ever laid eyes on, since she walked in not a minute later wearing a fucking leather shirt."

"Really?"

I set my beer down. "It was fake leather, but at first glance I thought it was the real deal."

He nodded. "And you and she got busy."

I nodded. "Used both fuckin' condoms for all the good it did either one of us, Tor."

He pressed his lips together and wobbled his head. "I don't know, man. If she's on the pill, then you just have to get your ass tested again."

I took a deep breath and tried not to let my anger get the best of me. "That's pretty short-sighted, man."

He twisted a hand up. "What else are you gonna do? Doesn't sound like you got her number."

I sighed. "No, I didn't. But she deserves to know about this shit. And I got no way of finding her. Hell, I had Jordan's address and his fuckin' phone number and couldn't get in touch with him, how am I supposed to find her again?"

Torque set his empty beer bottle on the dresser. "Social media? College girls love to post on Instagram."

I scoffed. "Maybe ten years ago, but all I have is her first name."

He shook his head. "What about the bar tab? Tell the bartender you need to—"

"I put her food on my tab and charged it to my room. My ass didn't even pay attention when she whipped out her college ID."

Torque poured another shot for himself. "You ain't gonna like this, but I'm a man who looks for the silver lining." He downed his shot and leveled his eyes on me. "At least that cunt, Josie, didn't trap you."

I grabbed my beer and finished it. "Did she fuckin' leave already?"

Torque smiled and it was malicious. "No. I tied her ass up and she's in the closet in my room. Knew there was no way you were gonna let her off that fuckin' easy."

"Damn straight. My guess is she used needles to fuck up the condoms. Get Giant, Nelson, and Tuscon. She's gonna learn what it feels like to get needled."

A WEEK LATER, MY doctor called. I was clean of all STDs.

That was a relief.

Now if only I knew if Simone was pregnant.

CHAPTER 4

RED LIGHT SITUATION AT THE DONUT SHOP

SIMONE

IT TOOK WILLPOWER, BUT I left Steel sleeping in that hotel room bed. The blackout curtains were closed which was a bummer because I'd wanted to drink in his body and tats in the morning sunlight. It wasn't to be, though. While he cleaned up following the last time – even better than the first because he'd been so damned gentle – I'd gathered my clothes and tucked them close to my side of the bed so I could dress quietly and quickly.

I hadn't done many walks of shame, but note to self: wearing dressy clothes makes it easier. That was until my neighbor across the hall opened her door just as I was unlocking mine.

"Simone," she said, chipper as could be. After she gave me a once-over her tone down-shifted. "Oh, you must have spent the night at Jordan's new place. Are you moving, too?"

For the life of me, I couldn't remember her name. It happened every time I saw her, and I was too embarrassed to admit I'd forgotten her name.

I shook my head while pressing my lips together. "Nope. I'm here for a while."

Her eyes widened. "Are you getting a new roommate?"

With luck, I'd be getting a job at the firm I'd interned at this past semester, but that wasn't her business.

I smiled. "Probably, but it's up in the air for now. You look like you're going to work out, I don't want to keep you."

She pointed a finger at me. "Before I forget, there was a man here yesterday looking for Jordan. I let him know that he moved."

That got my attention. "What kind of man?"

Her head tilted with her grimace. "I'm not sure. He was older, forties or so, but I didn't ask him why he wanted to see Jordan."

I paused. "Was he wearing leather, like a leather vest with lots of patches on it?"

She frowned and shook her head. "No, but he had fantastic tattoos. He left before I could ask who he was."

I nodded. "Thanks for letting me know. I'll pass it along to Jordan."

Only half of what I said was true. It was good to know because with Jordan's inability to communicate, maybe he had a debt collector calling on him. However, the last statement was a lie. If I had anything to do with it, I wouldn't see or speak to Jordan again.

Inside the apartment, the emptiness hit me like a slap in the face. With nobody else here to talk to or distract me though, I couldn't ignore my feelings. It hurt that he'd pulled one over on me, and I couldn't believe I'd missed the signs. After living together for so long, his suggestion of moving out was an alarm bell like no other. Yet... I'd fallen for his excuse that he needed to focus on his studies and I was a distraction. For all of my book-smarts, I'd certainly let my heart get stupid.

I grabbed a tissue and wiped the tears from my face. After I blew my nose, another realization hit me. Tennyson lived in the same complex as Chet.

My stomach lurched at the idea that they'd already been together. No, that went too far. Jordan wouldn't do that. Still, as close as she stood to him and the way she held the door for him like a loyal puppy, they were definitely involved in some way.

The anger and betrayal I felt forced me to get my shit together. I wasn't going to cry any more for him. It might hurt every now and again, especially at nights – but I was better off without him.

And who knew, maybe I'd look for someone older than me in the future.

—

"ARE YOU SHITTING ME?" Alexandra shouted.

I had just told her about Jordan's crappy stunt yesterday evening, and I pulled the phone from my ear a moment before she blew out my eardrum.

I put the phone back to my ear. "Wish that I were."

"But, but... in front of all your friends?"

My lips twisted to one side. "Pretty sure their actions... or inaction, says they were always Jordan's friends and not mine."

She scoffed. "That isn't the point. Nobody does something that shitty."

"Jordan did."

"And he oughta pay," she muttered.

I loved Alexandra's ruthlessness, and I often wondered if it came from Uncle Cal or Aunt Mallory. Odds were it came from them both, but the viciousness of her tone... I suspected Uncle Cal played a big role in her protectiveness of me.

"As Mom would say, it's his loss."

She sighed and kept quiet for a moment. "I get the feeling you're leaving something out."

For whatever reason, I couldn't tell her about Steel. It wasn't that I was embarrassed, I just wanted to keep him to myself for a day or two.

After a beat, I said, "I am, but I promise to tell you soon."

She gasped. "Soon? How soon? Oh God, you're gonna have me quoting one of my mom's favorite songs. Just tell me what else happened. Jordan's clearly a jackass."

I wheezed with laughter. "You're absolutely right, Lex. You had his number from the jump."

After a lengthy pause, she said, "I should hold off on this, but now that he's moved out, when can I move in?"

"Commencement is on Tuesday. The next day, I'm coming home for Christmas and staying until just after New Years. So, I guess any time after the second. Does that work?"

"You betcha. Bonus, you'll be in town for the big Christmas bash. The Biloxi brothers always come out for that."

———

THE HOLIDAY PARTY WAS in full rip-roaring swing. I came out of the tiny bathroom tiny bathroom only to dodge a new prospect leading a woman down the corridor.

"Simone," Abby called from the end of the hall.

"Auntie Abs," I murmured, and trudged toward her.

She grabbed my hand. "You okay?"

I nodded.

"I heard you're done with Jordan."

My brows arched. "I didn't realize Alexandra had told you, but yeah."

She gave me a wry grin. "At least you can make a fresh start in the new year. You didn't need him anyway."

My eyes widened at her. Seemed everyone had an opinion about him except Dad. Then again, he never had opinions about my boyfriends.

He'd once told me, "An asshole puts a ring on your finger, I'll pay closer attention."

He wasn't fooling me, though. He paid *very* close attention to everyone I dated, and especially the man I'd lived with for two and a half years.

Abby eyed me for a moment. "You look... different."

I grinned. "It's the look of being single."

Her head shook ever so slowly. "No, it's something else. You're not as torn up about him dumping you as I would have expected."

Alexandra wandered up to us, handing me another beer. "That's because something else happened after he broke it off, but she won't tell me. I'm dragging her to Mom and Dad's tomorrow for mimosas, brunch, and Sunday gossip. If she met someone, we need all the deets."

Abby glanced from Alexandra back to me – her eyes assessing. "You had a fling, didn't you?"

How was Aunt Abby so damned intuitive about relationships... or lack thereof?

Alexandra gasped. "Oh my God! That look says that she can't believe you figured it out."

I shook my head. "No, this isn't the time—"

Abby gave me a pointed stare. "She doesn't drag you to Cal and Mallory's, I damn sure will."

I survived Sunday brunch and felt like I got one over on all the ladies since I just glossed over the fling with Steel. Bonus, Mom wasn't there and neither was Dad – which meant they hadn't found out.

Though, I suspected Aunt Abby would spill to Mom soon since I'd been back in Gainesville for over a week. It was Monday, and Alexandra had moved in this past weekend.

Someone knocked on the door and through the peephole I saw my landlord standing in the corridor wearing a big heavy toolbelt, which was unusual unless there was a problem.

"Hi, Mr. Brown. Is everything okay?" I asked.

"I thought I'd stop by and meet your new roommate," he said, pulling a screwdriver from his belt and fiddling with our doorknob.

"What's going on?" I asked.

"I'm changing your locks."

My brows drew together. "But I have Jordan's key, we don't need new locks."

He leveled his stern hazel eyes on me. "He left his key for you, but that don't mean it was the *only* key. I met your dad, he's a good guy, and smart as heck. I woulda thought he'd have taught you that."

I didn't expect Jordan do anything psycho, but I supposed a girl could never be too careful.

While he put finishing touches on the new locks, he said, "Besides, Ines across the hall told me about that man showing up looking for Jordan. You don't know if that boy got into some trouble before he left you."

Ines was her name.

I still knew I'd forget it in ten minutes.

I nodded. "You're right, Mr. Brown. I wasn't thinking. Thanks for taking care of things."

He handed me two new keys and put his tools away. "You're welcome, and remind your new roommate, no blocking the dumpster – ever."

"You got it."

Alexandra had gone to the campus bookstore in case they had a couple textbooks that had been in short supply.

Half an hour later, she had to knock on our door since her key no longer worked.

"What the hell, chickie? You lock out all your roommates on their first day?" she asked when I let her inside.

I laughed. "Mr. Brown changed the locks when you were gone. Your key is on the counter."

"Oh. That makes sense. So, what's the plan for tonight? Are we hitting that pizza joint so you can pick up another older man?"

I gave her a dry look. "Why do I bother telling you things?"

She grinned. "Because I make your life better."

"Let's get sushi. I'll show you the best place in town."

"Fine, but I'm buying. It isn't every day someone starts their first job in the real world."

I MADE IT THROUGH my first week of work without any problems – other than being dead-on-my-feet tired every single day. I'd heard that working for the man would tire you out, but this was ridiculous.

Friday night, I rolled inside at five-fifteen, hung my purse on my chair at the kitchen table, and went straight to the pantry for a box of cereal.

Alexandra watched me from the sofa. "Seriously, Simone? You're having cereal for dinner again? What gives? It's Friday night, we need to let loose. They're having some big party since it's the last Friday before classes start."

I put the cereal box on the table. "I'm sorry, honey. I didn't think office work would kick my ass like this, but I'm so freaking tired."

She twisted her lips to the side for a beat. "Maybe it's remnants of the bad sushi you had on Monday."

I shook my head. "I don't think that was bad sushi though. You didn't get sick, right? It was probably stress or something."

"But why are you so tired?"

I shrugged. "Some months my cycle's really intense and I get tired just before my period."

"Okay. So, are we streaming a new show or are we going with a comfort watch?"

I stifled a yawn as I pulled a bowl out of the cabinet. "Sorry, but I think I'm gonna crawl into bed. I hate that I'm not showing you all the ropes."

She swatted a hand at me. "Don't worry about that. Ines, across the hall, told me about this party. Maybe I'll see if I can tag along with her."

I nodded and dumped some cereal in the bowl. "Be careful though. I'm not tight with her, and some of these parties are cool, but there are still creeps lurking and waiting for newbies like you."

"Okay, Dad," she said in a deeper tone.

Talk about a knife to my heart.

Not because she'd called me out for being protective, but because it instantly reminded me of Steel. And how I'd wanted to say the same thing to him.

"Like I'm being parental right now. Besides, I know you'd obliterate any moron stupid enough to fuck with you."

"Nice save. If you need anything, call me."

"Goes both ways, Lex," I said, pouring milk on my cereal.

She scoffed. "You'd never hear your phone! I yelled at the TV last night when the basketball game went into overtime and you didn't even blink."

"I was in bed."

"On the couch," she chided.

I crunched on some Honey Nut Cheerios. "You're right, I'm sorry."

Alexandra chuckled. "Woman, you've got nothing to be sorry about. I'm just giving you grief. I'm more concerned about what's making you so tired. But tomorrow's Saturday, so you sleep in, got it?"

In the morning, I found a note from Alexandra on the fridge.

Hey sleepyhead!

The party was a bust and I got in before midnight. Ines is taking me to her Zumba class this morning. I have my phone — let me know if you want me to bring back donuts.

I loved donuts, but then that's why she'd offered. With a grin, I dug my phone out of my purse so I could text her.

Only if the donuts are Krispy Kremes. Otherwise, why bother, right?

She responded with a mind-blown emoji

The idea of coffee turned my stomach, and that, too, was strange. Nothing went better with a Krispy Kreme than a cup of java. I opened the calendar app on my phone. Then I plopped onto the couch.

My period was over a week late.

How was that possible?

Maybe it was stress.

No, it had to be stress.

We had used protection. Hell, the sight of Steel rolling a condom on his cock had replayed in my mind on the daily for the past four weeks. My vibrator failed at delivering anything close to the pleasure Steel gave me.

I should have woken him up that morning, but I hadn't been thinking about how difficult it would be to find another man who could weave such a spell with his tongue.

We should have exchanged numbers.

Ugh. That was ridiculous.

I hadn't wanted to jump into another relationship – that was outrageous.

Still, I hated when my period was late. It didn't happen often, but when it did I found a new appreciation for clichés like 'sweating bullets'.

My phone vibrated with another text from Alexandra saying she'd be leaving soon.

With a deep breath, I mustered some courage and called her.

"What? Are you gonna strangle me if I don't wait for that magic red light to go on at the Krispy Kreme?"

"I was hangry that day," I said in my defense.

She laughed. "If you say so. You never call, so what's up?"

I sighed. "I need a favor and you have to keep your mouth shut. If you rode with Ines, you can't let her know about this."

"Geez, what's with all the cloak and dagger?"

I bit my lower lip for a moment. "I need you to get me a pregnancy test."

Other than random background noise, silence filled my ear.

"It's only January, so this isn't some early April Fool's Day prank, right?"

My eyes closed, I shook my head, and I whispered, "Lex."

"I know, it's just... that is the last thing I expected, but I meant it, Simone. Anything you need, I'll get it. Should be home in fifteen minutes – depends on the red light situation at the donut shop."

Forty-five minutes later, it was the first time I didn't want to eat Krispy Kreme.

Lex had brought home three different tests, and after reading the instructions, I used all three. Every one of them had the same result.

Positive.

Yeah, we should have exchanged numbers – Steel and I.

What the hell was I going to do?

SUNDAY MORNING I DOWNED a yogurt with some granola, then vegged out on the sofa.

Alexandra curled up on the matching loveseat catty-corner to me. "We would have to take a road trip for this, since we live in Florida, but... you have choices, you know."

I paused the show and tipped my head to the side to catch her gaze. "Do I, though?"

She heaved a heavy sigh. "He would never know—"

"I would know. I don't think I can handle an abortion. I'd feel so much guilt."

"You're right, but you don't know who he is."

I gave a feeble shrug. "I haven't tried to find him yet."

"You said you never got his full name, just his last name. He's not from here, and he wasn't ever coming back. I don't see you tracking him down. You're going to do this all on your own? That's scary as hell."

I nodded. "Yeah, but at this point, it's too soon for me to make any firm decisions. Deep down, I can't see myself giving a child up for adoption, either."

She nodded and we were silent for a while. Then she said, "Your whole life's gonna change."

I stared at the watercolor print on the wall. "Yeah, but it'll be good... I think."

"Your job might decide—"

"Pretty sure there are laws about that sort of thing, Lex."

"Daycare—"

I found myself growing defensive. "You think Aunt Abby or Trixie won't help me?"

She put her hands up in surrender. "No, no, they would all pitch in, but... they're in Jacksonville. Where are you gonna live?"

That was a problem. I didn't want to move in with Mom and Dad... hell, my younger brother Bobby hadn't even moved out yet. Though he was away at college. The cost of rent was outlandish in Jacksonville – all over really, but the news had reported Jacksonville was tracking much higher than other cities.

I pressed my head back into the throw pillow. "I can't make a decision today."

Alexandra used a gentle tone when she spoke. "You can't wait too long either, Mony."

Damn, this was tough.

"One more thing since I'm playing the voice of reality."

"Oh, boy. What now?"

She exhaled a silent chuckle. "If you used a condom, and you're preggers... you need to get tested."

I nodded. "Yeah, you're right about that, too."

This conversation drove home how Alexandra was mature for nineteen... soon to be twenty. It likely resulted from Aunt Mallory and Uncle Cal's age when they had her. It still felt like she was my little sister, but it beat having this conversation with my mom.

I groaned.

"What?" Alexandra asked.

"I have to tell my parents. This is going to be so embarrassing."

Chapter 5

Payout or Bloodshed

Steel

Torque leaned against the bar in the clubhouse common room. "I hate to bring it up, but we should figure out how the hell Josie got in your room."

I sat on a barstool next to him and shook my head. This had been the first day thoughts of Simone hadn't assaulted me the moment I rolled out of bed. The last six weeks, I'd had dreams about her. If that wasn't bad enough, the craziest shit brought her to mind – and we'd only spent maybe twelve hours together.

"Hello... cat got your tongue? You got thoughts on this?" Torque demanded.

"How she did it doesn't fuckin' matter. It's done and it's *never* fuckin' happening again."

"So you're just gonna be what... celibate from now on?"

I glared at Torque. "It's not your fuckin' business, motherfucker."

Hard to say if my grouchiness stemmed from not getting laid since the night I was with Simone, or the fact I didn't want to even think about another woman.

The difference in our ages should make it simple. If she were twenty-one, that made me twenty years older than her. Most men would balk at the idea of seeing her again. Don't get me wrong, they'd jump at the chance to have a hot college girl in their bed, but they'd get their fill and move on – not dwell on that woman. I couldn't stop thinking about her, and my dick wouldn't stop getting hard at the thought of her.

It was almost enough to have me riding back to Gainesville to try and hunt her down, but I despised Florida for so many reasons.

"You're right. It isn't my business, but you're crankier than normal when you don't get laid."

"Prez needs to get laid?" A familiar voice asked from behind me, and Circles leaned over the bar and grabbed a bottle of vodka.

I turned to Circles. He wore jeans with a thick, black, leather belt. He had a loose, white t-shirt under his cut – though with his lanky frame, all his clothes seemed to hang on him. Today, his naturally-curly black hair was bound up in a man-bun. I caught his green-eyed gaze. "No, I don't need to get laid. You need to tell me what you found out about Corrupt Chrome. Are they still fucking with the strip club?"

Circles unscrewed the cap on the Grey Goose and downed a shot. "Not like they were, but they were at the Player's Palace. Can't exactly run them off without cause."

"We can refuse service for any reason," Torque said.

Circles looked past me to Torque. "Durham tried that two weeks ago. The cop who showed up said there was no cause to refuse them service. Not sure if that officer's just a straight arrow or if CC MC is paying him."

My patience slipped. "Where does that leave us, *today*? How many of those assholes were at the club?"

"Four of them. Their president, an enforcer, and two prospects. They gave me a message for you. Said, they aren't backing off on our territory without a pay-out or bloodshed. Either one works for them."

"Goddammit," I hissed.

Neither of those options were good. The Corrupt Chrome MC wasn't worth losing a brother, and we would never give them money.

"What's the problem, Prez? We pay them and it's all good," Circles said.

I glared at Circles. "Not a damn thing would stop those assholes from demanding more money the next fuckin' day. Get your head out of your ass."

After a beat, I asked, "Did they say anything else?"

"No, sir," Circles said.

My cell rang. I stood and went to my room to take the call.

"Steel," I answered on the fourth ring.

"Hey, it's Naomi."

Three months ago, the sound of her seductive voice would have been calming. Instead I dreaded this conversation.

"You busy? Feel like swinging by this evening?" she asked, her voice suggestive.

I dug that about her. She didn't throw herself at me. I had met her late one Saturday afternoon ten months ago after a ride by myself. I'd stopped at a small diner not far from my house. She sat at the bar eating an omelette and we struck up a conversation about my bike. While neither one of us had been looking to get laid, we couldn't stop flirting with one another. I took her to my place and we'd had random hook-ups ever since.

After the grief Torque had given me, I ought to jump at the chance to get my rocks off. Instead I said, "Sorry, but I'm not in the mood."

"That tone of voice alone, I can tell. And just to say, word got around about one of your club girls messing with your condoms. Good thing we always use mine, right?"

I sighed. "Not funny, Naomi. Also, the rumor mill gets shit wrong. The bitch fucked with my condoms in December. You and I haven't seen each other since October."

"You're right, I'm sorry. You know, we don't have to be physical, you can just swing by and chat. Might help to have a female perspective who isn't... a hang around."

"Not gonna do that to you, Naomi."

She chuckled. "You wouldn't be doing anything to me, I'm signing on for this."

"There's more to it than that," I muttered.

"There is?" she asked, and I heard the smile in her voice.

For a twenty-nine-year-old woman, she was damned intuitive and had a way of drawing things out of me. "Yeah, shit that isn't known to the fuckin' rumor mill."

"Well, I'll be," she whispered. "You met someone."

My body strung tight. "No."

"Okay," she chuckled. "It's your call, but just remember, I'll be here."

I sighed again. "Do me a favor."

"Sure."

"I appreciate that you'll be there, but don't wait for me."

"Steel—"

"Take care, Naomi."

I ended the call and threw the phone on my bed. A hot shower always helped me clear my mind, and I needed a clear head. The Devil Lancers couldn't allow a rival MC to encroach on our territory in any way. I needed to strategize. The idea of this problem dragging on for months and brothers getting injured, that was unacceptable.

For the first time since December, I was grateful Simone wasn't around because she would distract me like nothing else.

CHAPTER 6

MOST IMPORTANT PEOPLE

SIMONE

BY THE END OF January, I was nine weeks pregnant according to my doctor's calculations. Morning sickness had set in with a vengeance.

I still hadn't told my parents yet.

Since I was on a probationary period at work, I hadn't informed anyone there about my situation either.

Alexandra had done the impossible and kept my news to herself. Then again, the semester was in full swing, and she had very little time to gab with anyone back in Jacksonville. For that matter, she'd struggled to keep her gym dates with Ines. Turned out Ines was an excellent accountability partner though, and she wouldn't listen to Alexandra's excuses.

The two of them had left earlier for a Saturday morning run. They'd invited me along, but I barely had the energy to run to the bathroom some days. I wasn't going to risk it.

I heard a knock at my door and made my way there. "You forget your key?" I asked, as I lowered my eye to the peephole.

I blew out a sigh at the sight of Jordan on the other side of the door.

I'd given myself away, so I opened the door.

"Jordan. Do you need something?"

He dragged a hand down his face. "I, uh," he trailed off as he stared at me. "You look ill."

I nodded. "Yeah, I've felt better."

His eyes widened. "You aren't contagious are you? I'm traveling next week and—"

As tired and nauseous as I was, I slipped. "Not unless you sprout ovaries and a uterus."

It took him a moment to catch my drift. "You're pregnant?"

I watched as he worked through a mental calendar. His deer-in-headlights expression shifted to outrage. "That was fast. Is it mine? It's only been—"

My temper flared and I crossed my arms on my chest. "It's been almost two months since we split, but well over three months since we had sex, Jordan. So, it isn't yours."

"Then whose is it?" he demanded.

My eyes slid to the side. "It doesn't matter."

He crossed his arms. "If it's one of my friends it does."

With a scoff, I shook my head. "He's not a student. He was just visiting town, back in December. Why are you here?"

He lowered his arms and shoved his hands in his pockets. "I didn't know if you got any of my mail. I'm expecting a check from my dad."

"Sorry, haven't come across any of your mail. I'll ask Alexandra when she gets back if she's seen anything, but I know she would have told me." I tilted my head. "You could call and ask him to resend it."

Jordan's lips curled. "I don't want to call him. He'd probably insist I meet him at Bike Week or some shit, since that's coming up."

"In March, but he wouldn't make you wait that long, would he?"

He shrugged. "It's just four weeks away, and it wouldn't surprise me. Mom said he came looking for me back in December."

My head reared back an inch. "Oh. Maybe he was the man Ines saw... though she said he wasn't wearing a cut."

Shaking his head, he sighed. "Yeah. I don't know and I don't care."

"But you care about his money?" I asked, unable to stop myself.

He rolled his eyes. "It's complicated. Take care, Simone."

ALEXANDRA BUSTLED INSIDE WITH flushed cheeks and her hair falling out of her ponytail in whispy fly-aways. "Ugh. The way you're looking at me, I have the lion's mane going on, don't I? There's a hot guy moving in downstairs, he said hey, and of course, I look like Simba's older sister."

I chuckled. "No. You look fit as a fiddle."

She gave me some side-eye. "You look even more exhausted than when I left. What gives?"

"Jordan dropped by."

She aimed wide eyes to the ceiling, then leveled her gaze on me. "Every time his name comes up, I say the same thing these days. Are you shitting me?"

I laughed. "I shit you not, girlfriend."

"What the hell was he doing here? You didn't have a quickie with him did you? I hear pregnant women get really horny."

My lip curled. "No. I didn't even shake his hand. He came looking for a check his dad sent him. You didn't find any mail addressed to him in the past few weeks, did you?"

She dipped her chin and arched a brow. "No, but if I had, I'd have set it on fire."

"Alexandra!"

"What? He had that shit planned back in December, and I don't care that *you* gave him the benefit of the doubt, I bet if I befriended Tennyson, I'd get the scoop." A calculating look hit her eyes. "I should do that any damned way."

I pitched my voice lower to get her attention. "No, that's a waste of your time."

"You're right. So... Jordan needs dear old dad's help with money?"

I shrugged a shoulder. "Sounds like it." I dipped my chin to give her a pointed look. "You know it's not exactly cheap to go to school here."

She gave me a sassy head tilt. "Oh, I do know. I busted my ass to get scholarships to afford it. Did you tell him you're pregnant?"

My head tipped to the side. "It couldn't be helped. He noticed I'm a little green in the gills."

"Really?"

I shot her a small smile. "He can be observant, Lex."

"Did he offer congratulations?"

"No. In fact, he wanted to know if it was one of his friends... I shouldn't have told you that. Only gives you more fodder."

She grinned and pointed a finger at me. "Damn skippy. Only someone ready with their rebound would immediately assume you turned to one of his friends. I'm sweaty and sticky, so I'm hitting the shower."

ON SUNDAY EVENING, ALEXANDRA went to the library. I curled up on the sofa with some ginger ale and my cell phone debating making a call.

Ever since I moved to Gainesville, Mom and I had a standing date to talk every Sunday night. My hesitation stemmed from the fact I felt like this was an in-person conversation, but not knowing how Mom would react – I might be better off going the cell phone route.

The phone vibrated, and then rang, Mom's name on the display – she'd beat me to the punch.

"Hey, Mom."

"Hey, sweetie. How are you?"

"I'm good."

She asked after Alexandra, and I kept it to the bare basics.

"A little birdie—named Abby, by the way—tells me that you had a... tryst."

A sneak-attack, that figured.

I rolled my eyes. "A 'tryst,' you and the romance novels, Mom."

Her tone became dry. "That should be *us* and the romance novels, and stop changing the subject. Jordan dumped you and you had a one-time-only thing with someone?"

This seemed as good a time as any to lay it all on the table.

"Yeah. Are you sitting down?"

She chuckled. "Yes, but why?"

I took the deepest breath. "Because, I found out yesterday that I'm pregnant."

She chuckled again, but cut it in half. "You aren't joking."

"No, I thought about waiting to come home and tell you, but—"

"Have you told the father?" she asked.

I hesitated. "We didn't exchange numbers."

"Well, surely you can look him up."

After a long blink, I said, "He was from out of town – hell, I don't even know where he's from, just that he said he'd never be back here again. Not to mention, the only name he gave me is Steel. I don't know his first name, and as common as that surname is..."

I trailed off and the ensuing silence from Mom scared me.

Finally she whispered. "Okay, I can understand how that's challenging."

"Challenging?" I croaked.

She gave a long sigh. "Simone, the hotel didn't just take his credit card on a single name basis. Somebody there should be able to help you look him up."

That wasn't a bad idea, but my every instinct said it would be a waste of time.

"Mom, it was over a month and a half ago. I'll be lucky if they still have those records."

"You won't know until you go ask."

I frowned. "The hotel isn't just going to hand out someone's name to me. Besides, he wasn't the only businessman staying there that night, I'm sure."

Mom's tone shifted. "Sweetie, you can't tell me you don't remember the room number, and I know you recall the date. It was the last day of the semester."

Shit. She had me there.

She continued. "Your father will want to know you put in the effort, Simone."

I shook my head. "I'm not sure the hotel will have a cell number for him."

"You don't understand, Simone. He has a right to know, and frankly while your dad isn't going to care that you're preggers, he *is* going to care that this man doesn't know, because you and your brother are the most important people in the world to him. More than the brothers, more than his Harley, and... more than me."

"Not more than you," I scoffed.

Her tone softened. "If you and I are both in line to take a bullet, he's saving you, not me, sweetie. And I'd want it that way. *Try* to find this man. He decides to ignore you or not believe you, then fuck 'im. But you gotta put in the effort."

I shook my head. "They're going to protect his privacy."

Her tone became sly. "Rumor has it you met at the bar downstairs. The bartender might have some info."

I sighed. "Seven weeks is a long time, Mom, but I'll go by there tomorrow. See what I can find out."

"Good. I would have you talk to your dad right now, but he's in Memphis on club business until Monday. Call on Tuesday, so I can be there for it."

I nodded. "Okay, Mom."

———

THE NEXT DAY, I took an early lunch and went to the Pi House. If the same bartender wasn't there, then I'd hit the front desk. For some reason, I thought I might have better luck with the bartender... on the very slim chance he was still working there.

In theory, Mom's idea was great, but in reality, it was ludicrous and even more embarrassing than telling people I'd had a one night stand.

As luck had it, the bartender from that night stood behind the bar drying pint glasses.

He grinned. "Good afternoon. Does today call for Jack Daniel's Honey?"

I grimaced. "Unfortunately, I can't have that for a few months."

Understanding washed over his face, and his smile faltered. His flirty tone went flat. "Oh."

"Yeah. As if that isn't enough, I'm trying to get in touch with that man. You wouldn't happen to have—"

He held up a hand. "We can't give out that information."

I knew it.

I gave him a jaunty grin. "Are you sure you can't make an exception?"

He shook his head. "Been in this situation before, ma'am. Made the mistake of trying to get the info from the front desk in the past. The information isn't available."

I settled on a bar stool. "All right, well, I guess I'll have a Sprite and two slices of pizza. One cheese and the other with ham."

While I ate my lunch, I used my phone to scroll through apartment listings in Jacksonville. Alexandra would be bummed about me moving out, but things were shaping up such that I knew this was the right decision.

The IT firm I worked for had offered me the chance to start working remotely now that I'd completed my first month. I'd jumped on that idea and even asked if they cared if I worked from Jacksonville. Since they had a small office there, they were cool with that.

I loved Gainesville, but I didn't see myself raising a baby here on my own. Plus, there were far more people in Jacksonville willing to help me if or when I needed it. Another bonus was that I could see my usual OB/GYN.

———

Tuesday evening, Mom called.

"Hey, Mom."

"Hi, there. I have your dad right here, I'm going to put you on speaker."

Great.

"Jacqueline says you have big news."

As fast as I could, I told Dad I was pregnant.

"You don't know who the father is, Simone? I'd heard you'd met someone right after that asshole gave you the run-around. Jacqueline said you had a name for him... she thinks he's a biker."

I gave a rueful chuckle. "No, Dad. He isn't a biker, I'd spot that a mile away. It's his last name. Lots of men go by their last names as nicknames and stuff. It's just a name that's good enough to be a road name," I semi-lied.

Everything about Steel had screamed power and leadership, but he wasn't wearing a cut and no way would a president of a club be at that bar not wearing his—

It hit me.

That bar didn't allow colors.

Shit.

"You need to get in touch with him, honey. He has a right to know."

I nodded. "Totally agree, Dad." Embarrassment flooded my system. "But I don't have his number – as humiliating as that is. Mom told me the same thing, but the hotel doesn't give out information like that."

"You..." he trailed off. His lengthy sigh didn't quite sound like disappointment...but it wasn't too far off. "You need to try to find him. What's his name? I can help you."

I shrugged a shoulder. "It's a common last name, Dad. But since you're determined—"

I heard his phone ringing in the background. It was Blood's ring tone.

"I have to take that. We'll talk more about this in person, Simone."

Alexandra trudged out of her room. "That sounded like a fun convo."

I leaned my head back on the couch. "Yeah. What are you doing this weekend? More fitness with Ines?"

"No. I wasn't sure what I was going to do, other than study."

I leaned my head up. "I'm headed to Jacksonville to apartment hunt."

"You're moving?" she asked, sitting down next to me. The disappointment in her eyes brought on the guilt.

"Honey, you're not gonna be able to study with a newborn in the apartment. I hate that I have to move, but my instincts tell me that's the smart thing to do." I gave her a quick hug. "And I'm not moving immediately. As crazy as rent prices are, I'm going to scope out places and figure out my budget and stuff like that. Do you want to come with... or do you need to stay in town?"

"Oh, I'm coming with you. I love touring houses and apartments."

ALEXANDRA HAD INSISTED ON driving us to various apartment complexes so I could 'weigh my options.' What I hadn't realized was that she'd planned for Jasmine and Aunt Abby to meet us at her parents' place afterward.

It didn't feel like an ambush until they insisted we sit outside by the pool and they proceeded to hound me about who Steel could possibly be or how I could contact him.

I drove my fingers into my hair at the sides of my head. "What? It's not like I had sex with Steel from the Devil Lancers. This man wasn't even wearing a cut, and he didn't have long hair or anything."

Abby's expression turned wary. "He's always been clean-cut-ish. You're right, though, it's crazy to think he'd be there. The man hates Florida. Hell, he spent all of Biketoberfest looking like he was constipated."

"You're a nurse, you think everyone looks bound-up," Aunt Mallory said.

Abby shook her head. "No, this was different. He frowned the whole time. There's no call for that shit when you're so close to the beach, easy access to great food and better music, plus all the hot bikes and even hotter women. That man can't stand Florida and he lets everyone know it."

Mallory gave a slight nod. "That's true. Plus, what business would he possibly have in Gainesville? A trip to God's country is always fun, but I trust Simone's gut."

"Not God's country, that's three hours away in Tally," Abby muttered.

"Aren't there any pictures of this Devil Lancer president?" Alexandra asked.

I gave her a look. "How many pictures are there of my dad floating around?"

"True, true."

"Where is the Devil Lancer mother chapter?" Jasmine asked.

I scoffed. "Why? You think I should just drive there and ask Steel to step outside?"

Jasmine shrugged. "Why not? My mom would do something like that."

Abby laughed. "You're assuming she could get in the damned gate, and Trixie did shit like that *years* ago, Jazz. Things are different now."

Jasmine stood up and dropped her beach towel from her waist. "Are they though?" she muttered that question and ran to the pool, executing a perfect cannonball into the water.

Just watching her made me yawn.

How could a group of cells the size of a lime suck so much of my energy?

Next to me, Aunt Abby asked, "You're coming to Bike Week, aren't you? It's the first year you can do everything since you're twenty-one."

I gave her a lop-sided smile. "Except I can't, not really."

Alexandra rubbed sunscreen into her arms. "You gotta go. Who else is gonna hang out with me and Gabriella?"

Aunt Mallory swallowed a sip of white wine. "Just go Thursday, Friday, and Saturday."

I shrugged. "I'll think about it. Aunt Trixie isn't wrestling this year — that's what made it worthwhile."

With her hands on the pool deck, Jasmine heaved herself out of the water as though doing a push up. She beamed at me. "I'm taking her place. That's reason to go right there!"

UNCLE CAL HAD COME out to grill chicken and steaks. I snuck back inside because the scent of the raw chicken turned my stomach.

Abby stood at the counter chopping tomatoes for a salad, a huge wooden salad bowl sat next to the cutting board. "I'm glad you came inside."

"You are?"

She dumped some tomatoes in the bowl and leveled her eyes on me. "I've been thinking about what I said."

I grinned. "You say a lot of things—"

"Ha ha. I might have said it was unlikely to be Steel with the Devil Lancers in Gainesville, but I remembered something about him."

I leaned against the counter with my forearms resting on top of it. "What about him?"

She stared at me for a beat. "He has a thing for younger women."

"Really?" I asked, my tone dry.

"Don't be so skeptical. I'm just saying – you'd be right in his wheelhouse."

I raised my chin in an exaggerated nod. "That doesn't make me feel any better. What's your point?"

She grabbed a cucumber and cut off the ends. "Jasmine was right. Except instead of hitting their compound, we're going to find their campsite."

My eyes widened and I straightened from the counter. "That's worse than Jasmine's idea."

She shook her head. "No, sweetie. It's smarter because women all come and go at rallies."

I shot her a pointed look. "Not with Riot patches, they don't."

Her head wobbled side to side. "Not usually, but I've been to their area before. If I go with you, it'll be fine."

CHAPTER 7

REALITY SUCKED

STEEL

"You sure you're reviewing the books, Prez?" Tie asked, while he stood in the doorway to my room at the clubhouse.

"Yeah, I'm reviewing the books every time you say they need it. Why?"

He blinked. "You aren't pissed about what the Jacksonville chapter brothers are costing us? *Have* cost us? We haven't nailed down a new law firm to put on retainer, but every place we've spoken to the damned fees are at least triple. I could give a shit about the lost dues from their chapter. Losing our lawyers fuckin' sucks."

I dragged my hand down my face. "Yeah, I'm aware of the legal issues we got, Tie. And at this point, I'm not sure we should keep the Jax chapter, but that isn't official, so keep it quiet."

"Steel, I'm treasurer. I don't run my mouth. I want to know if we're gonna force them to pay next week in Daytona."

That sounded like a plan, but I knew better. It was a fuckin' five-hour ride down to Daytona. Bike Week down there was one of the *only* reasons I was willing to allow a second Florida chapter of the Devil Lancers. It gave us somewhere to stop off before or after the rally. In the spring it couldn't be beat. All the women, the beach...

...And there went my dumb-ass brain serving up visions of Simone and questions about whether she'd look better in a one piece or a bikini. The only right answer was nude.

Shit.

Reality sucked. Simone wouldn't be at Bike Week. A new graduate wouldn't have time for fun and sun around a bunch of rowdy bikers.

My son did, though. Or, rather, not my son.

No, that was wrong. Nothing was going to change the fact that Jordan was my son. Not him shoving me out of his life. Not DNA. Not a damned thing.

I loved him, even if I didn't know him very well any more. I'd changed his diapers, and been there when he took his first steps. He may not have known it, but I'd been at his basketball and baseball games – even though I'd had to lurk by the stands and behind the dugout.

His bitch of a mom had done a helluva job spinning a tale about me and convincing him to give me a cold shoulder.

Until he needed money, of course.

That was all I was good for... child support, even as an adult.

My phone dinged and I saw a complete surprise.

A text from Jordan.

The check never came.

I debated my response. The check never came because I never sent the damned thing. After my failed attempt to see him in December, I decided to be a jackass. He expected me to foot his bill for college... I expected to see him in person to do it.

He just didn't know it yet.

I'll be in Daytona all next week. It's a two hour drive from Gainesville. Come see me, you'll get your money.

Sending that undoubtedly cemented his hatred of me, but we needed to talk. He needed to man up and learn to deal with people he didn't like any damn way.

The world didn't owe him shit any more.

CHAPTER 8

LIFE'S BORING WITHOUT ME

SIMONE

ABBY SWEET-TALKED A BURLY Devil Lancer named Greco into letting us through the barricade separating the Devil Lancers from other campers. She grabbed my hand and dragged me across the field – narrowly dodging other people as we went.

We stopped short and Abby angled her body so she stood slightly in front of me. "Be very subtle, now. He's in that group of bikers standing under the awning for that white and blue fifth wheel camper."

I stared at her for a beat longer than necessary, took a deep breath and let my eyes naturally wander that way.

At first glance the men looked like any other group of bikers. The only thing that told me those seven men were Devil Lancers was the huge patch on their cuts. The patch seemed more familiar to me, but that had to stem from being surrounded by so many of their members.

Everyone in the group erupted into laughter except one man. I stared at him and noticed the tiniest up-tick of his lips.

Oh, shit.

It was *him*.

The moment my brain registered the knowledge, I felt that bizarre pull of attraction. I wanted to run right to him as much as I wanted to run away from him. Especially since a tall, thin, blonde woman lurked behind him. Only it was hard to say if she was with him or the man to his right. Hell, at Bike Week, she might be with them both.

"Did you see him?" Abby asked.

I turned to her. "Yeah. I don't think that's him."

She narrowed her eyes. "You're lying."

I shook my head. "No, Aunt Abby, I'm not. This isn't the time or place to go looking for—"

"You're not going to get a better place or time."

My head cocked to the side. "You know, this isn't something all his brothers need to know. I can come back."

She grinned. "I thought it wasn't him."

I shrugged. "I don't think it's him. It's still personal and not something a bunch of Devil Lancers need to know about."

She looked over her shoulder. "Oh, good. The half dozen or so brothers all cleared out. Now he's talking to some hang-around. Let's move closer and get a better look."

"No, no," I said, and tried to dig in my heels when she grabbed my hand.

Her eyes widened at me. "We aren't going to make an approach. You're right about this being private, but you're too far away."

With a sigh, I let her lead us through the crowd. Two steps later and I caught sight of the 'hang-around' with Steel. Dread and dismay coursed through me. I stopped and let go of Abby's hand. The crowd was a little thicker here, and she doubled back to me.

"What's wrong now?"

"That isn't just some hang-around."

She shook her head. "What do you mean?"

Not *ever* did I think I'd be a woman who slept with her boyfriend's... no, ex-boyfriend's father. Seemed life had a lesson to teach me about embarrassment, because whatever had embarrassed me before was *nothing* compared to right now. The idea that I had to confront Jordan *and* his dad made my stomach lurch. Or was that morning sickness in the afternoon? Pregnancy was fun... Not.

"Who is he?" Abby asked.

"That's Jordan with him."

Aunt Abby's jaw dropped. Very few things rendered her speechless. Looked like I was overachieving all around. "You sure know how to weave a tangled web, Mony."

"Gee, thanks."

She nodded. "You're welcome, but we still gotta get closer."

"I don't want to run into both of them!"

Her patience slipped a touch. "Trust me. We're gonna lurk, eavesdrop, that kind of thing. Now stay close."

<hr>

TRAIPSING THROUGH THE CROWDS on this campground brought out a whole new side to Aunt Abby. It surprised me how flirty she could be with total strangers, and yet, after the stories I'd heard about her when she was younger... it made sense.

We slipped between the truck attached to the fifth wheel and another RV. She put her hand at the small of my back and pushed me alongside the truck. I stopped when we reached the truck tailgate, and we could hear Steel and Jordan's conversation.

"Please hear me out, Jordan," Steel said.

"I'm only here because you won't send me the check," Jordan said in a petulant tone.

My lip curled up. He only wanted money from Steel. In the years we lived together, he'd made it clear how much he despised his dad. If he hated his dad so much why would he want money from him? I hadn't realized Jordan could be so petty.

Steel sighed. "And I need you to know your real dad is serving fifteen years behind bars."

"Like I should believe you."

"You talk to your mom lately?"

Aunt Abby pulled me backward as a lumberjack of a man stalked in our direction. She scurried around the truck and I followed. We wove our way through the crowd and we lost him. Or he didn't care that we were lurking.

"That sucks," she muttered when we left the Devil Lancer's portion of the campgrounds.

"What sucks?"

She laughed. "You have to ask? Your dad is gonna freak. Your baby daddy's gonna freak twice."

I shook my head. "Why twice?"

Her chin lowered. "You're his boy's ex-girlfriend."

I twisted a hand up. "Sounded like he isn't Jordan's dad after all."

Aunt Abby scoffed. "Like that matters. For twenty years he's had a son. It doesn't just switch off because DNA results change."

The mention of DNA gave me an idea. Recalling how Jordan complained about his dad, did I even want to tell Steel? Find myself forced to share my child with him?

Ugh. How would that work? The Devil Lancers had always been a thorn in the side of the Jacksonville Riot MC.

His words from December replayed in my mind. *"Hard to say which '-ville' I hate more, Gainesville or Jacksonville."* Now it made perfect sense.

"What are you thinking?" Abby asked.

I grimaced. "That... maybe he *doesn't* have to know."

"Your dad wants you—"

My eyes widened. "Now that we know who Steel really is, I bet his tune would change."

Aunt Abby's face practically dimmed with solemness. "Think hard about telling him, Simone. You hide behind this excuse, you aren't the woman I thought you were."

PEOPLE WATCHING AT BIKE Week had to be one of my favorite things to do. I sat at a picnic table sipping a huge Sprite while watching the crowd and debating how to approach Steel.

"I'm surprised you didn't go back to the rental house with Alexandra," Blood said, sitting down at the other side of the picnic table.

With a closed-lip smile, I shrugged. "I won't get to do this next year, and probably not the year after that either."

He tipped his head to the side and he picked up a baby back rib. "You're probably right. Abby said you found the mystery man."

A plate loaded with chicken and brisket landed on the table. Dad sat down sideways next to me, straddling the picnic table bench. "You found Steel? When?"

My eyes went wide and I hesitated.

"Volt, I didn't say she found Steel."

Dad swiveled his head toward Blood. "No, you said the mystery man – she's only got one mystery man."

As cunning and devious as Blood could be, he knew what he was doing. He'd been Dad's VP for over a decade. He'd dropped that bomb, well-aware that Dad would hear it.

Why in the world would he want Dad to freak out now?

Then it hit me, in public, Dad almost always held his shit together.

My eyes wandered to Blood and he winked at me. I loved and hated him.

I nodded and turned to Dad. "Yeah, Aunt Abby and I found him."

Dad's jaw shifted. "Here? You found him here? Today?"

I nodded.

"Is he a weekend warrior?" Uncle Blood asked, his voice full of fake hopefulness.

My eyes slid to him and back to Dad. "No."

"Simone," Dad sighed.

"I had no idea at the time—," I started.

With an uncharacteristic roar, Dad grabbed my huge Styrofoam cup of Sprite and hurled it into the field behind us. Luckily, there weren't any groups milling around there. "I wanted you to break *out* of the life, Simone!"

"What the hell's going on?" Mom asked, as she hustled to us.

Aunt Abby scurried up behind her, but with one look at her husband Blood, she shook her head with defeat.

"Tell her," Dad ground out.

"Are you going to freak out hearing it a second time?" I asked.

"Simone," he said through clenched teeth.

I glanced up at Mom. "I found Steel, and he's the Devil Lancer president."

"Why on earth—" Mom started.

Dad interrupted. His temper still in full force. "Did you tell him?"

I tilted my head back. A few stars twinkled in the twilight sky but they didn't offer me any solace. I looked back at Dad. "Not yet, I'd rather not announce it to all of the Devil Lancers. I'm going to tell him tomorrow morning."

"Better hope Jordan's not there," Aunt Abby muttered.

"The fuck?" Dad asked.

"Aw, hell," Aunt Abby whispered.

I twisted a hand up and kept my eyes on Dad. "You and Jordan had something in common after all. He hated his dad, who turned out to be Steel."

Dad closed his eyes for a long moment. "What?"

I explained about the conversation we overheard.

Blood glowered at Abby. "Woman, you didn't tell me that part. You snuck around behind Steel's camper! Do you know how fuckin' dangerous that was?"

Dad stood and stalked away. Mom turned to follow him, but he quickly returned.

He put his phone on the table. "That's the phone number I have for Steel. Call his ass, and get it over with."

I grabbed my phone, but Uncle Blood put his hand on my wrist. "No, sweetheart. That asshole isn't gonna answer an unknown number. You gotta use Volt's phone."

I stared at him, then glanced over my shoulder at Dad. "No disrespect, but this should be shared in person."

Dad crossed his arms. "Why? You told me over the phone."

I tapped Dad's phone before the screen went dark. As fast as I could, I entered the number into my phone so I could save the contact.

I stood and faced Dad. "Believe it or not, I need to see his reaction. I'm planning to keep my baby, but I'm within the time frame where I could...terminate the pregnancy. If he suggests that, I want his sorry ass to look me dead in the eyes when he does. That shit isn't the same in a video chat, and it damn sure doesn't come across in a phone conversation."

His body sagged, he reached out, and pulled me into a fierce hug. "Simone," he whispered.

I returned his hug and willed myself not to cry. As usual, that failed, but I kept it to just three tears and wiped them away before anyone else could notice.

I backed away a touch. "It'll be okay, Dad. Thanks for his number, though. It might come in handy if he won't give me the time of day."

"He doesn't give you the time of day, you tell me," Blood said.

I looked over my shoulder at him.

"Blood," Dad muttered.

"Oh, no, man. This is part of my job as VP. I keep your ass from gettin' in a sling, and if he gives her some shit, I'm gonna beat his ass, so you won't get blamed when you *really* beat his ass."

Dad's body jerked with his chuckle. "You're crazy as fuck."

Uncle Blood grinned. "Life's boring without me."

Chapter 9

Good to Know

Steel

By the middle of Bike Week, I always felt my age. This year, I wondered if Bike Week was making me crazy.

Earlier that afternoon, my eyes had played a trick on me. I thought I had seen Simone milling around in the campsite crowds. She looked even more gorgeous than in December. Almost as though she were glowing, but the beach did that to some women. She also looked tired and I wondered if she were hungover from too much Jack Daniel's Honey. Before I could break away from my brothers, a woman stepped in front of Simone, and *that* woman wore a Riot MC patch.

Of all the damned patches, it was the Riot MC.

But that had to be wrong. It had to be some weird mindfuck as part of getting over my epic hangover.

Greco manned the gateway to our campsite, and he damned sure knew not to let Riot members – or their bitches – into our camp.

Next thing I knew, Torque had signaled for the brothers to clear out because Jordan had showed. I couldn't dwell on that shit.

He had his money. I'd told him what he needed to know – whether he listened was a whole other matter.

The sun had set hours ago. Under the awning outside my camper, I sat in a folding camp chair with rockers on the bottom. The damned thing posed a hazard to drunks because it was easy to go ass-over-teakettle when sober, let alone tipsy. As I sat rocking, I saw a woman striding my way.

"Fuckin' A, what are the odds," I whispered to myself and rose from the chair.

Ten feet from the awning overhang, Simone stopped.

I held myself still. Something about her reminded me of a skittish doe. Instincts told me to wait her out.

"Steel?" she said my name as if it were a question.

"Yeah, Simone."

She took a step forward and I heard her deep inhale. "Can I have a minute of your time, please?"

I moved out from under the camper awning so only a foot separated us. I stared at her for a long moment. It felt just like that moment she'd told me to show her how bossy I could be.

Fire burned through my body. In the faint light from my camper, I saw she had become even more gorgeous than I remembered.

"Sure. Come with me," I said, grabbing her hand.

I ushered her into my camper and slammed the door closed.

She pulled her hand from mine. "I don't mean to bother you, but—"

Actions spoke louder than words, and I wrapped her up in my arms and kissed her hard. Hopefully my aggressive kiss said she would never be a bother. I deepened the kiss. She moaned, raised her leg up alongside mine, and shoved her hands around my waist to my back.

Yeah. I had to have her. Though, I'd limit it to this one last time.

She tore her mouth from mine. "God, Steel. I almost forgot how great a kisser you are."

That dazed look in her gleaming brown eyes – I could eat it up.

I reached for my wallet and the thought of a condom stopped me. "We need to talk."

"Yeah, that's why I'm here."

I gave a slight head shake and cut right to the chase. "Someone fucked with my condoms back in December. I found out when I got home, but by then... I had no way to reach you."

Her brows drew together. "Who would – another woman did that?"

I leaned my head back with a sigh.

Time to face the music.

My eyes locked with hers. "Yeah. She's been taught a fuckin' lesson. Seriously, Simone, I'd have called you that day, but we didn't exchange numbers."

Her eyes rounded, those lips pressed together, and she nodded once. "Yeah, I wish we'd done that since I've been wanting to get in touch with you."

A hollow feeling hit me. She hadn't freaked about the condoms.

"What about?" I asked.

The way she looked me dead in the eye, I knew she wouldn't sugarcoat whatever was coming my way. "I found out in January that I'm pregnant. At first it made no sense to me since we'd used protection, but... now it makes sense. Someone actually tampered with them?"

"Yeah. What's your tie to the Riot?"

Other than the shift of her chin, she gave nothing away. But, I caught that minute movement that said I'd caught her off-guard.

"How do you know—"

"Thought I saw you earlier this afternoon. Then I saw a woman wearing a Riot cut step in front of you. If so many of my brothers hadn't been jacking their jaws, I'd have tracked your ass down right then and there. But... other things came up and I figured my eyes were playing tricks on me."

She rubbed her index finger along her brow. Her fingernails were well-manicured with a black and orange color scheme. Harley colors, if I had to guess. "Would those other things include Jordan showing up?"

I clenched my fists and unclenched them. "What the fuck do you know about Jordan?"

She turned her hands up. "Jordan and I lived together for a little over two years, and he's the douche – no offense – who couldn't be bothered to tell me things were over. Before I left the campground this afternoon, I saw him talking to you."

"It was Jordan, but... You're his ex-girlfriend?"

She rolled her eyes and I wanted to punish her. Sexually.

No. We needed to figure shit out and move on.

I tilted my head to crack my neck and caught sight of the time on the microwave. It was five minutes after midnight.

She wasn't traipsing through the campground alone this late.

Not a fuckin' chance.

Shit.

That meant she'd have to stay here... or I'd have to find someone to take her to wherever she was staying.

"Are you camping out here?"

She sighed. "I'm staying somewhere else."

"And your tie to the Riot?"

Her lips were almost pouty. "You won't like this either, but I'm Volt's daughter."

I couldn't stop my wheeze of laughter. "That's fuckin' rich. No, seriously. How do you know Abby?"

She nodded her head like I was dense. "Yeah, Aunt Abby is Uncle Blood's old lady, and he's Dad's right hand slash VP. If it had been up to Dad, I'd have just called you using his phone because he said there was no way you'd take a call from an unknown number."

I shook my head. "That's true, but plenty of people refuse calls from unknown numbers."

"Anyway, I insisted on telling you in person."

She was stunning, but her exhaustion could be seen plain as day. "Why did you have to tell me in person?"

Her eyes slid to the side for a beat. "I'm not yet at fifteen weeks. Some men might encourage me to have an abortion."

My stomach roiled at her words. "Stop. I'm not some men, or most men. I'm not going to ask you to do that. This isn't exactly a shock since I've known about the condom fuck up for a while. But it's still a shock since I'd hoped I hadn't harmed you because of that bitch's scheming."

"Harmed me?" she asked.

Fuck me, I wanted to kiss her.

"Yeah, harmed you. Pregnancy can go bad, Simone. My check-up was clean in June, and again in December, but I hadn't been a choirboy."

"Oh," she whispered. "My girlfriend encouraged me to get tested too, once I found out I was pregnant. But that wasn't real harm."

I gave her a half nod. "Yeah, but you also haven't delivered the baby, so I don't like that I put you in that position."

"You didn't know."

I kept eye contact with her even as my head moved in infinitesimal shakes. "Yeah, well, I should have done better."

She leaned toward me. "Unless you're psychic, there's no way you could have."

I turned and stalked to the tiny-ass fridge in the kitchenette.

"Anyway, I'll get out of your hair. If you see an unknown number from the nine-oh-four area code, it's most likely me."

I speared her with a look. "You aren't fuckin' leaving, Jade."

"Why not?"

"It's late, which wouldn't mean shit any other time, but it's Bike Week and plenty of people don't know their limits. You aren't getting into an accident when you can sure as hell sleep here tonight."

"You're serious?"

I nodded. "Very." I jerked my head toward the back. "You can sleep in my bed. I'll take the couch."

She shook her head. "I'm a big girl, Steel. I can get back to my car just fine, and it wouldn't be the first time I was on the road at the same time as drunks."

I crossed my arms. "You're staying here, woman."

She laughed. "Okay. If you say so."

When was the last time a woman fucking laughed at me?

Her hands went into her pockets and she dug her keys out. If she hadn't done that, she might have gotten the jump on me. She took one step toward the door and I stopped her.

I had my arms wrapped around her from behind. "You aren't going anywhere."

She rested her hands on my forearm at her belly. We were both enjoying this moment. That was wrong and I forced myself to let her go and step away.

She moved to the couch and sat. "If you're going to keep me here, the least you could do is tell me about your club. Everything I've heard is from my dad – and that's," she gave a scoff mingled with a chuckle. "Precious little information to say the least."

I twisted my lips while I debated how much to share. "I run the mother chapter. Twenty chapters roll up – including the Augusta chapter."

"Augusta, Georgia?"

"Yes."

"You live there?"

"Outside of there, but yeah."

Her eyes locked with mine. "Good to know."

Those words, and her in my camper.

Fuck.

I wanted her, but I knew better.

Not only did I want to avoid another run at parenthood, I didn't want to put her in the cross-hairs of me and Volt.

I'd have hit her with the dark shit some of the chapters did, but being the daughter of an MC president it wasn't likely to faze her much. Bastard that I was, I did it anyway.

"Shit varies by chapter, but we don't shy away from running guns, dealing drugs, every chapter runs the largest titty bar in town and if they slip to a competitor, they get fined."

Her head went up and down in the slowest single nod. "Anything else?"

I nodded. "We provide security and run legit businesses for... tax purposes, you might say."

Her eyes lit with borderline humor. "Wow! That's looking out for number one. Gotta clean the cash."

I widened my eyes at her. "What do you think Cal's window and door business is all about? Or that damned storage center?"

Her expression shifted to offended. "My dad wouldn't..."

She trailed off.

I smiled, but it was mean. "Yeah. They've 'cleaned up,' but it could go back the other way, Jade. At any time."

She frowned. "So, your chapters are—"

"Don't you dare say dirty."

Again with that slow nod. "Okay, but I'm guessing the strippers do more than dance."

I shrugged a shoulder. "If they do, that's news to me."

She stared me down with a 'That's bullshit' expression. I fucking enjoyed that, and so did my cock.

Everything about her did it for me.

No, I shoved that thought out of my head. I was *not* doing parenthood again.

I shrugged a shoulder. "It would be news to me because the Augusta chapter has a few prostitutes who work for us."

She blew out a small sigh and looked away for a long moment. When she met my gaze again, she asked, "Do you want this baby?"

Part of me wanted to watch her grow more pregnant with each passing day, but I couldn't.

Time to pull the Band-Aid off. "I've done the dad thing before, and I won't do it again."

The way she stared at me. Her disappointment was palpable, and I knew she could see right through me.

She gave a slight head-tilt. "Good to know."

That struck deep and I hated myself even more.

It became clear Simone would talk my ear off instead of go to bed – even if I could see the fatigue all over her face. Using my bossiest tone, I told her she had to go to bed and she complied.

I stretched out on the cramped sofa in the living room, and recalled how Simone had snuck out on me back in December. I grabbed my phone and texted Jackhammer and Warden – two brothers from the Jacksonville Devil Lancer chapter. They were the only two long-standing brothers in that chapter not serving jail time, and that was by sheer dumb luck. Subsequently, they were on overnight gate duty all week.

You see a brunette leave my camper without me, follow her.

On the surface, this didn't make sense. If I didn't want to do parenthood all over again, why did I give a shit where she ran off to? If I were honest with myself, I'd have recognized that her being pregnant with my kid affected me. But she didn't need a man twenty years older than her in her life. Hell, our kid deserved a younger dad. The idea of another man raising my child pissed me off, but shit. They both deserved someone far better than me.

In the morning, I found my bed empty, the sheets rumpled, and no sign of Simone.

Frustration mounted, but I held it at bay.

Warden had sent me a text at four-fifteen this morning.

Following the brunette. Do you need the address?

I smiled. Then I frowned since I had to meet with Crank, Walker, and Shark – presidents of chapters out west. That couldn't be put off since I didn't feel like riding out to San Diego, Dallas, or Las Vegas in the coming months.

I texted Warden back.

Yes. But keep watch on her until I can get there. Won't be until around one.

He texted back a thumbs-up emoji, which surprised the fuck out of me. I fully expected guff since he'd been up a good eighteen hours now.

Maybe the brothers from Jacksonville weren't all colossal fuck-ups, after all.

"I THINK THE SHIT with Corrupt Chrome is just in Georgia, Steel," Walker said in his deep Texas drawl.

Of all the presidents, he had an arrogance I didn't encounter often. Most of the time I could overlook it, but it rubbed me the wrong way today.

"That's great, but I'm ordering you to stay vigilant about it. Shit can change and I don't want any chapter to be caught unaware."

He swirled a toothpick in his mouth. "Not often you issue *orders*."

Walker and I were sitting under the awning outside my camper. It wasn't ideal for privacy, but Walker had arrived with a lit cigar and I opted to sit outside before the temperatures rose. I hadn't smoked in over six months, but the stress was getting to me.

I took a long drag off my cigarette. "That should tell you how serious this is."

He stared off to the side for a beat. "No disrespect, but if you nip this shit in the bud in Georgia, I don't have to be vigilant about it in Dallas."

"You want to tell me how to run the club, Walker? Come to Augusta and take the fall for killing off five or more members of the Corrupt Chrome MC?"

He sat back. "No need to bite my head off."

I stubbed out my cigarette in the ash tray on the camp table.

"If you think that's biting your head off, you've gone soft. Torque and I will ride out to Dallas in June. In the meantime, you know where to find me."

Walker blew out a plume of cigar smoke and wandered back to his RV on the other side of the camp site.

Shark, the president of the Las Vegas chapter, should have been here by now. I dug my phone out of my back pocket and saw a text from him.

> Hung over, Steel. Got time to meet tomorrow? I'll pay the fine for wasting your time.

I ran my hand through my hair. That asshole should have been able to meet with me even if he was hung-over. That meant he probably had a woman, or more than one woman, with him.

Part of me wanted to stalk over to his camper and bang the fuckin' door down, but this worked out. I could go check on Simone.

I wasn't known as Steel for nothing though. I had a will of steel and I liked to run the club with an iron fist.

Damn right you'll pay a fine – *triple* the fine, mother-fucker. Be here at nine tomorrow morning with breakfast.

CHAPTER 10

NOT ALL GODDESSES ARE GOOD

SIMONE

ALEXANDRA CLAPPED HER HANDS after zipping her suitcase closed. "How is it noon already and why do all the fun things have to happen the exact same weekend?"

I shrugged. "Murphy's Law, I guess? I feel like we should offer this place to someone else. I bet—"

She crossed her arms. "Not a chance. You deserve to be here, in a real bed, where you can get some rest. *And,* you can swim at the beach without dragging your tired self through a hotel lobby or some crap."

'Here' happened to be a three-bedroom house at the beach that Alexandra had found on VBRO. We'd rented it for the week so I could work remotely Monday through Wednesday, because I only had the last two days of the week off.

Alexandra took her beach bag and backpack out to her car. She came back inside looking worried.

"What's wrong?"

"There's a guy out there just sitting on his Harley. I mean, it's Bike Week so maybe that's normal, but I called Dad just in case and made sure the guy saw me on my phone."

I scurried to the window and peeked through the blinds.

The guy had his back to the house now, and his Devil Lancer patch couldn't be missed.

"I really wish you hadn't called Uncle Cal."

"Why?"

I gave her a dry look. "Dad's gonna swing by here now, and lose his mind all over again because that isn't just some guy. He's a Devil Lancer and my hunch is that Steel had him follow me home since he'd asked me to stay the night last night."

Her eyes widened. "That should be good news. Why'd you come home?"

I chuckled but it sounded hollow. "He doesn't want the baby. I guess you could say I stayed part of the night there since I didn't get home until after four. He can't be mad about that. This is overkill."

"Oh, honey. I had no idea. He didn't ask you to get an abortion, did he?"

"No, so that's a relief."

Before I could grab my phone, I heard the distinct sound of two Harleys coming down the street.

Alexandra stood at the window. "Oh, good. Dad's here... and you were right. Your dad's here too, and getting in this guy's face."

"What?" I asked hurrying to her side.

"I'm kidding, but he's definitely *having words* with that guy."

To my dismay, another bike roared up the street and I got my first look at Steel on his bike. I thought he couldn't get any sexier, but I was dead wrong. He wasn't wearing a helmet and his wavy hair had an incredibly sexy, wind-blown look to it. His eyes were hidden behind his dark-tinted wrap-around sunglasses.

"This just got awkward," Alexandra said, turning to me.

"No thanks to you," I muttered.

She chuckled. "I didn't know. I'm getting out of here, now, so give me a hug."

After a brief hug, I walked her to the door. She lugged her suitcase to her car. I followed her out, but stopped short on the narrow sidewalk outside the house.

Unlike Dad and Uncle Cal, Steel had pulled his bike up the drive and parked it behind my car.

Uncle Cal broke away from the huddle between Dad, the other Devil Lancer and Steel. He put Alexandra's bag in her trunk and aimed a look at me. "You need to get back inside."

I tossed a hand out toward the curb. "They don't need to be arguing in the middle of the street."

"They aren't arguing."

Steel tipped his head at the other Devil Lancer, turned on his heel and stalked up the drive way.

"Go inside and lock the door," Uncle Cal said.

"She has nothing to fear from me, Callous."

I didn't think I had anything to say to Dad or Steel, so I turned and went in the house. Steel was right on my heels and followed me inside. I started to close the door and saw Dad coming up the walk.

"Is Uncle Cal coming too?" I asked Dad.

"No. Shut the fuckin' door," Dad said after he came inside.

I didn't like his tone, but I closed the door.

"I'll tell you what I told Warden. She doesn't need your fuck-ups leading a threat right to her!" Dad shouted.

"Dad!"

Steel locked eyes with me. "He isn't wrong. Nothing but dumb luck kept Warden out of a raid."

"You don't make any sense, Steel. Told her you don't want the baby, but now you're protecting her, as if you've claimed her, even though you haven't."

Well, Mom had a big mouth. She'd called me at eight-thirty demanding to know when I was going to hunt Steel down. I'd shared that I'd already done it late last night and he didn't want the baby.

His eyes widened. "I said I wouldn't do parenthood again. Not the same as not wanting the child."

Dad's nostrils flared and his eyes slid from Steel to me and back to Steel. "She's my daughter and part of the Riot – we'll keep her safe."

Steel smiled. "And so will I. Two MCs protecting her are better than one. She'll be well taken care of."

I blew out an exasperated breath. "Okay, since you've forgotten I'm standing here, nobody has actually threatened me."

Dad's dry look spoke volumes.

Steel opened his mouth to speak, but I held up my hand. "Fine. A rival MC won't tell me they're going to fuck me up, they'll just do it. But nobody's—"

"Word gets around, Jade. Hell, other MCs fuck with our club bunnies in an effort to fuck with me."

Dad inhaled through his nose, and I suspected the comment about club bunnies bothered him like it did me.

"Fuckin' hate this," Dad muttered.

Steel chuckled. "It's good I'm not contrary."

"Seriously?" I asked.

His eyes were remorseful, but I was done. "Both of you leave. I've got a gun and I'm capable of taking care of myself and my lime-sized peanut."

I stormed out of the room, but only got as far as the mouth of the hall before Steel caught my bicep in a firm grip.

"Don't be that way."

My lips pressed together. I stared down at his hand on my arm and up at him. "Don't be an overbearing Neanderthal and I won't *have* to be that way."

He chuckled.

"Are you laughing?"

He failed to clear his expression. In fact, his smile grew wider. "Never."

"There's nothing funny."

"'Lime-sized peanut?'"

I fought a smile. "You had to be there."

He pressed his lips together. "Wish I had been, Jade."

The moment felt like a bubble growing between us.

Until Dad cut through it like a knife. "Are you leaving yet?" he asked.

Steel cocked a brow at him. "I know she's your daughter, but she's an adult. No need to see me out of her space."

Dad low-key glared at me.

I shrugged. "It's fine, Dad."

"It isn't," he fumed.

After a moment I understood and shook my head. "That isn't happening, Dad. And just to say, I can't get *more* pregnant."

Dad spoke through clenched teeth. "Not fuckin' funny, Simone."

I twisted my hands up. "If I don't laugh, I'll cry. So... sorry, not sorry."

"Give me a hug before I leave."

I closed the door behind Dad after hugging him.

Steel hadn't moved from the mouth of the hall where he'd stopped me earlier. He stood there, his straight white teeth pressing into his lip.

After a groaning sigh, he said, "I'm not taking Warden or Jackhammer off you."

"Who's Jackhammer? Dad only mentioned Warden."

He had his arms crossed, and it accentuated how hot he was in his cut. "They're both brothers from Jacksonville. Get used to them."

"I don't need—"

"Non-negotiable, Jade."

My lips twisted to the side to hide my confusion.

"What's that look for?"

"I'm wondering why you had to bite your lip when thinking about my protection detail."

He dropped his arms and stepped toward me. "If I'm thinking about you, it's always a struggle."

"Right," I muttered.

The sexiest smolder hit his eyes. "It is right. I struggle to keep my hands, my lips, and other parts of me away from you."

My chin dipped and I shot him a skeptical look. "You're besting that challenge as we speak."

He laughed and came two steps closer. Four feet separated us. The more I stared at him, the more my breasts tingled... and I felt the same struggle.

My more rational side reminded me that saying there was a difference between not wanting parenthood and not wanting the baby was bullshit. A baby and parenthood went hand in hand.

I had to keep that at the forefront of my mind because it meant more than this crazy attraction.

"You raising the baby in a college town?" Steel asked.

I shook my head. "I'm moving into a place in Jacksonville next week."

He stroked his chin. "Your parents going to help out?"

I shrugged. "I guess. We haven't talked about that yet."

"Yeah," he whispered.

That single whispered word held so much regret, but then how could it?

"You don't want parenthood again, so what do you care?"

"Fuck," he hissed. "Because part of me nearly asked you to move to Augusta. But that's also because I can't control myself around you."

I laughed. "Again, you're managing quite well."

He shook his head. "You don't need an asshole like me fucking up your life. Or, fucking it up further."

I tilted my head. "A baby doesn't fuck up someone's life, Steel."

His brows shot up. "It does when that baby is used against someone. To get child support, to force me to bend to some other club's demands."

I stepped toward him. "Has someone threatened our unborn baby?"

Those gorgeous brown eyes shone with malice. "No, they did it to Jordan when he was five fuckin' years old."

I heard Jordan's bitter voice in my head, *"Dad left when I was five."*

Another piece fell into place, and I realized I had been right. I'd told Jordan no decent biker would abandon his kid without reason.

Steel narrowed his eyes at me. "That doesn't fucking faze you?"

I shook my head. "I wouldn't say that, but let's say some of Jordan's attitude makes sense now, especially if he hasn't heard that from *you*. Because that pain is right there in your tone."

"Leave Jordan out of this."

That pain in his voice – I wanted to hunt down Jordan's mom and throat punch her.

"Fair enough. To sum up, you don't want our baby—"

"Didn't say that."

"Same thing. But your rationale is because of a yet-to-happen threat. The threat of a threat, if you will."

He widened his eyes. "You're my son's ex-girlfriend and twenty years younger than me."

"The 'ex' means it's *over* and age is just a number."

He shook his head. "It's still wrong."

I arched a brow. "Funny, it wasn't wrong back in December."

"Simone."

"Now, I'm Simone."

"No, now you ought to be bent over my knee getting spanked for that sass."

My lips tipped up. "If only you had the energy, old man."

His hands settled on his hips. "You're goading me."

"You aren't the only one struggling."

He closed his eyes and sighed.

I tiptoed to him, cupped his cheeks, and touched my lips to his.

He grabbed my hands and whispered against my lips, "Jade."

"What?"

"This has to be the last time."

"Second to last time," I countered.

His eyes narrowed.

"You got stamina. I want you twice for sure, three times if you can hack it."

His arms locked around me and he crushed my body to his. "I can hack it, woman." One of his hands reached for his back pocket. "I only have one condom."

I leaned back an inch. "I can't get more pregnant and my tests are all clear. Have you been with anyone else?"

He shook his head.

"Then who needs a condom?"

"You're evil."

I smiled. "Not what you said the first night. Then, I was a goddess."

He returned my smile, but his was wicked. "Not all goddesses are good, sweetheart."

"I'll take your word for it. What are you waiting for?"

His arm gave me a squeeze. "A bolt of lightning to knock some sense into me."

I slid my hand down his body. His jeans bulged with his erection and I stroked it. "Do you know how many times I wished I'd woken you up that morning?"

He stopped my stroking, except he held my hand there, pressing it harder against him.

I gazed up at him. "You wanted that, too?"

"Stood in the bathroom doorway, staring at you like a fuckin' stalker, at three in the morning. Talked myself out of waking you up."

My other hand tugged his shirt free of his jeans.

His body stilled. "I should resist you."

I stared up at him. "The door is right behind me. However, you sure like pressing my hand to your cock."

"Is your pussy wet for me?" he asked, his voice husky.

I shook my head.

"I can check."

I smirked. "It isn't wet. It's soaked and aching."

He shrugged off his cut and tossed it over the top of the couch. I shoved his shirt up and he pulled it over his head. His body was divine. I nipped at his chest while my fingers fumbled with his jeans.

His hands pushed inside my panties from behind, rubbing his palms on my ass. He shoved one hand farther and his middle finger skated through my folds.

I gasped and pushed my ass out to get more.

"How could I forget how greedy you are?" he rasped.

I yanked my shirt off, took a step back, and lost my sleep-shorts and panties. "Very greedy."

I pushed on the button of his jeans, but he swatted me away.

"Let me look at you."

I dipped my chin. "Needs to be a two-way street, Steel."

He undid his jeans, but left them hanging open.

I decided he'd seen enough and dropped to my knees. In no time, I had my lips around the crown of his cock. I managed two bobs before he hauled me to my feet. He toed out of his boots. Then he stepped out of his jeans and underwear. He picked me up. My legs wrapped around his hips.

I tilted my hips to rub him against my pussy. "Oh my God, Steel. Hurry."

"Patience, greedy girl."

With a growl, I put my mouth to his neck and sucked.

"Keep that up, you'll get double spankings."

I chuckled and kept at him.

"Yeah, my girl loves to be naughty."

I loved hearing him call me 'my girl.' My hips moved again.

He put his hand to my ass cheek. "You don't stop, I'll fuck you against the wall."

"Yes, please."

He growled and my back hit a cold wall.

His mouth found mine and he kissed me like it was the last kiss he could ever have.

Finally, I felt his tip line up and I tore my lips free. "Fuck me, Steel."

He pushed inside further. "This will be really fucking fast, woman. But after that, you're in trouble because I'm gonna fuck you all afternoon and into the night."

I squeezed my legs around his waist. "I'm holding you to those promises. Show me what you've got, Steel."

His hips bucked and his thick cock drove inside. I exhaled with sheer pleasure.

He nipped at my neck and I moaned.

His hips pulled back for a second before he thrust forward. "God, you're fuckin' tight. You feel even better than before. I love it."

He kissed me and picked up his pace. I wished I could meet his thrusts, but in this position, I had to hold on and enjoy what he gave me.

His feet shifted and he fucked me harder. He started grinding at the end of his thrusts and I felt my orgasm building. He broke the kiss, cupped one of my breasts and lowered his mouth to my nipple. He dragged it through his teeth and sensation shot through my body.

"Yes," I hissed.

I drove my fingers into his hair.

"Missed that," he groaned.

I kissed him and he bucked his hips faster.

"Get there, Simone," he whispered against my lips.

That wasn't likely to work, but then he swiveled his hips and thrust harder. He dropped his head to my other breast and ran his teeth over that nipple. The sensations ripped through me again and I came.

He gave a shout as he came not long after.

I liked feeling him come inside me. If I were honest with myself, I liked it too much. I ignored that and kissed him.

He unwrapped my legs and put me down. "You showered yet?"

"No, is there a problem?"

He traced his finger down my neck and between my breasts. "Nope. We're gonna shower together."

I STEPPED OUT OF the bathroom and drank in the sight of Steel in the bed. The sheets rested at his belly button, and his tattoos had my fingers itching to trace them.

He smirked at me. "Are you just gonna stare at me? Isn't that what you asked me back in December?"

"Sounds like something I'd say, but yeah. I could just stare at you."

He shrugged a shoulder. "As long as you do it standing there naked, that works."

I chuckled silently and wandered back to the bed. He reached out and pulled me to him under the covers. "I'm starving. I don't know if I'm keeping you from serious club business, but—"

"We'll Doordash whatever you want."

I bit my lip. "For being so worried about the threat of a threat, aren't you paranoid someone will tamper with your food?"

He gave me a slight smile. "In Georgia, absolutely. Here, I'm just another biker."

I swirled my index finger around a tribal tattoo that resembled the rim of his Harley's front tire. "A psycho Doordasher gets a pick up for two orders, he could poison both and come back to fuck with you."

He rolled on top of me. "Are you trying to make me more paranoid?"

I smiled. "Nope. Just saying, the extra protection is just being... *extra*."

"I'll show you being extra with my cock."

I laughed. "You did that twice already."

His eyes were hypnotizing. "And I want to do it two more times."

"If you feed me, you can. Actually, I can feed both of us. Lex picked up stuff for tacos if you want."

His hand drifted down my body to my center. "This is the only taco I want."

I rolled my eyes. "So original, that one."

He grinned. "We'll eat whatever you want, Jade. I'll even cook for you, but I'm a terror in the kitchen."

"A terror?"

He settled more of his weight on me. "Burn shit, spill it, you name it and it's hit or miss if the damned food is edible."

I nodded. "All righty. Not a culinary master."

"Who's Lex?" he asked.

"Alexandra. She left when you showed up."

He nodded. "Gotcha. You enjoy pissing off your Dad?"

"That's random."

"Volt doesn't want you with me. Why not send me packing?"

I wriggled out from under him and sat up. "Believe it or not, the only people who have anything to do with this are me and you." I hesitated – unsure if I should share so much. "It's insane how attracted I am to you. I've never been like this and it's not the pregnancy hormones. That night at Pi House... I could have spent all night with you and that was *before* we went to your room. I didn't want it to end."

He shifted to his side and stared up at me. "But you walked out."

"Because goodbyes suck and I'd have embarrassed myself by being clingy or something weak like that."

He chuckled. "I'd almost like to see you being clingy."

"Anyway, you can go if you need to or you can stay. You don't want fatherhood again, but as long as you aren't going to ask or insist that I get rid of—"

He sat up. "Never."

I nodded. "Okay. Then I'll figure it out."

"Fuck," he hissed.

"What?"

He tipped his head back, the strong column of his throat tempting me. He looked at me. "I don't want you to 'figure it out.' But I won't be the reason another kid hates my guts when all I'm trying to do is keep my child safe."

That made sense.

If there were an actual threat.

"You know, I'm hell on wheels when people threaten me, too."

"Don't be cute right now."

"I'm not being cute. I'm nothing like Jordan's mom."

"What the fuck does that mean?" he demanded.

Uh-oh. I'd done it now.

"I heard you and Jordan talking yesterday."

He cocked his head to the side. "You didn't get near my camper yesterday."

I pulled the sheet up and covered my chest – for some stupid reason, this wasn't something I wanted to admit while naked. "Abby and I snuck around the back and were hanging out by the hitch."

"Eavesdropping?"

My head wobbled, and I pressed my lips together. "It wasn't cool. Hell, I don't know why I let Aunt Abby lead me back there, but she insisted we get closer."

His eyes narrowed. "You heard the whole conversation?"

I shook my head. "Just the part where Jordan wanted money, and you wanted him to know where his real dad happened to be."

He had such a stony expression, it was equal parts admirable and disturbing. I suspected he was mad, but if so, he was damned good at hiding it. Or he had quiet anger, and that scared me the most.

My stomach growled, and he stared down at the sheet. "Let's get you fed."

"Are you mad?" I asked.

He yanked the sheet down. "Very, but more at my men. The two of you shouldn't have been able to get back there."

"Why are you mad at me?"

He snorted. "Because you put yourself in danger. Considering that Abby's Blood's property, it would have sparked trouble between two clubs."

"What do you mean?"

"If my men had been doing their job, they'd have rounded the two of you up and they'd have been damned rough about it."

I grabbed the sheet, but his hand stilled my movement. I looked at him. "To be fair, there was a lumberjack of a man who came around, but we got out of there and lost him."

His hand moved to my breast. "I will punish you for that, beautiful."

I liked hearing him call me that. "Okay," I whispered.

He squeezed me. "You might not like it. In fact, I hope you don't like it."

"Why?"

"Only way punishment sinks in."

"Can I beg forgiveness?"

He grinned. "Too late, and you're not reading between the lines, woman. Nothing that I think should bother you does, so my guess is tying you up won't bother you, either."

I dragged my lip between my teeth. "Tying me to a bed or tying me to a chair?"

"What do you think?" he asked, gently pinching my nipple.

After a stilted exhale, I smiled. "Yeah. I've never done that, so... I probably wouldn't like it."

He leaned closer, running his nose alongside mine. "You're a shit liar when it comes to sex, baby."

I brushed his lips with mine. "I'll have to work on that."

His hand slid around to my waist, he fell to his back pulling me on top of him. "No, you don't. But I like the idea of you begging."

I had my hands on his shoulders and pushed up, but he kept me from going very far. "You want me to beg?"

His cock pushed inside me just a little. "No, beautiful. I'm going to *make* you beg."

I shook my head. "No, you won't."

He laughed. "Oh, those are bold words, Jade. You forget how greedy you are?"

I sunk down on him further. "Nope."

Fire burned through my ass when he spanked me. I gasped and glared down at him, but it held no heat. Crazy as it made me, I wanted another spanking.

"How'd you get your road name?" I asked once I situated myself next to him after I cleaned up.

"It doesn't matter."

"Sure, it does."

Silence lingered between us.

"You aren't going to tell me about your road name, are you?"

"Nope."

"You know, whatever I make up in my mind is going to be a thousand times worse than the actual story."

"No, it won't."

I stared at him. "What? You bludgeoned someone with a steel pipe?

His eyes slid to the side, and he shook his head. "Not telling you, Jade. No need for me to make you more jaded."

I shrugged a shoulder. "But you've killed someone, I take it."

His eyes narrowed. "You are so blasé. You should run the other direction from me, to think, let alone *know*, that I've done something like that."

"You're an outlaw. You aren't going to follow the rules."

"Never thought an MC princess would be my gig. You're cool with a cold-blooded killer in your bed?"

"I don't think you realize how early I became an MC princess. Since I could talk, I've loved motorcycles and everything about them. Hell, it's why Dad insisted I leave for college. He probably knew I'd find a brother who was a president, or about to become the chapter president."

"You don't think your dad knows what's best for you?"

I nodded. "It's more like he *thinks* he knows. But the truth is, between him and my mom, I was born to be a president's old lady, when the time is right."

CHAPTER 11

NOT IF I CAN HELP IT

STEEL

SIMONE HAD TO BE all talk. *Born to be a president's old lady*, that was too much. At the same time, she was right. Her spunky side only came out when it wouldn't bite her in the ass. She had the ability to keep her cool. Over the years, I'd found that hard to come by in most women – especially the women determined to be with me for my position.

We ate spaghetti on the deck. She had a recipe memorized and it had to be the best meat sauce I'd ever tasted.

If only I were ten years younger.

Jordan needed his head examined. After spending the entire day with her and learning more and more about her, no matter how much I loved Jordan, he was a massive moron to let her go.

The sea breeze had calmed down as the sun set. The encroaching darkness along with the heavy food in my belly, the time had come.

"That's an ominous look on your face," she said.

This had been a great day, but also reckless of me. I should have left when Volt did. Yet, I craved her even as I sat across from her.

"And now you're biting your lip again," she muttered.

I put my napkin on top of my plate. "I have to go."

She nodded and smiled. "Okay, gonna leave me with dish duty, after I cooked for you. That's... a choice."

My lips quirked. "Simone."

"What?"

"You make it hard to go."

She stood. "Now can you imagine if I were being clingy? Ride safe, it'll be dark soon and believe it or not, you're more likely to be on the road with drunks right now than at midnight."

A reckless idea struck me. I didn't put women on the back of my bike. Not even Naomi, for a ride around her neighborhood that she'd begged for the day she met me. Right now, I wanted to take Simone back to my camper, and I didn't want her driving there. Another upside was that she wouldn't have wheels to make a getaway.

Putting her on my bike made a statement though.

I didn't give a shit about statements. Not with Simone. The more I thought about having her at my back, the more I wanted it.

"Let's get your fuckin' dishes done, Jade. Then you need to put on some boots if you brought any."

She grabbed her plate. "Boots?"

"You're coming back to my camper tonight, and you're not driving yourself. You're riding with me, so yeah, motorcycle boots would be good if you packed any."

All that sass made for a great show as she cocked a hip, tilted her head, and smirked. "What kind of MC princess doesn't pack her motorcycle boots? Seriously, Steel, this isn't my first Bike Week."

I grinned. "Hurry up woman, or we'll never leave, and that's a fuckin' problem since I got a meeting at nine tomorrow."

Her lips twisted. "Tomorrow's Saturday. I need my car."

I walked past her and led the way inside to the kitchen sink. "What for?"

"I'm not missing the wrestling. It's the entire reason I came down here."

With the hot water turned on full blast, I gave her a pointed look. "Not to corner me? Or eavesdrop on me?"

She put her plate on the counter and grabbed a Pyrex dish with a lid. "That was pretty much Abby's idea. I wasn't going to look for you since it seemed crazy that you could be the father, but Abby and my friends wanted me to get a look at you. Jasmine suggested I drive up to the mother chapter compound, but Abby said the campsite would be easier."

While she loaded the leftover pasta into the glass dish, I grabbed her plate and washed it.

It seemed strange that other people wanted to hunt me down and not her. "Would you have made the drive to Augusta?"

She chuckled. "If I had a death wish, I suppose."

I shook my head. Our reputation preceded us, but for once that wasn't a good thing. "You would have gone on without ever finding me?"

She gave a very slow nod. "Probably. Dad and Mom were adamant I find the father. Hell, I went back to Pi House to talk to the bartender."

"Bet that made his day," I muttered, rinsing the pot.

Dish towel in hand, she grabbed the pot and dried it. "Right until I mentioned that I was off the Jack Daniel's Honey for a few months."

I choked on laughter.

"What's that for?"

I shook my head and washed the empty pot. "Serves the fucker right."

Her head reared back. "You're possessive."

"Damn straight. Wanted to punch him that night when he flirted with you about fuckin' Old Fashioneds. What'd he tell you?"

She dried a plate. "That he wasn't able to give out that information."

I nodded. "If the wrestling is the only reason you came down here…" I trailed off when an awful thought hit me. "You're not planning to wrestle are you?"

She tilted her head back and burst with laughter. Her joy and humor was contagious. Not since that night in December, had I smiled and laughed this much.

Christ. Being around her felt natural and right. I didn't get much of that in my life.

Her laughter waned and she dabbed at her eyes. "Oh, that's funny. No. I won't be wrestling."

I nodded and pulled the drain stopper on the sink. "That's right. Who's the Riot woman who wins every year? She belongs to Roll, is her name Tricia?"

She laughed again, loud but short. "You mean Trixie, and she isn't in it this year."

"Get the fuck out."

Her smirk gave her the barest hint of a dimple. "No, her *daughter* is taking her place. I damn sure can't miss that."

I yanked the dish towel out of her hold, dried my hands, then threw it on the counter. Grabbing her wrists, I pulled her closer and wrapped my arms around her. "Guess not. What time is that tomorrow?"

She rested her hands on my chest and gazed up at me. "Around lunch, I think. Why?"

"I'll take you."

She closed her eyes for a moment. When she opened them, I saw wariness and caution there. "You're sending a fair number of mixed signals, sir."

My cock twitched hearing her call me 'sir.' That didn't feel natural and right, it felt like a balm.

I stayed focused. "You're right, but you're not leaving my side this weekend. I'm a total bastard for this, but if you can hack it, I'm gonna spend the next two days with you and to hell with the consequences."

Her head tilted and her eyes narrowed. "If I can hack it?"

I grinned. "As long as you don't expect more. Don't get attached. I'm a selfish asshole and I want as much of you as I can have all weekend. After that... we go our separate ways because I'm bad for you."

"Bad for me?"

I dipped my chin. "You and your lime-sized peanut deserve better."

The calculating look on her face, I expected an argument.

Instead, she grinned. "I'll go get my boots and a change of clothes."

Perfect.

"IS THE COAST CLEAR?" Simone asked, coming out of the bedroom in my fifth-wheel.

For the second time that morning, I admired her figure in her dark purple baby-doll dress. The damn thing made me war with myself.

"It's clear, but you're in trouble, baby."

She grinned, and hell if I didn't see the outline of her nipples against the cotton dress. That had my blood rushing south.

"Why am I in trouble?" she asked, her tone light and innocent.

I crooked my finger at her. "You know exactly how fuckin' sexy that dress is and you wore it around one of my chapter presidents. Had him drooling over you so bad I almost punched him, which forced me to send you to the bedroom."

She smirked while strolling toward me, slower than normal, putting some extra sway in her sexy hips. "Like you weren't going to do that anyway? No way are the two of you meeting while I'm within earshot."

I hadn't moved from my seat on the couch, but she now stood within a foot of me. We'd maintained eye contact the entire time. My hand darted out, grabbed hers, and I yanked her onto my lap.

She let out a surprised yelp, but quickly shifted so she straddled me. Her beaming smile twisted me up inside.

"You wearing this just to make me jealous?"

Her brows drew together. "No, crazy man. I'm wearing it because it's sexy as fuck, I knew you'd like it, and the open criss-cross cut-out in the back keeps me cooler than my tank tops do."

I rubbed my hands up and down her rib cage, slowing at the top so my thumbs grazed her nipples.

She leaned toward me. "And I was right. You really like it."

I slid my hand around to her back – my fingers dipping under the criss-cross straps to stroke the skin of her back. "Yeah, I do. Now kiss me, baby."

As much as I wanted to fuck her in this scrap of a dress, the front door was wide open with just the screen door keeping the bugs out. I wasn't down with putting her on display like that.

She lowered her smiling lips to mine, and kissed me. I let her take her time about it. Her tongue explored my mouth, gentle and almost tentative. My other hand went up to her neck. I angled her head, and took control of the kiss.

A knock sounded on the metal door just before Tie's voice filled the camper, "Hey Prez... Ooh, sorry, I'll come back."

I pressed Simone's face to my neck. "What is it?"

I felt her lips curl and then she nibbled my neck. I tightened my grip on her waist and neck. My naughty girl redoubled her efforts and sucked. I swallowed a groan and concentrated on Tie's words.

"That problem I mentioned last week back home... got a new firm lined up, same cost, but you can meet with them next week."

I dipped my chin. "Set it up."

Tie nodded and grinned. "You got it, Steel." His eyes cut meaningfully to Simone and back to me. "And, I like that for you."

My eyes widened. "Are you trying to piss me off?"

He chuckled. "No. I was gettin' worried. You ain't been yourself since December. She's just what you need. Later."

I glared at his back as he walked away, then shifted to break Simone's suction on my neck. "Give me your naughty mouth, baby."

She smiled and lowered her lips to mine. We both lost control, the kiss was so wild. I shoved my hands up under her dress. Groaning at the feel of her bare ass. The thong she wore had to be the skimpiest one I'd ever felt. She drove her hands in my hair, those nails grazing my scalp and making me growl. Moments like these were dangerous, but I lived for danger.

In that moment, one word filled my brain. The one word that had to be the craziest idea: *mine.* She was mine.

I couldn't and wouldn't leave her. I might not want to be a dad again, but this sassy vixen had it right. She wasn't Debra. Nothing about this was the same, and sticking by her side was the least I could do.

Whether I'd move or ask her to move remained to be seen. The Jacksonville chapter had been a problem for years now, and I'd let it slide. At a bare minimum, I could find the right person to lead that chapter and help him find prospects to join their ranks.

I pulled one hand free of her dress, then I wrapped her hair around my hand and pulled.

She tipped her head back with a gasp. "Love when you pull my hair, Steel."

My teeth sunk into her neck. She laughed.

I took her mouth again and, somehow, she pressed even closer to me.

"Dad, or I guess I should call you Steel," Jordan called before the screen door squawked as he opened it.

Simone's body tensed, and she shoved her face to my neck again. Neither one of of us wanted to face Jordan like this, but I couldn't have a conversation with him while Simone sat on my lap. Then again, I'd struggle to talk to him with a hard-on too.

Fuck.

Jordan eyed us and his lips curled while he rolled his eyes. "Think you can send your *young* woman away, so I can talk to you?"

Simone pulled her head back, but she focused on me. Those brown eyes burned with ire.

With as much subtlety as I could muster, I gave her a stern look. "Yeah, Jordan."

I pulled my other hand free of her dress.

Jordan blew out a sigh. "Aren't you forty-five or some shit?"

"Forty-one," I bit out.

Simone stood, kept her face angled toward me, but her expression said she was holding it together by a thread.

I rose and wrapped an arm around her shoulders, planning to keep her face pressed closed to me while I hustled her into the bedroom.

Jordan glanced at us from the corner of his eye. "God, is she even legal?"

Simone snapped, pulled free of my hold, and put a hand on her hip. "Yes, Jordan. I'm legal."

"S-s-simone?" he spluttered.

"Yeah, Jordan. That's me."

"Why are you with him? How do you even know him?"

"Jade, head to the back," I muttered, pulling her gaze from Jordan's.

She opened her mouth as though she might argue, then nodded. "Yeah."

Watching her saunter down the narrow hallway, I couldn't fathom how Jordan could cast her aside.

Once the bedroom door closed, Jordan said, "You call her Jade? That isn't her name."

I met his angry gaze. "No, but it suits her."

He sneered. "You know I lived with her for two years?"

I nodded once.

Disbelief clouded his face. "Do you know she's pregnant?" His head turned a fraction and his jaw dropped open. "You're the man from out of town, aren't you?"

I bit my lower lip. "Why'd you come by, Jordan?"

He either didn't hear me or ignored me. "How did you meet her? Or did you decide you wanted my sloppy seconds?"

I closed the distance between us. "Anyone else said that shit, they'd be laid out on the fuckin' floor right now. You're my son, and I'm giving you a pass, but that's the last time you disrespect her or me. Now, what do you want, Jordan?"

He gaped at me as it hit him that I cared about her. "She's my age!"

"I gave you the fuckin' money, so what do you want?" I whispered.

It took him a moment to get his shit together. "It doesn't fuckin' matter. Mom was right, you always want the younger, prettier, shinier model. Said you love to rob the cradle. Hell, you killed a man for pointing it out when you were prospecting."

I cocked my head to the side. "That's a fuckin' lie, Jordan. I killed a man. Not because of that, but because he bad-mouthed your Mom, and age had fuck-all to do with it."

"Whatever," he muttered, turned on his heel and left.

I shut the front door of the camper, locked it, and went to the small fridge for a beer. While I had it open, I grabbed a soda for Simone and moved to the bedroom.

She sat on top of the bed with her legs folded.

I put the soda bottle on the tiny end table next to the bed. "Know you heard all that shit. You got something to say about it?"

She pressed her lips together. "I didn't hear all of it. Not after he said I'm his age."

I swallowed a slug of beer. "Are you disgusted by the difference in our age?"

"Hell, no," she said, unfolding her legs and scooting further up the bed. "Are you pissed?"

"No, I'm... Did you want to hit him for calling me sloppy-seconds?"

"I fuckin' say what I mean, Simone."

"You didn't, just because he's your son?"

I closed my eyes and exhaled. "Yeah."

"Is it wrong that I wanted you to punch him?"

I opened my eyes. "You wanted me to hit him?"

She nodded. "I don't like him judging us... even if there won't be an 'us' after this weekend."

"Wrong," I said, pulling my boots and socks off.

"What do you mean 'wrong'?" she scoffed.

I already had my cut off and yanked my t-shirt over my head. "I mean you're wrong about that."

My hard-on had dissipated while Jordan was here, but Simone in that baby-doll dress, wearing no bra and a tiny thong, had me hard as a rock. I carefully dropped my jeans and underwear.

"You are so sexy," she muttered, licking her lips.

I grabbed her legs and yanked her across the bed so she was laying down. My control was slipping, but I pulled her thong off without destroying it. I dragged my index finger through her folds. She was sopping for me.

I loved that.

"So are you, baby. Get your dress off or I'll tear it off and I really fuckin' like that dress."

She smiled. "I'm glad."

When she tossed the dress on the floor, I pinched one of her taut nipples. "But the next fuckin' time you wear it, you *will* wear a bra, you hear me?"

"Yes, sir."

I lifted her legs and surged inside her. "Do you know what you fuckin' do to me, calling me 'Sir'?"

"Maybe. Are you gonna show me?"

"Yeah, because it's time to take your fucking."

Between the lengthy make-out session earlier and my pent up anger, I fucked her hard, wild, and fast. So damned good... the best.

While we both came down from our orgasms, she traced her tongue along my collar bone. "I love how you work my body, Steel. It's fantastic."

I loved being buried inside her. That was even better.

Watching my fingers slide her hair off her forehead, I said, "You were wrong earlier."

"What am I wrong about?"

I grabbed her hands, pinned them to the bed, and gave her more of my weight. "You said there wouldn't be an us after this weekend. That's wrong."

Her eyes widened. "That's not what you said last night."

I nipped at her lower lip. "And I've changed my mind, woman."

Her head tilted. "You're fuck-drunk."

I threw my head back and roared with laughter.

She got the drop on me and rolled me to my back, dislodging my cock from her pussy.

I grabbed the globes of her ass. "I could be, as addicted to you as I am, but that isn't what prompted me to change my mind."

"Really?" she asked, lowering her torso to mine.

My lips curled into a smile while I gathered her hair in my hands. "Yeah. Deep down, I don't want you having to figure it out for yourself. That's wrong. Then there's what you said about how you're different from Debra. The more I thought about it, the more I realized how true that is. Hell, it's what drew me to you that night. You didn't want me because I'm president of a mother chapter. You didn't know shit about me."

She rested her forearms on my chest and propped her chin on top of her arms. "Yeah, but I... I'm gonna ask this anyway, are you sure you won't bail on me like you did with Jordan? I won't be cool with that, and I want to be in on that kind of decision... 'cause you don't understand how much I'll fight back with someone who fucks with my family."

I gave her ass a squeeze. "I can't make that promise, but we'll take it one day at a time."

Her eyes rounded. "I'm not moving to Augusta, I just put a deposit down on an apartment and I want my doctor to be—"

I put my finger on her lips. "One day at a time, baby. My club's had issues in Jacksonville for a long-ass time. You're in Jacksonville. I have to make a visit there to solve the fuckin' problems. I've decided I'm gonna be in town for a while. That means I'm staying with you, but we'll take precautions."

Her lips tipped up. "Right, that sounds like a plan."

I liked the excitement lacing her tone. It almost had me looking forward to a trip to Jacksonville.

She stared at me like she couldn't believe what I'd said. My gut said my next words would wipe that look off her face.

"One more thing, Jade."

"What?"

"Most of those weekends, I'll have to go back to Augusta. You're coming with me as often as possible." Her eyes went wide. "And it'll kill me, but that won't be on the back of my bike."

Yep. Her expression drooped like a wilted flower.

"Sorry, baby, but how many pregnant women do you see on the back of a Harley?"

She rolled her eyes. "It's annoying when you're logical."

I rubbed my hand up and down her back, squeezing her ass every chance I got. "Is Volt gonna freak the fuck out again?"

She grinned and slid her eyes to the side. "Most likely. But, he'll get over it as long as you don't fuck me over."

Those words made my lungs freeze. The word 'never' sat on the tip of my tongue, but life had a way of fucking things up. "Not if I can help it, darlin'."

CHAPTER 12

SCALE OF ONE TO TEN

SIMONE

"I DIDN'T GUILT YOU into this, did I?"

He tipped his head back on the pillow and he laughed long and loud. "You won't believe this, woman, but I'm not known for laughing much. That first night with you, I laughed more than I had in over a year."

"You didn't laugh much then, either. They were more like chuckles."

"You've made me belly-laugh at least twice in the past hour."

"So you needed a comedienne in your life?"

"No. You believe you're made to be a president's old lady. Well, I'm certain only a woman like you would be able to make me laugh."

"Fair." My eyes darted to the side and back. "Um, I don't move to Jacksonville until late next week. I'll be back in Gainesville tomorrow night."

"Right. My bike is getting dropped in Jacksonville. I'll ride to Gainesville with you, it might give me a chance to patch shit up with Jordan. But Tuesday, I'll have to hit Jacksonville for the rest of the week to start laying the groundwork for shit there."

Nosy by nature, I asked, "What kind of groundwork are we talking about?"

He cocked a brow. "Not gonna tell you that, woman. How much club business does your mom get from Volt? Damned little, if I had to guess."

I returned his brow arch. "You're not Volt and I'm not Mom."

99

He nodded. "You're still not getting that info from me. Thought you wanted to see the wrestling today? Or would you rather spend all day in bed?"

I smiled and lowered my mouth to his ear to whisper, "The wrestling, but I'm wearing my dress sans bra, baby. It'll drive you wild all afternoon."

His head tipped back and he groaned.

It was music to my ears.

WE ARRIVED IN THE nick of time to see Jasmine win her first coleslaw-wrestling round. Steel stood ten feet away while I congratulated her.

After she wiped a hand towel across her face, she asked, "Is that him over there? All broody, dark, and handsome?"

Jealousy flared inside me, even though I knew she wasn't interested. "Yeah."

Her eyes locked with mine. "Not my type, but he's fuckin' hot."

"Yeah," I whispered. "So, you move on to another round, right?"

"Technically, yes, but it's up against the woman who always lost to mom. Dad's hell-bent on me bowing out with just the one win."

My eyes widened. "You're not going to do that are you?"

Her eyes scanned the area around us. "They don't know I'm only seventeen. That bitch will rat me out... hell, I suspect she'd claim I'm seventeen even if I were older."

I frowned. "That sucks."

She shrugged, a couple strands of coleslaw falling off her shoulder. "Nah. I'll be eighteen by October and it gives me plenty of time to practice."

Her older brother Rafferty lumbered over to us. "All right, Jazz, let's go. Your ass is falling out of your bikini bottom. Nobody needs to see that." He nodded at me. "Simone. I'm surprised you're here without your roommate."

I smiled. "My roommate has a name, and Alexandra headed back early yesterday."

He made a strange humming sound. "You take care, Simone. C'mon, Jazz."

Jasmine rolled her eyes. She leaned forward to hug me, then realized she was covered in coleslaw and backed away. "He needs to get over his shit with Alexandra, but I'll see you soon."

Steel's arms came around my waist from behind and he rested his chin on my shoulder. "She going to get ready for the next round?"

I sighed. "No. It's a long story, but let's just say Biketoberfest will be one to remember."

His hands moved down to cup my small, but growing belly. "It sure as hell will."

A tiny smile played at my lips as I caught his meaning. I'd be a new mom by then since the baby was due September eighth.

"You wanna get some food?" he asked at my ear.

I nodded and turned in his hold. "Yeah, that'd be good."

He smiled down at me. "Barbeque beef? Noticed you made a face when you were near chicken."

"Yeah, brisket would be great."

We carried our food to an empty picnic table. I hadn't seen any Devil Lancers around, and I had no idea where the Riot members were at either.

Steel sat on the bench sideways – straddling the bench. When I sat down, he guided my hips so I sat between his legs.

I turned my head to him. "Are you trying to send a clear message to people or something?"

He scratched his stubbled cheek and stared past me for a long moment. His eyes met mine. "Yeah, I am. Every asshole who looks at you needs to know you're with me."

I nodded. "Okay, then."

Three shadows formed on the table. I glanced over my shoulder and saw one of my favorite people, Uncle Yak. Uncle Roll and Uncle Rage stood on either side of him. They all looked unhappy.

Yak spoke before I could greet him. "You get lost, Simone? The rest of the Riot is on the other side of the food truck with the wings."

I widened my eyes at him. "Well, I definitely don't want to sit over there. The smell of chicken makes me nauseous these days."

His eyes cut to Steel. "Yeah, I heard about that."

Uncle Yak's glower deepened when Steel's arm came around me, resting just under my breasts. "She's not sitting with the Riot today because she's with me."

Rage stepped forward. "Find someone else to sit with you, Steel."

"There isn't a problem here," I said.

He widened his eyes at me. "There isn't a problem here? Think again, Simone. It's because of this man that Lisa and Nora were—"

I shifted so I could look at Rage and Yak without twisting my neck. "It isn't his fault directly. He didn't even know what had happened until after the fact."

Uncle Roll spoke in his firm, even tone. "You think long and hard about what you're doing, girlie. Maybe you need to talk to my niece about what Steel's brothers—"

In a fluid movement, Steel rose from the bench. "Stop right fuckin' there, Roll. I had no fuckin' idea about those two members. And the whole fuckin' chapter lost their charter because of that shit. Waited over three years before approving another charter, but that's the past. Right now, Simone's carrying my baby and I'm not bailing on her."

"That's not what you said yesterday," Dad muttered from behind us.

Could this get any more awkward?

"Fuckin' A," Steel hissed and turned toward Dad.

I stood and put an arm around Steel's waist. "Things changed, Dad. This isn't really the time, though, don't you think?"

"You're not gonna negotiate your way out of this," Uncle Yak said.

Dad shook his head. "Thanks, Yak, but you, Rage, and Roll can join the others. I'll handle this."

"There's nothing to handle, Volt," Steel said.

Dad set his full plastic cup of beer on the table and sat. "The hell there isn't. You say you aren't bailing, but you aren't moving her to Augusta either."

Steel guided me back to the table and I sat down. "I am an adult with free will, Dad."

Rather than sit sideways, Steel settled next to me facing Dad. "For all intents and purposes, there's only four, maybe five members who make up the Jacksonville Devil Lancer chapter. That's a problem."

Dad's eyes lit with something like mischief. "I'd think that when you run the mother chapter, you'd know this, but it seems to me if you want a decent chapter in Jacksonville, you'll have to lay the foundation yourself."

Steel stared at Dad for such a long moment, the similarities between their personalities couldn't be ignored. In tense situations with heated emotions, Dad always took his time before speaking or acting. The only problem now was that I didn't know Steel well enough to say if he was angry or just thinking.

Finally, Steel nodded. "Yeah, the only upside to Jacksonville needing my direct attention is that Simone will be there, too."

Dad took a long pull on his beer. "Are you claiming her?"

Steel's jaw shifted. "At this time, no. Me claiming her puts a visible mark on her—"

"Glad you don't have your head up your ass."

"Dad," I scoffed.

Steel put his arm around my shoulders without losing eye contact with Dad. "But I'm taking her to Augusta on the weekends."

Dad's eyes flared for a moment, then he focused on me. "And you're cool with that?"

Part of me was cool with whatever Steel would give me, but not only did that reveal too much, it might have been my lust talking.

"For now, I am."

Dad turned back to Steel. "Do you intend to bail Ghost and the others out of jail?"

Steel shook his head. "That's not your business, Volt. But… out of respect for you and your daughter, I'll tell you that I'm not. Their patches haven't been stripped publicly, but notices went out that they're no longer members of the club."

"If they were granted parole tomorrow, you wouldn't welcome them back in an effort to build up the ranks?" Dad asked.

Steel shook his head. "No. Hell, every one of them has been inside for fifteen years, so they'd all owe well over nine grand in back dues."

"You don't waive that for time served?"

"In this case, no."

Dad's eyes cut to mine. "You still moving into that apartment on the westside?"

I nodded. "Yes."

His eyes slid to Steel and back to me. "You're sure you're not staying at their fuckin' clubhouse?"

My eyes widened. "I'm sure, Dad."

Steel gave my shoulders a squeeze. "I'll be staying with her, so I can help with the move."

Dad's jaw clenched. "What the hell changed your mind so fast?"

Steel raised his chin and ran his hand down his neck. "This isn't your business either, but Simone pointed out that she isn't like Jordan's mom. I still think she can do better than me, but I'll be damned if I let her figure this shit out alone."

"She wouldn't be on her own," Dad bit out.

Steel gave a single nod. "Maybe not, but now I'm gonna be there, too."

Dad stared at me for a beat. "I love you. Wanted you to try civilian life. Are you sure—"

I grabbed his hand. "Dad, I love everything about MC life and you know it."

He sighed and stood. "All right, I'll trust you on that, sweetheart."

I smiled. "Thanks, Dad. I love you, too."

His eyes traveled down to my dress and he shook his head. "If you love me, when you get home, do me a favor. Burn that fuckin' dress."

"Bye, Dad!"

Once he was out of earshot, Steel nudged my bicep with his. "It's official. I'm framing your dress when you get home. Then I'm gonna buy you fifty more of 'em."

I burst with laughter.

"I'M SO GLAD I got to help you mark something off your bucket list, Steel," I said, standing on the beach blanket, toweling my hair dry.

With his back to me, he adjusted his underwear. "Hurry up and get dressed, Jade. I don't want to court either of us getting arrested for indecent exposure."

I grinned. "Already done, baby. Another perk of my favorite dress, easy off, easy on."

He glowered over his shoulder at me. "And your underwear?"

I shrugged. "Wearing a thong is fun, but wearing a *sandy* thong is not." My gaze slid across the horizon. "Riding on your bike is going to be more of an experience tonight."

He yanked his jeans up with a growl. "I should spank your ass for that."

"I know."

"Woman."

"What? I get the feeling I'm keeping you young, Steel. When was the last time you had this much fun?"

He bent and grabbed his boots now that he'd shrugged into his t-shirt. "Get your shoes, baby. It's time to make tracks."

"Did you have any fun?" I asked, trudging through the sand next to him.

He squeezed my hand. "Sex with you is always fun, Jade."

I shot him some side-eye.

He stopped us on the trail to the parking lot. "Yes, baby. I had fun. More than I've had in a long-ass time."

I smiled. "Good, but you seem awful grumpy for having had so much fun."

He lowered his lips to my ear. "You haven't been paying attention, Jade. I fuck you once, I want seconds very soon afterward. But I'm not doing sex on the beach, and the thought of your pussy on my bike getting wetter and wetter from the rumble of those pipes...it's gonna be a fuckin' challenge to get us back to the campsite."

I turned my lips toward his ear. "You could always fuck me *on* your bike when we get back."

He made a growling noise and kissed me hard. "Not happening, woman. Not there, anyway. Hell, I don't even think I could trust my brothers not to watch us at my clubhouse."

I pressed my lips together. "Bummer."

THE FOLLOWING THURSDAY, ALL my stuff had been moved into my two-bedroom apartment. To my chagrin, Dad and the Riot brothers had worked well alongside Steel to move my crap.

Now, it was closing in on five o'clock. Mom, Abby, Alexandra and I were sitting around in the living room staring at my boxes. The men had all left. Steel had things to do with a couple of the Devil Lancers and the Riot men had all gone to the clubhouse, which was only a couple miles away.

Alexandra wandered to the breakfast bar where she'd left her phone and keys. "I have to get back to Gainesville. It's cool that Ines could take over your part of the lease, but I'm gonna miss having you as a roomie, Simone."

"I'm sorry, sweetie," I said.

She gave me a reluctant smile. "Don't be. Aunt Jackie can disagree all she wants, but I think Steel is really good for you. You're so happy now. I mean, you're still turning into a pumpkin at five-fifteen every evening, but man... I want some of what you've got, chickie."

"Don't let Cal hear that," Mom said.

Alexandra shook her head. "I don't mean with a Devil Lancer. I just mean... well,—"

"You want the look of being well-fucked on the regular by someone who knows what they're doing," Aunt Abby suggested.

Alexandra blushed.

Aunt Abby and I cackled.

Mom sighed.

I walked Alexandra to the door to avoid Mom's judgment or disappointment. At this stage, it felt like they went hand-in-hand.

After I locked the door, Aunt Abby stood at the kitchen counter with a bottle of chardonnay in hand. "My man's picking me up here, so Jackie, unless you want another glass, I'm polishing this off."

Mom took her red Solo cup to Aunt Abby. "No, you're splitting that with me."

Aunt Abby held the bottle aloft. "Why? Because you're stressed about Simone's new living arrangements?"

"Yes, amongst all the other things, Abigail."

She stared at Mom for a moment before she poured the wine. Aunt Abby caught my eyes. "How good is he?"

Mom gasped. "Abby, I don't need to know—"

She wagged a finger at Mom. "Jacqueline. Every woman deserves happiness. Happiness includes a healthy sex life. So what if he leads the fuckin' Devil Lancers. As long as he's good to our girl, that's what matters."

Mom glared at Abby. "It'd be nice if she had a good man in her bed."

Abby shrugged a shoulder. "Good men come in all shapes and sizes. There are people who think your man isn't very good. But you and I know they're wrong."

"This isn't the same," Mom muttered.

"Oh, but it really is, Jackie."

Mom threw her hand out in my direction. "She could go to jail! Then what happens to my grandbaby?"

Abby's head tilted in question. "Has Volt *ever* put you in a position where you'd be incriminated?"

Mom kept quiet.

"Right. Nor has Blood done that to me. Open those eyes, Jackie. The way Steel looks at her, he's not gonna do that either."

"He fucking better not."

Aunt Abby's head dipped. "Right. And if he does, I'll lead the brigade to cut him into eighty-five little pieces and scatter his sorry ass across the Southeast."

"Geez, eighty-five is rather specific. Vengeful much?" I asked.

Aunt Abby made big eyes at me. "Very. Now, how good is he? Scale of one to ten."

I didn't hesitate. "Best ever."

Aunt Abby's expression fell. "Really?"

"Definitely."

Mom downed her wine. "We're so fucked."

Aunt Abby grinned. "No, she is. And I'd say, that's how she wants it."

"What are you so worried about, Mom?"

That earned me a glare. "Oh, I don't know... you moving to Georgia, getting hurt, all of it."

I nodded. "If the tables were turned, you'd tell me to have faith. That you and Dad know what you're doing."

She shook her head. "Simone, that doesn't work here."

I shrugged. "Fine. I'll tell you what Steel keeps saying, one day at a time."

"One day at a time! That's easy for him to say. At least he didn't insist you move closer to the Devil Lancer compound, then—"

"She'd be on the same side of the river as your house," Steel said, walking inside.

I made a mental note to ask him how he unlocked the door so quiet and stealthy.

He came right to me. His hand cupping my belly while his other curled around my neck. He kissed me quick. "Hey, Jade."

He nodded at Mom, "Jackie."

Then he did the same with Aunt Abby.

Mom nodded back at him. "How do you know where we live?"

Steel grinned. "I don't. Simone said you live across the river. I do my research, but I haven't looked into you or Volt."

"Oh," Mom whispered.

At the same time Aunt Abby muttered, "Yet."

Steel chuckled. "Listen, we don't have issues with the Riot. The shit in the past is past. Seeing as the Riot isn't in the same... trade as us, I don't anticipate problems."

Mom choked on laughter. "Trade? You call what you do—"

"Mom," I said.

"No, Simone. You should know about their *trades*."

"She does," Steel said.

Mom's eyes danced between us. "She doesn't."

"I do."

"And it doesn't bother you?" Mom asked.

I took a deep breath. "I'm not entirely down, but the Riot runs Platinum's right down the street."

"Yeah, that's the one area of overlap," Steel murmured.

"Are you hearing this?" Mom demanded.

I nodded. "Yeah. That's a problem for Uncle Yak and Turk."

"That's our girl," Aunt Abby said.

Mom ignored her. "Simone, you can't be that dense. More goes—"

Steel's voice became stern. "She isn't dense and we discussed it."

With her plastic cup to her lips, Mom stared at Steel. She sipped her wine, then put the cup down. "Are you certain you can keep her safe?"

Steel's lips twisted a touch. "Are you certain you're always safe? There are risks being a president's old lady."

Mom's eyes lit with triumph. "She isn't your old lady, so the risks to her are increased seeing as she wouldn't have your protection."

His dark eyebrows lowered and he stared at Mom. "Whether or not you mean to, you're twisting this around. Not being my old lady doesn't mean she isn't protected."

Aunt Abby tossed her empty cup in the trash. "I don't think Jackie's trying to twist your words."

"But if she's yours, that would come with heavier protection, wouldn't it?"

I shifted out of Steel's hold. "Mom, you need to stop."

"You need to stop and think about these things."

"I have. Everyone keeps talking about a threat, but no details." I pointed at Steel. "You should share if there's more information, by the way." I turned back to Mom. "But, there's a risk being Dad's daughter, too."

"Old ladies and kids are off-limits."

"Not always," I said.

Mom's eyes widened. "When have you ever been threatened?"

"You were threatened when you and Dad first met."

"That was before he claimed me, so you're only proving my point."

Steel shook his head. "If the rumors are true, it was non-bikers who threatened you, so in reality, Simone's right. There are risks to being anybody. Wrong place, wrong time happens plenty." A sly gleam hit his eyes. "A woman who speaks up for her best friend when she's been done wrong in such a heinous way garners the wrong kind of attention."

Mom's jaw shifted. "Thought you didn't look into me and Volt?"

Steel grinned. "Not your address." He tipped his head toward me. "She's got spunk, and I asked a few people what they knew about how you and Volt met."

Aunt Abby's lips pursed and she narrowed her eyes at Steel. "Who would run their mouth about that?"

"Hard to say," he said, looking at Aunt Abby.

From his expression, I realized he was telling her something else. I shook my head. "Uncle Blood would never."

She turned her head to the side. "Sonuvabitch. I knew I should have stuck closer to him that last night at Bike Week." She glanced back at Steel. "But you weren't around for that conversation."

He turned his hands up. "No, I was somewhere else."

Mom grimaced. "This is getting awkward. I just want to know she and her baby are going to be safe."

Steel nodded once. "She will be safe."

From the set of Mom's lips, I knew her irritation had amped up another notch. "Seeing as you aren't claiming her, forgive me if I don't believe you."

"Someone fucks with her, it's the last damned thing they'll ever do, Jackie. I'll burn their whole fuckin' world down. Do you believe that?"

The conviction and malice in Steel's tone alone had me believing him.

After a beat, Mom nodded. "Yes. I believe that." She pointed a finger at him. "But let's make sure it doesn't come to that."

Steel chuckled. "Yeah. That's the plan."

CHAPTER 13

TYPICAL TRIP TO TARGET

STEEL

THINGS IN JACKSONVILLE WERE worse than I'd suspected.

Very few hang-arounds meant no fresh blood to revive the chapter. Worse, if the rumors were true, the Corrupt Chrome MC was making inroads with the Southside Slayers – our main competitor in drug distribution in Jacksonville.

Jackhammer and Warden took direction well, but neither one of them had leadership skills. From what I could see, neither one of them *wanted* to lead a chapter.

On top of that, I'd been too lax with this chapter. Some neighbors had complained to the code enforcement department about the state of the clubhouse. The last president had gone the cheap route for the building. Two single wide trailers were on the property and they were connected by a ramshackle roof. The walls were nothing but screens.

It was embarrassing.

Maybe Tie was right. We should cut our losses and eat the lost dues coming in every month. It wouldn't take much to convince Warden and Jackhammer to move to another city.

If we went that route, I'd see far less of Simone.

It also left things open for Corrupt Chrome to gain more ground, which would bring them more money and it stood to reason that they would funnel that money toward their efforts to fuck with us in other cities. Augusta first, if I were running that club.

This was a complete clusterfuck.

I had to confront this head-on, and to do that, I'd need other brothers to come to town. I could bring the whole Augusta chapter down here, but that wasn't ideal either. With a sigh, I ran my hand through my hair. Atlanta could spare a few brothers for this, and possibly Raleigh as well, but none of them would be eager to make such long rides on the heels of Bike Week.

A few of them had narrowly escaped being arrested earlier in the month.

Tough shit. They'd have to suck it up and pitch in for this.

"I'm sorry about Mom," Simone said, as she settled in the armchair adjacent to the couch where I sat.

I stretched a leg out and locked eyes with her. "Come over here."

"What's wrong with where I am?"

"It's not close enough for me to put my arms around you."

Her lips pursed, but I didn't miss the way her head reared back a fraction of an inch. She rose and sat between my legs, resting her back on my chest.

I wrapped one arm around her waist and slid my other hand down her arm until I found her hand and laced our fingers together. "Don't apologize about Jackie. Hell, I'd be more concerned if she didn't bust my balls."

She chuckled and twisted her head to look at me. "Oh, she wasn't busting your balls. She's just overprotective of me."

"And she should be."

"Not like this, I don't know how you kept your cool."

I squeezed her hand. "Her questions were all valid. The situation between us is tenuous and the moment someone puts it together, you're going to be in danger."

"Here we go again," she breathed. After a beat, she shifted more of her weight on to me and rested her head against my shoulder to make eye contact. "Who exactly is going to put me in danger when they realize we're a thing?"

"A thing?"

She tossed a hand out. "I don't know what else to call this. So, who are the bad guys here?"

"You don't—"

She sat up and twisted her body toward me. "Oh no, you're about to say 'You don't need to know' or I don't need to worry about it, or some variation on that theme. But you're wrong. Knowing who and what I'm up against is good strategy, Steel."

I took a breath and held it. "This isn't about strategy."

She dipped her chin. "Bullshit. I'm better off knowing if the threat is from a street gang or some rival MC, so which is it? Or is it both?"

"It's a rival MC, but depending on things, there could be a street gang involved too."

"Sweet."

I choked on a chuckle. "That is not sweet, Simone."

She smiled, reminding me how much I loved seeing her eyes light with her grin. "It's sweet because it'll keep me on my toes. Might have to tussle with a biker one day and deal with a gang member the next."

With a low growl, I pulled my leg up and shifted so I could look in her eyes. "You aren't doing any of that shit. You're pregnant."

Her eyes widened. "Yeah, and most people don't even know since I'm not quite showing yet. Pregnant doesn't mean I'm an invalid."

"It also doesn't mean you're an MMA fighter."

"Who said anything about fighting?"

"Tussle?"

Her lips twisted into a smirk. "A gun cuts any tussle short."

I traced my finger along her cheekbone. "And if that gun gets wrestled away from you, what then? You end up shot, and I'm gonna be pissed."

"Really?"

My eyes widened at her. "Yes, really. You were there when I told your mom I'd burn down the world for you."

She shook her head. "That's just an expression."

I lowered my chin. "Not in my world – and you know it."

She sighed. "Well, I wouldn't want you going to jail."

I shook my head. "I'd rather not have to go after anyone because they fucked with you."

We were quiet for a moment as she mulled that over. She turned to me with a quizzical look. "Something in your tone sounded off. Have you been to jail?"

I nodded once.

"But you got out right away, right?"

Her eyes held so much anticipation.

I pressed my lips together. "No. I served nine months for manslaughter."

She attempted to hide her surprise, but I could read her. "How did you get out after nine months?"

"Club lawyer appealed, got it overturned."

"Wow," she whispered.

"Yeah, I'm not the nice guy Jackie would have picked for you."

"Like mother, like daughter," she muttered.

"What do you mean?" I asked.

She twisted toward me. "Grandpa told me how much he, and especially Gran, wanted *anybody* but Dad for Mom."

I grunted, imagining how much they'd despise me. Not that I'd care. "Do they know you're pregnant?"

She frowned. "They passed away a few years back."

"Sorry to hear that, sweetheart."

The way her eyes warmed when she looked back to me... I hadn't felt a punch like that in ages. "Yeah, me too." She stood and went to the kitchen. "So, there's maybe one glass of red wine in this bottle someone left, and six chicken wings left over in the fridge. It's not a decent dinner, but I haven't hit the grocery store yet."

I suppressed a groan and stood. "Then put your shoes on. We're going to get some seafood and then we'll hit the store on the way back."

"On your bike?" she asked.

"No, you're driving, Jade."

———————

"You should dial it back on the aggression when you're driving," I suggested.

She turned just enough to give me side-eye. "And you might dial it back on the commentary, sir."

I shook my head. "Now you're fucking with me."

"You started it. I'm surprised you want to come with me to the grocery store. Aren't you headed back to Augusta the day after tomorrow?"

"Yeah, but I still have to eat. And you're going with me to Augusta."

She turned into the parking lot for a Super Target. "On your bike?"

"No, I'll be on my Harley. You'll follow me."

That didn't earn me side-eye, it got me one helluva dirty look. "It oughta be that you're following me, because I got news for you, I might not be showing, but hell if I don't have to pee like a mother all the damned time."

I couldn't help but grin at her choice of words.

"What are you smiling about?" she asked, pulling through an empty parking space so the SUV sat nose-out.

Once she shut down the vehicle, I unbuckled my seat belt. "Your choice of words, Jade. You have to pee like a mother because you're soon going to be one."

She let out a cute growl. "Let's get this done, smart guy."

I hustled out of the car since she made such a quick exit. Once I fell in step next to her, I said, "You're pissed."

"No, but now who's got jokes, saying I'm pissed?" she asked.

I bit back my laughter and followed her inside the store. She reached out for a cart, but I grabbed her hand and pulled her to the side. "Why are you angry?"

She glanced up and over my shoulder while taking a deep breath. "I'm not angry. I'm irritated."

I shifted to catch her gaze. "You're splitting hairs. What's got you 'irritated'?"

She stared at me, looked away, and kept quiet.

"Not being on my bike," I guessed.

She exhaled, and turned back to me. "Maybe, even if I know it shouldn't bother me, it does. I'm sorry."

Again, laughter threatened, and that would only irritate her further. I let go of her hand and wrapped my arm around her waist. "You have nothing to apologize for. If something bugs you, it bugs you. But you're pregnant, I'm not putting you on my bike with a four-hour ride ahead of us."

She took a deep breath, her tits brushing my chest. "You say things like that and I want to think you care ... and maybe you do ... but you aren't going to stick around."

I kept eye contact with her, and it nearly gutted me, but I dismissed her words. "Let's get this done."

Some people despised grocery shopping. If it wasn't too crowded, most of the time it didn't bother me. The way Simone maneuvered the cart through the aisles, she didn't like getting groceries one iota. We had the cart half-full and from her demeanor, we couldn't finish fast enough.

"You, uh, do a lot of grocery deliveries in college?" I asked.

She whipped her head toward me, her eyes narrowed. "Not any more than any one else."

I did a slow nod. "Right."

With the cart angled toward the pre-packaged salads and spinach, she turned to me. "What are you getting at?"

Some twisted part of me found her attitude refreshing. "I'm not getting at anything, Simone. Just seems that you'd rather be anywhere but here."

She glanced to the side for a beat, then back to me. "It's not my favorite, but I know it needs to be done and the quicker we start the sooner we finish." Her eyes darted to the salads and back to mine. "Do you eat salad or can we skip the obligatory rabbit food?"

I choked on my laughter. "Obligatory?"

"Salads are supposed to be good for you, but I can't stand them."

"That's a first," I muttered without thinking.

Her head tilted. "What's a first?"

I sighed. "Most women love salads. You might be the first one to admit to hating them."

She grinned. "Mom loves them enough for me, my brother Bobby, and fifty other people over fifty."

I felt a sneer hit my lips and my head twisted. "Your mom isn't fifty."

Her eyes widened. "Yeah, even more reason for her to lay off the green stuff."

"If I didn't know better, I'd say you're hangry, but... I saw how many shrimp you put away during dinner. So, what's the story, Jade?"

"You dodged whether you're going to stick around. But more than that, you dodged whether you care or not. I suppose the latter will become clear soon enough, but going it alone... that's something I'd like to know sooner rather than later. And somehow, I think you know if you're going to bail on me for Augusta and your club."

Damn, she did not mince words. I loved that about her. I hated the idea of leaving her to go it alone.

I grabbed hold of the cart handle and pushed it around the corner to the next aisle. "I'm not certain what the future holds, but if my club needs me, then I'm gonna have to hit the road. Like this weekend, though you're coming along."

"A tag-along," she muttered.

"Didn't say it like that," I muttered.

She sighed. "You're right. I'm sorry. I don't know what my problem is." She grabbed a small jar of green olives and looked to me. "Do you eat olives?"

I shrugged a shoulder. "Not usually, but if you want 'em, get 'em."

She put the jar in the cart and moved to take control, but I held firm to the handle.

"You cool now?" I asked.

Her brown eyes gleamed in the florescent lights. "I will be."

I nodded and let go of the handle. "Good."

We faced forward and saw two bearded men walking our way. They both wore leather cuts with the Corrupt Chrome logo dominating the left side. As they came closer I saw one had the road name 'Scar,' and the other went by 'Pump.'

"They're not from here," Simone muttered.

"Be quiet, and let me handle this," I whispered.

"You're a hard man to find," Scar said, propping his foot on the bottom rail of the shopping cart. He stood an inch shorter than me, but it appeared he had at least twenty pounds on me. Probably fat, but I didn't want this to get physical with Simone next to me. His hazel eyes bored into mine, and I wondered if he even knew anyone else was around.

Pump, however, had his eyes locked on Simone, practically salivating the way he licked his lips. "Who's your friend, Steel? She a secret daughter you been hiding?"

Simone opened her mouth, and using my index finger I gave a subtle tug on her belt loop.

My gaze never left Scar and through clenched teeth, I asked, "What do you want?"

After a long, loaded moment, Scar's eyes shifted to Simone and back to me. "Knuckles asked you for a sit-down before Bike Week, you too good to respond?"

"He didn't ask me, since this is the first I'm hearing of it," I said.

Scar narrowed his eyes. "Your club runs the titty bar in Augusta. He left word there."

I shrugged a shoulder. "I'm busy."

Scar glanced around the aisle as though he'd never been in a grocery store. "Sure, so busy you can wander around a fuckin' grocery store."

"Why did you follow me here? Why not talk to my VP?"

Pump's blue eyes slid to me. "Don't think we didn't. He's gettin' a message right now."

Scar nodded. "Same one you're gonna get."

Three things happened at once. Scar made to shove the cart into me and Simone, but she'd already jerked the cart back. Pump reached for a gun, but didn't pull it free before Simone's voice cut through the air.

"Freeze right there, asshole," she had taken a gun out of her purse —which sat inside the top of the cart— and had the gun aimed at Pump. "I will shoot your balls off."

Surprise suffused both men's faces.

"Jade," I said in a warning tone. "Put the weapon away."

"I will, when they calmly *walk* away."

The way Scar stared at her, like he was cataloging everything about her, I wanted to carve his eyes out.

"Jade's a pretty name," Pump said. "And it's easy to remember."

Her head cocked an inch to the side and I knew she had a smart retort.

"Keep quiet," I ordered.

A woman pushing a jumbo-sized cart with room for two kids entered the opposite end of the aisle. Scar glanced over his shoulder and I saw why he likely had his road name. A thick scar lined his neck and I wondered how he'd survived such a vicious cut.

He turned back to us. "We'll leave, but your time is up, Steel. We're taking over whether you like it or not."

A lecherous smile twisted Pump's lips. "And we might take more than just your territory."

Scar turned on his heel and Pump trudged after him.

In a very low voice, I said, "Uncock that piece and put it the fuck away, woman."

She did as I asked, then glared up at me. "Why are you pissed at me? I kept those assholes from getting the jump on you."

I widened my eyes. "I told you to let me handle this shit."

She shook her head. "Thanks to the fabulous nickname you gave me, they don't even know who I am."

I scoffed. "They know who you are now. Grab your purse, we gotta ditch the fucking food or they'll follow us to your place."

She dipped her chin and smirked. "Honey, not to be cocky, but I can lead those morons on one helluva wild goose chase on the way home."

I tore a hand through my hair. "Not happening. I'm driving and we're hitting the Devil Lancer clubhouse."

"That's out by the docks."

"Yep."

She started pushing the cart forward. "No. I'm not heading there, Steel. They aren't forcing me out of my home."

Grabbing the cart, I halted her progress. "They found us already. We need to be where I can protect you."

She twisted her body so she could put a hand on her hip. "And we can do that at my place. However they found us, they probably already know where I live."

The mom with her two kids pushed past us and I waited until she was out of earshot. "My bike stands out, Simone."

She nodded. "Right, and seeing as it's parked outside my apartment, that means the die is cast. Let's have these mofos arrested or take them out ourselves."

I shook my head. "This is real life, Jade, not some episode of a biker show."

She straightened. "Believe me, I know that. But I told you I fight back when someone fucks with my family."

A warm sensation gathered in my chest. "I'm not your family."

Her brows arched. "You're my baby-daddy, so think again, tough guy."

She motored the cart out of the aisle and moved toward the check-out. I couldn't remember the last time a woman was so stubborn. For some bizarre reason, I enjoyed the fuck out of that about her.

I stopped the cart. "Will you humor me and go to the clubhouse tonight?"

She grinned. "Sure, if it's the Riot clubhouse. First, we need to pay for the food."

"We need to ditch the cart and go, Simone."

"Why? So they can follow us *and* we'll have bare cupboards. You could call Warden or Jackhammer to help you out."

That was the next thing I was going to do... maybe an MC princess wasn't the right choice for me.

At my lengthy silence, she aimed a shy smile at me. "Oh, did I take the wind out of your sails with that one. Sorry. I've spent most of my life watching Dad call in brothers for support or handle 'situations' that I wasn't supposed to know about."

I dug a credit card out of my wallet. "Go pay for the damn food."

IN THE PARKING LOT, I wished the sun had already set. Instead, there was more than enough light for bystanders to see Scar and Pump standing at Simone's SUV along with a third man. He had his back to us and no club colors stitched on his cut.

"You know this new guy?" I asked.

"Shit, that's Rafferty," Simone hissed.

"He got a thing for you?"

She laughed. "Not a chance. He'd tell you otherwise, but he's got a thing for Alexandra."

"Then, why's he following *you*?"

"If I had to guess because he thinks it'll make him look good to my Dad and the other brothers. They haven't approved him to be a prospect yet."

I wondered why they'd keep him from prospecting, but kept focused on the situation at her vehicle. "How would he know to follow you? Did you realize he was following us?"

"No to your last question, and I have no idea how he'd know to tail us. Maybe he thought I'd lead him to Alexandra."

"Not likely. How about you hang back at the doors?"

She pointed a sly smile my way. "Not likely, tough guy."

I sighed. "Keep your damn gun in your purse, then."

She faced forward. "I make no promises."

"Jade," I said in a warning tone as we came within earshot of the men.

"Don't worry," she whispered.

Rafferty had a thick build, dark hair, brown eyes, and a firm grip on a nine millimeter he had pointed at Scar and Pump.

"Is there a reason you're pointing a gun at these two in broad daylight?" I asked.

"Really, the sun's setting," Simone muttered.

"Jade, don't."

To my relief, Rafferty didn't flinch or show any confusion at the nickname.

"These two were looking into her car, and I approached."

"He with you, Steel?" Pump asked. "Devil Lancers must have lowered their standards."

A hot-head would rise to that bait, yet Rafferty ignored it. He'd make a decent Devil Lancer if he weren't loyal to the Riot.

I locked eyes with Scar since he seemed to be the smarter one. "The two of you are foot soldiers at best for Corrupt Chrome. Tell Knuckles, I'll meet him next Saturday."

Scar's eyes narrowed. "That's nine days from now, motherfucker."

Rafferty shifted his stance as though he were offended.

After a beat, I shrugged a shoulder. "I got shit to do before I head back. He can leave word at the Player's Palace strip club if he's down or not."

While Scar mulled this over, a police squad car pulled into the lot. He noticed my gaze shifting and glanced over his shoulder. His demeanor changed instantly. "Let's go, Pump."

They hurried toward their bikes. In a smooth motion, Rafferty tucked his gun into his waistband, then leaned against Simone's Ford Escape. His head tipped toward the cart. "Need help with the bags?"

"Sure," Simone chirped.

We had half the bags loaded in the back when the Jacksonville Sheriff's Officer drove by with his window down.

"There a problem here?"

"No, sir. Just loading the car," Simone said.

She didn't blink at the officer's hard stare.

Finally he nodded. "I'll leave you to it."

We closed the hatch and she blew out a sigh. "That wasn't my typical trip to Target, but let's go home."

"You aren't serious," Rafferty said.

More and more, I liked this kid.

Simone tossed her hands out. "They approached us inside and were milling around my SUV. They probably already know where to find me." She jerked her head my way. "He set a date for a meet. It's done. I'll take all the back roads home to be safe. But there's no point and you know it."

Rafferty lowered his chin, his anger plain in his eyes. "A clubhouse would be better and *you* know it."

Yep, I definitely liked him.

With a grin, I said, "Now, you're outvoted."

She leveled a dry look at me. "Or it's a tie because the baby likes me sleeping in my bed. And we need to leave before I have to pee."

Rafferty shook his head. "Guess I'm watching your new pad all night."

Simone chuckled. "Not necessary. I think Jackhammer has that duty tonight."

Rafferty's eyes slid to the side and back to her. "He'll have company then."

WE MISSED THE GREEN light to leave the parking lot. While we sat at the red, using the side mirror I watched Rafferty on his bike behind us. He wore a helmet with a visor, preventing me from seeing his eyes.

"Why isn't he prospecting? Do you know?"

Her head turned toward me. "Why? You gonna recruit him?"

I glanced at her. "Yeah."

"What? Are you serious? Why?"

The light turned green and I tipped my head toward it. "Focus on the road, woman. To answer your question, he stepped in without either one of us there. Kept his cool more than twice during that encounter. I respect the hell out of that, and I don't see it every day."

"Wow," she whispered.

"So, why isn't he a prospect?"

She sighed. "Honestly, I don't know. My hunch is that they're waiting for him to turn twenty-one."

"How old is he?" I asked.

"Nineteen, but he turns twenty soon." She paused. "I could be completely wrong about the reasoning Steel. The last four years, I've been in Gainesville and that isn't info Dad would tell me anyway."

"Fair enough."

"His mom's gonna lose her mind."

"But not his dad?"

She chuckled. "Him too, but Aunt Trixie loves the club with her heart and soul."

I hummed as her words replayed in my mind. "Wait, he's Roll's son?"

"Yeah."

I chuckled. "Then I *really* don't understand why he isn't prospecting early. It's in his fuckin' blood."

"Yeah, I don't get it either. Seeing as you know the Riot is in his blood, maybe it'd be a good thing to keep searching for your next recruit."

"No," I said.

"No?"

With a curt nod, I said, "No, and that's final. Should be his decision any damned way."

"Can't argue with that."

Chapter 14

Free-Fall

Simone

Guilt gnawed at me. I probably shouldn't have said anything about Rafferty not prospecting with the Riot, and I felt like a traitor for sharing. Yet, over the last week, I had developed a soft spot for Jackhammer and Warden – maybe it was only by association with Steel. Who knew? Either way, I felt like I'd put myself in the middle of an untenable situation.

I made a mental note to text Rafferty and ask why he'd been following me. That wasn't just something Steel wanted to know. Had Dad put him up to it? Or was he trying to impress all of the brothers?

The thought of Raff becoming a Devil Lancer made me cringe as much as it made me smile. Part of me thought it would be fitting for him to join that club. A vision hit me of Aunt Trixie when she found out and I snickered.

"What's so funny?" Steel asked.

"The thought of Aunt Trixie if you convinced Raff to join your ranks. You really know how to stir a hornet's nest."

"Not me stirring anything, Jade. It's up to him. Not my fault if I can spot leadership potential at a glance."

"Leadership?" I blurted.

"Potentially. Character is what you do when nobody's watching. He didn't know we'd be right out and approached those assholes anyway. It could have gone wrong for him, but it didn't."

It struck me with razor sharp clarity that *if* there were a Steel and me, this would be my life. Feeling like I sat in the middle all the time.

"Do you have a concealed carry permit?" he asked.

"Sure do."

"How often do you practice?"

"I'm due, but I usually go once a month at least."

He shifted in his seat. "I'd prefer it if you didn't carry your weapon."

I glanced at him and back to the road. "Do you expect me to say yes to that?"

"It'd be nice."

A small smile crossed my face. "Yeah, well, I can't do that."

From the corner of my eye, I saw him give me a hard look. "Either of those fuckwits could have taken that gun from you."

"What about Rafferty?"

Steel faced forward. "He's not the subject here."

I stopped at a traffic light and looked at him. "They could have taken Raff's gun, too. Or is it because I'm female?"

He met my gaze with earnest brown eyes. "Rafferty isn't carrying my child. He probably has ten pounds on Pump, where you're at a forty or fifty pound disadvantage."

My eyes went back to the road as traffic flowed forward. "I held the gun. He'd have to be a huge moron to come for it in close quarters like that."

Steel nodded. "There's a reason Scar did all the talking, sweetheart. Pump *is* a moron. May have just met him, but it rolls off him like an odor."

I swallowed down my sigh. "How am I supposed to take care of myself without a weapon? You know, considering that fifty-pound weight difference?"

"I was there, Simone, and I would have handled it."

My temper flared. "Is this a blow to your ego? I pulled the weapon and what? You got embarrassed? I kept that fuckwit from getting the upper hand, tough guy."

He leaned his head back on the seat. "I love that you're a firecracker, but you gotta dial it down right now."

A rueful laugh bubbled out of me. "Oh, I'll dial it back when you give me the honesty."

His head came forward and twisted my way. "The honesty is that *you're* the one on security footage holding a weapon on those assholes. Not me – you. That pisses me off."

I scoffed. "They aren't going to report it."

"Not the point. That mom could have screamed bloody murder. Hell, security footage gets reviewed at stores like that; you're lucky they didn't see you when it was going down."

I took a deep breath and eased my SUV into the lot for my apartment. "I hadn't thought about that at the time."

He nodded. "I know. That's why I want you to stop carrying."

After I parked the SUV, I powered off the engine and faced him. "Why? Because I didn't consider the security cameras? They threatened us."

"With words, not weapons."

"He reached for his—"

"He'd deny it," he said in a firm tone.

Shit. This reminded me of arguing with Dad.

"You went quiet."

"I'm not giving up my gun."

He heaved a heavy sigh. "They shoot you, I could lose you and our baby."

I bit back a grin. "So you changed your mind about peanut?"

He leaned toward me. "Simone, please. Put my mind at ease."

"Answer my earlier question. What do I do instead? Carry a knife? Mace? How am I going to protect myself? Because you might have noticed that I take care of myself."

His eyes heated. "I'm gonna take care of your sass in the bedroom, but we'll talk about it later."

Rafferty tapped on the back hatch, and our conversation ended.

Once out of the SUV, both men behaved as though this were the Olympics and their event was the grocery-delivery two-hundred-meter freestyle. I understood wanting fewer trips to the apartment, but they were one-upping each other for no good reason. We got all the bags inside on the first go, but they went back for the cases of soda, seltzer water, and Steel's beer.

Not to be left out, I followed them back to the lot. They stood at the open hatch in an intense conversation.

Steel whipped his eyes to me. "Go inside, Jade. We got it."

I tilted my head. "You got an agenda is more like it."

From the impatient look crossing Steel's face, I'd pushed his patience to the brink. "Jade, humor me."

"Fine." I pointed at Rafferty. "I'm texting you and you better respond."

"Whatever, Si—Jade. Go inside."

Twenty minutes later, I had everything put away when Steel led Rafferty inside, telling him where to put the boxes of Bubly seltzer water.

"Productive pow-wow?" I asked.

Rafferty straightened from the pantry where he'd stacked the water. "Simone, cool it. He told me who those assholes were and what you did in the store. I can't believe you brought out your gun inside a Target."

"I kept most of it hidden by my purse."

Rafferty widened his eyes. "The cameras in the sky will see that shit."

I threw a thumb toward Steel who leaned against the breakfast bar with a shit-eating grin on his face. "I got that from this guy already, Raff."

"Someone's gotta make sure it'll sink in."

I narrowed my eyes. "Don't you have somewhere to be? Say... Gainesville, perhaps?"

His jaw ticked. "You aren't funny, Simone. No, I'll be in the parking lot. Jackhammer should be here soon." His gaze moved past me. "Later, Steel."

Steel lifted his chin. "Let me know what you decide."

Part of me wanted to call Aunt Trixie, but more of me wanted to call Alexandra. In the end, I was too damned tired to call either. I stifled a yawn and moved toward the master bedroom. "I'm taking a shower and going to bed."

He grinned and twisted the top off his beer. "No, *we're* taking a shower and then I'm taking you to bed."

My lips twisted. "Fine. But it'll have to be a quickie. I'm not kidding, this baby is draining my energy."

***

I WOKE UP TANGLED in Steel, his legs were twined with mine and his arms were wrapped around me. Under any other circumstances, I'd have loved this, but my bladder felt ready to burst.

With careful and precise movements, I adjusted his arms, slid my legs free, and extracted myself from his grip. After doing my business in the bathroom, I spied the blue digits of my alarm clock. Two-o-two in the morning. That was a little later than I normally had to go pee, but then I'd gone to bed a little later compliments of Steel's insistence to take care of my sass.

The sheets rustled, and Steel's husky voice filled the air. "What's goin' on?"

"Go back to sleep. I had to pee, that's all."

He rolled out of bed and came toward the bathroom. When he drew even with me, his hands cupped my cheeks and he gave my lips a peck. *That was surprisingly sweet.*

I climbed back into bed and wiggled around until I was comfortable again. The pregnancy books all warned me that in my third trimester, getting comfortable would be a serious challenge. I made a mental note to buy more pillows.

Steel came back to bed and wrapped his arms around me from behind, his hands sliding down to my belly. "Make me a promise, Jade."

"A promise?"

"Yeah. Promise me, you won't fall for me," he whispered.

My lungs froze. I rolled toward him, but he held me in place. "I can't do that, Steel."

"Do it anyway."

I bit my tongue, unsure how honest I could be. It was the middle of the night. We were both tired. Still, I couldn't make that promise because I'd already started falling for him. At this point the question was how much farther did I have to fall? Because it already felt deep – deeper than anything I'd ever experienced.

"Can you do that for me, stubborn woman?"

"No, and not because I'm stubborn, but because I'm already in free-fall."

He lowered his forehead to my shoulder and sighed.

Never one to leave well-enough alone, I asked, "Why shouldn't I fall for you? Is there a reason or something?"

He pulled his hands away, allowing me to roll toward him. In the dim moonlight streaming inside, I saw the seriousness in his eyes. He cupped my cheek. "I could name at least five reasons. One reason is that I'm not invincible, Jade."

"Nobody is, Steel."

"Most men don't get guns pulled on them at the grocery store."

"And most men don't interest me."

"Simone."

"Raymond."

His head reared back. "How do you know my name?"

I grinned just thinking about putting his credit card back in his wallet earlier and spying his driver's license while I was at it. "I have my ways."

He let out a quiet sigh. "When I told you to put the credit card in my wallet, you got nosy didn't you?"

"Not exactly, it was staring me right in the face."

"I'm dangerous, Simone. You should keep that in mind."

I dipped my chin. "I will. Can we go back to sleep now? This man who doesn't want me to fall for him did an excellent job of fucking me earlier and I'm a wee bit wore out."

He lowered his mouth to mine, and gently sucked on my lower lip. "You got it, Jade."

I edged away from him. A moment later, he shifted to his side and spooned me. Yeah, this man was crazy if he expected me to promise something as outlandish as not falling for him. A strange thought hit me.

"Did you want that promise so you wouldn't fall for me?" I whispered after a couple minutes.

He exhaled in a heavy, steady rhythm and I figured he'd fallen back to sleep. Men seemed to have that uncanny ability, not that I was jealous. I was *completely* jealous.

I closed my eyes and willed my mind to clear.

Then I heard him whisper, "No. I'm in free-fall, too."

For the first time in a very long time, I fell asleep with a small smile on my face.

———

MY BOSS HAD APPROVED me working a half day on Friday because he knew I'd moved into a new apartment. This might have been the only reason I was willing to have a moonlight chat with Steel at two a.m. Though I was grateful I did. Knowing we were both in the same boat — free-falling for each other — gave me a reassurance like nothing else.

Steel's phone vibrated before a tinkling alarm filled the bedroom at seven-thirty. I rolled away from the sunshine pouring into the room through the flimsy blinds, while Steel slid out of the bed and hit the shower.

The sound of water always made me drowsy and I dozed for a few more minutes. I cracked one eye open when I heard the door open. Steel sauntered out of the bathroom with a navy blue towel wrapped around his waist. His sparse chest hair failed to hide his luscious tattoos. I wondered how he kept his abs so ripped because I wasn't the only one putting away fried shrimp and fish last night.

"Rest, woman. There's no time for you staring me like that."

I tossed the covers off and got out of bed. "No time in *your* schedule. I have plenty of time today, but I'll let you get to it...whatever *it* may be."

He dropped the towel and tugged on a pair of boxer briefs. "I'm not giving into your attempt to fish information out of me Jade. But, I'll be back by six – maybe sooner depending on how shit goes."

I nodded and went into the bathroom, closing the door behind me.

After I washed my hands and brushed my teeth, I opened the bathroom door to find Steel in a pair of faded black Levi's and a black t-shirt. My hands itched to run up and down his chest.

He grinned and shook his head. "You're easy to read when you wake up, baby."

I shrugged. "Can't say I was trying to hide anything."

"Does your buddy, Rafferty, have a truck? Or just a bike?"

I twisted my lips as I thought about it. "If he has a truck, it's a beater, but he and I haven't kept in touch that well while I was in Gainesville. I can ask him."

He shook his head. "Don't bother."

"What do you need a truck for?"

A secretive smile made his eyes twinkle. "I'll let you know later. Now come give me a goodbye kiss."

I stepped into his space, and he wrapped his arms around me. What should have been a goodbye kiss quickly turned into a hot and heavy make-out session. Steel broke the kiss and rested his forehead against mine. "Goddamn, Jade."

I smiled. "You can say that again."

He pulled away, but not before kissing my forehead. "Be good today."

I rubbed my hands along his biceps. "I normally am."

"Hate to say it, but you need to stay inside as much as possible."

I nodded. "Also the plan, since I have boxes to unpack, and I need to get onto the network and do half a day's work."

His chin dipped in a slow nod. "Sounds good, but you always have a way of surprising me."

I shook my head. "Not today, tough guy."

He gave me a quick peck. "Later."

I locked the deadbolt behind him, and heard my phone ding with a notification.

Unlocking my phone, I saw it was a text from Mom.

> **Dinner tomorrow. Six-thirty.**

Sorry, Mom. Won't be able to make it.

The little dots weren't jumping around on my screen. Maybe she was texting someone else. My phone rang and I should have expected that.

I swiped up to take the call and Mom spoke before I could.

"Your brother is coming home for the weekend, Simone. Why did you text me that you can't make it for dinner tomorrow?"

I sat on the sofa. "I'll be in Augusta tomorrow, Mom. And Bobby's home for Spring Break, not just the weekend. I can catch up with him during the week."

"Ha! I'll be lucky if I see him after that first dinner. I wanted to have both of you at home, together."

"How about we shoot for Thursday? Make Bobby's favorite dinner, he'll be there for sure."

"His favorites are things you can't stand."

I shrugged. "I'll suck it up and deal with it. Will that work?"

"I suppose. Why are you headed to Augusta so soon?"

"It's not 'so soon' really, but think about it. How often is Dad away from the club for three weeks at a time?"

"It hasn't been three weeks."

"Steel was at Bike Week from start to finish, then followed me back to Gainesville, spent a week in Jacksonville, then helped with my move. We're coming up on three weeks, Mom."

"Hmmph," she muttered. "Well, I can't wait for you and your brother to be here on Thursday."

I smirked. "Can I bring Steel?"

After a long moment, she said, "Sure. Tell him to wear Kevlar because your father will probably shoot him."

"You're joking."

"Only a little, but you can bring him."

I nodded. "He might be busy, but it'll be nice to extend the invite."

"Are you saying he doesn't like us either?"

I chuckled. "Not at all. I'm saying he doesn't want to be in an awkward situation any more than you do."

"I'd ask who taught you about guilt trips, but that would be me. Fine. The ball's in your court, and I'll welcome him with an open mind."

"And Dad?" I asked, even though I knew the answer.

"I'll do what I can."

"I love you, Mom."

"I'll always love you more, pumpkin."

A DULL HEADACHE FORMED along my brow late in the afternoon as I reviewed programming code. I glanced at the time on the lower part of the computer screen. Four o'clock. No wonder I had a headache, I hadn't eaten anything in hours.

Setting my laptop aside, I went to the kitchen and grabbed a package of peanut butter on cheese crackers and a can of lime Bubly. I heard a key slide into the lock and a moment later Steel came inside.

Exhaustion rolled off him and his eyes looked defeated.

"What's wrong?" I asked.

He shook his head. "No offense, baby, but this town sucks."

My head reared back. "Why's that?"

"Too many reasons to count, but the fuckin' building department, code enforcement, the awful traffic, and a fuckin' HOA to start."

My brows furrowed. "An HOA?"

He huffed out a derisive chuckle. "Yeah. I'd terrorize the shit out of those pretentious, ignorant, motherfuckers, but it'd be too damned obvious."

I pressed my lips together to keep from smiling. Not that I found his anger funny, but rather he was really freaking sexy when he was pissed – as long as it wasn't with me.

The doorbell buzzed and I shook my head. "Who could that be?"

Steel took a deep breath and wandered toward the door. "It better be Rafferty."

He opened it, and Rafferty came inside handing a key fob to Steel. "Gray Tundra, parked near the retention pond. Don't have a ramp, but I brought a sheet of plywood to get your bike in the bed. You need straps?"

Steel shook his head. "No, I got those. Can you be here in the morning? Don't want to load the bike until I'm ready to leave – otherwise those assholes will know exactly which vehicle to follow."

Rafferty nodded once. "You leaving at five?"

"Six, if Jade isn't dead to the world."

Rafferty nodded, then looked at me. "Hey, Simone."

"Hey, Raff."

He locked eyes with Steel. "I'll be here at five-thirty, then."

Steel shot him a skeptical look. "You won't be out partying tonight?"

He shook his head. "No, sir. I'll party tomorrow night – if the mood strikes."

"Nineteen-years-old that mood should always strike," Steel said.

Rafferty's brow ticked up and down. "Not always, not for me anyway."

"You want something to drink?" Steel asked.

Rafferty shook his head. "Nah. Gonna get rolling," he pointed a finger at Steel. "That general contractor I used to work for got back to me. He's willing to take a look at the structure, but can't get out there until Monday afternoon."

Steel nodded. "That works since we'll be back by then."

"Cool," Rafferty said.

"By the way, Bobby will be in town for Spring Break – in case you feel like hanging with him tomorrow night," I said.

Rafferty nodded. "I heard. Be safe, Simone."

He left, Steel locked the door behind him, and turned to me. "Bobby's your younger brother, I take it?"

I nodded. "Yep. I'm having dinner with him, Mom, and Dad on Thursday night. You're welcome to come with me."

"I doubt that," Steel muttered.

"Nope. Mom said she'd welcome you with an open mind."

"Is that so?"

I nodded. "Yes, though she did say to wear Kevlar since Dad might shoot you, but I think that would have been at her request, so it's all cool."

He laughed. "Not sure it's *all* cool, seeing as yesterday she was worried I knew where she and Volt live, but I'll keep the dinner in mind. What time on Thursday?"

"Six-thirty."

His lips ticked to the side and his brow went up and down. "It'll depend on how shit shakes out that day, that's for damn sure. Might have to meet you there, which isn't ideal."

I shook my head. "Sure it is. If you're spending time at the Devil Lancer compound, then meeting me there saves you two trips across the river."

He lowered his chin. "But it doesn't keep you safe."

I tossed my hands out. "I could always ride over there with Dad, he's usually on this side of town during the day and you can bring me back."

He gave me a chin lift. "We'll play it by ear, Jade. Are you packed?"

I scoffed. "No. I have another hour of reviewing code, then I can call it a day and focus on packing."

"It's just a weekend."

I smiled. "And I'm rapidly approaching the halfway point of this pregnancy. Most of my clothes aren't fitting half as well as I'd like."

"You're hardly showing."

I chuckled. "I am a little if you know where to look, but that doesn't change the fact that my pants are tighter, and I probably ought to buy a couple new bras."

His eyes heated, he stepped into my space, and wrapped his arms around me. "Get another one with the cherries on it."

I grinned. "I'll see what I can do, baby."

He gave me a long, gentle kiss. His dark eyes held warmth after he broke it and stared down at me. "Good. I gotta shower. The AC isn't working at that clubhouse and I've been sweating all day. You get back to work."

CHAPTER 15

REPLACE YOU

STEEL

AN HOUR OUTSIDE OF Jacksonville, Simone cracked open a diet soda. "Not to look a gift horse in the mouth, but did you rent a truck just so you didn't have to follow me?"

I felt my lips quirk. "Sweetheart, I'm not sure I'd have been able to keep up with you, the way you drive. At least not without getting a ticket, and the way the last two days have gone, a speeding ticket would've been a sure thing."

She made a tsk-ing sound, but smiled at me. "I don't have that bad of a lead foot."

A chuckle rumbled from my belly. "It sure isn't a light foot though."

"True. Why did Rafferty have to get the truck?" she asked, sipping her soda.

"Is the doctor cool with you drinking diet soda? Won't it harm the baby?"

"One a day is fine, and it has less caffeine than coffee, which I can't seem to stomach, and that's a bummer. You aren't changing the subject on me, though. Something's up – are you on some do not rent list or something because you spent time in jail?"

I laughed. Her ability to coax things out of me should alarm me, but it didn't. "No, I didn't have a ton of time yesterday, and the only rental place I went to, the prick behind the counter took one look at my license and gave me shit about how I couldn't take the vehicle out of state."

She stared at me, her left eye narrowing. "You're leaving something out."

"We got the truck, that's all that matters."

"Oh, no, no," she said, wagging a finger in the air. "There's a story here, handsome."

"I lost my temper. Not enough sleep does that to me. It wasn't cool, but—"

"So you kind of *are* on a do-not-rent list."

"No. Just not at that location."

She laughed and I glanced at her. The joy and happiness on her face made her more beautiful, and hell if she wasn't glowing with pregnancy. **Damn, she was gorgeous. How had Jordan fucked shit up with her?**

Where the hell did that question come from?

Deep down, I wanted to repair my relationship with him. A paternity test couldn't erase the years I'd spent with him and Debra or the years watching him grow up from afar. No matter how much shit Debra had spewed about me, and how much of a brat Jordan could be, I held hope that he and I could have a relationship as adults. His headstrong nature posed a problem – especially when he should be willing to hear my side of things. My relationship with Simone was only going to be another obstacle.

Still, I had to wonder why he'd string her along instead of manning up and making a clean break.

Rather than ask her that outright, I asked how she liked her new job.

"It's good. Challenging, that's for sure."

"Are you in over your head?"

"No, it's just different from learning about it in school, that's all. What do you do for money? I suppose you take a cut from club members' dues every month?"

I grinned. "Yes, but officially I work for one of the businesses the club owns."

"Really? In what capacity?"

"Silent partner."

"Convenient," she muttered.

"It is. Keeps me from having to pay self-employment taxes, which are much steeper."

From the corner of my eye, I saw her nodding. "You know, it was taxes that got Al Capone caught, right?"

"I'm aware. What's your point?"

"Just being cautious. Seems silly to take precautions about speeding tickets, but you could end up in the big house for tax evasion."

"I'll keep it in mind, Jade. You need to pee again?" I asked, when we passed a sign for an nearby rest area.

"Not quite yet, but I could stretch my legs."

"You ever been to Augusta?" I asked as I veered the truck onto I-16 West.

"No, I haven't," she said.

"Not sure what you do at your computer job, but the city's known for the Cybersecurity facility."

"Yeah, but that's part of the Army."

"There are likely contractors that work with them."

She turned to me. "Are you trying to talk me into moving?"

"I'm just letting you know some things that might interest you," I hedged.

We needed to have a conversation about where she wanted to raise the baby. I didn't want to split my time between two cities, so I knew she wouldn't want to do that with a newborn in the picture. But, I figured I could put that off – after all, it flew in the face of what I'd said to her at Bike Week about taking things one day at a time.

"Do your chapter presidents ever come in for visits to the Mother chapter?" she asked.

I glanced at her and back to the road, exiting onto Highway 25. "How do you know... Volt tells you when he's visiting the mother chapter?"

She wobbled her head. "Not exactly. He and Har, the president of the Biloxi chapter, talk about it."

My gaze cut to her. "You overheard them talking about it, you mean."

"That's neither here nor there. Does your club do things like that?"

"I try to make that shit happen at rallies instead, but sometimes they do. Surprised you would be in a position to overhear Volt and Har discuss anything. Most chapters seven hours apart don't see each other that often."

"Aunt Abby went to college with the daughter of the Biloxi president before he was taken out in a crash."

"The president before Har."

"Right. And then there's Stephanie and Suzie, they're sisters who both wound up with Riot members."

"So it's women that tie the two chapters together. Typical Riot."

She looked at me askance, irritation shining from her eyes.

I shook my head. "I'm not saying it's a bad thing."

She scoffed. "You're not saying it's a good thing either."

I tilted my head. "It's unusual, that's all."

"Probably so. Are we hitting the clubhouse first? Or your pad?"

I chuckled. "I have a four-bedroom house, I wouldn't call it a pad."

"Wow. Why so many bedrooms?"

"I'd intended to move Debra and Jordan in there as a surprise once the threat to Jordan was resolved, but a week before closing on the house, I found out she was cheating with a member of a different MC."

"That's... harsh. And you never tried to find someone else or thought about selling it?"

I shook my head. "It's a fuckin' great house with everything I ever wanted, plus my nearest neighbor is five miles away."

"Anti-social, much?"

"I prefer the term 'private.'"

She nodded. "That makes sense."

"Why would you say that?"

She grinned. "Five miles gives you a fair amount of leeway if you have someone there against their will."

I drew the truck to a stop at a traffic light and looked at her. "Simone, I would never bring an enemy to my place."

Her head dipped. "It doesn't mean they wouldn't follow you there."

The light changed and I faced forward. "And you think I'd kill someone in my own backyard?"

"Maybe. I think you'd shoot them and ask questions later. If it's five miles to your nearest neighbor, I'm guessing you got a fair amount of property and you have somewhere you could hide a body – and by hide, I mean bury."

I grabbed her hand and gave it a squeeze. "You're a crazy woman. My nearest neighbor is five miles away because my property sits between two tree farms. You've been watching too much television. It's a shitload of work for one person to bury a body."

"Enter your brothers, maybe prospects, but that depends on how much you trust them."

Before I could disspell her vengeful ideas, my cell buzzed, Torque's name on the display.

I accepted the call and put the phone to my ear. "Yo, I'm about twenty minutes from my place. Let me call you back."

"Shit. Is there anyway you can come here first? Knuckles and his enforcer put a beat down on Circles and two of his direct reports."

None of the brothers had 'direct reports.' Circles dealt with prostitutes though, which meant two of the girls had been beaten, too.

"I don't have you on speaker, but how do you know who was behind it?"

"Circles didn't report into Tie as scheduled. Tie found him just before the ambulance showed. Circles had just enough energy to tell him who did that shit."

I blew out a sigh. "Yeah. I'll be there in fifteen."

"If you're twenty minutes from your house that puts you half an hour from the clubhouse."

"Yeah, I'm picking up the pace."

"Don't get a fuckin' ticket, man. The cops are itchin' to bring you in for any fuckin' thing they can."

I let my foot off the gas. "Right. Thanks for the reminder. Be there soon."

I set the phone back in the console.

"No grand tour of your home, I take it?"

"Not yet."

"I get to see your clubhouse instead?"

"Seems so."

"You sound disappointed."

"Shit's hitting the fan, Jade. Didn't want to drag you into this, but I guess I'm gonna see what you're really made of."

***

Torque running out of the clubhouse forced me to park the truck closer to the front of the compound than I'd have liked. I hadn't seen him haul ass like that in years.

I leapt out of the cab. "What's wrong? Is Circles gonna make it?"

Torque stopped a few feet from me, breathing hard. "It's not Circles. We got another problem."

"Yeah, you doing a fuckin' hundred-yard dash told me as much, Tor."

He gave a feeble grin. "I still got it, motherfucker. But Debra's here."

Simone had come around the hood of the truck and stood next to me. "Debra... as in Jordan's mom?"

Torque's blue eyes darted to her, then to me. "Yeah. You didn't tell me you were bringing her with you."

I didn't tell him a lot of things – for many different reasons. To be fair, I'd hoped to keep Simone away from the clubhouse this trip. As usual, that plan was shot to hell already. I gave a small nod. "Now you know she's with me."

Torque raised his arms over his head, getting his breathing under control. "Want me to give her a tour of the compound, show her the fire pit, keep her away from Deb and the other catty bitches."

"It's okay, I can handle it. This isn't the first time I've been to a clubhouse," Simone said.

A thoughtful expression took over Torque's features. "You think you can handle it? Debra alone in there, sure. The catty club whores on their own, probably so. But all those women at one time, sorry... Jade, I'm puttin' my money on them breaking you."

Simone looked up at me. "He knows who I am?"

I turned to her. "He knows I call you Jade. Simone, meet Torque. Torque, this is Jade as far as anyone around here is concerned. She's Volt's daughter."

Torque's eyes widened at me. "Fuck. You didn't tell me that."

I pressed the tip of my tongue to my canine tooth, thinking. "And she's Jordan's ex-girlfriend, which is likely what brought Debra here."

"Yeah, she's been ranting about that non-stop. You really know how to step in it, Steel," Torque said, turning around to lead the way.

The front door of the clubhouse slammed open and Debra stormed toward us. Her brown hair with blonde highlights was pulled into a high ponytail, which should have made her look younger. Instead, she seemed to be trying too hard. The anger in her eyes put me on alert. I'd never seen her so riled.

"Get back in the truck," I muttered to Simone.

"She's already seen me, Steel. I'm not running. Not from her."

I gave my head a short shake. "That kind of anger, she's unpredictable right now, Jade."

She gave my hand a squeeze. "I can hack it."

"Stop right there, Debra. You need to cool your shit," Torque said, stepping between us.

"Don't play go-between right now, Tor. He says he gives a damn about his son, but he's screwing Jordan's ex-girlfriend."

A handful of the club girls had followed Debra outside, because those bitches ate up drama with shovels, not spoons.

"It's all right, Torque. Get those bitches back inside the clubhouse or they can be kicked out of the compound – permanently."

"You got it, Prez," he said, and strode to the front door, waving his arms as he went. "Get inside or you'll get tossed out – forever, bitches."

Debra's hazel eyes cut to Simone. "That's what he does. A woman makes him uncomfortable and he tosses her aside."

Simone stared at Debra, obviously considering her words. "He didn't do anything like that. Whatever you have to say to us is private. Those women try to eavesdrop, that's offensive in many ways. He hasn't tossed anyone out – yet."

I fought off a smile, because she was good. Zero attitude in her words, and all truth aimed at Debra.

"He'll replace you," she said in a venomous tone.

She shrugged. It irritated me that Simone could even *think* I'd do such a thing. "Maybe, but I shouldn't have to tell you that he can't *replace* his baby's momma. Oh, that's right. You're a baby-momma, but to some other man."

So much for being good.

"Simone," I muttered.

The way Debra's lip curled, the gloves were coming off. "And *you* cheated on my son with his *father*!"

Simone tilted her head. "Actually, Jordan dumped me in front of our friends and didn't have the spine to do it in private. I had no idea who Steel was when I met him."

She flicked a finger toward my cut. "His name's right there, or can't you *read*?"

Simone's voice returned to the calm tone she'd used earlier. "Both the restaurant and the hotel prohibit wearing colors inside. So, while my reading capability is excellent, he wasn't wearing anything to indicate he was with an MC."

"Don't get condescending with me, Missy."

I interrupted before Simone could argue any further. "What the hell do you want, Deb? To bust my balls? You did that, now leave."

She narrowed her eyes. "You're done in Jordan's life. Any relationship you wanted with him is gone."

I shrugged a shoulder. "You made sure that would happen his entire life, bitch. But he's an adult now. It's up to him whether he has a relationship with me, though, if he wants his last semester of college paid for, he'll have to treat me with respect."

She aimed a fake smile at me. "You already gave him the check."

That was true, but when I'd checked my bank balance yesterday, the check hadn't cleared.

I kept a stony expression as I bluffed, "He hasn't cashed it and I'll put a stop-payment on it today, if you press this any further."

Her eyes went wide. "You wouldn't."

I leaned toward her. "You're fucking with me, and you know good and damned well how I treat bitches who fuck with me. Now, get gone."

She stared at me for a long moment, then locked eyes on Simone. "And to think I liked you for Jordan."

With that, she turned on her flip-flop and stalked to her car.

"I don't think she's finished," Simone muttered.

I moved in front of her. "She is for now. I got other shit to deal with in there. My plan wasn't for you to see the clubhouse like this."

With a small smile, she said, "It's all right, Steel. I know things get crazy at clubhouses."

I put my hands on her shoulders. "My club isn't anything like the Riot."

She nodded with wide eyes. "Yeah, that's clear from the number of nosy club bunnies who followed her out here."

My eyes closed and I took a calming breath. I opened them and lowered my face toward hers. "Torque has an old lady. Hell, Shelly might even be in there."

She nodded. "Okay."

My brows arched. "And he might have one or even two of those nosy club bunnies – who *aren't* his old lady – in his lap. You get me?"

Her jaw shifted. "I get you, but I'm carrying *your* baby, not Torque's. Do you behave that way, too?"

I shook my head. "No. The reason he's got multiple bitches hanging on him is for two reasons. The first is because he gets off on the extra attention. The second is because they know he's VP. Shit happens to me, he's in charge. Those women don't give a fuck about him. They give a fuck about being the President's old lady and the edge it gives them with the other women."

She chuckled. "Like that means anything."

Skepticism twisted my lips. "Your mom doesn't get special treatment?"

"Not really. All the old ladies matter, but club girls also know their place."

I dipped my chin. "And there's the difference in our clubs. Somebody made it clear to Riot club girls how shit works. Around here, I don't get involved in club girl shit. Hell, I used to enjoy a decent cat-fight. But hear me, Jade, I don't want you getting in a fucking cat-fight. You understand me?"

She nodded. "I do, but I'm not going to shy away from standing up for myself."

I tipped my head back, caught sight of a smattering of clouds, exhaled, and looked back to her. "Where's your gun?"

She smirked. "Still in the glove box where you made me put it four hours ago. Should I go get it?"

"No. Leave it, please. It will make me feel better."

"Funny, it would make me feel better putting it back in my purse."

I couldn't fight my grin. "Being cute here isn't going to help you, sweetheart."

"Fine. Should I just hang in your room, or would you prefer I get to know the club bunnies?"

I took her hand and led her toward the clubhouse. "Now who's anti-social?" She responded with a fake grin. "You can hang in my room if you want, but you might be better off to try making some in-roads."

She nodded. "You're right, but out of curiosity, if I need to get into your room, is there any chance I can get a key?"

I ran my thumb and forefinger along my chin, then I dug my keys out of my pocket, and pulled my room key free. "Yeah, that's a good point. Here's my key. My room is across the hall from where we have church, so you don't need to wander upstairs or down the main hallway."

She took my key and nodded. "Got it. No *Alice in Wonderland* shenanigans."

CHAPTER 16

CONNIVING AND DEVIOUS

SIMONE

WITH HIS HAND AT the small of my back, Steel guided me into their clubhouse. It was brighter than I expected, since they had florescent lighting throughout the common room. To my immediate left I saw at least seven aluminum baseball bats hanging from a wooden wall mount. That was convenient... and telling. I glanced over my shoulder at Steel.

"Keep moving," he murmured.

I kept moving and realized none of the women were here. "Torque didn't mess around."

A member across the room sauntered to the bar. "No, he doesn't. Tor knows how to scare 'em off."

His voice sounded vaguely familiar, and I noted his name patch read 'Tie.'

"Did he go outside?" Steel asked, moving beside me and I caught a whiff of his crisp, woodsy cologne.

Tie huffed out a laugh. "Probably. He ain't got no shame."

Torque entered the room from hallway to the right. "I'm not outside, asshole."

A mischievous smile crossed Tie's face. "My bad, Veep."

Torque rolled his eyes at Tie, then faced Steel, but not before giving me an unimpressed look.

I shoved the key to Steel's room into my pocket. "I'll just head out back."

Steel looped a finger into the belt loop of my shorts. "Jade."

I turned to him, wondering if he wanted a kiss before I left, but the earnest look in his eyes stopped me short.

"Remember what I said."

My eyes slid to Torque and back to him. Something about this byplay irritated me, but I didn't know why. Through a small miracle, I kept my temper in check. "Hard for me to forget."

His brows drew down, but I pulled free of his hold, ignored Torque, and walked to the back door.

Before I made it outside, I heard Torque ask, "Why did you bring her here?"

Tie called out, "Who cares? I'm glad he did."

The door closed behind me before I heard if Steel even responded. Compared to the front of the clubhouse, which had oaks and pine trees shading the entry, there weren't many trees out back to block the sunlight. It took a moment for my eyes to adjust to the bright sunshine. I stood on a slab of concrete, which vaguely reminded me of the Riot Clubhouse, but there weren't any picnic tables and I knew this wasn't an area for loitering.

To my left, was more of the building and from the small window, I realized it was their kitchen which jutted out into the back – as if it were an addition to the original structure.

I shielded the sun from my eyes with my hand. The backyard gently sloped down and I saw a humongous pit with a low circular brick barricade. From the remnants of wood in the center, I assumed it was a firepit. A few feet away from the bricks were anti-gravity lounge chairs, plastic Adirondack chairs, and a couple of free-standing porch swings hanging from metal frames.

From my right side, Rafferty's deep voice made me jump a foot in the air. Luckily, I covered my mouth to keep anyone from hearing my yelp of surprise.

It took me a moment, but his words finally registered. "The club girls say they have bonfires almost every weekend," he'd murmured.

I blew out a breath and turned toward him. "What are you doing here?" I whispered.

"After I helped Steel load up his bike at the ass-crack of dawn, he invited me to come up here."

My eyes widened and I shook my head. "You're spending the night here? As a hang-around?"

He shook his head. "No, I'm staying at his place, but he told me he'd meet me here after he dropped you off. I'm guessing something came up since you're actually here, when that wasn't his plan this morning."

My mind was reeling. I loved that I had a familiar face here, but he wasn't here for me. Raff was here for Steel. On the one hand, I couldn't ream out Rafferty since he'd been invited, but on the other hand, I thought he was more loyal.

"Are you even interested in this club?" I asked.

"Keep your voice down. I might be. Not sure yet. Steel seems pretty solid. I won't know what I want if I keep my head in the sand, or keep dicking around waiting on Dad and the others to approve me as a prospect."

I stared off into the backyard. At the sight of what looked like half a dozen spindly logs leaning vertically toward a single point, I asked, "Why are they having a bigger fire to the side of a perfectly decent fire pit?"

Rafferty chuckled. "Look closer, uh... Jade. Those logs are held up with chicken wire to make a see-through tee-pee."

I shifted a foot forward, and the metal wire became more discernable. "Oh. That's cool, like for star-gazing."

Rafferty choked on laughter. "Yeah, because bikers lay around *star-gazing*."

I glanced back to him. "What are you getting at?"

"Think about it, woman. There are cushions inside each one, which means those are for fucking. If a brother wants privacy, he can put a blanket around it."

My attempt to hide my lip curl failed.

"What's with the face? Aunt Abby would fuckin' love this."

A silent chuckle shook my body. "She and Uncle Blood are probably the only ones, that's for sure."

His eyes darted toward the kitchen and back to me. "Be careful. This place isn't anything like back home, and those women are..." he trailed off and he thought for a long moment. "Let's just say they're different."

I dipped my chin. "You can do better than that. I'm guessing they're conniving and devious. Hell, half a dozen of them came out to eaves-drop on Steel's ex laying into him."

His chin lifted in a slow nod. "That's what that was all about."

I nodded. "Yeah. Wait, how did you know?"

A sly smirk curled his lips. "I was inside at the time. All the bitches except one chased out after Debra. Then a short while later, Torque ordered everyone to get the fuck out. The woman who had stayed inside with me led me to the hot tub before the rest of the women came outside. She wanted me to get in with her, but I turned her down."

I eyed him up and down. "Obviously."

He shrugged. "Just saying, you want to meet them, that's where they are. All of them."

"In one hot tub?" I asked.

His expression turned mischievous. "It's a split-level tub. I've never seen anything quite like it before. You should check it out."

I struggled to envision it. "You going to lead the way? Introduce me?"

His eyes bulged. "Fuck, no. You were right. They're all devious as shit. I'm gonna go for a ride and see the rest of Augusta. Tell Steel, I'll meet you two at his place around five."

With three strides, Rafferty darted around the side of the clubhouse leaving me alone. I debated going back inside and checking out Steel's room. After hearing what Rafferty said about the women, I didn't expect them to be very accepting. Not to mention I had a low tolerance level for petty bullshit – especially from women.

If Mom had taught me anything, it was that females had enough to deal with in life. Adding more bullshit to another woman's plate was just rude.

If *Dad* had taught me anything, it was to tackle things I didn't like head-on. Putting it off wasn't likely to make this any easier. If nothing else, I'd get to see what a split-level hot tub looked like.

I STEPPED OFF THE concrete, turned to the left, and walked along a path of square, coral-colored pavers that ran along the back of the clubhouse.

For late March, the sun beat down on me relentlessly. Relief swept through me at the sight of a medium-size, metal-roofed open-air pavilion. Four wooden picnic tables sat in the center and two hexagonal picnic tables flanked the outside. Piles of clothing were heaped on one of the hexagonal tables.

Then I took in the hot tub which sat in between the clubhouse and the pavilion. It looked as though two hot tubs had been set side-by-side, but one was raised up to the height of an above-ground pool. It sat four feet higher than the other tub. On the outside end of the shorter tub, there was a bar and a couple of bar stools. Cans of beer and hard seltzer littered the surface.

As Rafferty said, all of the women were in the tub. Four in the lower tub, and three in the elevated tub where two of those women were making out.

"You're lucky Steel didn't see you earlier. Takes a lotta nerve to come back here after what you did," a woman with kinky curls said from the lower level. Her eyes were aimed at one of the women in the upper hot tub.

Another woman in the lower level who had wavy auburn hair shook her head and scoffed. "That was months ago, never mind that. Since Kendall and Bella decided to make out up there, are you coming down here, Josie?"

"Not yet, Tessa," Josie said, looking over the ledge at the other woman. Her eyes caught my movement and she glared at me. "Oh, look, y'all, it's Jordan's ex-girlfriend."

Embarrassment rolled through me, but I powered past it. Something about Josie seemed off. The other women were looking at me with clear disdain, but Josie's expression held something... extra.

I heard water sloshing and the two women who were making out had come to this edge of the tub to get a better look at me. One had blonde hair piled high on her head in a sloppy, but cute, top-knot. The other had wavy, shoulder-length brown hair and light brown eyes.

"Oh, you're pretty," the one with brown hair said. I had a feeling she'd been the one to stay inside with Rafferty.

"Kendall, you think everyone's pretty," Josie sneered.

She shot Josie a look full of attitude. "Well, everybody is, in their own sweet way. Even you."

Bella tucked a stray lock of blonde hair behind her ear and said in a low, warning tone. "Kendall."

Kendall stood giving me a full view of her bare, voluptuous, double-D breasts. Yep, I bet she stuck around with Rafferty instead of following the bitch brigade outside. "What? I work at the Palace. You give as many lap dances as I have, you come to appreciate beauty in all forms."

"Like that makes you some kind of expert, bitch," Tessa said.

Kendall gave her a look and smiled at me. "You should get in. Take your clothes off, we don't care if you're naked. Most of us are strippers, so you don't have anything we haven't seen."

To stall, I looked up toward the pavilion and noticed security cameras. They were all aimed away from the hot tub, so that was good. My eyes darted to the clubhouse and saw another camera which was pointed directly at the tub. Not so good.

I returned Kendall's smile. "Sorry, I'll have to pass."

Josie didn't hide her snicker, and a few of the others joined in afterward.

Kendall's eyes darted toward the building. "Oh, if you're worried about the cameras, Tie likes to keep a watch on us. I mean, what's the point of security if some jackass barges through the gates and attacks us, right?"

From the lower tub, a brunette with a deeper voice said, "Yeah, Kendall, that's what he's doing. Protecting us. You know men are pervs."

"Well, you're welcome to one of my White Claws," Kendall said.

I really liked her. With a regretful smile, I shook my head. "I appreciate it, but I can't."

"How come? Is it that stick up your ass?" Josie asked.

I cocked my head to the side. "No. It's for the same reason I can't get in the hot tub. Pregnant women aren't supposed to drink, and while I have a bun in the oven, hopping in that tub could *actually* cook my baby. That isn't happening on my watch."

Josie's snide smile fell away and it struck me. She had messed with Steel's condoms 'months ago'.

I found it odd that she was on the property, that took a lot of nerve. While this place seemed wilder than the Riot clubhouse, not one brother would tolerate a conniving bitch who had messed with his stash being on the grounds – let alone using their hot tub. I had half a mind to mention it, but something told me keeping that nugget in my back pocket would serve me better. Steel had said she'd been taught a lesson. Did her being here mean she'd been forgiven?

I heard footsteps approaching. Josie's eyes darted past me and a mixture of lust, excitement, and trepidation crossed her face.

Steel wrapped his arms around me from behind and put his lips below my ear. "What are you doing, babe?"

I turned in his arms, slid my hand up his chest, and grinned. "You know, just taking care of our baby." I said loud enough for the women to hear. Then, in a lower voice I murmured, "And stirring the hornet's nest."

With that, I slid my leg up alongside his, and nipped his bottom lip because I had found he really liked when I did that. As expected, he groaned and took control of the kiss. His hands went to my ass and he lifted me up.

Next thing I knew, I heard the hollow clattering of empty aluminum cans and my back was on the bar of the hot tub. Steel pressed his chest to mine and kissed me harder for another couple minutes. In the background, I heard water sloshing and women complaining, but my attention was all on Steel.

He gently broke the kiss and his lips moved to my ear. "Don't do that shit again, Jade. I don't know what you're trying to prove, but don't force me to lose control, again. It won't go well."

Being reprimanded always sucked, and while he'd kept it somewhat private, I still felt embarrassed. After a moment, he helped me off the bar and I looked around to see the women had all left.

That was weird.

Steel read my look. "They know not to watch me with any woman. That's why they left."

I nodded.

In a low voice he said, "You're pissed."

"Apparently, so are you," I muttered.

His small smile stood out against his stubble. "I'm actually not."

I narrowed one eye at him. "Then what's with reprimanding me on the bar?"

He cocked a brow as though he hadn't just done that and the idea intrigued him. "Didn't reprimand you, baby, but I know when I've been played. You need to know I don't like it."

I decided to change the subject. "Do you know that a security camera is trained on the hot tub, those women know it and basically put on a show for whoever's watching? Or is that a side hustle for your club?"

That small smile turned into a grin. "It isn't a side hustle, but that sounds like a great idea, smart girl."

My eyes widened. "Are you serious?"

"What? I'd pay some of them. Hell, most of those women work at our strip club already. They want extra cake, I don't have a problem with that."

My eyes couldn't get any wider, but my outrage had tripled.

"I'm kidding, Jade. Hell, you think taxes will get me thrown in jail, that kind of porn would get us shut down in a heartbeat."

I waved my arm toward the camera. "That's my point. Are you *certain* a brother isn't uploading six minute or twenty minute clips somewhere behind your back?"

His eyes hardened along with his tone. "If he is, it's the last fuckin' thing he'll do and he damn well knows it."

I nodded. "Good to know. Can we get out of the sun?"

He smiled. "Do you one better. We're gonna get in the truck and grab some food."

"Excellent," I said smiling, but it was short-lived. I dug his key out of my pocket with a small frown. "Here, I never got to see your room, but I think you need this back."

Rather than take the key, he took my whole hand in his. A pensive look on his face. "I'll show you my room – next weekend."

I cocked my head to the side. "Why not this weekend?"

He grinned. "Too much shit going on, and I need time for the things I have planned for you, in my room, and especially in my bed."

"All right, honey," I said, my breasts tingling and definitely looking forward to the next visit.

Back inside the truck, I waited until we were rolling down the road before I asked, "Steel, what's the deal with inviting Rafferty, but not telling me?"

"The *deal* is that I don't discuss club business with you. Period. That includes who I'm approaching to prospect with any of my chapters."

"He's like a brother to me, though."

Steel shook his head. "Like a brother doesn't make him your brother. What I plan with him isn't your business, not any more than what I plan with you is his."

I scoffed. "Strange. He knew you hadn't planned to take me to the clubhouse."

"Simone, I'm not your father, this is not his club, and I'm not gonna do the shit he does."

I tipped my head back on the seat. "I get that, Steel. "

His jaw ticked. "I don't think you do."

"Trust me, baseball bats hanging by the door tell the tale."

"You think that makes the clubs different?"

I shook my head. "No, I *know* that makes your club rougher than my Dad's."

"Why are we arguing?"

I widened my eyes at the windshield and shrugged. "Because I dared to ask you a question, but you assume I'm questioning your leadership."

He laughed. "Jesus."

"What are you laughing at?"

He shook his head. "I can't remember when a woman took such an attitude with me."

I chuckled. "Just you wait, we have a little girl, she's probably going to be my carbon copy, if not in looks, then definitely in attitude."

"Don't be so sure, woman."

"Oh, I can be sure. It's very likely that I'm the person she's going to be around the most, and sorry to say, my snark can't be restrained all the time."

"That's for sure."

"Are we done fighting or are we just letting sleeping dogs lie?"

"Fuck if I know, you started it."

"What?"

He shook his head. "We weren't fighting."

I gazed at his profile. "But you don't care that I'm close to Raff?"

"No, I *can't* care that you're close to him. Hell, that's reason enough to either dismiss him or make it a thousand times harder on him."

That was true.

"All right. I'm sorry I asked."

He reached out and squeezed my thigh. "No, I shouldn't have overreacted. I'm hungry – in more ways than one, and we have to wait before I can fuck you because we're going to one of the best barbeque places in town, if not all of Georgia."

"Cool."

"What's cool is that it's five minutes from my place."

My eyes widened. "That is cool. By the way, Rafferty said he'd be at your place around five."

His eyes cut to me for a moment. "Did he text you that?"

I shook my head. "No, he snuck up on me right after I went out the back door. Scared the hell outta me."

"Is he always stealthy?"

The thought of lying crossed my mind, but that was wrong. "When he puts his mind to it, you bet your ass."

Steel nodded and hung a right onto a two-lane road. If it weren't for the occasional dip and hill in the road, it would have reminded me of rural Florida. Tons of pine trees, a smattering of oaks, kudzu climbing trees where the land wasn't maintained. On the cleared lots, the homes ranged from double-wides to ranch-style houses.

After a few miles, Steel hung a left. We passed a church before the restaurant came into view. The lot was crowded, but Steel snagged an open spot by the end of the building.

He powered off the truck, draped an arm along the back of my seat, and grinned. "Prepare to have your world rocked."

CHAPTER 17

UNITS OF MEASUREMENT

STEEL

THE WAITRESS SET A plate full of beef brisket in front of Simone and a chopped barbeque plate in front of me.

Her eyes widened. "This is a ton of food."

I smiled. "It is, but we'll take home whatever you can't finish."

She devoured her food like she hadn't eaten in days. Then I recalled that the last time she probably ate was in the truck around ten-thirty. Seeing as she was eating for two, I was stunned she hadn't bitten my head off sooner.

After she swallowed a bite of her cornbread, she tipped her glass of water toward me. "You have to tell me, where does one find a split-level hot tub? Or did an engineering brother jerry-rig that for you?"

I laughed. "You liked that, did you?"

Her lips quirked. "No, I wasn't able to get in it. I just know some people who'd love that sort of set-up."

Figured I knew who'd love that set-up, but kept that to myself. "As they say, anything can be had for a price. It was special order, not jerry-rigged."

"Good to know."

"Any of the women give you a hard time?"

She blinked at me. "More like only one of them *didn't* give me a hard time."

"Kendall, I assume?"

She nodded. "She seems so nice."

I nodded. "She is the nicest person you'll ever meet, and every man in a fifty mile radius takes advantage of that."

Her mouth dropped open. "What?"

With a short shake of my head, I grimaced. "She sees goodness where there often isn't any good."

She nodded. "That's sad. Is that why she's a stripper at the Palace?"

"She told you that?"

"Not directly, but it was mentioned."

"Yeah, I don't remember how she got started. With as much money as she makes, she should be financially set but she isn't."

Her lips formed an angry pout. "Now that makes me mad."

I lifted my hands. "She's gotta make her own decisions."

Those words reminded me of Circles. After Simone had gone outside, and after Torque, along with Tie, busted my balls about Simone, Torque ran down all the injuries. Both girls had broken noses and bruised ribs. One also had a broken arm and a deep cut on her other arm. Circles took the brunt of it. The doctors put him in a medically-induced coma to help his brain swelling because he'd taken many hits to his face and they believed he was repeatedly kicked in the head. From the lacerations, the authorities suspected brass knuckles had been used.

I figured it could be brass knuckles, or whoever did it wore enough rings they didn't need brass. It was one of the main reasons I kept two rings on each hand.

Torque had told me that if Circles made it through the night, that would be the best sign for his recovery.

Simone shook her head and stared off to the side for a moment, pulling me from my thoughts. Then she focused on me with urgency. "Why was Josie there?"

My eyes closed for a long beat. No way I heard her right. I refocused on her. "What do you mean, Josie was there?"

"She's the one who really gave me a hard time. Snickered when I wouldn't get in the hot tub with them, not that I gave a damn, but boy did I take the wind out of her sails when I mentioned having a bun in my oven. Doesn't take a super-sleuth to figure out she messed with your protection."

I pulled my phone from my back pocket. "Yeah, and she shouldn't have been there. My guess is she snuck in with another groupie, but it still shouldn't have happened."

Her eyes lit up. "Don't run her off on my account, honey. It'll be fun to mess with her later."

I stared into her gorgeous brown eyes. "Jade, you're better than that."

Her head reared back. I loved surprising her. She stared down at her plate and then looked back at me. "Fine. You're right. I should've had my fun when I had the chance. I'm just glad to know you didn't forgive her for that shit."

I glanced up from my phone. "No, I damn sure didn't forgive that shit."

The text app opened and I sent Torque a message to make sure she wasn't anywhere on the property. For good measure, I sent a separate message to Tie in case Torque had left the compound.

"Is it normal for you to have a possible prospect spend the night at your house?" Simone asked.

I nearly choked. "Come again?"

"Rafferty said he isn't crashing at the clubhouse. I find it odd that you'd have him stay at your place while we're here."

Leaning back in my chair, I weighed my words. "You're right, but I sprung this trip on him. Not cool to expect him to throw down for a hotel or motel room at such short notice. Plus, I'd like him to really see what my club can do for him. It's difficult to show him that in Jacksonville since that chapter's been fucked up for such a long time."

She mulled that over for a bit. "Your place is fancy, I take it?"

I shrugged. "I wouldn't say that, but it's been remodeled with everything I want in a house."

"And what do you want in a house?"

"Four bedrooms, split floor plan. Huge-ass covered deck with outdoor kitchen for entertaining the other chapter presidents when they're in town. In-ground pool, great backyard, and a metric fuck-ton of privacy."

She laughed. "I love it. Some people mix metaphors, you mix your units of measurement."

"Privacy doesn't have a unit of measurement, sweetheart."

She nodded. "For you it does."

I gave the waitress my credit card when my phone dinged with a text from Tie.

Since when do you give a shit about the club bitches?

It hit me that not all the brothers knew about the situation with Josie. I tapped out a reply.

> **Since that bitch fucked with my wallet and condoms, making me a Dad. Get her the fuck out.**

Simone tossed a napkin on top of her plate. "I shouldn't tell you this, but you're freaking hot when you're pissed."

My eyes lifted to hers. "No, you shouldn't tell me that."

She stared at me. "Why not?"

I leaned forward and crooked my finger at her to do the same. Once her face was inches from mine, I whispered, "Because now I want to fuck you in the truck and that would get us arrested."

She leaned back and laughed, long and loud. Three different men in the restaurant turned and stared at her. It took effort, but I kept myself from glaring at all of them. No question, she was stunning, but it hit me – she had that pregnancy glow. Her words from two days ago replayed in my mind.

The die is cast.

That was the truth. Watching her laugh like that, I couldn't wait to watch her throughout the pregnancy.

She contained her laughter and shot a serious look at me. "That reminds me, were your security cameras installed by someone in the club?"

My brows drew together and I nodded. "Pretty sure, why?"

"Were they part of a kit?"

"Not sure, but probably."

She nodded. "And they transmit through your Wi-Fi?"

"Hell if I know. Why do you ask?"

She nodded. "You need to reset the default password on the cameras if they're on a network."

"Why?"

She exhaled through her nose as if she were hiding a chuckle. "Most of those do-it-yourself camera networks have a default password and people don't personalize it."

"Your point?"

"It isn't that hard to hack a default password, and with one of those cameras positioned on club girls in the hot tub, if someone hacked in they could stream or download footage of that and post it to certain types of websites." Her eyes darted around to make sure no one was listening. "You know, sites that would get you the wrong kind of attention since I'm sure there's probably something that makes it clear where the hot tub is located. Hell, your IP address would do that if nothing else."

I tapped a finger on the table. "Let me make sure I understand what you're saying, if the cameras have a generic password someone could hack into them, right?"

"Yes, that's part of it."

"Right, and if they did that, how could they...stream or post our video? Wouldn't they only be able to watch?"

"They could do either. All I'm saying, is make sure you've changed your password to access the cameras. Though, repositioning that camera pointed at the hot tub would be a good idea too. Even if according to Kendall, Tie likes to watch in order to protect them."

"Is that right?"

She widened her eyes at me. "I didn't tell you that. I don't need Tie being pissed at me on top of whatever grudge Torque has with me. Honestly, I cry bullshit on the protection excuse and so do some of the other women. That camera could easily be repositioned and still alert members to outside intruders."

She was right. Seemed I needed to have words with my officers.

The waitress returned with my credit card, I scribbled in a hefty tip on the slip, stood, and led Simone toward the exit.

My ears were attuned to the sound of bikes and I paused midway to the door. Through the windows I saw three bikes roll into the parking lot. They weren't Devil Lancers, and I acted on instinct.

"Don't argue with me, go to the bathroom. It's to your right. Stay in there until I text you."

She gave me a hard look, nodded, then hurried to the restroom.

I strode outside, so this wouldn't be public – or, *more* public.

The three men swung off their bikes and I saw it was the Corrupt Chrome road captain, Flip; their enforcer, Mug; and their Vice President, Sledge.

Sledge had brown frizzy hair styled in a mullet. He got toe-to-toe with me. "What the hell are you doin' here? Where's your fuckin' bike?"

"What do you want, Sledge?"

He squinted his beady, brown eyes. "You givin' us some kind of bullshit? Scar gave us your message. You aren't calling the shots. Now that we know you're in town, you're meeting with Knuckles, tonight."

After he gave me the run-down on Circles and the girls, Torque had told me about Mug cornering him at the Player's Palace Thursday night. Seemed Mug needed to work on his enforcing skills because Torque had seen the attack coming, and laid Mug out on the sidewalk outside the club.

"Wrong. I won't be in town tonight. He can meet with me next Saturday, or better yet, you assholes can get the hell out of Augusta and stop fucking with my club."

Flip smiled at Sledge. "Guess we'll have to run *circles* around this moron."

I kept my eyes pinned to Sledge, but I saw Mug's roundhouse coming my way and I ducked. Sledge moved closer, landing a sucker punch to my gut.

"What the fuck are you assholes doing?" a deep voice bellowed from behind us.

I straightened, still struggling to get my breathing back to normal. Jesse, the owner of the Great Times Barbeque restaurant lumbered out from the side of the building. He wore faded denim coveralls with a rust-colored t-shirt and a gray Georgia baseball cap which he'd turned backward. Very few people ever messed with Jesse because he had the build of a Mack truck and his six-foot six-inch frame towered over most people.

He came closer, his eyes narrowed on Sledge. "I asked you a question."

Sledge stared at Jesse. "Our friend is having stomach problems. Maybe it's food poisoning."

Mug chuckled.

"Don't fuck with me. I know he ain't your friend. Unless you want real problems, get out of here before I call the police."

"We didn't do anything wrong," Flip muttered.

"I saw you assholes corner this man, and so did half a dozen other customers. One of them might have it on their cell phone."

Sledge blinked and turned his head a inch toward Flip. "We're leaving," he whispered.

"I thought so," Jesse said.

My breathing had regulated, and I stood next to Jesse in the parking lot. We watched them leave.

He clapped a heavy hand on my shoulder. "You got that kind of trouble, I don't mind you doin' that Doordash shit instead of bringing those thugs to my door."

I sighed and nodded. "You aren't usually outside during a lunch rush. How did you know—"

"I might have had something to do with that," Simone said from behind us coming around the side of the building – the same way Jesse had.

"I told you—"

She shook her head. "And I kept a low profile for as long as I could. The moment I caught sight of those bastards, I knew you needed reinforcements."

Jesse grinned. "She's a smart lady. My wife woulda charged right out here."

I gave Jesse a dry look. "She wanted to do that, too. I happened to tell her not to before I came out here."

"Shee-it, you know if you got trouble, you tell me, Steel."

I nodded once. "Understand that, Jess, but this was something I had to handle on my own."

He crossed his arms over his massive chest. "Posturing is gonna get you killed. You have the chopped platter?"

I nodded. "And she had—"

"The brisket, I already asked her. Another thing that makes her smart. Told Winnie to get her a tub of banana puddin', then I'll tell you to do the same thing as those assholes. Get out of here."

———

I walked Simone to the truck, watched her belt herself in, and closed her door. While I rounded the tailgate, I debated my next move. My every instinct said she hadn't listened to me, but I didn't know that for sure yet.

At the red light about half a mile from the restaurant, I said, "I don't like you coming to my rescue."

She kept her gaze on the road, but I saw her lips twist. "Jesse rescued you, not me."

"You were supposed to stay put."

Her head turned toward me. "I'm not a figurine you can play with and put away. I'm going to do what I can to help you."

"I didn't need your help."

"Sure, unless you wanted to spend the night in the hospital."

"It wouldn't have come to that."

She scoffed. "Really? If Jesse had come out any later, Flip would have hit you in the kidneys and Mug would have landed that roundhouse you dodged. Nice move, bee-tee-dubs."

The way she said the letters shined a light on our ages.

I glanced at her before turning right onto Winter Road. "You think I wouldn't have caught them off-guard?"

"I know that when Flip pulled his gun, you'd have been in trouble."

Aggravation welled inside me. "Did you ever go in the bathroom like I asked? Hell, how do you know their names?"

From the corner of my eyes, I saw she was staring at my profile. "I went in and turned back around. My gut said there was more than one bike out there and that concerned me. I grew up in the life, Steel. First thing I do is read a brother's patches. No matter the club."

Shit. She had a point.

Most other women I dealt with didn't have a clue about men like me. Still, I needed to drive my point home. "In the future—"

She put her hand on my headrest. "If there's a future, please consider I'm *nothing* like those bitches at your club. No offense to Kendall, she's the only nice one of the bunch. From what you said, she's a doormat though, which makes those others even *bigger* bitches because they should help her see the light."

I opened my mouth to speak, but she kept going.

"I don't dig you because you're at the top of the Lancers' hierarchy. I dig you because you're sweet as hell in your tough-guy way – which makes it even better – and we're both part of the same lifestyle. I can be myself around you in a way I can't with anybody else."

"Is that all?" I asked, giving her a brief dose of side-eye before turning back to the road.

"There's also your wicked and devious tongue. It's freaking magic."

With a small head shake, I ignored her comment about my tongue. "You couldn't be yourself with Jordan?"

She sighed. "He made me feel ashamed every damn time. It's why I'm falling for you."

My chest warmed and tightened at those words.

She kept talking. "I may not love what your club does, but I love being at your side to help you in my own way. Even if it apparently freaks you out."

She was dangerous.

I pulled halfway down my hidden drive, put the truck in park, and faced her. "You won't always be able to help. The past two times were flukes and those need to be the last two times you help me."

With a pointed look, she said, "Me giving you head didn't relax you last night? The security checks I recommended at lunch – closing off an opening for a breach is a way for me to help you."

I stared into her bright, brown eyes. "You can't mouth off about that, though. My brothers hear that a woman's influencing me, we're both fucked."

She made a skeptical face.

I leaned forward. "This isn't the Riot MC. We'll both be fucked."

"I don't quite see how, but I'll take your word for it."

I exhaled a chuckle. "Do you really want to be by my side? Old lady to the mother chapter President – at your age?"

Her brows slowly rose. "Well, I wasn't kidding about your tongue. It's fucking divine."

In a flash, I caught the side of her neck in my mouth and gently bit her. She inhaled sharply, her nails driving into my hair. I pulled back. "I'm serious, Simone."

She laughed. "Yeah, I got that. Honestly, I didn't plan pregnancy at my age, but I'm rolling with it. And the more I'm with you, yeah, the more I want to be by your side."

My eyes searched hers for any hesitation or insincerity. There was nothing there but openness and honesty. God, I loved that. Finally, I said, "You'll have to move."

She gave a small shake of her head. "At some point. What do *you* want? Can you handle an ol' lady like me – at your age?"

With my hand at the back of her neck, I pulled her face to mine and kissed her as hard as I could. "Smart ass, you're gonna get fucked in the truck instead of in my house."

She grinned. "That sounds great, but you didn't answer my questions."

I nipped at her lips. "No, I didn't. Guess I'm in the same boat. Didn't plan on getting you pregnant, but I thought about you for weeks afterward. Now the more we're together, the more I want you around." I kissed her again. "And I can handle you at any age, baby."

She reached across the console for my jeans. "Good. You going to fuck me now?"

I kissed her again, but guided her hand back to her lap. "No. Gonna do that shit in the house where I have room to move."

CHAPTER 18

NOT FREE ANY MORE

SIMONE

EVEN THOUGH I WAS tired, I couldn't wait to see Steel's home and to find out what he did with 'room to move'.

The narrow, paved drive gave way to a bumpy road, and I realized the drive had brick pavers. Steel's house filled my vision and I almost gasped. The outside of his home reminded me so much of Mom and Dad's house, it wasn't funny. On one side, there was a two-car garage; the drive split off into a horseshoe shape in front of the house. The exterior was a creamy, khaki-colored siding with navy trim. A narrow walkway led to a double front door. Where Mom and Dad's house had traditional looking French doors, these doors were a dark navy blue with vertical, chrome bars for door handles.

I hadn't even set foot inside and I loved his house. It was stately and masculine, and it didn't hurt that it looked like a show home.

"This is gorgeous," I said.

He parked the truck. "You're gorgeous. This is just a house."

"As immaculate as the outside is, Steel, this is *way* more than just a house."

He grinned. "Let me show you inside, and then I'll come back and grab our bags."

Steel unlocked the front door, moved to a small alarm panel and disarmed the system.

I stepped inside the foyer and stopped short. Outside, I'd noticed a wide chimney in the middle of the roof line. Standing inside, I realized the wall was the backside of a fireplace. The brick had been painted navy blue. Ordinarily, I'd call that a crime against bricks, but in this instance it seriously worked. A huge painting hung in the middle of the bricks. The background was a lighter shade of navy blue and in the foreground were wide, white stripes that looked like a pound-sign, but weren't organized enough to be that symbol. Against the bricks though, the painting gave me the faint feeling of being in a jail cell.

I turned to find Steel staring at me. "Who painted this?" I asked, even though I suspected I knew the answer.

"I did."

I nodded. "When?"

"Doesn't matter."

"Okay, then *why* did you paint it?"

He stared at me some more. For so long, it was almost unbearable. Finally he said, "Haven't even shared this with Torque. That's a reminder – of where I've been, and that I don't ever want to go back there."

"Jail," I murmured.

His mouth opened, closed, and then he speared me with his eyes. "I didn't say that."

"You didn't have to, honey."

"Fuck, you're too much," he bit out, stalking to me.

I smiled. "I'm not really. If anything, I can read you, Raymond."

His eyes closed, he turned his head to the side, and he groaned.

"You don't want me calling you that?"

He turned to me, his eyes open and boring into me. "Far from it. I *love* hearing you call me that." His fingers came to my shorts working at my fly. "Fuck, I need be inside you, Simone."

"Good," I whispered, my hands moving to his belt.

He shoved my shorts down and I stepped out of them. His hand grabbed mine, and he tugged me around the brick wall and into a sunken living room full of cozy, overstuffed furniture. He led me to a huge light gray sectional where he quickly took off his boots, socks, pants, and boxer-briefs. I followed his lead and removed the rest of my clothes.

His arms came around me, he grabbed my ass, lifted me and laid me down on the sectional. I wrapped my legs around his waist, his cock lining up with my pussy. I arched in an effort to bring him inside me, but he pulled back and looked down at me.

"Christ, you're so fucking beautiful spread out on my sofa." His hands massaged my breasts, and since I'd told him how sensitive they were during our four-hour drive, his touch was incredibly gentle. "Such perfect tits."

I took his cock in my hand and gave him a stroke. "I'm glad you like them, but I thought you needed to be inside me?"

The way his eyes locked on me, I expected him to say something. Instead, he leaned down while surging inside me, filling me like nobody else.

"Yes, baby," I whispered.

"You got that right, Simone," Steel said.

The urgent way he started, I expected a fast, furious fucking, but instead, Steel took his time. Savored every kiss, each stroke, and worked us both up higher than before which made it more explosive when we both found our release.

While he caught his breath, I ran my fingers through one side of his hair. He caught my gaze, and I wanted to say it. The words were right there. Yet, I didn't want to break the spell.

His eyes searched mine. "It's not free any more."

My lips tipped up. "What isn't free any more?"

"The falling isn't free. You don't want this with me, Jade, you better decide because there's no going back. I love you."

Part of me thought I misheard him, but I'd listened so closely, the beautiful words were carved into my mind. I'd replay this moment at will.

My teeth sunk into the side of my lower lip. "I love you, too, tough guy."

He kissed me and we made out for a while before he lifted me from the couch and took me to another room. I opened my eyes and found we were in a huge master bathroom and Steel had set me on a marble counter between two sinks.

In front of me was a walk-in shower that had to be twenty feet deep and twenty feet wide, seeing as a huge bathtub sat on the far left side. A glass wall with a glass door separated it from the remainder of the bathroom. The wall on the right side had a bench running the entire length of it and there were two shower heads.

"You could birth a baby in that tub," I blurted.

"Come again?"

I looked at him. "It's a thing. Some people have water births."

His brows lowered. "What the fuck?"

I held a finger up. "Don't worry, this may be my first pregnancy, but I can tell you right now, I'm not going that route. I'm just saying, that's a big-ass tub."

He pulled a washcloth from a basket behind me, getting it wet under the nearby faucet. "It is. You want to take a bath, we can do that tonight. We're already naked."

My eyes danced around the room. "As fancy as this bathroom is, I'm dying to see the rest of your house, sir."

He leaned in and nipped my neck. "Plenty of time to do both, sweetheart."

I took the cloth from him. "Let me get cleaned up."

***

WEARING ONE OF STEEL'S Harley-Davidson t-shirts, I stood in what served as his dining room, which sat between the sunken living room and the kitchen. "The whole freaking house is decked out like a show home. Who did this for you?"

The round eight-seater dining table appeared to be custom made, and the wet bar behind the table had nearly every detailed touch. The only thing missing was a beer tap.

From his dry look, I shouldn't have asked. "Oh."

He shook his head. "Not that it matters, but I had no intentions of ever fucking her. The moment Debra showed her true colors, I decided to thank my interior designer."

I glanced around wondering where that might have happened.

He chuckled. "Don't worry. It was sixteen years ago, and that piece of furniture is long gone."

My gaze wandered to the kitchen on my right and I waved my hand that way. "For a man who says he's a terror in the kitchen, who actually cooks in there? You? Or do you have a personal chef?"

He sauntered toward me. Unlike me, he wasn't wearing a shirt, just a pair of boxer-briefs. "I can cook breakfast, that's about it. Tor's ol' lady comes in and cooks if I've got two or three chapter presidents in town. On the rare occasion I let Augusta brothers swing by, I either have shit catered or pay a chef."

I shook my head. "Pity. That kitchen is to freaking die for. I mean, a *six-burner* gas range? Thanksgiving and Christmas dinners here would kick ass."

Again, that got me his dry expression. "Raymond Reynolds, you have this pristine kitchen and don't do the holidays here? That's—"

He slid an arm around my waist. "Going to change this year from the sound of it."

I grimaced. "Well… normally, I'm at the Riot clubhouse or Mom and Dad's for Thanksgiving."

His lips pressed together, he did a slow nod and stared at a point over my head. "That will make things interesting."

I slid my hands along his chest, tracing his tattoos. "It will, but one thing at a time, right?"

With a grin, he nodded. "Right. Let me show you the deck."

I felt my eyes light up. "A deck? Do you have a pool?"

"Yeah, I mentioned that at lunch."

My smirk couldn't be restrained. "I forgot. Somebody rocked my world over on that sofa."

"You became my world over on that sofa."

My smirk fell away, that was so unexpected. I cupped his cheeks and laid a hot and heavy kiss on him. He slid his hands to my ass and gave me a squeeze. I broke the kiss, breathing hard. "I love you, but you can't say things like that to me and not pay the price."

This close to him, I felt and heard his rumbly chuckle. "If that's the price, baby, I'll pay triple."

I stepped aside while he unlocked a sliding glass door and I followed him onto his deck.

If the front of the house reminded me of Mom and Dad's, the back of the house was *all* Uncle Cal's place. A kick-ass in-ground pool stole my attention before Steel opened a wine-fridge and brought out a bottle of sparkling water. That would have been where Uncle Cal kept the kegs for his two built-in beer taps. There was a huge grill and a sink, but Steel's set-up was much more top-of-the-line. Ironic, since Uncle Cal was a great cook, but Steel wasn't.

I took in the rest of the deck. "A fireplace?"

"Darlin', this isn't southern Georgia, this is north Georgia and we're very close the South Carolina border. It doesn't snow here often, but it gets damn cold. I'm not gonna let that keep me from being outdoors."

I nodded. "Does that mean your pool is heated?"

He smirked. "It does, but we aren't going swimming right now."

I returned his smirk. "It's for future reference, my man."

"I'm gonna go get our bags."

"In your undies?"

He shrugged. "I'll put on jeans, but who the hell's gonna see me, Simone?"

"Rafferty, maybe? He said he'd be swinging by around five."

Steel drew his fingers along his jawline. "Yeah, and it's not even two-thirty, Jade. We're gonna take a bath, catch a nap, and see what your buddy thinks of Augusta."

TURNED OUT, STEEL GAVE good baths – if you wanted a bath with multiple mind-melting orgasms that left your body completely limp.

The man was a machine, though when I shared that, he claimed it was me being a vixen. Either way, we'd dried off and fallen into his bed and conked out.

Now, late afternoon sunshine glared into his bedroom but he wasn't in bed with me. I shrugged into his t-shirt and tugged on my panties and shorts. Through the blinds, I saw the backyard. Spring was in full swing with pollen dusting everything in yellow. I wondered what his backyard looked like in the fall.

I wandered out of the bedroom, through the living room, and to the kitchen. No sign of Steel.

The murmur of male voices came from the other side of the kitchen, and I realized there was a fourth bedroom there.

"This room is on the opposite end of the house from mine. You'll be fine," Steel said.

"If I get followed, I'd rather not lead anyone here," Rafferty said.

"Why would you be followed? Did you do something?"

"No. Just rode around town, got the lay of the land." That hesitation in his voice sounded familiar – like when he'd fib to his parents or Alexandra's.

It wasn't cool of me to eavesdrop, but I couldn't charge in there now. I had to see if Steel caught on to him or not.

Steel chuckled. "Right. I believe you rode around town, but you aren't pulling anything with me, Rafferty. What'd you do?"

He sighed. "I left my cut in my saddlebags, went to the Player's Palace and hung out. Watched two Corrupt Chrome members give the girl serving drinks a ration of shit she didn't fuckin' deserve. I left before I got too fuckin' pissed and interfered. Still, they followed me out, saw me at my bike and asked if I was interested in a club."

"That's unusual," Steel muttered.

"That's what I figured, but I played dumb."

"Do not try to get inside their organization," Steel said, his tone firm.

"I'm not, but why are they looking for new recruits? Seems like they'd have plenty of interest if they're as flush with cash from drugs and shit like they say they are."

"You have a certain look about you, Rafferty. Clubs always need fresh blood, and it takes time to move from hang-around to prospect to fully-patched member. They'd be idiots not to approach you. Hell, that says they're more observant than Tie or the others give them credit for."

I wasn't that close to the room, so I shuffled my feet and called out, "Steel?"

"In here," he called.

I padded that way and leaned against the doorway. "Hey, Raff. How's it goin'?"

Seemed I wasn't the only one who could pick up on tone. "It's goin' great, Simone. Something bothering you?"

"No."

Steel's eyes caught mine. "You overhear some things?"

"Hard not to in this house. The floor plan is rather open."

His jaw shifted and he rubbed his cheek. "I'm letting that slide, but you've noticed how much I like privacy. Don't get in a habit of doing that."

I wanted to ask 'or what,' but he had a point. Keeping his business private mattered, and I needed to respect that.

Rafferty asked, "Why do you live in the middle of nowhere?"

Steel chuckled. "Not the middle of nowhere, but this type of set-up provides extra security. Nobody comes here by mistake. Not even UPS."

Rafferty nodded. "That's smart."

A gleam hit Steel's eyes. "You gotta be smart to lead an entire MC."

"Yeah. Are you hitting the clubhouse tonight?" Rafferty asked.

Steel shrugged. "Not sure yet, but you feel free. Should be a bonfire tonight – you'll get the full Devil Lancer hang-around experience before you decide to prospect."

Rafferty's eyes cut to me and back to Steel. "Back in the day, my family had an issue with your Jacksonville brothers."

Steel dipped his chin. "That chapter was shut down for three years because of that."

"Are all of those members gone? Or did some transfer to other cities?"

"What are you asking?"

"Prospects have to eat shit. I want to know if I'll be eating shit from an asshole who fucked with my cousin who was seventeen at the time."

Steel's sharp gaze on Rafferty made me uncomfortable, but Raff withstood it. "You got a grudge?"

Rafferty scoffed. "Wouldn't you? But yeah, that's the issue. Those assholes will assume I have one and that I'm joining in order to carry out a vendetta or some shit."

Steel crossed his arms on his chest. "They find out you're related to the Riot, they'll assume that anyway." His eyes slid to me for a beat. "The way you two are together, it's gonna come out."

"Doesn't that put him in danger?" I asked instinctively. I knew Rafferty could handle himself, but I still felt protective.

They spoke simultaneously.

Rafferty said, "Don't worry about me."

Steel said, "Sure, but he withstands it, he'll prove himself in a way few other brothers have."

I nodded.

Rafferty shook his head at me. "You didn't ask if it puts *you* in danger."

I grinned. "Don't worry about me."

Rafferty rolled his eyes. "Right." He turned to Steel. "What time are you leaving in the morning?"

Steel pondered that. "If you two can shift your schedules, I'll leave before dawn on Monday. That lets you live it up tonight and we'll be back in Jax in time for me to meet with that contractor."

The idea of getting up so early didn't appeal, but I wanted to see more of Steel in his element. Plus, I wanted to take in more of Augusta.

Rafferty dug his keys out of his pocket. "Sounds good. We loading your bike tomorrow night?"

Steel nodded. "Yeah, but in my truck, and you'll drive the rental back. We'll load your bike into the bed of the rental truck sometime tomorrow."

This sounded like a production, but such was biker life.

"Got it. I'll see you at the bonfire, or I'll be back late." Rafferty moved past Steel, drew even with me, and said, "Later, Simone."

I wandered toward the kitchen, but realized Rafferty must have gone out some other exit because there was no sign of him. Then I heard his Harley and it sounded as though it were outside the garage.

Steel went to the fridge. "You hungry? I have the banana pudding Jesse gave us, eggs, beer, and whatever you packed in your 'snack bag.'"

"Is there food at the bonfire?"

He shut the refrigerator door. "Do you want to spend more time at the clubhouse? I got a fire pit in the backyard, we can stay here if you'd prefer."

I shrugged. "I may not be a hang-around, but I think I need the full Devil Lancer experience, too."

He nodded. "True." His teeth sunk into his lower lip and he came to me. "I love you, and you're having my baby, but so far only my VP and treasurer know that. I can't claim you this visit. Are you going to have a problem with that?"

With my lips pressed together, I did a slow nod. "I don't have to be claimed, but are you also saying you'll be with another woman in front of me? Or let a club girl hang on you?"

He grinned. "Are you jealous?"

I cocked a brow. "More like I'm possessive, and considering it seems that Jordan might have snuck around behind my back, I'm not cool with another woman touching you."

He nodded. "That's fair."

Thinking about Jordan brought Debra to mind. "Why was Debra at the clubhouse anyway? Was it really just to bust your balls? I can see where Josie might have snuck in with another club girl, but your ex? How does she get inside the gate, let alone the clubhouse? And how did she know you'd be there?"

He frowned. "Unfortunately, Torque's old lady had everything to do with that. She overheard Tor talking to me yesterday afternoon. He said he'd see me at the clubhouse. She ran her mouth to Deb, and from there, Deb's good at convincing the prospects at the gate to let her through."

I shook my head. "That doesn't make sense. Are she and Debra tight?"

"No, Jade. It's the biggest downside to Torque screwing around on Shelly. She bends over backward to fuck with him. When she can't fuck with him directly, she knows anything that causes me problems will cause Torque problems."

"Sounds like quite the couple," I muttered.

He bit back a grin. "That reminds me, why do you think Torque has a grudge against you? He doesn't even know you."

My brows arched. "He's certainly a master of the cold shoulder."

"He's doing his job and making sure I'm not being taken advantage of, sweetheart."

I couldn't hold back my scoff. "Where was he when Josie messed with your wallet?"

He shook his head. "He's not my housekeeper or some shit. Besides, Josie admitted to being in my room to check which brand I use. Then she bought her own box, tampering with those at home before showing up to the club to make the swap. It was an in-and-out kind of thing."

I widened my eyes at the pun. "Ba-dum-bum."

He tipped his head back and groaned. "You know what I mean, woman."

"Yeah, I do. I'll keep that in mind if I run into Torque again."

"*When* you run into him again."

"Right. So, at the bonfire, do you use one of those big, open-air things set away from the actual fire?"

"You mean the tee-pees?"

"Yeah."

"Not normally, but we can do that if you want."

I nodded.

He lowered his face toward mine. "If you start something with me though, I will drape a tarp over it so nobody sees us."

I grinned. "You wore me out, honey. I just want to watch your brothers and see the stars."

***

IT COULD HAVE BEEN that everyone gave us a wide berth because Steel 'never came out to the bonfires,' or it might have been the way he kicked another couple out of the tee-pee.

True to my word, I didn't start anything. It had been a long day that would soon take its toll. I enjoyed sitting back and watching the dynamics of this club while occasionally staring up at the stars.

Steel shifted next to me on the cushion. "When you look out there, what do you see?"

The fire light made his features appear more pronounced. His stubble sharper, lips fuller, and his eyes looked more intent.

I glanced back to the wide field before us. "I see a much larger club than what I'm used to. This group is definitely rowdy, and they're younger than I expected."

He laughed. "Younger?"

I smiled up at him. "Yeah. There's at least half a dozen guys over there who are in their twenties. Most of the members in Dad's club are well over thirty."

"That's still young."

"Yeah, you're right. Okay, I'll put it this way, I don't see many veteran members around."

His arm around my shoulders gave me a squeeze. "We've got those members too, they prefer to stay away from the bonfires."

I shook my head. "But why?"

He grinned. "Most of them have kids that are either teens or will be soon. They don't need to be around this crowd – not like this."

I nodded. "Yeah, the obvious drug use would be a problem."

That was one thing that put me off. The scent of marijuana in the air was one thing, but seeing people doing cocaine was something else entirely.

"That bothers you."

My eyes met his. "The police attention it gets bothers me."

A brother with a head full of brown curls trudged by and stopped. In the dim light, I saw his name patch read, 'Nelson.'

"This is crazy, Prez! You never hang out here. You wander around and hide out in your room during bonfires. I don't know who she is, but she's good for you, man."

If Steel had anything to say to that, I'd never know because Nelson delivered that and moved to the fire pit.

"He might be nice," I muttered.

Steel chuckled. "Nice and sloshed, sure."

I shrugged. "Better than being mean and sloshed."

He moved in and gave me a slow, soft kiss. "You had enough of this, yet?"

I chuckled. "Why? Need to hide out in your room?"

"Yeah. My room at my house, Jade. I gotta hit the john, meet me at my truck."

We walked side by side for a few feet, then I slowed and watched Steel make his way up to the back of the clubhouse. He had a fabulous ass.

I veered left to get to the truck. There were a few trees here and there, and I watched my step, since some brothers didn't care where they partied – in fact, the darkness made it more enticing.

From a few feet away I heard a female voice ask, "Who are you? I've never seen you before. Are you a new prospect?"

Then I heard Rafferty say, "I'm just a hang-around right now."

I focused in their direction and saw one of the women from the hot tub standing very close to him. Her hair was dry now and she wore a face full of makeup, but I was pretty sure it was Tessa. "You can come hang around me... or I can grab one of my friends if you like it like that."

"Three's a crowd," Rafferty muttered, but his voice sounded husky.

I stepped on a twig and Rafferty looked around and spotted me. Tessa did too, but promptly focused on Rafferty again.

I gave him a look.

Even in the dim light, I saw him cock a brow. "She isn't here, so don't look at me like that."

"Oh, there's someone else?" Tessa asked, running her hand up his chest and under his cut.

"Yes, Tessa, there's someone else," I said.

She ignored me and smiled at Rafferty. "I don't mind. Makes it more fun."

She had no shame.

Rafferty ignored her and kept his eyes on me. "She doesn't want me, and she's made that clear. Repeatedly."

"Whoever she is, she's dumb," Tessa said, earning her extreme side-eye from Raff. And that was all the proof I needed to know he really wanted Alexandra.

With a short headshake, I turned away and climbed the small hill leading to the parking area.

I found Steel's truck and heard footsteps behind me. I thought it might be Steel, but Rafferty was stalking toward me.

"Why'd you follow me? I bet Tessa liked *that*," I said in a low voice.

He shook his head. "Five men who might be brothers, or might be hang-arounds, watched you walking this way. I had to make sure you stay safe."

"What are you thinking?" I whispered.

Rafferty stopped a foot from me and lowered his voice. "Maybe I'm not thinking, Mony. I'm here, I'm horny, and I don't have to jump through half a dozen hoops for any of these bitches. They're gagging to give me whatever I want because they're desperate to wear a brother's cut."

I tried to hide my sneer. "You can do better than a clubhouse whore."

"I'm the son of—"

I saw red. "Don't you *dare* insult Aunt Trixie that way, she's the strongest, bravest woman either of us knows."

His eyes widened. "I'd never insult my mom like that, but my *dad* spent years staying away from her trying to protect her and give her what she really wanted. I'm my father's son because staying away from Lex gives her what she wants. Pretty sure we both know *she's* the strongest, bravest *young* woman we both know."

I lowered my voice. "She's strong, but she's not like your mom. Believe it or not, unlike Aunt Trixie back in the day, Lex doesn't actually know what she wants."

Rafferty dipped his head almost in concession to me. "I can only take her at her word. Not gonna force her or any damn woman into something they don't want. Ever."

"Even though she's all you've ever wanted?"

He tossed his hands out. "I might be young, but life's taught me that some things aren't meant to be, babe. In the meantime, I have to live my life."

I looked around, trying to see if there was anyone else around in the darkness. "And you want this? Are you sure?"

He shrugged a shoulder. "Won't know if I don't see what this club is all about."

I sighed. "Fair enough."

CHAPTER 19

GET BLOODY

STEEL

EARLY SUNDAY MORNING, I left Simone sleeping in my bed.

While at the bonfire last night, I'd received a message from Jeremiah, a member of an Augusta street gang. Motorcycle clubs and street gangs didn't work together very often, but I hadn't shied away from doing things for street gangs in the past. With the threat from Corrupted Chrome, I'd cashed in markers with three different gangs.

Jeremiah's message included the day and time for CCMC's next drug supply arrival and the address where Knuckles routinely met his mistress, Farah. I'd heard that he always spent Saturday night somewhere near the Aragon Park area in Augusta and the address was in that neighborhood.

Since this could easily be a set-up from Jeremiah – there was no honor among criminals, thieves or otherwise – I drove the Tundra to the address, kept going, and parked at a small school at the end of the block.

There were no sidewalks in this neighborhood. The homes were older, brick construction, but not all of them were well-maintained. Knuckles rode a black Harley-Davidson Street Glide, and it sat in the driveway – parked backward no less, probably a futile effort to keep people from knowing he was there. This house appeared to be kept up, at least on the outside. The driveway had a sheen that likely came from a recent pressure wash, the bushes were trimmed, and a brick mailbox sat at the end of the drive.

There weren't many trees in the neighborhood, so I couldn't lurk for much longer. The front door opened, and I crouched behind the brick mailbox.

I heard the jangle of keys and slowly stood.

Knuckles zeroed in on me, and he reached for his saddlebag. "I should shoot your ass. But that would start a war."

That went both ways. The easiest solution would be for me to shoot Knuckles right now, but there would be too much blow-back. Not just on the Devil Lancers, but also on Jeremiah and his crew for giving me the information.

In theory, nobody should know how I found Knuckles, but information had a way of getting out once someone was killed. Then I'd have Corrupted Chrome *and* Jeremiah gunning for me and my brothers.

I took a step forward. "You're right."

Knuckles had long russet brown hair that was pulled back in a low pony-tail. His beard had a smattering of gray hairs and looked like it could use some grooming. He frowned. "Torque's a wildcard."

The upside to Torque fucking any woman he met was that he told them all sorts of shit about himself. That shit became rumors which somehow became legend. Torque was only a wildcard with women.

If Knuckles took me out, Torque would find him and make him watch all his brothers die before flaying him and bleeding him dry.

"Why this power-play? You can't expand in your own cities?"

Knuckles rolled his eyes at me. "Why should we, when you have what we want? And we can just take your customers. No need to waste our time laying the groundwork."

"You can try," I said.

"Already undercutting your prices on drugs in Augusta and other cities. It's just a matter of time."

He couldn't keep that up forever, but I kept that to myself.

"You're taking the lazy approach," I muttered.

Knuckles crossed his arms on his chest. "What you see as lazy, I see as smart."

I stepped forward again. "Not smart to wail on prostitutes. That gets around."

His lips twisted. "Keeps the bitches in line."

"It scares off the johns, too."

He smiled. "No, they know they're next if they fuck around with us. That's where the Pussy Lancers fucked up."

I ground my molars together at the insult to my club. He was wrong. Johns who didn't pay or messed with the girls in any way got theirs. We didn't have to beat the girls in our rotation to prove the point.

Knuckles put his hands on his hips. "Know what the best part is? We took out your best pimp, and ran off two of the top whores in your stable."

Top whores. That was Tie's idea. Every one of our prostitutes claimed to be the best one. He said it was basic marketing – fake it until you make it. If the girls said that shit enough not only would they believe it, but so would the clients. I'd thought it was ridiculous at the time, because how many johns were going to believe that bullshit? Now it seemed to have been a possible stroke of genius since Knuckles *thought* he'd targeted our best.

"Why did you send Scar after me for a meet?"

Knuckles threw a hand out. "Give up your drug territory."

I widened my eyes in question. "Where? Here?"

Knuckles gave a single shake of his head. "Anywhere there's a Devil Lancer chapter."

"Why in the hell would we do that?"

"You got other businesses. We're going to take your drug business. I'm giving you the chance to save face."

I took a deep, quiet breath. "Right. I give up our drug business, then what? I saved face for you to move in on how many other dealings we have? Fuck off, Knuckles. That shit isn't happening."

He swung a leg over his bike and put the key in the ignition. "It's going to get bloody."

I took a step back. "Considering what you did to my brother, it already has. If you want us out of the drug trade, why attack two of our whores?"

Knuckles started his bike and shrugged. "Why not? It was fun."

He walked his bike forward, twisted the handle to rev the engine and be an annoying show-off, then he roared off down the street. He turned right, and away from where I'd parked the truck.

I SAT IN THE truck debating my next move. It was early enough, Simone should still be sleeping. For some reason, I didn't want her to wake up with me not there. Being an MC princess, she probably wouldn't bat an eye at my absence, but I wanted to be there when she woke up.

At the same time, I needed to meet with Torque, Tie, Nelson, Greco, and Tuscon at a minimum. Really, this demanded a full session of church.

I tapped out a quick text to Torque, Greco, and Tie telling them to get word to everyone about church at noon. Then, even though I could have texted, I wanted to fuck with Rafferty so I called him.

With a thick, husky voice, he answered on the first ring. "Hey, Steel."

"Hey. You at the house?"

"Yeah," he said, sounding groggy.

I nodded. "Do you know if Simone likes donuts?"

He wheezed out a laugh. "Yeah. She doesn't like them, she *loves* them. If you have a mom-and-pop shop, those are normally her favorites, but otherwise, she can put away three or four Krispy Kremes on her own. Or at least she used to. Not sure with the pregnancy thing going on."

I liked that she loved donuts so much. Knowing that, I wished I had time to drive across town to Belair Donuts, but that was a hike from where I was and then getting back to the house. "Krispy Kreme works since there's one on my way. She gets up, tell her I went to get donuts. I'll be back soon."

"Awesome. Later, Steel."

My phone rang in my hand. "Yo, Torque."

"We're having church while Circles is in a coma?" he asked.

I started up the truck. "I just met with Knuckles. They're coming for our drug business in every city where we have a chapter. He said they beat Circles, Heather, and June for fun."

"Fun?" he bit out.

"Yeah. I'm fucking pissed, and it's time to retaliate."

"We gotta warn the other chapters."

"Yeah, you call Raleigh, Atlanta, Vegas, Richmond, Reno, and Milwaukee. Tell Tie to handle his six cities, and I'll deal with the rest."

"You on your way to the clubhouse?"

"No, I'll be there around ten-fifteen."

"What's the hold up?"

"The hold up is that I'm in a shitty part of town, and I got other shit to do."

"Simone," he muttered.

"Get the chip off your shoulder, Tor."

He hesitated. "Not a chip on my shoulder, man. You've been happier since you've been around her."

"Yeah, so what's your problem?"

"You aren't as methodical since you've been with her," he said.

I wanted to argue, but he was right. "You find out a woman's carrying your baby and neither one of you expected that shit, it fucks with you."

"Yeah, well, get your head on straight, Prez, because this shit's serious."

"WHY DON'T WE JUST kill Knuckles and be done with it?" Nelson asked.

"Are you still fucking high?" Tie demanded.

Torque locked eyes with Nelson. "If we did that, it would start a war."

I nodded. "Hell, Knuckles wanted to shoot me on sight, and said the same shit about war."

"What are we going to do? Match their bottom-feeder prices? We'll be operating at a loss in no time," Tie said.

The room went quiet and I debated how much to share. I had an idea, but it needed time before we could execute it.

I looked at Tie. "Problem is, if we don't drop our prices, we'll be operating at an even bigger loss. For the next three weeks, we'll meet their prices – but do it on a case-by-case basis."

Greco's thick dark brows lowered. "Due respect, Prez, but why three weeks?"

"Circles is in a coma right now, and if a Corrupt Chrome member ends up dead, the cops are gonna look at us first. Three weeks isn't enough time for that to die down, but it's as long as I can tolerate to let this shit go unanswered."

Most of the men at the table nodded their heads.

"This is going to get ugly, not that that's going to bother any of you."

"Damn right," Nelson muttered at the other end of the table.

"Knuckles said it would be bloody – so watch your backs."

"Where are you going to be?" Torque asked.

"I'm rebuilding the Jacksonville chapter. Went too easy on Jackhammer and Warden. They have four patched members and three prospects. Obviously, they haven't been recruiting like they should have been. The clubhouse is a fuckin' shambles which turns off most hang-arounds and creates a vicious cycle for filling the ranks.

"I'm meeting with a contractor tomorrow to see what can be done. Code enforcement was called out and we'll be lucky if the damn buildings aren't condemned."

Tie shook his head. "There's more than one building?"

I nodded. "Yeah. It's a cluster. I'll fill you in later since we'll need to pay some fines."

Tie twisted a hand out. "All the more reason to shut that chapter down and be done with it."

I shook my head. "Corrupt Chrome has already struck an allegiance with a local street gang down there. We leave, they take that business. If I'm Knuckles, I'm using all of that to make matters worse for other Devil Lancer chapters."

Tie bowed his head. "Hadn't thought of that. Dammit."

I nodded. "Yeah. I'll be back here on weekends. I'm gonna hit up two or three of you to ride down to Jacksonville and help find new recruits and get that chapter in order."

Never one for formalities like a gavel, I banged my fist on the table to end the meeting and stood.

Greco grinned at me. "Hey, Prez, are the women down there as gorgeous as your woman? If they are, I'm in."

Torque glared at him. "Just for that, you're out."

I smiled. "Damn straight. If you're concerned about the women, you won't be focused on the club."

***

"Hey, Steel. You here by yourself?" Tessa asked as I entered the common room.

She had auburn hair that she usually wore piled on her head, but today she'd left it down. Her green eyes were wide with anticipation. She moved closer, but I held a hand out.

"Sorry, Tessa, I'm headed out."

I ignored the disappointment stealing across her face and pushed out the front door to my bike.

"Doesn't she ride?" she called out, following after me.

I stopped and turned around. This was the part of being President that I hated. Club bunnies twisted shit and watched me like a hawk. It had been tolerable ten years ago, but now... no.

"She rides, but—"

"Her bun in the oven is too precious?" she said, her tone dripping with catty attitude.

I stared at her, and unlike Simone, Tessa squirmed. Finally, I said, "It is, and so is she."

A conniving expression fell over her like a shroud. "You'll get tired of her, too. Especially since she lives in Florida."

"How do you know that?" I asked.

She couldn't hide her satisfaction at catching me off guard. "She knows Rafferty and he's from Florida, so..."

"You just assumed."

"Yeah, but she knows Rafferty awfully well."

"Why do you say that?"

She shrugged. "Why else would she give him such a hard time about being with me? Unless she has a thing for him. I'd hate to see you get hurt, Steel."

"No need to worry about me," I muttered.

The front door opened and Greco stalked out, looking for someone. "There you are, Tessa! Get your ass in here."

I turned and mounted my bike. Seemed I needed to have a word with Simone. Rafferty might be like a brother, but she couldn't go butting into his business like that no matter which club he joined.

Whether she realized it or not, she'd given Tessa more info than she'd probably intended. While it didn't matter in the big scheme, it could have had different results if Tessa were a bunny who hung with another club.

For Simone to be my woman, I needed to know she wasn't going to butt in on a brother's love life. She had to stick to the 'live and let live' mantra. It used to be that was the Riot way.

Fifteen minutes later, I pulled my bike to the far side of the driveway.

I walked into the kitchen from the garage. Simone stood at the counter, eating a Krispy Kreme donut over the sink.

She smiled at me. "Hey, honey. Did I thank you for the donuts? Because these may be the best Krispy Kremes I've ever had – that manager deserves a raise."

I nodded. "Did you confront Rafferty in front of Tessa last night?"

She took her time licking icing from her fingers. "Yes. I take it Tessa mentioned it to you."

"Could have been Rafferty."

She smiled knowingly. "It could have, except he came into the kitchen ten minutes after you left, looking like death warmed over. Plus, five minutes ago he came out for 'lunch,' which was three donuts, and he just went back to bed. He's been in no shape to communicate like that."

"Yeah," I whispered.

"You seem pissed – or disappointed – so let's have it. I was, what? Supposed to ignore him last night?"

"No," I said with a headshake.

"Okay."

"But you can't do that shit if I claim you."

Her jaw shifted just like the first night when I'd caught her off-guard. "You're thinking of claiming me? I didn't think we were there yet."

I cleared my throat. "I'm not keeping you by my side for my health."

"Right, but you can't claim me is what you said last night."

"That had to do with the club – we have problems that need to be dealt with, sweetheart. I love you, and at some point I plan to claim you if things don't change."

"Okay," she whispered.

"You gotta understand, there's enough bullshit with the brothers and other clubs. I don't need female drama, too."

She nodded. "To be fair, I shouldn't be around Raff and Tessa again in that sort of situation."

"You're right." I jerked my head toward the guest bedroom. "You said he went back to bed?"

"Yeah, he looked rough."

I grinned. "I'm about to make it rougher. Hit my room if you don't want a headache, too."

I bent to a cabinet and took out a skillet and a pan.

She gasped. "You wouldn't! That's mean, Steel."

My grin became a smile. "He prospects with us, it'll be a hundred times worse."

She shook her head. "Does he really deserve that, though?"

I pointed the skillet at her. "You're being protective again. He's out of town, underage, and not an official prospect. Not a good idea to get hammered to the point you're hung-over, and that's the lesson he's gonna learn, Jade."

"Are you playing father-figure to him?" she asked hesitantly.

I chuckled. "Far from it."

Her eyes cast down at the counter and I sensed she had something else she wanted to ask. I waited her out.

"I have a question, and I don't want you to think it's coming from anywhere but me."

I narrowed an eye at her. "That's a strange start, but go ahead and shoot."

"What happens if Raff decides he doesn't want to prospect with your club? What if he wants to be part of the Riot?"

"Why don't you want him to be part of my club?"

Her eyes closed for a moment. She opened them and shook her head. "It isn't that I don't want him to join your club, it's that... "

"What? It's complicated? I don't think it is."

She lifted her chin. "For the most part you're right, but if he joins the Lancers it's going to cause a lot of... friction."

"With his parents? He's an adult."

She sighed. "No, with Lex. Call me a romantic, but those two are peas in a pod and always have been until high school. This would... sever that beyond all hope."

She had such a huge heart. "I feel for you, but it isn't your business. And you might be surprised what people can overcome with an open mind and some understanding."

Her head tilted. "Sounds like that comes from experience."

I shrugged a shoulder. "To an extent." Something struck me and I narrowed an eye at her. "Are you trying to distract me from waking Rafferty?"

She failed to bite back her smile. "I would never."

I gave her a lopsided grin. "You better be this protective of our baby."

She widened her eyes and she chuckled. "You say that now, but our baby is gonna want me to loosen up."

"Good. Now, get out of here because I'm about to bang these pans together like cymbals in a marching band."

She shook her head and went to the sliding glass door. "I'll be out on the deck."

***

MONDAY AFTERNOON, RAFFERTY'S FORMER boss, Brian Smith, stood in front of me, and his posture alone told me I wouldn't like what he had to say. He stroked his sparse beard. "You're already facing fines from code enforcement, so this won't be what you want to hear—"

"Don't tell me what I want to hear. What's going to solve this problem and let us move forward?"

"The enclosure between the two structures can't stand because of the code enforcement violations. Since it has to come down regardless, the easiest thing to do is get rid of one of those trailers and build a new building with enough room away from the first single-wide. Or, you could get rid of both trailers and start from scratch the whole way around, but that would be the most expensive option and it will take the longest, too."

I dragged my hand down my face. Tie's words from weeks ago came back to me again. Maybe he'd been right. We should get rid of this chapter and be done with it. How many times could we say they were snake-bit before we acknowledged this wasn't a good fit?

Fuck.

"I'm sorry that's not what you want to hear," Brian said.

I let my lips tip up in a small smile. "It isn't that, Mr. Smith. Honestly, I half expected you to say that, and if you hadn't I'd be on alert. It's been a long day and this Monday is only half done."

He grinned and pulled his wallet out of his back pocket. "I hear that. If you want to move forward with us, here's my card. Either option is doable with my firm – though, if you start from scratch, that would be easiest."

"Right," I whispered with a slow nod.

He tipped his head toward the trailers. "If you decide to off-load both trailers, I might have someone interested."

"Can they move them?"

That was the other problem with trailers. Sure, they were movable, but it came a steep price all things considered.

Brian pressed his lips together. "Not sure, but I'll ask if that's what you decide to do."

I held out a hand and we shook. "Thanks for your time, Brian. I appreciate it."

"No problem. Talk to you later."

Rafferty strode toward me from his bike on the other side of the property. "You look like you sucked on a lemon. Was the news that bad?"

I nodded twice. "Worse."

His eyebrows shot up. "Really?"

"Yeah. You have any problems dropping the rental truck?"

He gave a small smile. "No. Problems dropping Simone, yeah."

My eyes narrowed. "How so?"

He shrugged. "Nothing unusual. She was just being nosy and shit."

I stifled my sigh. "She's got to stop that."

He dipped his chin. "Got your work cut out for you then."
With a heavy dose of side-eye, I muttered, "I fuckin' hope not."

OPEN MIND

SIMONE

"YOU SOUND DIFFERENT," ALEXANDRA'S voice on the speaker of my cell filled the apartment.

"I have you on speaker," I said, spooning meat sauce into a lasagna pan.

"No... that isn't it. I don't want to say you sound unhappy, but there's definitely something wrong. You've never been good at hiding things from me."

My lips quirked to the side. "Nothing is wrong," I fibbed. Rafferty joining the Devil Lancers would be all kinds of wrong to Alexandra. "I'm just tired. Growing another human takes it out of you."

"You're in the second trimester. You're supposed to get your energy back right about now."

I grinned. "That's still a week or two away, Lex. And just to say, some women *don't* get that extra burst of energy or whatever is supposed to happen."

"Be optimistic, Simone. How was Augusta?"

"It was good. Steel's house is so awesome."

"Really?"

I fought an eye-roll. "Yes, really. Don't sound so surprised. I mean, how great is your parents' house?"

"Okay, you're right."

I laid lasagna noodles on top of the sauce. "Speaking of your parents' house, you'd have loved his deck... or your dad would have, definitely."

"Really?"

I nodded. "Only thing missing was beer taps, but his outdoor kitchen is seriously sweet."

"I'm sure our pool is better."

With a spoonula, I spread the ricotta and mozzerella cheese mixture over the noodles. "It's debatable. Steel's closest neighbor is five miles away."

"Mm-hmm. It's Wednesday, so how have things been now that you two are back?"

"Pretty good, I have to say. I love him."

She went quiet. "You didn't tell him that did you?"

I paused. "He said it first, Lex. To be fair though, I'd already started falling for him."

"That fast?"

My brows drew together. "I wouldn't call it fast."

"Besides that one night, you've spent two weeks with him."

I dipped my chin and grabbed the mozzarella cheese. "I'm also having his baby, which means we have to co-exist at a minimum, or we build on the initial spark of attraction."

"Okay—"

I didn't want to hear any words of caution. "He's more than just the Devil Lancer President."

"Of course, but—"

My hackles were rising and I fought against my irritation. "But what? He's thoughtful, strategic, generous, and occasionally more logical than I'd like, but I've never felt this way with anyone else."

"Felt what way? Are you sure it's not hormones?"

I laughed. "I'm sure, Lex. He gets me, and I love that. He doesn't judge me. That might stem from his maturity, but he's just... the person I've been looking for even if I didn't know it."

She hummed and kept quiet. Then she said, "I'm glad you have that because my last two dates have been bullshit."

I shook my head. "Do you even have time to date?"

"Not really. One was a guy from my statistics class – that was a dud. The other was someone Ines introduced me to, but he's more interested in Ines. He's just too damned scared to say so."

"That sucks. I'm sorry, Alexandra."

"It's okay. Is Steel an eight-to-five kind of man, and you're just seeing him when he's done with club business? Or does his club business extend into the night?"

"He's normally home for dinner, but I suspect that will change as…" I trailed off realizing I was probably sharing too much.

"As what?"

"As he puts the chapter back together, but I didn't tell you that."

She scoffed. "Who am I gonna tell?"

"You know how secretive bikers can be. How's rooming with Ines?"

After a pause, she chuckled. "Let's just say I'm getting used to the scent of burnt bagels."

"I'd have never guessed that about her."

"That makes two of us. Are you hanging out with your brother, since he's home for Spring Break?"

I smiled. "I'm having dinner with him, my parents, and Steel tomorrow night."

She choked. "Did you say Steel's gonna be there too? Does he have a death wish?"

"Mom said she'd keep an open mind," I said, spreading another layer of sauce onto the lasagna.

Alexandra laughed. "Yeah, open to ways she can take him out."

I shook my head. "This isn't helping, you know."

"I'm sorry. It'll be fine, just make sure everyone leaves their guns at the door."

"Alexandra."

"That's the last joke, I promise. But you better call me Friday. I want to hear how this goes. I'd call Bobby, but he'll give me like two-word answers, and I need more than that."

I wanted to change the subject to Rafferty so bad, it wasn't funny, but I couldn't do that without running my mouth about the Devil Lancers. Instead, I said, "Well, you call me on Friday. I never know when you'll be out and about, Miss Social Butterfly."

"Far from it, but I'll check in. Later, Simone."

I hit the button to end the call and finished layering the lasagna.

The door opened and Steel came inside. "Hey, Steel."

He sauntered to me. "Hey, yourself. Is that lasagna?"

I smiled. "Yep."

"I fucking love lasagna. I hope yours is good."

I tilted my head. "I like to think so. Mom's mom was Italian, and I make the sauce from scratch."

His eyes widened. "Well, shit. If I hadn't already told you I loved you, I'd tell you now."

My head shook while I tore off a piece of aluminum foil and wrapped the pan. "You definitely know how to make a girl feel special."

He wrapped his arms around me. "Oh, I'm gonna make you feel special all right. Let's hit the bedroom, this can wait."

My jaw dropped open. "No, it bakes for an hour and a half. Once I put it in the oven, I'll have that much time to be with you."

His hands traveled down to my ass and gave me a squeeze. "You better, Jade."

THURSDAY AFTERNOON, DAD DROVE his GMC Acadia and picked me up at the apartment. He didn't come inside because it was closing in on four o'clock and he wanted to beat the worst of the early rush hour traffic on Blanding Boulevard.

"You and the baby are okay?" he asked after I buckled my seat belt.

Reflexively, I rubbed my belly. "As far as I know, but I go to the doctor next week."

He nodded. "That's good to hear."

Once we were on I-295 he turned down the volume on the radio. "I'm not gonna harp on this, but I wanted more of the civilian life for you."

I turned and took in his profile. His goatee had more gray. "Why? That's what I don't understand. You and Mom love the life and the brotherhood."

His lips twisted for a moment. "Sure, but there are things that come with the life – extra police attention, and even if you dodge that there's plenty of other judgmental assholes out there."

I shrugged a shoulder. "Who cares? Fuck 'em. They aren't living my life, I am."

He chuckled and blew out a sigh. "Jacqueline was right. You are my daughter, but saying that doesn't change how hard it can be looking over your shoulder all the time."

"You don't do that now," I muttered.

"Are you kidding me? I've done it more the last two weeks because you're with Steel."

I gave him a sideways glance. "I'm with Steel, not you. That sounds like paranoia."

Dad gave a conciliatory nod. "To a degree, you're right and *that's* what I didn't want for you."

We were silent for a while as we rode up San Jose Boulevard. We crossed Goodby's Creek and I realized how close we were to their house. "Are you going to be cool tonight?"

He took his time before answering. "I'll deal with him being in my house, and, yeah, I'll be cool."

I nodded. "And Mom? You won't let her goad you into anything?"

He grinned. "No, I won't, but she hates this more than I do."

Typical. They were playing this off each other.

"If you say so."

"Have you seen Rafferty lately? He wasn't around this weekend."

I glanced out the window as we entered the Lakewood area. "I haven't seen him since just after Bike Week," I lied.

Dad said nothing to that and a few minutes later we pulled into the drive. We both got out and I noticed a truck headed our way. Steel sat behind the wheel of his Nissan Titan wearing his wrap-around sunglasses.

Dad sidled up to me. "Are you sure about him, pumpkin?"

"Very."

Dad didn't hide his grimace as he hissed, "Shit."

Steel pulled the truck into the drive, powered it off, and unfolded from the vehicle. He met Dad's gaze. "Do you mind me parking in your drive or should I move to the street?"

Dad shook his head. "You're fine there."

Steel lifted his chin and tucked one arm of his shades into his shirt. He came to my side, slung his arm over my shoulders, and kissed my cheek. "You doing okay?" he whispered at my ear.

I nodded. "I'm good, honey."

"Good," he whispered.

Dad watched us for a beat. Then he turned on his heel and called over his shoulder, "Come inside. Not sure what time the food will be ready, but we can have a beer."

"You can," I muttered.

"WHEN DO YOU HAVE your first ultrasound?" Mom asked ten minutes into dinner.

I swallowed hard to keep from choking. Part of me suspected Mom had planned this inquisitive ambush, but that might have been stretching things since it was a valid question. The halfway point of my pregnancy was in three days.

After a sip of water, I said, "Next week, assuming the schedule doesn't change."

Mom's eyes darted to Steel. "Are you able to go with her? If not, I can—"

Steel moved his hand from his lap to my thigh and gave me a squeeze. "I'm definitely going to be there."

Her eyes held Steel's and she nodded. "That's good to hear." She looked at me. "Can you have more than one person with you?"

I shrugged. "I don't know. I'll have to call the office tomorrow and find out."

Bobby pointed his fork at me. "If you're having a boy, name him Robert."

Even though my brother was impervious to my pointed, dry expressions, I gave him one anyway. "I'm thinking Steel might have ideas about that, *Robert*."

Bobby aimed remorseful eyes at Steel. "Sorry." He looked back to me. "I'm just saying, don't give your kid a biker name."

I blinked at him feeling embarrassed.

Steel laughed, though. "Your Dad and I both have regular civilian names for all the good it does us. Got a feeling it won't matter what we name the baby."

Bobby nodded. "I mention it because Killian told me about the crap he put up with in school with his name and other kids finding out his dad's in a club."

Dad shook his head. "That's no reason to give a kid a normal name, Robert. Kids are gonna find ways to single others out no matter what. I'm sure dealing with that built Killian's character."

"Or his familiarity with the principal," Mom murmured.

Dad caught my gaze. "Are you going to find out what you're having?"

"No," Steel said.

At the same time, I said, "Yes."

Steel looked at me. "Why?"

I laughed. "Being pregnant has been as much of a surprise as I can handle. I want to know everything I can about this baby. Why do you want it to be a surprise?"

He shrugged a shoulder. "Life's full of surprises, but this is one of the happiest surprises you can get... and I suppose it doesn't matter to me one way or the other. The point of that ultrasound is to make sure the baby's healthy. I don't care if it's a girl or a boy."

Dad looked down at his plate. "You'll care if it's a girl."

My head whipped toward Dad. "What?"

Dad tipped his head up. "I've worried about you since the moment we saw you on the ultrasound."

Mom grinned at Steel. "I bet that's really why you don't want to know. You won't have to start worrying until you hold a little girl in your arms."

Steel sipped his beer. "It's not my first experience with a baby being born. I figure there's plenty of time for the worrying to begin. Right now, she should just enjoy the ride."

Bobby swallowed a bite of garlic bread. "I thought Jordan isn't yours."

I tilted my head back wondering how the hell he'd found that out.

"Bobby," Mom said in a reprimanding tone.

He had the gall to look offended. "What? Jasmine told me—"

"And you should know to keep some shit to yourself, son," Dad said.

With a patient smile, Steel shook his head. "It's all right, Volt." He cocked a brow at Bobby. "Your dad's right, though. You're better off not letting people know how much information you have on them. As for Jordan, the DNA doesn't matter. I was there in the early years... hell, I was there after, even if his mom kept him from knowing I was around."

Bobby's brows furrowed and his lip curled up. "She did?"

Steel nodded. "Yeah. It's messed up, but that's life. Bottom line, I'd like to be part of Jordan's life, but that won't happen if he doesn't open his mind."

"How did you find that out, anyway?" Bobby asked.

"Oh my God, are you eight or eighteen, Bobby?" I asked.

He glared at me. "It's a valid question. How does he know that bit—woman didn't do something else to scam him?"

Steel tipped his head to the side. "My dad died seven months ago. He was serving time in jail. He got sick, didn't get to the doctor until things were advanced. In the hospital, they discovered prostate cancer. They didn't even get to treat the cancer before he developed pneumonia and passed away. I wanted Jordan to attend his funeral.

"Since Jordan never took my calls, I had no idea if he would have read a text."

"He wouldn't," I muttered without thinking.

Steel nodded. "Right. I went to Debra to explain things. She's bitchy with me most of the time, but that evening, she was drunk on top of it and she let it fly that Jordan wasn't mine."

"Are you shitting me?" Dad asked, outrage lacing his tone.

Steel's eyes cut to him. "No."

"I should have let her have it last weekend," I said.

"You met her?" Mom asked.

I shrugged.

Steel kept speaking. "I thought she was lying and said so. Deb's always had to have the last word with me., She dug a file out with a paternity test."

"Wait," Bobby cut in. "She had the test done?"

Steel nodded. "She'd been cheating on me. When she turned up pregnant, she didn't know who the father was. In her mind, it was supposed to be an insurance policy."

"But it shows someone else is the dad?" Bobby asked.

"Right. It backfired on her, but at twenty, I was a moron. Had no idea she was cheating. Found that out five years later. Should have put it together at that point, but I didn't."

Bobby's eyes were wide.

I tipped my glass at him. "This is why you have to be careful who you date."

He arched a brow. "Because you were so careful yourself." His eyes slid to Steel. "No offense."

If I wasn't mistaken, Steel sat a little straighter. "That wasn't her fault. A woman hanging around the clubhouse heard me lose my temper about Debra trapping me. That bitch tried to do what Deb hadn't. Problem was, she didn't expect me to be with anyone outside the club."

The hum of the fridge filled the room, such was our awkward silence.

Dad exhaled and looked at my brother. "That's an example of why you keep your info to yourself, Rob. No disrespect intended, Steel. I can't imagine I'd have reacted any better."

Steel's hand still rested on my thigh. I put my hand over his and gave it a squeeze. "I'm sorry you lost your dad."

He dipped his chin and locked eyes with me. "Thanks, Jade."

A mixture of love, gratitude, and wonder filled his eyes. I loved how expressive his eyes were.

"Why do you call her that?" Mom asked.

Steel's eyes moved to Mom. "The necklace she wore when I met her was a ring of jade with a dragon. The look on her face when she sat down, she looked jaded. It suits her. Plus, calling her anything besides her real name keeps her safe."

Mom arched her brows at Dad. "I told you her birthstone would have been a better idea."

Steel burst with laughter. I fought a grin while my cheeks flamed with embarrassment.

WE SPED DOWN SAN Jose Boulevard. "When were you going to tell me about your appointment?"

"Later tonight. It was just pregnancy brain that kept me from telling you sooner."

He grabbed my hand. "I'm not reprimanding you or mad. Just wanted to be sure you were going to include me."

After what he'd shared tonight, there was no way I'd *ever* cut him out.

I gave his hand a squeeze. "I'm definitely including you. I hope it doesn't interfere with club business."

He picked up our hands and gave them a small shake. "I'll make it work, woman."

"I'm sorry my brother has zero manners."

The truck cab filled with the sound of his deep chuckle. "It's all good, Simone. It's crazy but I'm pretty sure it made your parents see me differently."

I nodded. "Yeah. What was so funny about Mom's comment on my necklace?"

He grinned at the windshield. "Jackie thinks that a different necklace wouldn't have gotten my attention. The reality is I'd have been drawn to you regardless."

"Yeah."

"I also love irony, and it seems to me your parents giving you that necklace pushed us together. It reminded me of jewelry I'd seen at Bike Week."

"Fate is a crazy thing."

"Yeah, and it's part of what makes life fun."

Chapter 21

Cross-Hairs

Steel

WHILE I WOULDN'T GO out of my way to spend time at Volt's home, the dinner last night went much better than I'd expected. Even when Bobby was being nosy. Volt and I would have to coexist once the baby was born, because he wouldn't turn his back on his grandchild.

Thoughts of Volt and other clubs brought Corrupt Chrome to mind.

I swallowed a sip of coffee while I leaned against the kitchen counter watching Simone eat a blueberry yogurt. "Is your dad an early riser?"

She twisted her lips in thought. "It depends. Most weekdays he's up by seven. Why?"

"Was thinking of giving him a call. Got a club issue and crazy as it might be, I thought he might have an opinion."

She shook her head. "Why not just ask Torque or Tie? And even though I haven't spoken to them much, Jackhammer or Warden might have thoughts about it."

I stared at her for a beat. "Let's just say, I understand Volt has more direct experience with this sort of issue."

Her eyes held an expectant look for a moment, then she focused on scraping yogurt out of the container. She knew I wasn't going to share with her. For some reason, seeing that anticipation and then her turning away, it almost hurt. I still wouldn't put her in the middle of this.

"Funny thing is, I've never heard him mention Corrupt Chrome before."

I finished my coffee. "I'm not talking about them specifically, sweetheart. I love you, and keeping you and our baby safe is what matters most to me. That means keeping you out of the loop is for your own good."

"I hear you, but why drag my dad into it?"

I took a deep breath as I deliberated my words. "Not dragging him into it so much as I'm asking him for references."

She mulled that over. "Call me crazy, but have you considered that I can help you—" She held up her spoon when I opened my mouth to speak. "—on the down-low," she finished.

"You're crazy."

She sighed. "I'm not trying to get your badass-man card revoked. I have a computer science degree, Steel. There are ways to cause Corrupt Chrome serious problems, and they'd never know it was you."

Her getting involved – even remotely – was too risky. "No. If a company figured out their system was hacked, they'd bring in a government agency, but if Corrupt Chrome figured out someone – you – fucked with them using technology, they'd hunt you down. Either way, *you* would be on the hook. Not any different than you pulling the gun at Target."

Her lips pressed together and she fumed.

I put my mug on the counter and approached her. "I like where your head is at, but it's not happening. Besides, I don't want them to have problems, I want them gone. Completely."

"You're going to k—"

I put a finger on her lips. "Stop. I didn't say that."

She took her yogurt container to the trash can. "I don't see Dad being able to help you with that."

A small smile crossed my face. "Funny, he convinced me to dismantle the Jacksonville chapter years ago."

"Yeah, but it didn't *completely* get rid of the chapter, seeing as that's why you're back now."

I nodded. "That's true, but that situation was different all around."

"How so?"

My reflex was to shut this conversation down, but part of me wanted to share. "Volt was far more diplomatic about shit for many reasons. I confronted Knuckles and diplomacy isn't going to get me anywhere with him."

Her mouth dropped open. "When did you do that?"

Fuck.

And this was another reason I didn't share with women. Too easy for me let shit slip that should have been kept quiet.

"Before I brought donuts back on Sunday."

Her eyes went wide, she turned her head to the side, and then back to me. "Okay, no more of that."

I couldn't hold back my laughter if I tried. "Or what, sweetheart?"

She shook her head. "Listen, Raymond 'Steel' Reynolds, the last thing I want is to be a single mom because I'm a widow!"

"I'm not going to make you a widow."

"You can't promise that. Especially if you're meeting with men named 'Knuckles'!"

I fought off my laughter. "Sweetheart, you were fine with me setting the meet at Target."

Her eyes widened again. "Yeah, because that gave you time to set up cover for yourself. Not leave it wide open to get ambushed."

I closed the distance between us. "Pretty sure it's easier for him to ambush me with that much time for planning."

"Whatever. You were there alone – not even Rafferty or anyone knew where you were."

I shrugged. "This has to get resolved and I prefer to go straight to the source."

She frowned. "I love the efficiency, but going to the source won't matter if you're *dead*. Just saying, I will make that man's life hell if that happens."

"No. Our son or daughter needs their momma. Not to be an orphan."

"You're right. But don't underestimate me."

"Are you sure you were born to be a president's old lady? This comes with the territory. A year or two from now it could be some other club coming for me."

She blinked and sighed. "I'm cool with it."

"You won't go back on that, right?"

"No, but what about Mom's concerns? *Would* it be better for me to be your old lady? It seems like it would give me more protection."

"Yeah, if there's another threat, by then you'd be claimed and that *should* make you off-limits. Right now, my gut says it's better not to draw attention to you like that. The shit Pump said about you at Target and especially the way he looked at you, Knuckles doesn't give a damn about women or children and his brothers know it."

She gave a slow nod.

"Besides that, you deserve more than me claiming you in a rush. Are you working from home all day?"

"Yes, sir. My brother might swing by for lunch, but that's assuming he's awake before eleven A.M."

I nodded. "If you leave, take your gun."

She grinned. "I always do."

IN THE APARTMENT PARKING lot, I mounted my bike and my phone rang.

Volt's name lit up the screen.

"Volt," I answered.

"Steel. You at the apartment?"

"Yeah, though I'm about to leave."

"Do you have time to meet me at Platinum's Gentleman's club? It's about five minutes from the apartment."

"Sure. There a reason for this?"

"Yeah. I'll see you at Platinum's in ten minutes. Park around back."

Ten minutes later, I had put the kickstand down on my bike and watched Volt ride his Harley into the lot, followed by another brother.

Volt sauntered toward me and I dismounted. Blood followed behind Volt, and I wondered what this was all about.

"Sorry, Steel. I didn't want to do this over the phone. I don't trust Simone not to eavesdrop."

"I can understand that."

"Blood got a call last night. Are you having problems with Corrupt Chrome MC?"

I glanced at Blood and to Volt. "What makes you think that?"

Blood glowered at me. "Does it matter?"

Volt shook his head. "I may have stopped breaking the law outright, but that doesn't mean I ignore what's happening around me."

Since I hadn't spoken to Rafferty today, there was a slight possibility he might have mentioned following Simone and confronting Scar and Pump. "What's happening around you?"

"Why can't you answer his question?" Blood demanded.

I locked eyes with him. "Because he asked for this meet, so clearly there's an agenda. I don't give up information freely, and my guess is, neither do you."

Volt shrugged a shoulder. "I got word that Corrupt Chrome has an alliance with the Southside Slayers because they both deal drugs. The reason they forged this alliance was because they want to get the Devil Lancers out of the way."

That didn't warrant a response, so I kept quiet.

Volt dragged his hand along the back of his neck as though relieving tension, then he looked at me. "I ignored this information until I got a message late last night from a Riot chapter out west. Shit seems to be heating up between the Devil Lancers and Corrupt Chrome out there, too."

Since he said 'out west,' I surmised that Volt was referring to their Vegas chapter. Shark, our Las Vegas chapter president, hadn't called me. He might have called Torque... but even that should have gotten back to me.

While I debated how to respond, Volt said, "I don't intend to get in your business, and really don't care about this... except, I need to know if Simone's in the cross-hairs. Especially since I called some other people, and word is the Devil Lancers are dealing with the same shit across the board."

I nodded. "Those assholes are causing issues for me. I asked Simone this morning if you were an early riser because I wanted to call you."

"What the hell for?" Blood asked.

I couldn't decide if I liked or hated how protective he was of Volt.

With my eyes locked on Volt's, I said, "You convinced me to dismantle a chapter a few years back. That won't work with Knuckles. Did you have a plan in the event I *didn't* agree to shutting down the chapter?"

Volt shook his head. "I'm not answering that until you answer my question. Is Simone in danger?"

Honesty was the only way to go here, and my gut clenched at the thought. "Not right now."

"What the fuck does that mean?" Blood asked.

Volt's jaw shifted and he jerked his head toward Blood. "What he said. What the fuck does that mean?"

"They followed me and Simone the day she moved. We went out to eat, and then to get groceries. Two assholes made an approach."

"An approach?" Volt asked.

I nodded. "Your daughter pulled out her gun, though she did it with subtlety. Problem was, later they were hanging around her SUV and only left when a cop pulled into the lot."

"So, she's in the cross-hairs," Blood said.

I shook my head. "I don't refer to her by her given name in public. Even the night I met her, I called her Jade. Being with me comes with risks and I do my damnedest to lessen those."

"That's not much help," Volt said.

If the tables were turned, I'd feel the same way, but I kept that to myself. "She's got good instincts, and can handle herself."

"How would you know that?" Blood asked.

I decided I hated how protective he was of Volt and Simone. My eyes locked with his. "She didn't fully bring out her gun, which kept another customer from seeing it. Might have kept the in-store cameras from seeing it, but I doubt it. Bottom line, she's shown she has grit." I looked at Volt. "You won't like this, but she says she was born to be a president's old lady."

Volt slowly turned his head away. "You're right, I don't like that."

"Since we're talking about things you don't like, there have been a couple cook houses that blew up in Riot cities."

"Riot didn't have anything to do with that," Blood said.

If he hadn't responded so fast, I might have believed him.

I ignored Blood, keeping my gaze on Volt. "One of those was here and authorities pointed to the Southside Slayers or faulty cooking methods, but neither of those explanations ring true."

Volt shrugged a shoulder. "Why not? Cook houses blow all the time."

"Not all the time, and the Slayers aren't into explosives."

"Neither are we," Blood said.

I looked at him and back to Volt. "The other house is in Biloxi. And rumor has it one of those brothers is good with explosives. I'd like to talk to him."

Blood shook his head. "Those rumors are exaggerated. He launches fireworks. He can't help you."

Volt kept his eyes pinned on me. "Let's say he has time to chat. What's in it for us?"

"A marker to start."

"That's not worth much since we've cleaned our act up," Blood said.

"What are you planning? You want to burn down cook houses in twenty cities where you have chapters?" Volt asked.

I shook my head. "Clubhouses, not cook houses, and it would be more like thirty."

Blood's head reared back. "Why clubhouses?"

If Torque were here, he'd tell me to shut up and move on. Maybe being involved with Simone was marring my judgment, but I trusted them enough to share. Not to mention I might need their help beyond just information.

"Corrupt Chrome wants all of our business – one type of business – but even if I give into that bullshit, where does it stop?"

"But clubhouses? That's extreme," Volt said.

I nodded once. "They want to take over. I want to take them out."

"That's gonna bring a shitload of heat," Blood said.

I shook my head. "My club only has chapters in twenty cities. Why would we go after those other ten?"

Volt shoved his sunglasses on top of his head. "What does all this do for you? They can rebuild – it'll take time, but that doesn't get rid of them."

I dipped my chin. "You're right. But it makes them more vulnerable."

Blood turned his head and took a deep breath. "You're gonna go after those assholes in their homes."

I turned my hands out in question. "How am I gonna know where they live?"

With an arch of his eyebrow, Blood said, "Wouldn't be you doing the dirty work."

Volt shook his head. "I don't think you need help from Roman with this. If you want to burn down their clubhouses, then have someone set a fire and be done with it. Explosions are going to get even more unwanted attention."

He was right, but part of me wanted to send a message. Not just to Corrupt Chrome, but to *any* MC thinking of fucking with the Devil Lancers.

I nodded. "Thing is, Biloxi is one of the cities where the Lancers don't have a presence, but Corrupt Chrome has a chapter there."

Blood's eyes widened. "You can't expect our Biloxi brothers to do you a solid."

I shook my head. "I only need information and to talk to... Roman, was it?"

Volt crossed his arms. "This might be the perfect time to clean up your club."

"You aren't serious," I said, laughing.

Volt nodded. "Very. You got a kid on the way and *anything* you do is going to earn retaliation from them."

"That goes both ways, Volt."

He cocked his head to the side. "How do you know you aren't being played by the cartels? I assume you get your drugs from a larger supplier."

I narrowed my eyes. "What do you know about cartels, Adler?"

He chuckled. "Plenty. It was a big part of why I joined the Riot. I wasn't patching into a club where I could be someone's pawn. It seems to me that your club and the Corrupt Chrome MC are just middle-men. If their cartel forces CCMC to shove your club out of the trade, then that cartel makes more money."

I nodded. "Or they could be doing this on their own because Knuckles is a cocky motherfucker."

Volt's head wobbled side to side. "Either is possible, so why not look into legitimate enterprise?"

This was turning into a waste of my time, and I dug my keys out of my pocket. "That won't fly with my brothers. I appreciate your concern for Simone. She knows about the threat. I've already told her to be vigilant when she leaves the apartment, but I'll make sure she gets the message again."

Volt glared at me. "Anything happens to her, I will end you."

I nodded once. "Something happens to her, I'll deserve that."

AT A QUARTER AFTER eleven, Torque and Tie rode through the gates of the Jacksonville compound. I shook my head, wondering why they hadn't texted me that they were on their way down today.

I strode to where Torque had stopped his bike. "What the hell? I'm riding up to Augusta tomorrow morning. Could have saved yourselves a trip."

Torque shook his head. "We came down here to discuss the ongoing problem we have, and I'm not talking about that shit over the phone."

I glanced around the property. The general contractor had pulled permits and had a full crew of half a dozen men here to start the renovations. I tipped my head toward my bike. "Follow me. It's almost lunch time, we'll hit a hole-in-the-wall diner."

Fifteen minutes later, we sat at a picnic bench outside with our food.

Torque launched right in. "We gotta deal with this problem. Greco found Flip and Mug outside the house of one of his customers. Luckily the customer wasn't home."

I shook my head. "Why is Greco visiting a customer when they aren't home?"

Tie looked over his shoulder and back to me. "Because a female customer called him and said Mug and Flip had just been to see her. Told her she had to do her business with them."

"Did they force her to call Greco?"

Torque and Tie shared a look.

"Didn't ask that," Torque said.

I stroked my chin. "That would be good to know. They might have done that to ambush Greco."

Tie nodded. "Thing is, we got calls from six other chapters and they had similar shit go down today."

"It's time to take a stand, Steel," Torque said.

"I agree. My plan was to level their clubhouses and take those assholes out in their own homes."

Torque shook his head. "That's too much. Grabs too much attention."

"Killing off Corrupt Chrome members in twenty different cities is going to draw attention also."

Torque sipped his coffee. "Are we giving up to them? If we aren't, that needs to be clear."

I sighed. "Someone suggested letting them have the drugs and going legit."

Torque's angry expression could have melted wax. "Your new—"

"Don't finish that, and it wasn't her. The idea of us turning legitimate is ludicrous."

Tie shrugged. "Doesn't have to be. We'd have fewer legal fees, that's for sure."

Torque glared at Tie. "And that's all we'd have, Tie. Almost all of our members live for the thrill that comes from getting away with the things we do." He glanced around the area to be sure we weren't being overheard. "We get out of our current business, we're gonna lose a ton of brothers."

I finished my pancake. "Is Corrupt Chrome still sending members to Player's Palace?"

"Yeah, what are you thinking?" Torque asked.

"Have Bella and Tessa offer them lap dances in the back room."

"Are you sure about that?" Tie asked.

I nodded.

Torque grinned. "They'll get more than a dance, if I'm reading you right."

"Call the other chapters facing the same issue. If they have Corrupt Chrome members in their titty bars, implement the same set-up – but reinforce those dancers have to be girls who can be trusted."

Tie frowned. "Someone's going to report them missing."

I smiled. "Prospects will wear their colors, get on their bikes and take them to where the CCMC does their dirty work. Pretty sure all the CCMC chapters have places outside of town. Prospects leave the bikes there, and have the prospects get a ride back with a stripper."

Torque's face lit with his smile. "That's what I'm talking about. Thought you'd lost your touch, brother."

"No, but this shit is getting old."

Tie's eyes widened. "Are you stepping down?"

"No, but I wouldn't mind downsizing our involvement in the business that got Circles in trouble."

Torque shook his head. "Dancing can only bring in so much money. The bars tend to feed that operation."

"And maybe it shouldn't any more."

"Maybe you should step down," Torque muttered.

"Maybe. But not right now."

Tie swallowed some soda. "Are you gonna make Jackhammer or Warden a president down here?"

"No. Neither one of them wants that and neither of them has real leadership potential."

Tie shrugged a shoulder. "They got a decent hang-around somehow."

I chuckled. "They didn't do that, I did."

Torque nodded. "And a hang-around isn't the same as a prospect."

"Right, so the next six to nine months, I'm gonna be here. A couple of members are down this week from Raleigh. They aren't sure if they want to make the move."

"Can't blame 'em," Tie said. "It's not cheap to move and we've only had bad shit happen here."

I put my fork on my plate. "We get enough local interest we should be able to build a decent chapter."

"And you're here until it happens?" Torque asked. To anyone else, he had hidden his dissatisfaction, but I'd known him for eighteen years. He was very unhappy about this.

"Until December. Do you expect that to be a problem?"

Torque kept quiet for a long moment. "It will be a problem if Knuckles leaves to follow you down here. You don't have as many of us here to help you – and even if you did, none of us would know where the hell

Knuckles is staying or even where to begin to look for him. Until he's dealt with, it'd be better if you were in Augusta."

Tie leaned in and lowered his voice. "Or if he gives the order, we eliminate him outright. Gives Steel an airtight alibi since it's over four hours back to Augusta."

Torque's eyes slid to Tie. "He's gonna want that for himself."

I gave a small head shake. "Not if it means I watch my kid grow up from the wrong side of a Plexiglass prison window."

Ever the pragmatist, Tie asked, "Do you have a timeframe in mind? The way these assholes are fucking with us, I don't think we can put this off very long."

"I'm thinking another three weeks or so."

Torque stared off to the side. Then he turned back to me. "Why three? We go with two, everything goes down during the Masters."

I shook my head. "In Augusta it does, but that doesn't help the other chapters with what they're facing. Besides, along with the extra tourists comes extra police presence. We don't need to do this shit when that's happening, Torque."

He grimaced. "Yeah, you're right. I just figure it's easier to have two members of their club go missing during the Masters since we have so much extra business."

"It's better to keep the dancers focused on all the tourists. We make a killing that week, and we need everyone on their toes."

"So really, we're looking at four weeks from now. The Masters starts three weeks from this coming Monday," Torque pointed out. "It doesn't wrap until that Sunday, which means you got three more weekends of coming back to Augusta."

I dragged a hand down my face. When he put it like that, it gave Knuckles and his crews plenty of time to fuck with us further. Yet I didn't want other chapters going into this half-cocked.

Torque leaned on the table. "It'd be better if you came back for a week. What are you really accomplishing here? You got the building moving on the right path. Other brothers are here and can recruit new members."

"Not happening this week," I said.

"Why not?" Torque asked.

I glared at him. "I have a baby on the way, man. The ultrasound is next week and I'm gonna be there."

Torque's lips pressed into a thin line as he turned his head to the side. He looked at me. "I liked it better when you didn't know how to get in touch with her."

Tie narrowed his eyes at Torque. "That's cold. How the hell do you get bitches all the time with that attitude?"

Torque smirked. "The bitches want my dick and they don't give a fuck about my attitude."

CHAPTER 22

BINGO CARD

SIMONE

THE ULTRASOUND TECHNICIAN HAD to reschedule my appointment from Tuesday to Thursday. It was a relief since I had fading hickeys from the weekend in Augusta.

Rather than spend our time at his house, we spent the whole weekend at the Devil Lancer clubhouse. Many things were the same as a Riot clubhouse, but it had a different vibe – rougher and rowdier.

Saturday night, Steel had tied me to his bed and done wicked things to me. He hadn't only marked me with love bites, but also with his cum. That had to be the most erotic thing any man had ever done to me. I'd never felt so wanton and yet revered at the same time.

"What's wrong?" Steel asked, sitting next to me in the waiting room at my OB-Gyn.

Thinking about that night while filling out medical forms wasn't a good idea. I let out a quiet chuckle. "Nothing."

"From that grin, it must be something."

I shook my head. "I'm just wondering how we'll top last weekend."

That earned me his rumbly chuckle. "We'll top it all right."

I didn't think Steel was a dominant, but boy did he like his control. Not that I was complaining. Nobody had taken care of me the way Steel did.

"Oh, good. I'm not late," Mom said, bustling into the cramped waiting room.

I shot a furtive glance at Steel, and whispered, "You sure it's all right?"

"First grandchild for her, yeah, I'm sure," he whispered back.

Mom sat on the other side of me. "I'm so excited. Aren't you?"

"Yes, but—"

"But what?" she asked.

"But remember, he doesn't want to know."

"I know." Mom glanced past me. "How are you, Steel?"

He nodded. "Jackie."

I kept at Mom. "That means no trying to change his mind in the exam room."

"I know, sweetheart."

My phone dinged in rapid-fire succession. I saw three texts from Alexandra.

What's the deal with Rafferty?

Jazz says he's hanging with a club, but it isn't the Riot!

Do you know anything?

"Oh hell," I whispered.

"What? Are you okay?" Mom asked, her posture stiff.

I smiled at her. "I'm fine. Calm down, I'm only four months along, no worries."

She widened her eyes. "*Only* four months? Simone, every month of pregnancy can give you something new to worry about."

I rolled my eyes and the woman sitting across from me gave me a commiserating smile. After a deep breath, I turned back to Mom. "It's all good. I got a text from Alexandra, that's all."

Mom nodded. "Say no more. She can be very dramatic."

I choked on laughter while the woman across from me snickered outright.

Mom looked from her to me. "What's funny?"

Steel leaned forward. "Pretty sure it takes one to know one."

Mom gasped.

The door opened and a nurse called out my name.

EVEN THOUGH I HAD seen ultrasound pictures before, I still had no idea what I was looking at as I stared at the screen while the tech moved the wand over my belly. She adjusted some knobs and the blur of white took on a different shape. Lines started to appear on the screen and I realized she was taking measurements.

"Since this is your first ultrasound, I'm measuring from crown to rump. It helps to give us a guide for development and better determine your due date."

I exhaled slowly. "Okay."

She grinned at me. "Everything looks fine so far."

I nodded. "He doesn't want to know the gender, but I do. Can we do that?"

"Sure. I'll write it on a piece of paper for you, and you can find out when he isn't within earshot."

Steel gave my hand a squeeze. "The baby looks healthy though, right?"

The tech tilted her head. "The doctor will let you know, but unofficially, I don't see anything to be concerned about right now."

"Good," I whispered.

It struck me that Mom had been too quiet. I turned her way and saw her fighting back emotion, but two tears had escaped her closed eyes.

I reached out and grabbed her hand. "It's okay, Mom."

With a watery glower she sighed. "It's better than okay, pumpkin. These are happy tears."

There was a knock on the door and my doctor came into the room. She spoke with the tech and looked at the various measurements, and looked at me. "You're still feeling all right?"

I nodded. "Just tired, but it's been that way the whole time."

She smiled. "Yes. You're starting the second trimester soon, so you might feel a little less tired."

"Enjoy that while you can," Mom muttered.

The doctor tipped her head at Mom. "Right. I'm referring you for a gestational diabetes test. It's standard procedure to keep you and the baby healthy. In the meantime, everything looks good and we'll see you back next month unless something changes."

The tech handed me an envelope. "I've written down the gender in there, that way he won't hear, and we've had moms-to-be change their minds and want a surprise after all."

"Thank you."

"You're welcome, and there are paper towels, so you can wipe off the gel before you get dressed."

"I'll wait outside for you," Steel said.

I squeezed his hand. "Okay. Are you coming back to the apartment?"

He checked the time on his phone. "We'll see."

As soon as the door closed behind him, Mom held her hand out. "Let me see. I'm dying to know."

I held out the envelope and kept hold after she grabbed it. "Don't tell me. I decided I don't want to know."

Outrage washed over her. "Simone Dolores, you can't be serious!"

"What? I'm not keeping you from knowing."

She scoffed. "Yeah, but I won't be able to tell anybody because your brother can't keep a secret, neither can Abby, and it's only because Alexandra has a big mouth that I knew about your break up with Jordan."

I gave her a closed lip smile. "There's always Dad."

Mom growled under her breath and took the envelope. "I'll keep this safe. At least I can think about baby shower themes."

I tilted my head. "Without giving away the gender, right?"

Her smile fell. "You really know how to rain on a parade, honey."

I chuckled. "Sorry... not sorry?"

She shook her head. "Do you need more towels for the gel?"

I wiped my belly one last time. "No, I'm good."

"All right. Will we see you this weekend?"

The paper on the exam table made a crinkling sound as I swung off. "I'm supposed to be in Augusta."

"Again? This is crazy."

I adjusted my blouse. "I have to figure out if I can handle living there."

She sighed.

"It's only a little over four hours away, Mom."

"Yeah, yeah but you're gonna miss us, and Abby, and Trixie."

I shook my head. "You're probably right, but it's not like I can't visit."

"I know. Now what did Alexandra text you about?"

"Nothing," I said a little too fast.

She gave me a pointed look. "It wasn't about Rafferty was it? Trixie's getting worried about him, and *that* is saying something."

I moved to the door and shrugged. "I don't know what there is to worry about with Raff, but she didn't text about him. Just some issues with a hard-nosed professor."

Mom shook her head. "She isn't majoring in the same subject as you. How would you know about a hard-nosed professor?"

"Because she told me about this issue during Bike Week," I said, opening the door.

"Something tells me you're lying."

I stopped at the check-out counter and locked eyes with her. "Mom, it wasn't about Rafferty. And even if it was, she wouldn't want me discussing it with you."

She nodded. "You're right. I've taught you too well." She smiled. "I hope you end up with a girl so you can experience this bizarre déjà vu of hearing yourself talk back to you."

A baby girl with Steel's eyes and bossy disposition. I was not *prepared for that.*

I smiled. "It's not my fault you taught me so well."

"Nice save. Schedule your next appointment."

FOR THE FIRST TIME since we started living together, Steel didn't come home for dinner. After the ultrasound appointment, he'd told me he'd be late because of club business, so it wasn't a surprise. I *was* surprised by the fact I fell asleep reading in bed at around five-forty-five. I hadn't done that since moving to Jacksonville.

So much for a second-trimester energy boost.

The rustling of the covers woke me and I rolled toward Steel. "Hey, Ray."

He chuckled. "It's a good thing you're cute. Nobody calls me Ray."

I hummed while I snuggled up to him. "Everything okay? What time is it?"

"Everything's fine and it's ten-thirty. Did you eat dinner? Or just zonk out?"

"Both. I ate at five-fifteen because this child of ours is turning me into an old lady, and then I brushed my teeth and curled up to read... only I fell asleep."

He kissed my neck. "I'd say I'm sorry, but you need sleep so our little boy can grow big and strong."

My eyes flew open, not that Steel could see that in the dark. "What do you mean 'little boy'? I thought you didn't want to know."

He chuckled. "I don't want to know. I was projecting what I want."

My head reared back. "That sounds very new-age-ish for a biker like you."

His arms tightened around me. "No, but I'm not exactly thrilled with the idea of a little girl. Don't get me wrong, she'd be so fuckin' beautiful, but her beauty would do me in. I wouldn't know what to do... kill first and ask questions later, or let her live her life like a decent dad would and deal with the fall out as it comes."

I giggled. "It's funny, Mom hopes I end up with a girl so I have to listen to someone be just as sassy as me."

He groaned. "Yeah. Definitely pulling for a boy, two gorgeous firecrackers in my life might kill me."

I kissed his jaw. "We won't both be sassy at the same time."

He laughed. "Don't make promises you can't keep, Simone. Let's get some rest. If you're up for it, I'd like to hit the road first thing in the morning."

"WHEN WAS YOUR CLUBHOUSE built?" I asked as Steel pulled through the gate to the compound.

"Early eighties. It was a small church which ran a pre-school. They fell on hard times. Can't remember if it was a preacher or someone else who pilfered their money."

"They ran a pre-school? That's odd because the way the kitchen is built, it seems like an afterthought."

He parked the truck under the shade of a huge oak tree. "That's because it was an afterthought. The building was outfitted to be a church – sanctuary, and area to greet and mingle with parishioners before or after services, and a few rooms for Sunday school. Someone got a wild hair about a weekday preschool, and they needed a full kitchen in order to do that."

I nodded. "That sort of explains the bizarre set-up."

"Bizarre?" he asked with an arch of his brow and his lips quirked up.

"There are rooms upstairs and down, but your room is on the opposite side of those and the common room."

He nodded. "Yeah, the previous president did his best to keep the renovations to a minimum. He wanted his room to be away from the others, so the pulpit and the area where the choir sat behind it was sectioned off. One side became our room for church and the other side became his room."

"That's why the ceilings are so high."

His chuckle filled the cab before he opened his door. "That's a big part of it, Jade. Let's go."

We went inside through the front door and Steel got numerous greetings from brothers and sweet-butts. I didn't see Josie, so I suspected the brothers got the message that she wasn't welcome. Nobody greeted me, but I didn't let it bother me. For all they knew, I would be out in a week or two. To my knowledge, Steel hadn't been vocal about my pregnancy to anyone other than Torque.

Steel set my suitcase alongside the wall near the door. "You need the bathroom first?"

I nodded. "Yes, I can't imagine what I'm gonna do when this baby's bigger and pushing on my bladder."

After I used the bathroom, I found Steel right outside the door. I smiled. "I'm starting to think you're a bathroom snob."

He closed his eyes, chuckled, and shook his head. "You're crazy, baby. The bathroom at my house is much better."

I nodded. "Yeah, but everything in there seems brand-spanking new."

"Not that new, but it's well-maintained. When a man like me needs a decent shower, I need room and power."

He moved past me and closed the door. I went to my suitcase and grabbed some fresh clothes and my toiletries.

Steel came out just as someone knocked on the door in a strange rhythm.

His brows furrowed. "What the fuck?"

He checked his phone, put it back, and put his hands on my shoulders. "I'll be back in a moment."

I nodded once. "It's cool. Since we left so early, I'm going to take a shower."

After I showered, I dressed in an over-sized lavender scoop-neck t-shirt and the light khaki maternity cargo shorts that I wore earlier. I loved that the shorts didn't make my baby bump too obvious. I grabbed my toiletry bag and went to my suitcase.

From the hallway, I heard voices, both of them familiar.

Jordan said, "You're so full of yourself. Why can't we do this at the bar?"

"Because I want privacy and I would think you do, too," Steel said.

Jordan's petulant tone couldn't be missed. "None of those people know me."

"Torque, Tie, and Greco don't know you? All three of them watched you grow up until Debra cut me out of your life. What do you need, Jordan?" Steel asked.

I heard a door squeak and I assumed he'd opened the door to the meeting room across the hall.

"I don't want to go in there," Jordan said.

"It's just a room."

"Yeah, and where's your room here?"

"You cashed my check last week, so last time, Jordan. What do you need?"

For a long moment everything was silent and I wondered if Steel forced Jordan into church. I needed to stop eavesdropping. It wasn't cool, but as much as I knew that I couldn't tear myself away.

Then Jordan asked, "You have Simone here, don't you?"

"Jordan, I don't have time—"

"You say you love me, but stealing my ex-girlfriend sends a message."

"You dumped her, so I didn't steal her."

"If you want a relationship with me, give up Simone."

Steel's voice rose. "She's carrying my child. I can't leave her to raise him or her alone."

"You did that to mom."

"At her fucking insistence."

"Not at first."

"Right. I left when there was a threat and when I came back, I saw Deb's true colors. Should have insisted on a paternity test then, but you were mine – no DNA test will ever change that."

"But you went out of your way to tell me last month?"

"Yeah, because I hate the idea of keeping it secret from you – unlike Deb. Hell, she'd find a way to blame me for that, too."

Jordan's voice rose, his tone angry. "Leave Mom out of this. Simone has to go, I can't be around her."

That stung. What the hell would make him say that about me? We lived together for almost three years.

"Okay," Steel said and my mind whirled.

Irritation welled up within me. *Okay*.

I suspected Steel had more to say, but clearly Karma was trying to teach me a lesson and I moved to the other side of the bedroom. Jordan was a tool to try manipulating Steel.

There was a side exit from Steel's room out to the backyard. He'd used it last weekend when we left. I slipped on my sneakers. Then I shoved my keys into my regular pocket, tucked my phone into a cargo pocket, and went outside.

Gusty winds whipped my hair around. A front was supposed to move through later this afternoon. Billowy clouds glided across the sky. I loved watching the clouds, so I walked down toward the fire pit.

I was a few feet from an anti-gravity chair when someone wrapped a thick arm around me from behind.

I screamed and threw an elbow backward. My attacker grunted. He tightened his grip. I yelled while stomping on his foot.

Then Josie wandered in front of me. "Stop fighting with Mug. You act like you know what you're doing, but you don't. You're just pathetic."

I arched a brow. "That's rich considering your failed attempt at trapping Steel."

Josie's eyes widened.

Mug's grip around my neck tightened some more. "What's she talkin' about, Josie?"

Quickly, Josie schooled her features and looked at him. "Nothin'. She doesn't know what she's talking about." She nodded at him. "Now, baby."

I struggled against Mug's hold and screamed. The fire pit was so far from the clubhouse, I wasn't sure if anyone would hear me. Worse still, the wind carried my screams in the wrong direction.

"Stop fighting," he grunted.

"Give me the damn thing," Josie said.

Mug handed her a small syringe. I didn't have a fear of needles, but terror ripped through me at the sight of Josie holding that needle.

"I'm pregnant! You can't shoot me full of drugs!"

A condescending smile curved her lips. "Are you scared for your baby? Good. You should be. I don't know what Special K does to pregnant women. Guess we're going to find out."

With all my might I shoved my weight against Mug's frame, but he held steady. I screamed and twisted my head down to keep Josie away. My efforts were futile though because Mug had the strength of an ox.

"Watch where you're aimin' that thing," Mug said.

Josie stood right in front of me. I felt a pinch, and in no time, the world went black.

———

"Are you sure she's the right woman?" Mug asked.

I forced myself not to open my eyes as I gained consciousness. The longer they thought I was out, the longer I had to figure out what to do next. Not to mention, I had the worst headache in my entire life, keeping the light out helped.

"Yes, I'm sure. He brought her around two weeks ago," Josie said.

"She don't look pregnant," he said.

My shirt suddenly lifted.

"See that? Those are pregnancy shorts, they have that waistband to support the belly," Josie explained.

It took effort not to open my eyes when my shirt fell back into place.

"Where's Knuckles? I want my money. I did what you assholes wanted, I need to get paid."

A voice deeper than Mug's asked, "What'd he promise you? Three hundred?"

Three hundred dollars to abduct another woman? Josie wasn't just a bitch, she had no sense of worth.

"That's not what he promised me. It's between me and Knuckles."

"Bitch wants more money, Sledge," Mug said.

"You think I don't know that?"

Josie's tone lost some of its bitterness. "I didn't say I want more money. I made a deal with Knuckles and he's the only one I'm going to talk to about it."

I let my eyes open just a crack and I got my first glimpse of Sledge. He had bloodshot brown eyes, and his frizzy hair looked like it was two months past a decent haircut. Though if he were aiming for a mullet, he'd hit that mark. He wasn't as well-built as I expected a second-in-command to be.

"I need a hit. Did you snort all the coke?" he asked.

That might have something to do with his physique.

"Nah, man. We just got back here half-an-hour ago," Mug said.

"Wake her up, she's takin' up too much space on the couch," Sledge said.

Since I didn't want anyone touching me, I shifted enough for them to recognize I was awake.

"Christ. Why didn't you tie her up? Get her wrists," Sledge ordered.

Shit. I might have enjoyed it when Steel tied me to his bed last weekend, but I didn't want these people restraining me.

"She's pregnant, she's gonna have to pee, you know," Josie said.

Maybe she had a conscience after all.

I slowly sat up and opened my eyes.

Sledge glowered at me. "Something about her is familiar. Josie, get her to the fuckin' john and tie her up after."

I stood before Josie reached me. With an arch of her brow, she led me to a cramped bathroom, if you could call it that. The entire space felt like an old closet that had been outfitted with a toilet and tiny sink. She stood in the doorway and turned her head while I took care of business.

One thing was official. This year wasn't shaping up the way I thought it would. Pregnancy hadn't been on my bingo card, and kidnapping sure as *hell* hadn't made the cut, either.

After I peed, I rinsed my hands at the sink – there was no soap. Shocker.

Josie rolled her eyes when she turned her head back to me. "Let's go. There's a chair with your name on it, Jade."

Thankfully, I hid my shock at her calling me Jade and Steel's words at my parent's house replayed in my mind. He'd called me that to protect me. With any luck, that might pay off. I had a bad feeling about Sledge, especially when he said I seemed familiar.

Josie led me to a chair. On the other side of the room, Sledge and Mug were snorting cocaine. I sat down, and Josie tied me up. Unfortunately, she probably did it tighter than Mug or Sledge. I had my circulation still, but I wasn't going anywhere.

CHAPTER 23

RUTHLESSNESS

STEEL

"OKAY," I SAID AND paused. Nothing was okay about Jordan's demand that I get rid of Simone. I swung my arm out toward the empty room for church. "We're both raising our voices right now. Let's go in here so we can sit down and get some things straight."

Jordan's lips curled as he took in the room and the huge table with our patch etched into the center. I couldn't believe Deb had raised him to be so judgmental. After a beat, he trudged toward the table, pulled out a chair, and sat down.

I shut the door, and sat across from him. "You and I can get along without Simone being an issue, Jordan."

He gave a short head shake. "The fact I used to sleep with her doesn't bother you?"

I took in a deep breath while I ground my teeth together.

"Yeah, that's what I thought," Jordan said.

I exhaled slowly. "I didn't say anything, Jordan. As long as you don't dwell on it, I don't see there being an issue."

He narrowed his eyes. "I suppose that's what you'll say about all the years you weren't around, too. If I don't dwell on it and rub it in your face, it's not an issue."

I dragged my hand along my jaw. "Believe it or not, I was there, Jordan. Every little league game, high school games. Hell, I was there when you took Robin to prom."

His jaw dropped open a touch. "No, you weren't."

"How do you think you were able to do all of those things? That shit costs money."

"Child support is what you're *supposed* to do, Steel."

I lowered my chin. "Yeah, and every sport and extracurricular activity cost money that went above and beyond what I was ordered to give your mom. I did more than I was supposed to because you're my son, and I fuckin' love you, Jordan."

He stared at me for a long moment. "I think Mom needs help."

I shook my head. "What do you mean? She was here two weeks ago and confronted me. What kind of help are you talking about?"

He shrugged. "I don't know. She's just so angry and bitter all the time."

There were many things I wanted to say to that, but I wouldn't disparage Deb in front of him.

"I'm not the person to help her there. She blames me for many things that I didn't do or couldn't control."

Jordan looked around the room, his expression saying he couldn't argue with that. He locked eyes with me. "Maybe you can point me in the right direction to help her."

I mulled it over. "You'll be better off to encourage her to see someone for help if you're concerned. And make it clear this is coming from you. She loves you very much. You bring me into this and... she's more likely to dig in her heels."

He nodded and stood. "Right. I'll, uh, let you get back."

I walked him out to the common room when Rafferty stormed in through the front door.

Everyone turned to him.

"What's wrong?" I asked.

His eyes darted to Jordan and then to me. "A prospect is out cold, by the gate. Wasn't sure if you knew about it."

Tie darted out of the room and upstairs to check security cameras. Greco went to the rack of bats by the door, grabbed one, and shoved outside.

Torque sauntered toward me. "Why should we believe you didn't have something to do with it?"

Rafferty aimed a dead-eyed stare at Torque. "Because forty-five minutes ago I was getting a speeding ticket from one of Augusta's finest."

"Speed trap on US 25?" Jordan asked.

Rafferty lifted his chin, then looked at me. "Is Simone here?"

I opened my mouth to says she was, but a bad feeling hit me. I knew when my instinct was trying to tell me something. "Let me check."

I turned on my heel and hurried to my room. The bathroom door was open, and I saw Simone's toiletry bag next to her suitcase by the wall. As quiet as the room was, I knew she wasn't there. The deadbolt on the side-door exit was unlocked. I shoved the door open and stopped four feet from the clubhouse. Everything was too quiet. The hot tub had a cover on top of it.

My gaze traveled down the slope of the back lawn. By the fire pit, something seemed wrong. I couldn't put my finger on it, but I ran down there. The mixture of dirt and trampled grass seemed more torn up than usual. I straightened and stared at the bikes and vehicles parked in the back. I recognized everyone's – even Rafferty's. My truck was still where I'd left it, so she hadn't driven off on her own.

My gut said someone had to have taken her. Anger surged through me, but I had to keep a lock on it. Hot-headed reactions weren't going to help me now. I hung my head as visions of her ran through my mind.

I focused on my boots, and noticed a small glass bottle. Only, when I stepped closer, I saw it wasn't a bottle, but a vial. The label indicated it was Ketamine. We dealt drugs, but we stayed away from things like Ketamine because it was so heavily regulated and getting access to it normally required breaking into a pharmacy or veterinarian's office. That didn't mean other members didn't use it every so often.

Yet, this vial still had a fair amount in it. Someone who took the risk of scoring Special K wouldn't lose it or drop it randomly.

But someone struggling with a woman like Simone probably wouldn't realize they'd dropped it.

I turned toward the clubhouse to yell for Torque just as Rafferty ran to me.

"You find any sign of her? Did she drive her SUV up today?"

I clenched my jaw and shook my head. "No, took my truck, which is still here. Go get Torque and Greco. I found this vial of Ketamine. Whoever took her, probably used this to knock her out."

Rafferty's eyes went wide. "What? She's pregnant... what the hell is that gonna do to her and the baby?"

"Fuck if I know. Go get Torque and Greco, tell Tie to review the security feeds, then you can check WebMD to find out."

If anything happened to Simone... I couldn't even stomach the thought. I'd find Knuckles, then kill all of his men in front of him. Then I'd burn him alive and feel no remorse.

I sure hoped my kid liked orange because they would have to visit me in jail.

Torque and Greco ran down the backyard with Jordan on their heels.

I started up the slope and met them half-way. "Jordan, you need to leave."

"No way. Where's Simone? You look like you're going to be sick or something."

My eyes cut to Torque and he nodded. "Jordan, you gotta leave. It's for your own good."

"If something happened to Simone, I want to help."

I tilted my head. "You want to go to jail?"

Confusion stole over him and he looked at me like I was crazy. "No. Why would—"

"Then *leave*."

The confusion cleared and I couldn't tell if his eyes held respect for me or a newfound understanding of my ruthlessness.

"I can keep my mouth shut," Jordan said.

Greco clapped a hand on Jordan's shoulder. "Damn right you can, but the three of us need to talk. How about you head out and see about your Mom. We'll call you as soon as we know something."

Jordan's lips set in an angry line. I expected him to argue more, but with a short head-shake, he turned and left.

"Corrupt Chrome has her," I said.

"We don't know that, brother," Torque said.

"Who else would take her?" Greco asked.

Torque looked from me to Greco. "She's the daughter of a Riot MC president. Could be one of their enemies, could be someone else looking to fuck with Steel."

Greco turned an outraged expression to me. "You hooked up with a bitch from the Riot?"

Before I realized what I was doing, I planted a fist in Greco's gut. "Don't ever fuckin' call her a bitch, motherfucker."

Torque pulled me away. "Calm your shit, Steel."

Greco kneeled over, panting for breath.

Rafferty ran to us. "Tie thinks Josie brought someone in here. He can't get a good angle on the name patch, but he's wearing a Corrupt Chrome cut. They knocked out the prospect at the gate, but kept outside the range of the cameras. Tie thinks Josie knew that nobody keeps an eye on the cameras on Saturday mornings, so nobody saw them."

Greco straightened. "Why are you trusting him? He isn't even a prospect."

I glared at Greco. "He saved our ass three weeks ago, and I need decent members in Jacksonville."

"Is he a Riot kid, too?"

If someone had said something like that when I was nineteen, I'd have lost my shit. Rafferty had one helluva poker face though. He also kept quiet.

"He is, but he's considering joining our Jax chapter if you don't do something stupid right now and fuck that up."

"Maybe we don't need a member like him. We hate the Riot MC."

I shook my head. "That's news to me, Greco. What the hell did they ever do?"

"Rancid died because of them, and we don't know where Snake went. If I had to guess the Riot killed him, and we never avenged his death."

"That happened years ago now, and considering how Rancid died, I'd say it makes shit even."

Greco opened his mouth to argue more – the man could argue about anything with anybody, but Rafferty spoke.

"Can we move on to finding Jade? If they gave her Ketamine, who the hell knows what else they'll do to her."

The back door to the clubhouse banged open and Tie joined our huddle. "Put in a call to Durham, he's managing Player's Palace today. Knuckles has been there since they opened the doors. Gives him a fuckin' alibi, I'm sure."

I nodded. "Is the cop that's on their payroll there, too?"

"How'd you know?" Tie asked.

"Fuck," I muttered, twisting my head to the side.

Rafferty pulled his phone from his pocket.

"Who are you calling?" I asked before he did anything else.

Rafferty looked up. "Her dad. They may have GPS tracking enabled on her cell. That'll tell us where she is – or are you certain they'd take her to their clubhouse? I thought they didn't have an Augusta chapter yet."

Shit. I didn't want him to call Volt, but there was no way around it. Rafferty was right. Corrupt Chrome didn't have a clubhouse to our knowledge and they could have taken her anywhere.

I nodded. "Do it."

Once Volt was on the line, Rafferty cut right to the heart of the matter. There was silence, then he said, "He's right here. You want to talk to him?"

Whatever Volt said, Rafferty closed his eyes and appeared to fight a smile. "I'll let him know." Rafferty ended the call and tucked his phone back in his pocket. "He's got to check the app, but he's pretty sure they still have that enabled. As long as the phone isn't dead or powered off, we should be able to locate the phone."

I nodded, while praying that neither Josie nor the Corrupt Chrome members were smart enough to check for her cell.

Rafferty cocked his head to the side. "He also said, he'd do his best hold Jackie back from scratching your eyes out when they got here."

I rolled my eyes and shook my head. "They're on their way?"

Rafferty shrugged. "I suspect they will be. Once he knows her location... and gets Jackie on his bike."

"Shit," I whispered.

<hr>

INSIDE THE CLUBHOUSE, RAFFERTY crossed his arms on his chest. "I get that the Devil Lancers don't give a damn about the law, but why aren't you reporting her missing?"

"They have a cop on their payroll, dumbass," Torque said.

Rafferty dipped his chin dramatically. "And this could help expose him for the corrupt cop he is."

"That's wishful thinking," Torque said.

Rafferty looked around the common room. "Where are all the other women?"

"Lookin' to get your rocks off already? Thought you cared about Jade," Greco said.

With a dry look, Rafferty said, "They might know where Josie is...or where she's been hanging out to meet a Corrupt Chrome member."

"Our strip club would be a start," Greco said.

I shook my head. "Josie doesn't dance. When would she have been at Player's? I think he might be on to something, though. Call the girls who aren't on shift. Hell, have Durham interrogate the girls who are on shift between their sets."

Rafferty's phone rang. "Hey, Volt."

His posture slumped and he looked away from me. Dread washed through me, and I rubbed the back of my neck.

I locked eyes with Rafferty when he said, "Yeah, they haven't reported her missing here because Corrupt Chrome has a cop on their payroll."

There was another pause, then Rafferty said, "Got it. Ride safe."

"He's not coming here, is he?" Greco asked.

My head swiveled toward Greco. "If you had a daughter go missing, wouldn't *you* ride out for her? Drop the fuckin' attitude or I'm gonna break your fuckin' jaw so you can't say shit for a goddamn month."

"Turning on your brothers isn't cool, Steel," Torque muttered.

"That bitch and any of those cocksuckers getting to her on our property isn't fucking *cool*, Tor." I looked at Rafferty. "What'd he say about the GPS?"

"She opened her own phone account over a year ago. Jackie's trying to persuade an employee at the carrier to make an exception, but without a warrant or a police officer there to corroborate her story, they won't help her."

I sighed. "And of course the fact we haven't reported her missing doesn't help either."

"Right."

"Why's he coming here, then?" Torque asked.

Rafferty appeared to be fighting for patience. "Because she's his daughter, but also because they have another set of people trying to hack into her phone and get at her location that way."

"That won't work," Greco muttered.

"It can't hurt to try," Rafferty countered.

My phone rang with Jordan's ring tone. "Yeah, Jordan."

"I have an idea."

I fought groaning. It wasn't that I didn't think he would have a good idea, it was that he'd never broken the law before. "Okay, what is it?"

"Well, first, when you told me to leave, I went inside the clubhouse and overheard Tie talking about Josie sneaking through the gate."

My head tilted backward. "Jordan—"

"What if I contact Josie?"

"And do what, son? She's involved with some seriously bad men who have it out for me and the entire club. They won't balk at harming you."

"I didn't say I wanted to bust in and save the day. I'm gonna make conversation with her. Figure out where she is."

I let out a slow exhale. "That would work except you're ten years younger than the men she likes and honestly, she's got her sights set on a hard-core biker."

He sighed. "Don't forget about me, Dad. I want to help. I… can see she means something to you, even if it doesn't make sense to me."

"Thanks, Jordan. I appreciate that. Not sure what brought this on, but thanks."

"Mom said some things. She was pissed that I went to talk to you at all before seeing her. I guess I'm finally opening my eyes."

"I'll let you know when we find her, Jordan."

Tie put a laptop on the table where we were seated. "I'm sending brothers out to find Mug, Flip, and Sledge. Since they spent so much time coming into Player's Palace the past few weeks, Croc took down their legal names from their IDs. We searched for property in those names. I'm gonna see about running a search on Knuckles."

"Why would they buy property in their own names?" Torque asked.

Tie held his hands up. "It might not be them – you're right. But it beats twiddling our thumbs."

"Any word from the girls?" I asked.

Tie wobbled his head "Not really. Kendall thought Josie had a small house, but that turned out to be wrong."

I looked at Greco. "Speaking of small houses, there's a place in Aragon Park—"

Torque slammed his fist on the table. "You're crazy, Steel. We can't take Farah because she hooks up with Knuckles every once in a while."

"I didn't say I was gonna take her. It's Saturday afternoon. That asshole thinks to visit her tonight, he's in for a surprise."

Greco stood. "On it."

My phone rang again, but with a standard ring tone. The number on the display wasn't one I knew. "Who's this?" I answered.

"I hear you got a bitch pregnant," Knuckles said.

"Where is she?" I demanded.

Knuckles spoke slowly. "She's safe. She's alive. And I'll let her go after you pay up."

"How much?" I asked.

"Well, that's a good question. I want the drug territory in all twenty of your cities *and* one-point-seven million."

I didn't have that even if I sold my house. The club had that, but I hadn't claimed her.

"And how am I supposed to give you that money? It's not like we have that kind of cash on hand."

"That isn't my problem, motherfucker. You got until tomorrow, but I'd hurry if I were you. I'm not feeding her, and babies need their food."

The phone beeped twice and I chucked it across the room. Croc was in its path, and he jumped in the air to catch it. He grinned at me. "Don't bust your phone, Prez. How's your woman gonna call you if it's busted?"

While Croc brought back my phone, Torque asked, "What'd he ask for?"

"All our drug territory – every city, *and* almost two million dollars."

"Almost?" Torque asked.

"One-point-seven million."

"That's a strange number."

"I thought so too, but didn't want to give him reason to raise the price. The asshole isn't even giving her any food. Sounded fucking proud of that shit."

"What happens if we don't pay?" Torque asked.

"What kind of question is that?" Rafferty asked.

Torque's eyes slid to Rafferty. "A good question. He doesn't have that kind of cash on hand. The club has the money, but he can't spend it just to get his girlfriend out of a jam."

I stared Torque down. "She's carrying my child. I fucking love her, Tor. She's more than just my girlfriend."

Torque withstood my stare. "She's also Volt's daughter. Let the Riot pick up the ransom. We're gonna be hurting if we give up drugs to Corrupt Chrome."

I shook my head. "That motherfucker is going to die."

Torque's eyes slid to Rafferty and back to me. "You don't mean that."

I looked Rafferty in the eyes. "Did you hear me say anything?"

His head moved in three slow shakes.

"I didn't hear a damn thing."

CHAPTER 24

WHO'S YOUR FAMILY?

SIMONE

THE DOOR SLAMMING BEHIND me scared me to death. Sledge and Mug focused on the doorway, and Mug appeared apprehensive.

A bear of a man lumbered into the room. His gaze met mine. Extreme unease coursed through me. Without casting my eyes at his patches, I knew. He had to be Knuckles.

His pale blue eyes scanned me up and down. The strawberry-blond goatee made him appear younger, but I put him in his late thirties. A nasty grin split his lips. Oral hygiene would do him good, based on his teeth.

"Don't she seem familiar?" Sledge asked much louder than necessary.

Knuckles turned to Sledge and shrugged. "Looks like any other brown-haired, brown-eyed snatch, except she's got a gut."

Josie sidled up to him. "Hey, Knuckles. Actually, she's pregnant."

Knuckles looked down his nose at her. "Why the fuck would Steel have a pregnant bitch around?" He looked at Mug. "You assholes grab the wrong bitch?"

Mug's eyes widened. "Josie said she's with Steel."

"You didn't verify that shit?" Knuckles demanded.

I couldn't help myself. "You could verify with me. And seeing as Josie messed with Steel's condoms, she oughta know I'm with him."

Josie glared at me and lied. "I didn't do that."

Knuckles narrowed his eyes at Josie. "Where's her phone?"

Sledge looked ashamed. "Oh hell."

Josie moved toward me.

Knuckles shouldered her out of his way. His breath hit me like a stale-coffee-scented gust in my face. "Where's your phone?"

To keep quiet or cooperate? I figured the former would have him pawing all over me going through both pockets, so I cooperated.

"My right front cargo pocket."

He pulled my phone free without feeling me up. Then he pointed the screen toward my face, which made the phone unlock. He turned it around and started scrolling. I didn't know what he was looking at and I struggled against yelling at him.

If he was checking my contacts, he probably wouldn't learn much without calling people since I stuck to generic names like Mom, Dad, and Lex for Alexandra. If he opened my photos though...it would be another story.

"Why are there pictures of Riot MC brothers on your phone?"

By now, I suspected Steel had to know I was missing.

This place was a hovel. Not a clubhouse. I wasn't conscious when they brought me in here, but the inside felt like a ramshackle building with a bathroom. In a place like this, I had no clue how Steel would know where to find me.

"Answer me!" Knuckles thundered.

"I have family in that club," I semi-lied.

"Who's your family?" Mug asked.

Sledge wandered toward me. "That's what it is." He stared at me, squinted, then snapped his fingers. "You look like one of the old ladies. She's property of a president. Can't fucking remember which one."

Knuckles wrapped his calloused fingers around my lower jaw and squeezed. "Who are you related to?"

Part of me wanted to keep that secret, but I didn't know if Steel was searching for me. Getting the Riot MC involved might be my best shot at getting help.

My stomach roiled with nausea. This nausea had an edge to it that felt like more than just morning sickness. I had no idea what Special K would do to my baby, but the sooner I got to a hospital, the better. Tears threatened as I imagined all the awful things that could happen to my peanut. I wouldn't cry in front of these assholes.

"My dad's the Jacksonville president."

"Does he know you're pregnant?" Josie asked.

I nodded.

Knuckles smiled and set my phone on a nearby card table. He pulled out his phone. It wasn't in a protective case, and I'd never been so happy to see an Apple icon. As long as Knuckles had his Bluetooth enabled, my AirTag would send a signal to my network... but who knew how tech savvy Knuckles was?

He tapped his phone screen, and put it to his ear. After a moment, he said, "I hear you got a bitch pregnant."

I closed my eyes and gritted my teeth as I listened to his demands. When he mentioned not feeding me and how babies needed their food, my eyes flew open. Knuckles had his back to me, but Mug noticed my alarm and chuckled.

Knuckles hung up on Steel, and switched back to my phone. He had to point it at me to unlock it again. After tapping the screen a few times, he held it flat. Then, I heard a phone ringing over the speaker as he paced to the other side of the small room.

"Simone! Where are you?" Dad demanded. The sheer worry in his voice wrenched my heart.

"Thought your name was Jade," Mug said.

"Did your mother name you Mug?" I muttered.

Mug stepped toward me. "Bitch, I oughta backhand you."

Knuckles turned and glared at Mug, but spoke into the phone. "She ain't gonna tell you that, Volt. You shoulda taught her how to take care of herself."

"Let her go," Dad said, his voice lethal.

"Oh, I'll let her go... after Steel pays and *you* pay, too."

Dad failed to hide his sigh. "How much?"

"Since she's pregnant, I figure you can pay double. Three and a half million."

"That kind of cash takes time."

"Too bad," Knuckles said.

"She's pregnant. Whatever you used to attack her... she needs a doctor."

Knuckles aimed a lascivious grin at me. "Good point. We have a club doctor, he'll love examining her."

"At a hospital, motherfucker!" Dad yelled.

"Time's wasting, Volt. Better call your mother chapter and your Vegas brothers to get you some money."

My stomach had lurched at how much he'd asked for from Steel. Demanding twice as much from Dad, I hated this man anew.

He ended the call and messed with my phone some more. "Need to send some of these pics to Pump. This friend of yours can't be more than eighteen."

I fought against an eye roll and prayed he didn't do that. My hunch was that he was looking at pictures of Jasmine, though it could have been Alexandra since she was a young-looking twenty. Either way, neither one of them deserved to be on the radar of an asshole like Pump.

A metalic-sounding pop from outside captured everyone's attention.

Knuckles widened his eyes at Mug. "Were you followed?"

Mug looked affronted. "No. Not a damn person knew we were there besides the moron prospect at their gate. I knocked him out cold. We were in and out."

Knuckles narrowed his eyes. "You got in and out of their clubhouse without being seen?"

A coy smile quirked Josie's lips. "She came outside and made it so much easier for us."

In hindsight, I should have stayed in Steel's room eavesdropping on him and Jordan.

No, I couldn't blame myself like that.

I had every right to walk down to that fire pit. Josie and Mug never should have been able to get into the compound the way they did.

Knuckles jerked his head to the side. "Go check out that noise. I don't trust it."

Mug shook his head. "Nobody followed us, but I'll go. Probably the sun beating on that cheap metal siding making it pop."

"Check it anyway," Sledge muttered.

Mug trudged out.

Knuckles glared at Josie. "Leave. You served your purpose."

Surprise rushed over her expression. "But I haven't been paid—"

He leaned toward her. "Go, or you won't get paid shit."

She glowered at him, then calmed herself, turned on her heel, and left.

Once the door closed behind her, Knuckles noticed the cocaine on the card table. "Dammit! You assholes are sampling the product again. Got enough fuckin' problems with the cartel breathing down my neck. I don't need y'all making it worse."

Sledge stood. "Still don't think Steel's gonna give up shit. Why should we wait? Kill this bitch, and go after all the Devil Lancers. Be done with it."

With a glower, Knuckles shook his head. "When are we gonna be in a position to extort money out of two fucking clubs again?"

I watched Sledge pace the small room. "Right. Forgot about that."

Knuckles crossed his arms. "You stop snorting our blow, you won't forget shit." He crossed to a small window and pulled the ratty curtain to the side. "Where the hell is Mug?"

It had been less than five minutes since Mug left. I didn't think he had anything to worry about. The idea that someone could be here to save me was wishful thinking.

Those odds were ever *not* in my favor.

Being a stubborn, independent twenty-something, I'd wanted a top-of-the-line smartphone and took advantage of a deal exclusive to new customers. It was a double win for me. Cut my dependency on my parents and it got me a fabulous phone. And my parents no longer had the ability to locate my phone by GPS

That would have come in handy right about now.

The keys in my pocket came to mind, but no way would Dad think to involve Alexandra or Jasmine in this. They were the only two people who knew about my keychain. If only Rafferty had come up this trip. He might know about the Apple AirTag on my keys. And no doubt, Raff would call Alexandra to ask her if she had any ideas on how to find me, but Steel hadn't mentioned anything about Rafferty yesterday or today.

I fought against a sigh because I was gonna be stuck here for a long while. I needed to think about anything *except* how hungry I was.

CHAPTER 25

BRIGHT IDEAS

STEEL

TORQUE'S CELL RANG. "GRECO, you good?" He stared at me and arched his brows. "You believe Farah? Why would he tell her that? She's trying to get rid of you."

I moved closer to him during another pause.

Torque squinted. "No street number for this place?" After another pause, he said, "I don't care. You stay with Farah until we have someone drive by the area."

He ended the call. Before Torque could update me, I heard Rafferty talking. His loud, irritated tone put me on alert. The way he let the shit that Greco and Torque gave him slide off him, I didn't believe there were many people who could annoy him.

"Lex, she's missing and I need to know if you can help me. Jasmine mentioned Simone having a tracker for her keys because she kept misplacing them. I searched Simone's purse and her keys are gone. If she's got them with her, we might be able to find her... but only if she shared that kind of info with you."

He closed his eyes and exhaled through his nose. When he opened his eyes, they went wide. "Don't worry about the Devil Lancers. Get the fuckin' password."

Torque sidled up to me. "What the hell's a password gonna do for us?"

"Shut it," I clipped out. My gut filled with low-level hope that this was our break.

Rafferty had an iPad in front of him. He tapped at the screen. "Yeah, Lex. I'm in Augusta now, but I need the passcode to her iPad before I can try to log in." He nodded. "Great. I'll call you—"

He paused. I hated not knowing what was being said, but I knew better than to interrupt right now.

"Lex, I'm not even sure if this will work. Once we know more, I'll text you."

He ended the call.

Torque tipped his head toward the tablet. "What the hell is that?"

Rafferty aimed a calm expression at Torque. "Her iPad. She has one of those AirTags. Lex verified it's on her keys. She kept misplacing them after she got pregnant."

"That helps us how?" Torque asked.

Rafferty gave a small nod. "If there are any other Apple devices with Bluetooth enabled near her keys, we can log into her 'Find My' network and locate them."

"Which could be out back," Torque muttered.

"Those keys are in her pocket," I said, my relief building.

But I'd only be fully relieved when she was out of harm's way and I'd ended Knuckles once and for all.

"How do you know?" Torque asked.

My eyes slid to him. "I watched her put them in her pocket when we got here. Not five minutes after we hit my room, you pounded on my door because Jordan was here. If Rafferty didn't find her keys in her purse, then I'm sure they're still in her pocket."

Torque nodded. "All right. Farah told Greco that if he's looking for Knuckles, he should try a place near the cemetery in Old Town. She didn't have a street address. Supposedly they use some shotgun house for interrogations, though I don't trust a damn thing that bitch tells us."

My head reared back and I recalled all of Torque's questions to Greco. I'd have asked the same things and been twice as skeptical.

"Yeah, send a prospect in a cage. I don't want a bike roaring through that area."

Rafferty shook his head. "That's a great plan, but if she didn't give an address, what's the prospect looking for? You think Knuckles would leave his bike visible from the street? I don't know Old Town like you two do, but I'm guessing it isn't an area where there's a neighborhood watch."

I tipped my head at Rafferty. "You're right, but we can tell the prospect to keep an eye out for Josie's car and Mug's chopper."

"Done," Torque said.

Rafferty tapped at the screen and his lips tipped up. "The password worked."

I moved to look over his shoulder, then thought better of it and paced to the bat rack. I grabbed one and swung it through the air. The thought of bashing Knuckles in the head appealed to me, but even that seemed too merciful for him.

"Been a long time since I saw that look on your face," Torque said.

"What look is that?" I asked.

He grinned. "You're gonna bring the pain to somebody."

I swung the bat again. Its unique sound filled the room. I fucking loved hearing that.

Yeah, there was going to be pain all right.

Rafferty looked up from the tablet. "The house Greco mentioned is near a cemetery, right?"

I crossed the room and looked at the map he had on display. It had been years since I last rode down Taylor Street, but I recalled a line of shotgun houses were there.

I nodded at Torque. "Seems Farah told Greco the truth."

"We riding out at dark?" Torque asked.

I snapped my gaze to him. "He isn't feeding her, Tor. We have to get her out of there."

"How do you plan to do that in broad daylight?" Rafferty asked.

Torque jerked his head toward my room. "Let's discuss this with Tie, Nelson, and with Greco on the phone."

I shook my head. "I know what you're trying to do, Tor, but Rafferty isn't going to turn on us. Not with Jade in the crossfire."

Torque sighed. "You're taking a lot of risks here, brother."

My brows shot up in question. "If it were your old lady Shelly, wouldn't you do the same?"

"Maybe... probably."

"That's cold," Rafferty muttered.

Torque's gaze snapped to Rafferty. "It's not your business."

My phone rang with a ring tone for Jeremiah. "Whatever you want, Jeremiah, I don't have time."

I could hear the smarmy smile in his tone. "Has to do with Corrupt Chrome MC."

"What do you have?" I asked in a neutral tone.

"Corrupt Chrome's supplier is after the cartel you use."

That had to be the biggest problem with drugs. We relied on a supplier and they set the base prices.

"Why are you telling me this?" I asked.

"Their cartel is the reason Corrupt Chrome is pushing the Lancers out of the market."

"We aren't out of the market."

He chuckled. "Not yet. That info I gave you last week changed. Knuckles has to meet with his supplier at ten tonight down by the river. I hear this cartel guy's gone rogue. Take him out, and Corrupt Chrome doesn't have supply to sell any more."

Traces of a plan formed in my mind.

"Thanks, Jeremiah."

"Thanks? I wouldn't thank me. Manuel – he's the cartel contact – he carves up people who double-cross him. You'll be lucky if you don't end up floating in the Savannah River if you're planning to take on these assholes."

I smiled. "Right now, that's a risk I have to take."

Nelson wandered behind the bar, folded his arms, and leaned his weight onto his arms resting on the bar.

Torque raised his brows as I tucked my phone in my back pocket. "What did he want?"

"Says the supplier for Corrupt Chrome has gone rogue. Knuckles is supposed to be a meet him tonight by the river." I jerked my head toward the iPad. "Taylor Street isn't too far from the river."

"We need to wait until night," Torque said.

"No. I've got to get her out of there. Then Knuckles is a fucking dead man. I don't care about the risk."

"You're going to kill him in cold blood?" Rafferty asked.

I shrugged. "He fucked with the woman I love. Hell, he fucked with two people I love even if I haven't met that baby yet. I know what I'm about to do is wrong, but I'm doing it for the right reasons."

"Your reasons," Rafferty countered.

I twisted a hand up. "Men like Knuckles can't just barge in and throw their weight around because they got involved with a bad cartel. You got a decision to make, Rafferty. If living by our code bothers you, then you're cut out more for the Riot than the Devil Lancers."

"It's too soon to head over there, Steel. Your woman can survive a skipped meal," Nelson said, sipping some water.

The glare I aimed at him should have incinerated him.

He straightened and held his hands up in surrender. "I know she's pregnant, but Torque's right. We have to be smart. Won't be cool if you're six feet under when she has the baby."

"Or in prison," Torque muttered.

I blew out a breath. "Right."

"You don't know who else is there. I'm not a member, let me see what I can find out," Rafferty suggested.

Nelson's eyes widened and he looked impressed. Torque tipped his head to the side, a ghost of a smile playing at his lips.

I leveled a stern gaze at Rafferty. "Be very damned careful."

He stood. "Goes without saying. Never been to this 'hood. Seeing as the place backs up to a cemetery, I shouldn't be spotted."

"Make sure you aren't," I said.

Torque stared at the door after Rafferty left. "He might have potential."

I shook my head. "The cemetery was part of my plan, too. No question he has what it takes to prospect with us."

Torque nodded. "I'll have to ignore him being a Riot kid."

I arched a brow. "Or admit that it's the Riot that makes him worthy."

Torque let that go. "What about the other chapters? Vegas is getting hit pretty hard."

I sighed. "Yeah, Shark and I had a talk last week about the ways Corrupt Chrome is causing them problems. Tell him to light a fire."

Torque pulled out his phone. "Raleigh and Miami, too?"

"No. More than one Corrupt Chrome clubhouse getting hit like that won't fly and would get us more attention."

Twenty minutes later, Nelson looked around at the bar. "What did you do with the Ketamine?"

My eyes locked with Torque's. "Did Greco have it?" He was one of the brothers who would use Special K if it was on offer.

Torque shook his head. "I saw it here while the kid messed with the iPad."

"Fuck," I hissed, grabbing my phone to text Rafferty.

> **I know what you took. Don't use it.**

He responded ten minutes later.

> **No idea what you're talking about.**

> **No. You don't know what you're doing.**

He sent back a smiling devil emoji.

"Goddammit!" I shoved my phone in my back pocket. "I'm going to follow him."

"Steel, if he gets nabbed with the Special K, that's his problem," Torque said.

I glared at Torque. "If he gets found dragging Josie or Mug into the cemetery or whatever hair-brained scheme he has in mind, they'll figure out Simone's connection to him."

Nelson stood. "You're gonna blow the opportunity to take out Knuckles. I'll go."

I stared at him for a long moment. That would work better all around. "Thanks, brother."

I sent another text to Rafferty.

Nelson is joining you.

He responded faster than before, and I suspected he was at the cemetery already.

Cool.

SHELLY EDGED INTO THE room, almost on tiptoes. "You need to eat something, Steel."

I shook my head. "Not a chance I can eat while she's out there... and being starved by that fucking sick bastard."

Her posture slumped, she bit her lower lip, and nodded. "I'm sorry you're going through this, Steel. You'll get her back though. I know you will."

"Thanks, Shell," I said, wishing I had the same confidence she did.

My phone vibrated with a text from Nelson.

Got a status update if you got time.

I called him and he answered immediately.

"Yo, they sent Josie away a few minutes ago. Knuckles, Mug, and Sledge are inside, though Rafferty says Mug did a walk-around the outside of the house just before she left."

If I showed up, there would be three of us against three of them. The problem was that Knuckles would hurt Simone at the first chance. A better option would be if we could get Knuckles in the house alone, but the only time he might be alone would be when he left for his meeting at ten.

Nelson kept talking. "Rafferty suggested drawing Mug outside again by throwing something at the house, but I think that's too risky. We'd have to knock him out and drag him back here to the cemetery. At worst, Sledge or Knuckles would catch us. *At best*, they'd figure something's up when he doesn't come back."

I nodded. "Yeah, you're right, but I like where his head is at. We'll hold that for later, if it's necessary. I'm sending Russ and a prospect to Josie's place, she's a loose end."

"Understood, Prez. I'll text if anything changes."

I ended the call and gave Torque the gist.

A prospect barged through the front door. "There are two Riot members out front. You want me to let them through?"

"Is one of them Volt?" I asked.

"Blood and Cal," the prospect said.

After a deep breath, I nodded. "Let 'em through."

Outside, the wind had picked up and the cloud cover had increased. Part of me wanted the clouds to dump the rain and get it over with, but the other part of me wanted the rain to hit at night, when I planned to kill Knuckles. It rankled that he wouldn't die a slow and torturous death, but I needed Simone back.

Blood and Cal trudged toward the clubhouse. Torque sauntered out and joined me.

"Why the hell are you here?" I asked when they were four feet away.

Blood yanked his sunglasses off. "Knuckles wants his fuckin' money... it's not something we can do through a wire transfer. That kind of cash requires security and multiple duffel bags."

"You brought the cash?" Torque asked.

"Fuck, *no*," Blood said. "But I brought all the tools to kill these assholes and hide their fuckin' bodies."

"Or not," I said.

Both men showed their surprise at my words.

"You want to go down for this shit?" Cal asked.

I shook my head. "Knuckles has a meet scheduled with his cartel contact. A source tells me that contact has gone rogue, though I'm not inclined to believe that yet."

Cal nodded. "Yeah, great way to set you up. You're keyed up to deal with Knuckles and instead that cartel contact takes you out."

This shit was exhausting. Maybe Volt had been right. Going legit looked better and better.

No. I had to see this shit through.

"Where is Volt?" I asked.

"Forty-five minutes behind us or so. He's not on his bike and he had to pick up Jackie," Blood said.

"I'm not sure you should be here," Torque said.

Blood stood straighter. "You can't hold us back. Watched Simone grow up, love her like she's my own. Not a fucking chance we aren't gonna get her out of this shit."

I stepped closer to Blood. "I'm getting her out of there."

Blood tilted his head. "Why does it sound like you know where she is? And you're sittin' around here doing fuck-all about it?"

I clenched my fists. "Ten minutes ago, I learned there are three men in the shotgun house with her, and they just let the woman leave who helped abduct her."

"Loose end," Cal muttered.

Blood jerked his head toward Cal. "Back to what he asked, you're gonna go down for Knuckles getting killed?"

I shook my head. "If the cartel contact is rogue, then I intend to make it look like he and Knuckles got into an altercation and they both shot each other."

Cal nodded. "That could work... assuming you know where this meet is going down."

"Where is Simone during all this?" Blood asked.

"Probably being watched by Sledge or Mug based on what we got from Nelson and Rafferty."

Cal narrowed his eyes. "Rafferty? You aren't talking about Rafferty Rolland, are you?"

"Taking our girl isn't enough for you?" Blood asked.

I locked eyes with Blood. "He was there after Scar and Pump made their approach in the store. Liked how he handled those assholes. It isn't my fault you haven't approved him as a prospect. I'm leaving the decision to him."

Cal crossed his arms over his barrel chest. "I know someone at the DEA. This might go against your grain, but why don't we just call them in and get her out."

Torque matched Cal's body language. "Because Sledge, their VP, is known for using their blow and he gets trigger-happy when he does. You send in the DEA or any other cops, that asshole's gonna kill Simone."

I nodded once. "The moment Knuckles leaves for his meet, we'll draw out Mug and Sledge. Hell, the two of you showing up with the cash could work as the perfect distraction. Then we'll get Simone out and burn those assholes alive."

"Surprised you don't want to do the same thing to Knuckles," Blood said.

I ground my molars together then forced myself to relax. "I do, but that draws too many questions. We aren't the only ones who know that Sledge likes to get high. Mug isn't always the sharpest tool in the shed. Them setting the place on fire isn't out of the question."

Cal stared across the yard for a beat. "So, these two coincidentally burn the house down while Knuckles gets whacked by a cartel member... who also gets killed. Have I got your plan straight?"

I nodded.

Skepticism shone from Blood's brown eyes. "Corrupt Chrome may not have an Augusta chapter, but sure as hell there's more than just the three of them in town to cause you problems."

Torque unfolded his arms and put his hands in his pockets. "You're right. We don't know where their road captain is in this, and Pump and Scar are in town from Jacksonville. All three of them need to be dealt with, too."

I angled my head toward Torque. "Call Durham. Ask him if any of those three are at Player's Palace."

Torque pointed a finger gun at me. "You're probably right." He arched his brows. "Lap dance time?"

I twisted my hands up. "As long as their police buddy isn't there, yeah."

"What's that all about?" Blood asked.

Before I could answer, a GMC Acadia towing a bike on a small trailer pulled up to the gate with Volt behind the wheel. Jackie sat in the passenger seat, looking pale and worried.

"Let him through," I yelled to the prospect.

"Damn. I had hoped he'd talk Jackie into staying home," Cal muttered.

"ARE WE LETTING THEM into our clubhouse?" Torque asked.

Cal and Blood were forty yards away, where Volt had parked his SUV. They were giving him and Jackie a run-down of what we'd discussed so far, if I had to guess.

I dragged a hand down my face. "If they can't find a hotel room, at least one of them will have to sleep here tonight while the others stay at my place."

Torque blew out a sigh that sounded like a growl. "Never fuckin' thought I'd see the day we let Riot brothers into our clubhouse."

"Me, neither, Tor."

Volt gave Blood a curt nod, focused on me, and stalked my way. I knew how pissed I'd be if something happened to Jordan. The idea of something happening to a daughter would amp up my anger exponentially.

Fuck.

He stopped a foot from me with his feet planted wide. His anger wasn't apparent until he spoke in a bristling tone. "You said she wasn't in danger."

With a slow nod, I said, "I didn't know one of the women—"

Volt's fist connected with my cheekbone. Even if I'd seen it coming, I wouldn't have ducked his punch. I deserved that and more.

Torque stepped between us. "All right, asshole. You got your fuckin' punch in, but that shit won't help us get your daughter back."

Volt's eyes burned at Torque. "From what they tell me, you assholes know where she is and aren't already on the move. That's fuckin' bull-shit."

I rubbed my cheek. "Let's go inside. You got any damned bright ideas, you can share them."

CHAPTER 26

BEEN BETTER

SIMONE

"BET SHE'S OVER THERE praying. She's had her eyes closed a long-ass time," Mug said.

My eyes had been closed for a long time, but not because I was praying... more because I was doing my best to tune out their lewd conversations about a woman named Farah, and I couldn't stomach watching them sitting around eating. Not because it was making me hungry, but because they were so damned disgusting, chewing with their mouths open.

Bleh.

They'd ordered a pizza, which was delivered ten minutes ago. Little did they know, pizza was the only kind of food I wasn't craving these days – besides coffee. Pizza gave me heartburn now that I was pregnant. My doctor assured me that would pass once the baby was born.

Hopefully we'd make it out of this alive.

Once I knew my peanut was healthy and safe, I was going to find out if we were having a boy or a girl.

Surprises be damned.

"She needs to be praying her daddy and Steel come up with the fuckin' money. Either of them stiff me, and she's dead," Knuckles said.

"Thought you told Volt, you'd get Doc here to examine her," Sledge said.

Knuckles shook his head. "He's back in Savannah."

"I can examine her, since you said Farah's off-limits even though you're through with her," Mug said.

I willed myself not to frown or grimace as his words made my stomach roil. The light in the room changed and I opened my eyes.

Sledge had moved to the small window and closed the ratty curtains. "Fuckin' sun is finally setting."

If the sun was setting, then it had to be closing in on seven-thirty. Thinking about the time made my stomach growl.

I couldn't believe I'd been gone for at least eight hours. Steel knew I was gone... what was the hold-up? Hell, Dad knew I'd been taken, but he had a four-hour drive.

"You want me to take your back when you meet Manuel?" Sledge asked.

Knuckles aimed a sour look at Mug. "No. Can't trust this fucker with her any more than I can trust you with the blow."

Well, that was nice of him... sort of.

"You should have somebody at your back," Sledge said.

Knuckles shot an annoyed look at Sledge. "You're right, and Flip's gonna do that for me. Spoke to him before I got here. He's at the strip club and he's gonna meet me by the river. Make sure Manuel doesn't have a bunch of men with him."

My phone rang and I jolted.

Knuckles grinned. "Looks like Daddy wants a chat." He picked up my phone. "Hello, Volt. Got my cash?"

He hadn't put it on speaker, and I wished I could hear what Dad had to say. The way Knuckles cocked his head to the side, I knew he didn't trust Dad.

"You got over three million that fast? Like you said, that kind of money can't be wired, and it's only been six hours since I called you."

Knuckles shook his head. "It'll have to be at midnight."

The thought of being here for another four hours didn't make me happy, but at least I knew Dad was on the way.

Knuckles paused.

"You want to meet at eleven, well, too fuckin' bad. If you want your daughter back in one piece, we do this shit my way."

I hoped Dad wasn't fucking with Knuckles because putting together a million dollars was hard. Three-point-five times as much?

Yeah, that didn't happen in a day's time.

Sledge shook his head. "They can't have the cash already."

Knuckles shrugged. "He says their strip club had cash on hand and so did a bunch of brothers. Either way, we're gonna find out."

"I think we should call Steel. Makes no sense that the Riot can get twice as much money together and we haven't heard shit from him," Mug said, staring at me.

He hadn't made me that nervous when Josie was here. But now, his undivided attention creeped me the fuck out.

Knuckles nodded. "Putting the pressure on the Pussy Lancers is always fun."

I despised listening to him call Steel's club names.

For some reason, this call he put on speaker phone.

Steel's voice filled the room. "What do you want Knuckles?"

Knuckles shook his head. "That's no way to talk to me – unless you don't care about your woman."

"Goddammit, I'm getting your money together as we speak," he said.

"Good. Have it by midnight. The Riot was able to get their cash together. You should be able to do the same."

Steel let out a growly sigh. "Fuckin' hell, Knuckles. This is between me and you, let Simone go."

Knuckles laughed. "You aren't calling the shots here, asshole. Get the fuckin' money and meet me at the Riverfront at midnight."

"Are you gonna have Simone there? Put her on the line. I want proof she's all right."

Knuckles hesitated, then crossed the room and put the phone near my chin.

"Hi, honey," I said, wishing Knuckles, Sledge, and Mug weren't in the room.

"Goddammit," Steel breathed out. "Are you okay?"

My lips tipped up. "Been better."

"Hang tight, Simone."

"That's enough. Have my money at midnight, or Simone pays the price," Knuckles said, stalking to the other side of the room and tucking his phone in his back pocket.

Part of me wondered if I was better off not knowing *how* I would pay the price, but the other part of me started listing all the ways he could make me suffer.

My stomach growled again.

Unfortunately, Mug heard it and laughed. "Should I offer her some crumbs?"

Knuckles glowered at him. "No. Ignore her, and stop staring, for fuck's sake." He pulled his cell from his back pocket just before it rang. "Manuel, is there a problem?"

Dread welled in my belly when suddenly Knuckles stood straighter. He arched his back and I heard a pop and realized I'd worried for nothing.

"Yes, we have a truck, our road captain is driving it in for the meet."

He held the phone to his ear for a long moment, then I heard the faint double beep. Holding the phone away from his face, he frowned. "That asshole. Always has to have the last word."

I suspected Knuckles was the exact same way.

Sledge and Mug shared a look that said I was right.

CHAPTER 27

NOT TO BE TRUSTED RIGHT NOW

STEEL

HEARING SIMONE'S SOFT 'HEY, honey,' gutted me. Hell, it gutted Volt and Jackie, too. I thought Jackie would lose her shit and give it away that we were all in the same room, but she kept quiet.

I hated that Knuckles had the upper hand in setting the meet times.

Torque's cell rang. "Durham, whatchugot?"

His eyes widened and a huge smile spread across his face. "Fuck, yeah! That's great news!"

Volt's dead-eyed stare was laced with cynicism.

I twisted my hands up at Torque.

He lowered his phone and put it on speaker. "Kendall, sweetheart. Tell Steel all that for us."

"Durham had me give a private lap dance to a man named Flip. He asked how my day was going, and I said fine except for the asshole who parked a huge box truck behind my car in the parking lot. I'd wanted to grab lunch on my break, and I couldn't because of it."

"Yeah," I drawled, not seeing the connection.

"He apologized because he said he drove that huge truck and needed to keep it out of sight from the main road."

Torque grinned. "They got a shipment... how else are they gonna haul that shit?"

I nodded. "Where is Flip now, Kendall?"

Durham answered. "I led him to another room like you instructed earlier."

He'd said that to keep Kendall from knowing exactly what was going on. "Good man. What about his buddies?"

Kendall answered. "Pump and Scar got a dance from Tessa. Before I led Flip to the back, I heard their *other friend* say he had to leave… something about 'the less he knew the better.'"

"Kendall, you deserve a bonus," Torque said.

"Promises, promises," she muttered.

"This time he means it," Durham said. "Go get ready for your next set."

We heard the phone jostle and then Durham's voice was no longer on speaker. "I got those assholes tied up in the back, but I'd rather get them inside that box truck, Prez."

I nodded. "Yeah, but you're better off with them in the back. Inside that truck, they could bang around and get attention before we're ready to move."

Volt waved a hand over the bar where we were seated. "I hate to interrupt, but how is this good news?"

I held a finger up. "I'll answer in a minute. Durham, you got your CDL still, right?"

"Sure do."

Torque tapped the bar with his finger. "If Croc's there, he's closing. You gotta drive that truck down to the river at ten."

I lifted my chin. "But keep close tabs on their phones. I don't know if Knuckles or one of his men are checking in with them regularly. If so, text back, don't answer any calls."

"Got it, Prez."

Torque grabbed his phone off the bar.

I turned to Volt. "That's great news because we'll have three fewer Chrome members to deal with, and it'll make it easier to get the drop on Knuckles if my men are posing as his men."

"You're gonna hold them at your strip club the whole time?" Blood asked.

"He doesn't need to tell you what he's gonna do with them," Torque said.

Volt leveled a vicious glare on Torque. "Those last two assholes threatened her at a Target. They deserve vengeance as much as Knuckles."

I nodded. "I agree. They'll get theirs."

Volt caught my gaze. "I'm here to help. We won't sell you out. Hell, we'd be accessories, or accomplices, depending. I'd rather make those assholes fuckin' pay."

Torque shrugged at me. "If you trust them, then I trust 'em."

"As much as I'd love for them to suffer, it would be better if we slit their throats in the box truck. If this is supposed to be a drug shipment gone wrong, having three Corrupt Chrome members dead in the truck makes it more believable."

"Jesus, this is complex," Cal said.

"You're right," I said. "I'd much rather storm the house and get my woman out, but I have to end Knuckles, then go get her."

"You could divide and conquer," Cal said.

"Would you let someone else save your woman?" I asked.

"I wasn't given a choice," he said. From his dry, disappointed tone, I could tell it still bothered him.

"I'm getting her out," I said, my eyes landing on Volt.

He nodded. "That's fine, but I'm gonna be right there." He looked to Jackie. "You're gonna have to stay here."

I shook my head. "No. I'd rather have her go to my place. I can give you directions if you want to drive there yourself, or I'll have Torque's old lady take you, which would be better since she's got the code to get inside."

Jackie shook her head. "Not a damned chance. The moment you save her, she needs to go to a hospital and have that baby checked out. I'll be at the nearest hospital."

Blood dipped his chin. "You were planning to have her checked out at your house, weren't you?"

I twisted my hands up. "A pregnant woman who says she was drugged garners not only the attention of the cops, but social workers and others. We don't need that. We need to know the baby's okay, and that she's okay."

Jackie's shoulders slumped and she turned her head to the side. "Shit. You're right."

"And seeing as the asshole hasn't fed her all day, I thought you would know what kinds of food will help her feel better," I said.

Jackie put her fist on her mouth and twisted her head for a moment, then she looked at Volt. "I don't give a shit, Volt. I want this asshole's balls cut off. Starving a pregnant woman..."

I caught Jackie's gaze. "Do you want to drive to my place... or would you like Shelly to—"

"I think Shelly should take me. I'm not to be trusted right now, because raining on your parade sounds like a far better plan."

Torque stood. "Follow me, then. I'll introduce you so you and Shell can get on your way."

"NOW THAT YOU CONVINCED Jackie to leave, what's next? Raid your arsenal?" Cal asked.

"You didn't bring your own guns?" Torque asked as he came back into the room.

Cal nodded. "Yeah, but something tells me we need to be well fuckin' prepared for these assholes. Cartels don't fuck around – with or without a rogue leader."

I stood. "Yeah. We don't have a lot of time, an hour and a half goes quick, especially since we need to load three bikes onto a box truck."

"What about Rafferty? You sending him back here?" Blood asked.

I arched my brows. "He's watching the house where Simone is. Hell, he's the reason we found her at all. Him and Alexandra. Another brother is with him—"

"They could be spotted," Cal said.

My lips tipped up. "Not likely, seeing as they're in a cemetery."

Cal shook his head. "Great... a cemetery."

"This way to the guns and ammo, boys," Torque said, leading the way out the back door.

Cal and Blood followed Torque.

Volt stopped me in the common room. "I'm not going to keep you from getting to Simone, but be reasonable. For all you know, Knuckles is going to have someone watching her in that house. If he doesn't check in or give some signal, she could end up hurt worse than she already is. She has to be rescued while Knuckles is at the river."

I bit my lip. What did I want more: her safety or revenge?

It was a no-brainer.

"Fine. I'll have Torque take point on ambushing Knuckles and Manuel. You and I can rescue her from that house."

———

I KEPT MY EYES on the speedometer, not letting it go over thirty on this residential road. When I'd looked at the map earlier, it had slipped my mind that this cemetery was less than a mile from the Richmond County Sheriff's Office.

Gravel crunched under the tires as I turned into the narrow drive of the cemetery. I navigated the winding drive until we were on the southern side of the property which would put us behind the house. Once I pulled the truck to a stop, I caught the gleam of Rafferty's Harley and Nelson's Triumph.

Volt and I made little noise as we walked across the grass.

When we were eight feet away, Nelson straightened from a crouch and gave me a chin lift. "Prez."

Rafferty turned around, holding a pair of binoculars. "Volt."

Volt dipped his chin and spoke in a low voice. "Later, we're gonna have words."

Rafferty shrugged one shoulder and tilted his head to the side like it didn't matter to him. Anyone would see through that show of bravado, though. Especially a man like Volt.

"Knuckles hasn't left yet," Nelson said.

I nodded and examined the fence. It was iron bars, and I didn't like the idea of trying to scale it.

Nelson followed my gaze. "Don't worry. There's a huge gap twenty feet away. Looks like the fence was damaged in that tornado that tore through here last fall."

"Good." I caught Rafferty's gaze. "Have you been able to see anything with the binoculars?"

Rafferty shook his head. "Only when Mug did his walk-around and Josie left. They got curtains covering all the windows."

I itched to make an approach and kill Knuckles now, but that would draw too much blow-back on the club. It took all my self-control to let this plan play out.

From the direction of the house, someone yelled, "Did this shit already, you're paranoid, man."

Rafferty turned back to the house and raised the binoculars to his eyes.

"Are they night-vision?" I whispered to Nelson.

He nodded. "Smart, right?"

"It's Mug again," Rafferty said in a low voice.

I sidled up to Rafferty and he handed me the binoculars. Mug trudged around the house so fast, he wasn't cataloging anything as he went.

Handing the binoculars back to Rafferty, I looked over my shoulder at Volt. "He half-assed it. Once he's back inside, we should get in position to find a decent place to break inside."

The sound of a motorcycle starting filled the air. I pulled my cell from my back pocket when I heard the engine rev.

"You texting Torque?" Nelson asked.

"Yes."

"How can you be sure it's Knuckles? Could be someone across the street."

I shook my head. "I confronted Knuckles two weeks ago, and before he pulled out of the drive, he revved the engine just like that. Loud and annoying."

Torque shot me a text back.

> Yeah, he texted Flip a few minutes ago saying he was leaving. We're on the move.

"Tor says Knuckles texted that he's on the way. Let's get my woman out of there."

Within minutes, we made our way through the gap in the fence, and quietly edged around the house. Along the back, all of the windows were closed, but the first corner we rounded, the edge of a curtain fluttered out of the open window.

Mug's voice carried outside. "Sledge, he said to go easy on our product."

Sledge's voice sounded like he was next to the window. "Motherfucker, mind your own business. This is nothing since he's getting a new shipment. Hell, I'd be with him to inspect it if you weren't such a fuckin' pathetic perv."

I gripped my gun tighter at the thought of Mug making Simone uncomfortable. Volt strode past me and led the way toward the front of the house.

He put an arm out to stop me. "Raff and I have Mug. You take Sledge. He's a bigger wildcard."

I lifted my chin. "Fine. But aim below the nose. I want to gouge his eyes out for looking at my woman at all."

Volt's head cocked at an angle. "You need this to be believable. Eyes being gouged out is too much."

"Thanks for the reminder," I whispered and moved past him to the front door.

My hunch was right. Mug hadn't locked it behind himself.

Luckily, the hinges didn't squeak when I slowly opened it. I tip-toed inside and crept down a very narrow hallway. A free-standing fireplace sat in an alcove to my left. It hadn't been used in over a decade, from the dilapidated state of it. A tiny kitchen was to my right. From this angle, there was a pass-through at the kitchen sink and I saw Simone bound to a plastic chair. Mug stood watching her.

Sledge had to be along the wall on my left since we could hear him so well at the window.

Volt crowded closer to me and I nodded.

We both entered the room together with our guns raised. Volt went straight to Mug, catching him off-guard. Sledge noticed the movement, and had his weapon in hand but aimed toward Mug.

"Yo!" I called to get his attention.

The moment his eyes met mine, I shot him in the shoulder. He dropped his weapon. Volt's words outside the house came back to me and I kept myself from filling him with bullets.

He charged toward me. I tucked my gun in the holster, and landed a punch to his jaw.

Nelson came around and grabbed Sledge from behind. He shifted and locked an arm around Sledge's neck, putting him in a sleeper hold. In seconds, Sledge's body slumped and hit the floor.

Nelson grinned. "Blood splatters, Prez. I'd stand back if I were you."

I moved toward Simone, but stopped short when Volt said, "A little help here."

Volt had pistol-whipped Mug, initially. He couldn't shoot him since Simone sat directly behind Mug. I looked for Rafferty and saw him slumped against a wall. I should have had another brother here instead of Rafferty. Mug was an enforcer for a reason, and had likely caught Rafferty by surprise. Volt had a split lip, and Mug had a bowie knife in his hand.

"You motherfuckers are gonna die," Mug said.

From behind me, I heard the strange sound of a toilet lid scraping. Nelson came back into the room and flanked Volt's other side.

"A toilet lid?" I called out to Nelson.

Mug's eyes slid to me and then his head turned toward Nelson. It was enough of a distraction that Nelson lunged forward while swinging the rectangular piece of ceramic. I didn't think there was any way he'd connect with Mug, but that cracking sound was one I would never forget.

Mug's body stayed upright for a second and then fell to the floor. Nelson pulled his knife out, and I had to look away when he slit Mug's throat.

I hurried to Simone, untied her hands, and scooped her into my arms.

"Thank God you found me. I didn't think you'd ever get here," she said, tucking her face close to my neck.

"Yeah, baby. It's been killing me not being able to charge in here."

"Why did he slit their throats?" she asked.

Nelson heard her and said, "That cartel they use likes to slit throats. Makes it that much more believable."

She pulled her face free and caught Nelson's gaze. "I think that toilet lid put a wrench into that plan."

Nelson grinned maniacally. "Nah. *Zombieland* for the win, baby."

Simone smiled and looked at Volt. "Aunt Andrea would love him."

Volt wheezed out a single laugh. "Goddammit, I love you, babydoll."

I put Simone down so Volt could hug her.

"Love you too, Dad. Thanks for coming."

"Let's get you and Rafferty the fuck out of here," Volt said.

"Did he get stabbed?" I asked.

Volt shook his head. "Not that I saw. You take her, and I'll get him out."

CHAPTER 28

OATMEAL

SIMONE

ONCE WE ARRIVED AT Steel's house, everything became a whirlwind of activity. Mom wrapped me in a fierce hug, then held me at arm's length to make sure I was all right. Aunt Abby – who'd apparently driven up separate from Uncle Blood – introduced me to a local doctor and they took me to Steel's room. There wasn't much they could do without hospital equipment, but the doctor asked me how much Ketamine I'd been given. To my surprise Steel had produced the vial that was used.

The doctor advised getting in to see my doctor on Monday, but the amount was small and our baby would likely survive.

"Thank fuck," Steel said, and wrapped his arms around me.

"That's a huge relief," I whispered.

"You need to get some rest," the doctor said.

"I'd rather shower first," I muttered.

The doctor nodded. "Understandable."

Once the doctor and Abby cleared out of the room, Steel led me to the bathroom.

"We're showering together, Jade. Need to have you at my side for a little longer. I love you so damn much, and the thought of losing you..."

I touched my finger to his lips. "You aren't losing me, tough guy."

Half-an-hour later, I sat at Steel's massive dining table with him sitting next to me. I had on one of Steel's black t-shirts and my favorite pair of sleep shorts – a prospect had swung by with my suitcase. I was so grateful; whoever the prospect was, they deserved their patch now rather than later.

Mom and Shelly served up a smorgasbord of food. I had inhaled a stuffed manicotti and garlic bread. Mom insisted I eat some salad, and I complied because I was so famished.

Steel's cell vibrated. Reluctantly, he peeked at the screen and shook his head. "I gotta take this, Jade."

I nodded and whispered. "It's all good, honey."

With his lips pressed together, he nodded, then wandered to his bedroom to take the call.

"That was a fuckin' rush, but damn am I glad we went legit," Blood said.

"I wish they'd go legit," Shelly muttered from the kitchen sink where she was washing dishes.

I felt bad not helping, but nobody would let me lift a finger.

"Volt suggested this could be the time for Steel to do that," Blood said.

"That would be nice," Shelly said.

Since Steel wasn't in the room, this was my chance. I twisted my head to the kitchen where Mom was drying dishes. "Mom, what am I having?"

She stilled with a damp pot and a towel in hand. Her expression softened. "Now, sweetie, don't let that asshole take this joyous surprise from you."

"I could have died not knowing, Mom."

Uncle Cal set his beer bottle down with a harsh thud. "You didn't and that shit is *never* happening again."

I focused on Mom. "Tell me, please. I know you peeked."

She shook her head. "I didn't."

My head reared back. "Seriously?"

"Seriously," she said, drying the pot.

"Get the envelope. I'm sure it's in your purse."

She shook her head again. "Left it at home."

"She's right," Shelly said. "Don't let Corrupt Chrome take anything more from you. It's the best kind of surprise to get."

I sighed. "Guess I should thank Josie the next time I see her. It's only because of her that I'm pregnant."

"You aren't *ever* seeing her again," Uncle Blood said.

I turned to him. "Why not?"

Shelly came to the table. She laughed while she grabbed the empty salad bowl. "Josie's a loose end. I don't know about these brothers, but Steel is incredibly ruthless. He does *not* leave loose ends behind.

Somebody comes looking for Knuckles, you think she's gonna keep her trap shut? Nope. Loose end. She's gone."

My brows furrowed. "But she helped me... a little."

Mom tilted her head. "She's also the reason you got taken. Serves her right."

"Wow," I breathed.

With a self-satisfied smile, Mom arched her brow. "Are you sure you were made to be a president's old lady?"

"Yes, I am."

"Then get something straight, Simone. Steel is the reason you're pregnant. Not anybody else."

I nodded. "I wish I knew what happened to Knuckles."

"Are you gonna thank him, too?" Blood asked.

I scoffed. "No, but I'd have liked to have punched him."

"He got his, sweetheart. Don't you worry," Cal said.

I stared at the sliding glass doors. It was dark and the entire room was reflected in the glass. I looked over to the living room. "Where did Dad and Rafferty go?"

"Not your business," Blood said.

"That's getting annoying," I muttered.

"Too bad," Blood said.

I leveled a pointed look at him. "I don't think anybody would have found me without him and Alexandra."

Nelson stood and tossed a beer bottle in the recycle bin. "We had a source who confirmed about the property where you were. We'd have found you."

"*Had* a source?" I hinted at my question.

Nelson gave me a regretful grin. "Also not your business. At least not unless Steel says so."

Mom settled in the chair next to me. "Eat some more food, Simone. Then you need to rest."

There was a hard, authoritative knock at the door.

Blood looked at Nelson. "Would Steel mind if I answer it?"

Nelson shrugged.

Blood grinned. As he stalked to the front door, it struck me how unusual it was that he had his hair in a man-bun.

His voice carried back into the room. "Good evening, officers. Is there a problem?"

"That crazy motherfucker," Cal muttered.

I laughed.

"He's here, Officer Perkins. Me and my buddy rode up today. We got here around five o'clock. Steel's woman is pregnant and we had a big dinner to celebrate. He's been here all day."

Nelson hurried back toward Steel's room, but he strode around the corner before Nelson got very far.

I heard the door catch, but I didn't hear it snick shut. Even though the voices were muffled, the conversation could still be heard inside.

"Where were you tonight at ten o'clock?"

"Here with Damon, Cal, and my woman's family."

There was a pause, then another voice said, "You need to come downtown for questioning."

"I'm not going anywhere without my lawyer present."

"Why do you think you need a lawyer?"

"I don't take any chances."

Nothing but silence after Steel delivered that.

Then Steel said, "I have a house full of guests. Are we finished here?"

"You need to come downtown for questioning in the morning."

"My lawyer and I will be there," Steel said.

I heard a different voice say, "It's just questioning, but it's your call."

The door clicked shut and Steel took his seat next to me.

Nelson leaned against the breakfast bar adjacent to the dining table. "'Just questioning,' my ass. Why do they bother with that? We all know the score."

Uncle Cal shot Nelson a wry look. "Believe it or not, lots of people *don't* know the score. That's why they bother with that."

Nelson tipped his head to the side. "Fair." He looked at Steel. "Do we even have a club lawyer any more?"

Steel slung his arm around my shoulders. "We do. They're new, and it looks like I'll get to see what they're made of first hand."

Uncle Cal caught Steel's gaze. "Are you sure you're cool with us staying here? I don't have a problem hitting the road if I get my hands on some Café Bustello before I go."

Steel grinned. "It's no problem, Callous. The better question is if you have a problem bunking with Rafferty."

"I'm not bunking with him. He's sleeping on the floor."

"Or I'll just sleep on the sectional," Rafferty said, coming in through the sliding glass door.

"You plan to prospect with any club, I think sleeping on the floor is exactly where you belong," Dad said, following him inside.

Rafferty shook his head and stopped next to me. "Did you call Alexandra?"

I dipped my chin. "In his truck. It was brief. I'm gonna call her in the morning."

"Good."

Before he moved away, I grabbed his hand. "Thanks, Raff. I mean it. Not everyone would think to listen to Alexandra or Jasmine. I don't care what Dad and the others say, that's really admirable."

He gave my hand a squeeze. "Glad you're okay, Simone. We all love you."

EVERYONE HAD GONE TO bed. Blood and Abby were in a guest bedroom on the same side of the house as Steel's bedroom, while Dad and Mom were in a bedroom on the other side of the house. Cal had taken over the room Rafferty had been using... and I had no idea if Raff had opted to sleep on the floor, the sectional in the living room, or take his chances at the Devil Lancer clubhouse.

I'd never been so exhausted. Yet, as excited as I was to go to bed, part of me feared that I wouldn't be able to sleep because I wanted it so desperately.

Steel climbed under the covers, twisted toward his lamp and turned out the light. "Hit your light, babe. I'm wiped out."

I ignored his request and twisted so I could snuggle up to him. "Are you really going in for questioning tomorrow morning?"

He wrapped his arms around me. "Sweetheart, the less you know—"

"Nope. I'm not putting up with that. I was there for some of this shit. I know that you took care of it, which means I'm not going to rat you out or anything. Give it to me straight. Is there any chance they have something on you? I'm sure you concocted an elaborate plan against Knuckles, but for all we know some informant sold you out."

He rubbed his hand up and down my back. "Jade, slow down. Yeah, you were there... for some of it. The news reported that Knuckles and his drug supplier had an altercation after Knuckles learned Sledge and Mug had been killed."

"After?" I asked, since I knew Mug and Sledge had likely been killed at the same time as Knuckles.

He dipped his chin, his lips quirking upward. "That's what the news reports."

"So, what about the supplier?"

"He was found dead at the meeting site, so were the few men who were with him. The cartel isn't claiming Manuel or the others, because he'd gone rogue, but that won't be in the news."

I nodded and stifled a yawn. "Bottom line, am I gonna have to visit you and wish you weren't wearing the drab prison uniform? Everyone thinks it's orange all the time, but really, it's the color of oatmeal."

His body shook with laughter. "You got a problem with oatmeal, Jade? I heard toddlers like it."

I stared at him in the dim lamp light. "You heard wrong. No, I don't have a problem with oatmeal, just when it becomes a color. That's wrong."

"I'm taking a lawyer with me, sweetheart. It should be fine."

"Why aren't you more certain?"

He blew out a sigh. "All of our chapters were facing similar issues, but not with as much intensity as us. I don't know that this 'questioning' isn't to figure out if I gave the order to do anything to other Corrupt Chrome chapters."

"Okay, fine. But your new lawyer better pull their weight."

He gave me a quick kiss. "They will."

CHAPTER 29

PREFERENCE

STEEL

OUTSIDE THE SHERIFF'S OFFICE, Torque leaned against an electric pole, waiting for me. A light drizzle fell as I crossed the street toward him. I walked past him and in a few feet, he fell in step with me.

"New firm work out, okay?" he asked.

"Yeah, might even like that lawyer better. How did you know when I'd be done?"

"I didn't."

I shot him a quick glance. "You're a little conspicuous standing across the street in the rain."

He chuckled. "Just started drizzling when you came out. I like overcast days."

"Besides checking in on the new law firm, is there a reason you're here?"

"Shark couldn't get a hold of you. He spent all of last night being questioned about the Corrupt Chrome clubhouse fire."

"And?"

"They believe his story. Vegas Metro brought in a drug dealer that had double-crossed Corrupt Chrome a few months back."

Shark had told me about that dealer. The plan was to set him up to take the fall.

"Have we heard from the other chapters?" I asked.

He jerked his head toward a small sandwich shop and I followed him inside. "The other cities are good, but Raleigh and Miami have some issues."

I nodded. "Heard about those this morning. Axe and Link shared their plans to resolve the issues."

"Did Axe mention anything about cleaning up?" Torque asked in a low voice, while we stood in line to place our orders.

Axe, the president of the Raleigh chapter, had wanted us to get out of drugs five years ago. At the time, he couldn't convince anyone else to get on board with giving up drug-running.

The man in front of us paid for his order and moved aside. I ordered bacon, egg, and cheese sandwiches and coffee for me and Torque, paid, and we wandered to a booth.

When Torque sat down, I said, "Yeah, I heard from Axe. Seems Link wants to clean things up in Miami, too. I almost wonder if they spoke to one another, but as messy as shit was in Florida, I can see Link changing his mind."

Torque's face twisted with a strange look. Our order number was called and he slid out of the booth to grab our food.

He returned, unwrapped his sandwich, and locked eyes with me. "Why do you sound like you want to clean things up?"

I lifted a shoulder. "We've made money in drugs, but... it's the riskiest thing we do. The smart thing would be to take that money and bankroll something else. Ideally, something legal."

Torque swallowed his food. "Jesus, I think the hang-around rubbed off on you."

I sipped my coffee. "We aren't getting any younger, Tor. This shit's getting old. I give it nine months, tops, before another club or a street gang fights us for the same turf."

"Right."

I shook my head. "I'm not doing any more time. Finally have something good and sweet to live for. If the last twenty-four hours have shown me anything, it's that I didn't give a damn about dangerous situations. I wanted the danger to feel alive. Now, I don't need that. Being with Jade has changed everything."

"So... you really want to clean the whole club? Top down?"

I shrugged. "Of the drugs, yeah."

He narrowed an eye at me. "That's gonna be a tough sell."

"Got two chapters that want to clean up, and one of those is our best market for drugs. Then there's Jacksonville, which isn't doing well in terms of sales. Even if that's because their membership is low, they didn't do well ten years ago either."

Torque gave a small nod. "Yeah, but what about our other seventeen chapters?"

I twisted my hands up. "I'm not sure. It'll take time and a decent plan, but we won't know until we float the idea to the members."

He crumpled up his sandwich wrapper, tossed it on the tray, and sat back in his seat, blowing out a sigh.

I stared at him. "What? After last night, you really want to stick with it?"

His eyes slid to the side while he mulled it over. "You got a point. Last night was pretty brutal."

I WALKED INTO THE kitchen at eleven-thirty and found Simone and Rafferty sitting at the breakfast bar with bowls of cereal in front of them.

"Where's everybody else? And why are you eating cereal? It's nearly lunchtime."

Simone tilted her head up as I approached her side. "Mom and Dad got on the road early. Blood and Abby followed suit, and Uncle Cal left about an hour ago."

I tipped my head at her bowl. "And the cereal?"

She shot a quick grin at Rafferty. "After Uncle Cal left, *he* decided to sleep a little longer in a real bed. So, I guess this is breakfast for him, and I never know what I want to eat, but cereal hasn't steered me wrong yet."

My woman was gorgeous, but the dark circles under her eyes told the tale. Yesterday had taken a lot out of her and she was still tired. "Once you're done, go grab a nap."

Her eyes widened and I anticipated an argument. Then she reluctantly said, "I will."

It didn't take long for Simone to finish her food and leave the room.

Rafferty had nearly finished his bowl.

I pulled out the chair next to his. "I want you to prospect with us, but that won't work if you decide mid-way to cut bait to join the Riot MC."

He kept his eyes locked on the fridge. "I know."

"The only way you get out of prospecting as a Devil Lancer is if you *don't* make the cut... and you've shown you have what it takes."

He shook his head and looked at me. "But I don't have it, since I was knocked out when it really matters."

His self-loathing tone hit me hard.

"How many bar fights have you been in?"

His eyes held a hint of irritation. "Two."

"That's not enough. I think you know that. Takes a hell of a lot of guts to go up against an enforcer for another MC."

He stared at me with that neutral expression. Then, I realized maybe I was seeing through it because there was something else working in his eyes.

"You made a decision."

"I wouldn't say that yet."

In the whirl of events from last night, I vaguely recalled how he'd nearly been sick at the sight of Mug and Sledge lying on the floor.

"Killing people isn't something that happens often."

He nodded. "Yeah, killing Mug and Sledge didn't bother me. It's sending someone after Josie. I thought women were off-limits."

"Normally, yes. However, Josie would rat us out. Hell, she led Mug right to my woman. She had no kids, had recently lost her job, and none of that justifies her death, but I'll never let anyone get away with harming Simone."

"And what about Farah?"

"We didn't kill her."

He arched a brow. "I don't believe that."

"She isn't dead. She left town."

Rafferty narrowed his eyes. "She owns a house."

My lips tipped up. "A house that is in foreclosure. So the hundred grand we offered to get her to leave was enticing."

His lip curled. "You blew money on her?"

I shot him a pointed look. "Knuckles had money to give his contact. Technically, he paid her."

"That's convenient."

"No, it's smart."

He picked up his coffee cup and held it near his lips. "But it won't always work out that way."

"No, probably not. And no matter how much time you take to plan and strategize, when shit's going down you gotta have faith it's going to work out. And typically, it does."

"How often does this shit happen?"

I tilted my head side to side. "To this degree, not often. But we deal with assholes trying to take our turf almost every day. It's unusual for another MC to target all of our cities at one time. The day-to-day shit gets handled by the individual chapters as they see fit. "

He kept quiet.

"Not usually with murder," I added.

"Right," he whispered.

I stood and put the barstool under the breakfast bar. "You've been active with us. You hang around for another two months. Then you have to shit or get off the pot."

Rafferty nodded. "Got it."

"JORDAN IS ON HIS way here," I told Simone when she came out to the deck where I was grilling steaks – the one culinary thing I could do well, as long as I wasn't distracted.

"So I have time to leave," she muttered.

I gave her a sideways glance. "Sweetheart, he offered to approach Josie to help find you."

"That wouldn't have worked."

I flipped the T-bones. "No, but he wanted to help, and he said he—"

"Wanted you to give me up."

I stared into her deep brown eyes – lamenting how thin the walls were at my end of the clubhouse. "I didn't know you heard that. He changed his tune when you went missing."

"Okay."

"He could see how much I care for you. Made it clear he may not understand it, but he was opening his eyes. That's why he's coming to dinner."

She settled on the outdoor sofa. "I hesitate to ask this... is he bringing Debra?"

I barked out a laugh. "No."

"Good. Here's hoping three isn't a crowd."

The doorbell rang.

The anxious expression on her face had me handing her the tongs. "You flip the steaks. I'll get the door."

I let Jordan inside, but didn't let him go very far. "Are you going to be cool?"

He met my hard stare. "Yeah, Dad."

Hearing him call me that never got old. I reached out and gave him a quick, fierce hug and led him to the deck.

"Want a beer?" I asked.

"Maybe with dinner."

Twenty minutes later, I smiled while Simone and Jordan laughed at a story I told about changing Jordan's first diaper. Her concerns about this being awkward were for naught.

Simone sighed. "I forgot about that with boys. Mom let me change Bobby's diaper once or twice when I was little, but I don't remember it at all."

Jordan grinned at her. "Do you know what you're having yet? Do you have a preference?"

Simone glanced at me, and back to Jordan. "At this point, my only preference is healthy. Though, Mom wants me to have a girl so I get a taste of my own medicine."

I swallowed a bite of steak. "Pretty sure she wants a healthy baby and doesn't care."

Simone nodded and looked at Jordan. "Will you graduate in May?"

He sipped his beer. "August. I'm starting an internship June first."

"That's awesome. The one you wanted last fall?"

I'd never seen it before, but Jordan's cheeks held a hint of pink.

He shook his head. "One that a friend told me about. It's in southwest Florida."

Simone sipped her water. "Tennyson's from there, right?"

That caught him off guard. "Why would you think she told me about it?"

She aimed a closed-lip smile at him. "The way she looked at you that night in December. And I recalled her living in the same complex as Chet."

This conversation could have had an awkward overtone, but Simone was relaxed and matter-of-fact about it.

Jordan nodded. "She's from there, but it was Chet who told me about the internship. Tennyson's gone to New York City with an old boyfriend."

She did a slow nod. "Ah. Sorry to hear that."

He smiled. "It's all good. I'm not as ready to settle down as I thought I was."

TREASURE

Simone

Six months later...

"Rayella," I said.

Steel ever-so-slowly swiveled his head to me. The dry, pointed look he gave me should have made me uncomfortable.

I grinned. "Raymonda? No, even I don't like that. How about Ramona?"

He did a long blink, then held our daughter closer, though I hadn't thought it was possible. "No. We're not naming her after me. Come up with something better."

A cavalcade of names sifted through my brain, but none of them fit. I thought back to Mom's side of the family, and Dad's, but that didn't work well either. The night we met came back to me... but I wasn't sure he'd like that idea either.

"You might shoot this one down too, but what about Olive?"

He deliberated it for a long moment. "Possibly. How about Felicity?"

I twisted my lips as I considered it. "Is there a reason?"

We were in our hospital room, and Steel had taken his shirt off for skin-to-skin contact with our two-day-old daughter.

He shrugged a shoulder. "I looked into the meanings behind some names. It's probably all B.S., but the name comes from Latin for 'good fortune.' Even though we hadn't expected her, and may not have planned on her, she is definitely our little treasure."

My mouth dropped open and I narrowed my eyes. "Did you just use the term B.S. because of our daughter? I don't think I've ever heard you refrain from cursing."

He looked abashed. "Focus, woman. If you don't like Felicity, then—"

"I love it. It's perfect, just like you."

He shook his head. "I'm far from perfect, but I'm fit to burst with the amount of love I have for you and this perfect little girl you've given me."

Emotion clogged my throat just as a nurse came into the room.

"Have you got a name yet? They're going to kick you out of here today, and I'd hate for you to have one more thing on your plate. Especially since we have staff here who can do it for you." She aimed her non-nonsense gaze at me. "Seriously, you don't need a trip to the Social Security Office with a newborn."

I chuckled. "Yes, we just decided on a first name... as for a middle name—"

Steel's eyes burned with intensity at me. "Felicity Jade Reynolds, that way she has a piece of you with her all the time, too."

Tears pooled and ran over my lower lids. "That's brilliant, honey."

He propped a hip on my bed and leaned in close. "No, Jade. It'll be brilliant when we get married two months from now, and both my girls have my last name."

I leaned up and gave him a soft kiss. He'd put his cut on me not long after my abduction. I wore it any time I was in the Devil Lancer clubhouse. Even though his brothers knew I was his and he'd claimed me, he still wanted us to be legally bound. I couldn't wait to get married, but I wasn't certain it would be in two months.

Figuring out a wedding dress while eight months pregnant was a challenge, but I had narrowed it down to three dresses. The plan was to try on those dresses in three more weeks, after I'd dropped a few more pounds.

The nurse bustled toward us. "That's a beautiful name, but it's going to take some time for one of you to complete this form."

With a small smile, Steel transferred Felicity into my arms and started filling out the form.

"She is so stinking cute," Alexandra said, holding Felicity and staring down at her.

We were sitting on my couch in the living room the morning after I'd been discharged from the hospital. Steel was in bed catching some sleep, since it had been a long night.

"Yeah. She's stolen my heart," I said.

"She'll be breaking hearts, that's for sure." Alexandra's gaze met mine. "You better hope she isn't half as good as you are at keeping secrets."

From her tone, I knew she was referring to me keeping the secret about Rafferty's hang-around status with the Devil Lancers. She had lost her mind almost as badly as Aunt Trixie had.

Almost.

Were Alexandra and Rafferty speaking to one another now?

No.

The sheer stupidity of that killed me, but Steel pointed out it wasn't my business.

Which also killed me.

"It wasn't mine to tell, Lex."

She nodded. "I get that. I do, it's just...I guess there aren't any sisters before misters in MC life."

I tilted my head. "It isn't about putting anyone above another...it's respecting Rafferty's right to privacy."

"And not sharing the Devil Lancers' business," she muttered.

I tossed a hand out. "Or the Riot's. If he'd been hanging around there, it wouldn't have been my place to tell Steel – hell, I felt like I'd done a bad thing just telling him he wasn't prospecting with *any* club."

She nodded and stroked Felicity's cheek. "Right. And he still isn't a prospect with either club."

I grinned. "You'd have to ask him why that is. His phone number's still the same. You could call him."

She shook her head. "I don't think MC life is for me, Simone. I'm too boring for it, I guess."

I chuckled. "You are *far* from boring my friend, and even if you don't want to hear this, you're more cut out for this life than you think."

Her hazel eyes filled with skepticism.

I widened my eyes. "Who wanted Jordan to pay for his stunt last December? Who wanted to befriend Tennyson to get the full scoop? That's so diabolical, it isn't funny."

After a moment she gave a nod. "Yeah, and that's the kind of thing that men like Rafferty can't handle. The idea of sitting back and keeping my mouth shut won't fly with me. If I can help someone, I'm gonna do that... and Rafferty especially hates when I help him."

This was news to me and it was all I could do to keep my eyes from lighting up.

"How did you help him?"

"It was stupid and it was just before graduation, but Rafferty's reaction really let me know where he stood."

Felicity started to fuss and I let Alexandra hand her over to me.

"The two of you are older now, Lex. You've both changed even if you don't see it, and I know you've both matured since then."

She shrugged. "You're right. It doesn't matter though, since I've been dating Porter for the last four months."

That name made me cringe every time I heard it, but I managed to hide it from her while I situated Felicity to breastfeed.

Once Felicity was latched, I asked, "Is it getting serious?"

She shook her head. "I don't know. We'll see. Dad really doesn't like him."

I had nothing to say to that because my Dad really hadn't liked me being with Steel, but I wouldn't give him up for anything now.

"Did Uncle Cal tell you why?" I asked.

She rolled her eyes. "Says I can do better."

"Yeah, I've been there," I said with a grimace.

She shook her head. "He has no idea how hard it is to meet people."

I nodded. "It is hard, but I'm pretty sure the right person will come along at the right time."

"I guess I'm impatient."

"Don't go getting baby fever. That will only make it worse."

"I'm glad you're happy, Simone. Steel dotes on you."

I grinned. "Yeah, I'm a very lucky woman."

Alexandra wandered to the kitchen and grabbed her water bottle. "How long are you going to stay in Jacksonville? After your baby shower at his house last month, I can't imagine not moving to Augusta. You weren't kidding, his place is the shit."

"My lease is up in December. The new clubhouse should be finished by then...or at least part of it. As long as Steel finds someone to lead that chapter by the end of the year, that's when we'll move."

The smile on her face didn't shine like normal. "I'm happy for you, really. But I feel like I'm not going to see you any more."

"You think Mom isn't going to hound me to come visit every chance I get?"

Her smile brightened. "Totes."

"Yeah. It's not like I'm on the other side of the country."

"But you won't be at the Riot MC clubhouse much. The holiday bash won't be the same."

I grinned. "I thought MC life wasn't for you?"

"You know what I mean."

I nodded. "You're right. I can still come for certain things. I'm not going to miss a low-country boil when the Biloxi brothers come to town."

"You sure?" she asked.

"Lex, you can take a girl out of the Riot, but you can't take the Riot out of the girl."

She smiled. "I better go. Let you get some sleep since that little girl looks like she dozed off."

Two minutes after she left, Steel wandered out of our bedroom wearing black draw-string pajama pants with orange Harley-Davidson logos all over them. "She leave?"

I nodded.

"You did good," he said.

I shot him a dose of my side-eye. "Now who's been eavesdropping?"

"Sorry, but I had to hear how you'd handle the stuff about Rafferty. You were perfect. Besides, if she'd blamed you still – I don't care whose daughter she is – I'd have had to set her straight."

I shook with laughter. "You're so protective. Felicity is in trouble when she gets older."

He shook his head. "No, anybody who fucks with her is."

"You got that right," I muttered.

He sat down next to me, wrapping an arm around my shoulders. "My house is the shit, Simone, but it's just a house. If you want to live close to your folks, I can sell it and we'll find a decent place around here."

"Wouldn't you have to give up the presidency to move here?"

"Not necessarily. My point is that it's a place, and we can always find a different house."

I widened my eyes at him. "And give up your privacy? No way."

His lips stretched out in a grimace. "Not sure how private it's gonna be. Harvest time for the tree farm on the left side of the property is coming up. My electric bill is gonna be outrageous without all that shade."

I grinned. "More sunshine is awesome. That means I could get a better tan by your pool."

His eyes took on a faraway look. "You're right, we're not moving."

Steel

I STARED AT SIMONE laying on the sofa with Felicity nestled on her chest. A year ago, I'd have never envisioned living in Jacksonville, let alone living here with a woman I intended to marry, and our daughter.

They were my whole world now. I'd do anything for them because they were everything to me.

I had an uphill battle in front of me with my club. Circles had survived his attack after a three-week hospital stay. To my relief, he wanted to see the entire club get out of drugs and prostitution – that part was a surprise, but understandable.

As expected, few of the other chapters wanted to give up their drug income. Walker and Crank were the most adamant that we continue with drugs.

Walker had gone so far as to demand I let Torque lead instead.

Link, Axe, and Shark stepped up and made it clear how costly the drug business could be when a concerted attack hit.

Over the past five months, Miami, Raleigh, Las Vegas, and Augusta were serving as an experiment to show exactly how losing the drug trade would impact chapters. Part of me believed this was futile because every market would be different, but Tie had taken point on this and the results were promising.

If they weren't, I would step down as mother chapter president. Leaving the brotherhood wasn't happening, but I would keep Felicity and Simone safe at all costs.

"What are you thinking about over there? I can practically hear the wheels turning," Simone said in a husky voice.

"I'm thinking about where to take you on our honeymoon."

She grinned. "You are a shit liar when you're worried about us."

I chuckled. "I love that you can read me, Jade."

Her eyes warmed. "I love that you're mine to read."

"You want me to take her so you can rest?"

"Let's put her in the bassinet. I want to sleep curled up next to you."

"Anything you want, sweetheart, I'm going to give it to you."

Thank you for reading.
If you want more of Simone and Steel, scan the QR coade below
to sign up for my newsletter and get their bonus epilogue.
The series will continue with **Break Away** *Rafferty & Alexandra's*
story.

Acknowledgements

Without you the reader, I wouldn't be able to do this, so thank you so much for reading! Huge kudos to the ladies in my reader group, your help is always invaluable.

Thank you to Ena and Amanda at Enticing Journey, and all the book bloggers and influencers who help make every launch a success. I'm grateful to Melissa at Wildfire Marketing and the influencers and bloggers who shared and read *Break Out*. It's not everyday an author launches a new series, and all of your assistance is greatly appreciated!

Thanks to Bee at Bitter Sage Designs (and to the fine people at the LIFT4Autism auction — if it weren't for last year's auction, I wouldn't have found Bitter Sage!). This cover is so much more than I could have imagined.

Thank you to Golden Czermak at FuriousFotog and cover model Joey Berry. I had a difficult time narrowing it down from five different images, but that just goes to show the photos are simply fantastic! It's a pleasure doing business with you.

I'm grateful to Melanie Harlow for taking the time to provide feedback on my original blurb and helping me tighten it up. You give back so much to the author community and I hope you know how appreciated it is!

Thank you to Barbara J. Bailey for your insights and editing prowess.

Thanks to my family and friends for supporting me in the crazy writing journey. Special thanks to my Mom, who always insists on getting her hands on my work... I know a next generation seemed odd at the time, but I'm so glad you enjoyed it!

DISCOVER OTHER BOOKS BY KAREN RENEE

Please visit your favorite retailer to discover other books by Karen Renee:

The Riot MC Series

Unforeseen Riot

Inciting a Riot

Into the Riot

Calming the Riot

Foolish Riot

Respectable Riot

Rough Riot

Fighting a Riot

Starting the Riot

A Friendsgiving Riot – a short story found in Romancing the Holidays

Riot MC Box Set (0.5, 1, 2, 3)

Riot MC Box Set (4, 5, 6)

Riot MC Next Generation Series

Break Out

Break Away

Riot MC Biloxi Chapter Series

Harm's Way

Brute's Strength

Roman's War

Cynic's Stance

Gamble's Risk

Block's Road

Tiny Problem

Finn's Fury

The O-Town Series

Relentless Habit

Wild Forces

Abrupt Changes

Holiday Fixation (An O-Town Short Story) – found in Romancing the Holidays Vol. 2

Standalone

Beta Test

www.ingramcontent.com/pod-product-compliance
Lightning Source LLC
Chambersburg PA
CBHW060704190726

48289CB00002B/533